TAKE THE WAR TO WASHINGTON

TAKE THE WAR
TO WASHINGTON

by

PETER VAN GREENAWAY

ST. MARTIN'S PRESS
NEW YORK

Every man must weep in his own way for Hiroshima, Ulster, Vietnam; any place where a child dies needlessly. This is my way.

P.V.G.

History is a bunker. Just lob in a couppla grenades. No problem.

Lieut. Henry Ford
(1st Motorized Division, US Army)

MURDER IS NOTHING but what you see in men's eyes; he'd worked that out in the long reaches between bad times. Slowly, imperceptibly, he was being done to death; the killing was just a formality.

'No-one's going to ask you a thing, Roberts. You're just going to stand there; stand in that enormous room full of senators, aides, the public and distinguished visitors. You'll listen to the whole story and in time you'll feel remorse for what you and your buddies did to America, you got that?'

'I had my trial.'

'Correct. The death sentence three times over, desertion, murder, treachery and all kinds. Problem—how do we kill you three times over? Maybe this is part of it, Roberts. A summons from Congress to bear witness to your infamy. Everything we hear in the Senate relates to you—simply because you still exist. It won't be easy.'

'I'll manage.'

'The country's in a lynching mood, Roberts. Why not say the word? Tell 'em you ran away because you'd had enough, right?'

'I ran with a purpose, like I told the court. It's as simple as that.'

That soft, caressing voice repeating: 'Simplicity can be an unhealthy symptom, Ed.'

He remembered Colonel Headshrinker's words as he stood in a kind of pillory on the left of the Senate Chamber with two hulking MPs either side of him gripping submachine guns to keep everyone breathing nice and easy.

They didn't even let the Press get too close and that, he knew,

7

was a sure sign you had third degree leprosy. Why, just touching him your antennae for detecting social deviants could fall off.

He had time to run film clips of old times through his head as he watched without interest the mix-out of animated dummies milling around him, keeping a distance, studiously ignoring his contaminating presence, as though, after all, he had nothing to do with it. Which was funny if you took another POV.

I mean they also ignored my presence in Vietnam, knowing I was killing those nasty Commie bastards.

'How about that!' *Associated Press* called to the *Houston Chronicle*, 'Roberts is grinning like he didn't have a care in the world.'

'Maybe he saw Lieutenant McKie sitting back of the public gallery,' *United Press International* offered.

That was worth a bitter smile to the *New York Times*. 'What's public about a gallery stiff with cops? I'm surprised they don't dig up Hoover and draft him for door duty.'

AP studied the scene, identified the stains still showing up on the floor—the Floor—the crimson splashes turned russet on the walls. It was depressing.

'Keep 'em there,' the Majority Leader had ordered. 'I want America to know, for all time, what happened this terrible year. Keep 'em there. They're better than monuments.'

The clock hands had slipped over the high noon mark, and though the bustle—the coming and going of important looking nobodies loaded with bulky files, the traversing of significant seeming maybes with even bulkier briefcases—had, if anything, increased, there was still no sign of the man who would set everything in motion.

Roberts noted the Press was grown restive. The photographers, sated with used negative, waited with the desperate patience of men blind to the world without a lens to give it focus.

Someone dropped a newspaper on his way by and his eye pounced eagerly on the headline 'US TELLS CANADA'.

'Tells what, for God's sake?'

They wouldn't let him have newspapers, so he had no way of

knowing what had happened to the outfit. But he knew its destination and the big, black words told him what he wasn't supposed to know.

They'd gotten there. They'd made it. Smile and be damned. He was glad and didn't care who knew it. Man, it's beautiful, not to mention implicational. We shot the balls off old Uncle Sam and now he wants his boys back. Sure enough he must've made strong representations to his uppity neighbour over the Forty-ninth. 'Now you see here, my friend, they belong on my side of the fence and they got something to answer for, d'you hear me?'

No dice—that's how the headline read to Roberts. Almost before the overburdened aide had whisked up the paper, the ex-PFC knew it was OK. They were all dead or free and he'd carry their packs for them while he had the strength.

Just because someone dropped a newspaper, he knew so much. That it had all been worthwhile, that he didn't run that day like they kept on telling him he'd done, that he couldn't have given himself up like they never stopped persuading him. He'd been captured, which could happen to any grunt in any situation. So it happened to him. Bad beans.

He relaxed a little for the first time since they'd started working him over. The trial hadn't worked; they'd thrown the whole process against his silence and retired baffled. Now they had a chance to show him as a regenerate to the Full Committee, and the going would be tough.

Meantime he tried to work out how it must have looked that dawn when a long line of tiger suits went bloodied, hobbling, limping aboard the plane, Marsh and Extra carrying Thu hai and Thu ba. Did two children ever have so many loving fathers?

While Roberts thought about his kids, their kids, the ones who'd started it all, things began to happen.

A few members of the Press, lingering for tit-bits on the Floor, hurriedly went their ways as Senator Winfield strode in looking purposeful and almighty grim. Time had been when he would give them a word, a smile and a sense of belonging. But that was very nearly long ago.

There would be no more press briefings on the Floor, at least,

9

not while these momentous hearings were in progress. There would be no questions and no comment.

A short session for queries would be permitted at the end of the day, otherwise, as the sharply worded hand-out inferred, the Press was to confine its activities to the gallery.

Any infringement of the new regulations would result in a claw-back of credentials.

That was why the delinquents scurried past the senior senator for Nebraska without daring a glance. A headline would have told all. 'PRESS IN DOGHOUSE.'

Winfield paused pointedly, long enough to see the dogs on their way, before striding to the Chair.

From which he surveyed a whole conflux of countenances, most of them familiar; the surviving senators, their aides, a few distinguished representatives who could squeeze in while their less fortunate colleagues watched the proceedings on closed-circuit television.

But he gave not a glance at the man with an almost symbolic responsibility for it all.

Roberts started and looked vaguely around him. Surely somebody had mentioned God? He listened in growing disbelief as the chaplain intoned. Unbelievable! Coming from that oddity with the filemot face, eyes that never rested between up there and down here, grey hair cut so short he might have been wearing a cap of penitence——

'...and we ask Thy blessing on this historical Committee of the Full Senate and its work in searching out the root cause of evil which brought desecration, sorrow and untold misery on our country and its stricken people.'

That was, it seemed, only the beginning of interminable formalities, including the roll-call.

The clerk began the long drone.

Alabama—James Alleyn. J. J. Marksman—Alaska. Michael Cotman, Edward Gravener, and so on through to Gill Manson of Wyoming, one of the few American Bald Eagles left in that State.

He needn't have bothered; they were all present excepting the senior senator for Minnesota, the senior senator for Montana, South Carolina's junior senator and Louisiana's veteran maverick, Cooper, who was right there, yessir, when they gunned down ol' Kingfish in Baton Rouge. But he was tired of it all, bewildered and sick. He'd never leave Houma again.

The others would never see Washington again.

They were already dead.

But the whole thing was ongoing and through the roll-call, expectancy began to take a firmer grip of the assembled. It showed in Nebraska's nervous fiddling with his pen; grave, dignified Pennsylvania meticulously arranging the papers on his desk; Texas stretching the longest legs on the Hill to ease a build-up of tension.

Everyone had shaken down into place, crowded six or more deep round the walls, seated tidily at desks, disposed by categories in the galleries above; so much human sediment had settled, leaving Roberts in conspicuous isolation, despite, or because of, the wooden hatracks on each side.

Isolated. Free to remember how it all began.

Thu hai and Thu ba.

Platoon Sergeant Floyd (Soup) Kemble, Lieutenants Racowiczs, Benner and Able Thompson, PFCs Helmut Marshall, Harry Newsman, 'Extra', Broken Cloud and all the rest of the guys—some, he didn't even know their names; a lot of them were dead. Well naturally, that was only to be expected. They'd all taken the inevitable into consideration, and accepted it; what else was a soldier conditioned to do for God's sake?

Accepted—right! The way they'd accepted the stringy boy with large, frightened eyes and the little girl with her cute face, lacquer black fringe and a smile as bright as a daisy chain.

The vision prompted a soundless chuckle. Those two sure had a lot to answer for.

Mississippi, J. C. Nessitt. Missouri, Swart Singleton, Thomas B. Ogleton. Montana...

Racowiczs, Benner, Marshall, Hapgood...

'Now how was that name again?' Gribble was still asking as he flung himself into an already overcrowded ditch beside Marshall.

Company A was taking a little mortar fire.

Marshall tried sticking his legs straight up ahead while his

11

near neighbours watched with keen interest. He was too tall for the ditch and there was the slimmest chance he might get his feet shot off 'and serves you damn right for indecent exposure, Marsh,' Hapgood observed. So he tucked them under Hapgood's folded legs and that began an argument about the world getting too fucken small for comfort. Marsh grinned, tipped back his helmet and fumbled around for his cigarettes.

'Hey Marsh, what d'you say that name was?'

Marshall never broke into a sweat when it came to answering. He was busy listening to the clatter of the Cobras as they passed over on their run-in. Listened, or just let himself drown in pure sound.

Eventually, as the last of them skittered away over to the north, he enquired amiably, 'What name?'

Gribble looked surprised. He seemed to have forgotten the question. 'What you talkin' about?'

'How should I know? You just asked me is all.'

'That's right. So what's the name of the place we just left? That's what I wanna know, ain't it?'

'OK. If it makes you feel better—Loc Ninh.'

'Loc Ninh. Man, you're really fluent.' Gribble sounded genuinely impressed. 'I can't seem to get it like you have it. How d'you spell it?'

Bored to hell and meaning it Marshall told him. Gribble thought for a moment.

'Why don't you pronounce the aitch?'

'Oh man, what would it do for me?'

'Yeah I guess you're right.' Another mortar round churned up the mud in a field across the road. 'Y'know Marsh, I still think you must've had a Vietnamese grandpappy or somethin' —I never knew a guy pick up the basics the way you do and it ain't the easiest language.'

Marshall tried not to look flattered. He just wanted a quiet drag and two minutes communion with his aching feet.

'One of these days,' said PFC Extra, hunched up on Marshall's other side, 'you'll learn Marsh is the smartest dingbat in this outfit.'

Extra fitted into any ditch, he was so tiny. His words came in short little monkey-runs, as though speech was less a matter

12

of communication, more a question of escape.

Nobody ever called him anything but 'Extra', not since Fort Benning. Every time he stood in line for a canteen meal the cry went up, 'Give this one extra—he'll never make it with enough!' So he got extra and the name stuck better than a label pasted over his surname which was Jones.

In eight months of rugged campaigning with A company he'd proved out; could give, as well as take, extra.

'Oh I knew Marsh was smart all fine,' Gribble smiled sleepily, white teeth stood well outside his black, good-natured face, 'but I couldn't know he——'

A mortar round hit the road, not too far from where Racowiczs' platoon had holed up.

There came that peculiar silence when men cast up their accounts in a split second. Then the losers start screaming. This time it was somewhere further along the dirt track away from Can Tho, the village they were heading for.

'That's B company,' Gribble mentioned, and hunched a little further into himself.

Whitney Fletcher looked puzzled. 'Which raises another point. We have three companies, not to mention airborne, surrounding this ville, right?'

Someone grunted, or groaned. There had to be a Napoleon in every company.

'And we have RPD and mortars incoming from outside the perimeter, right?'

Nobody bothered to reply.

'So why are we sitting on our asses around nothing with our backs to something? I mean—we should be fanning outwards, right?'

'Medvac!' Racowiczs shouted. His men looked startled, especially Sims Littleman. None of their boys were hit that he knew of.

'What's wrong, Lieutenant?'

'Would you mind doing minor surgery on Private Whitney Fletcher's mouth—like sewing it up for the duration?'

Everyone relaxed and grinned. Racowiczs always had the word and always at the right time. Like now, when they were going to be hit and knew it, and knew damn well that Fletcher was right as any man could be. So many times they'd been caught in this trap. VC suspected in this or that village. Zippo! A bowling alley didn't set up its pins with nicer precision.

Further along the line 'Soup' Kemble was chuckling himself into incoherency. 'That Private Fletcher sure dropped out of General Cumberland's ass one fine briefin' session.'

For everyone who heard, it was good for a laugh, cut out the screams from down yonder long enough to get them all back on base.

'Where you think you're going, boy?' Racowiczs was watching Daniels, a quiet studious-looking replacement, only six days old and showing it. Had said not a word since they took off on this mission.

He wasn't saying anything now, just hitching up, cradling his M16 like an unwanted child and climbing out of the ditch.

Racowiczs put out a hand, a firm hand, grabbed the man by his webbing. 'Going some place?'

'I'm going home. Had enough of this stinking mess.'

Even Marshall stopped looking sleepy.

'Hey, hey, LBJ! Someone's decided not to stay,' Gribble crooned softly.

'I wouldn't go that way if I were you,' Racowiczs. Casually. 'They've got the track covered. Why not wait till the Cobras flush 'em out?'

Daniels looked hurt, uncertain. The only way to handle slow-burning hysteria was to blow their certainty apart.

'Got to get myself killed some way,' he offered, but his heart wasn't in it.

The other men were watching him closely. If he made a sudden break someone was going to have to block on plan four.

Racowiczs stayed casual. 'Suppose you don't get killed? And we can't find you—so I can't get dust-off? And you're somewhere hurt bad?'

Daniels stared up at the sky and down at his boots. Somewhere in between he worked out a makeshift formula for survival. The others enjoyed a moment of relief as he ducked back into the ditch. Racowiczs knew how to keep a guy from falling apart.

Smoke was rising from beyond a line of trees hiding Can Tho

village. The last gunship made its run-in, the quad-60s pumping fire fit to baptize the devil, but nobody was interested. The awe-inspiring gets to be a drag the second time round.

When Racowiczs got word from Halliday, they stirred sluggishly, climbed out of the ditch with the elegance of guests arriving at a tramps' ball. Maybe their own mothers would have been proud of them. Maybe.

'Ed, you ain't on RT right now, you take point—but nice and close.'

'Why me, Sergeant?'

'Everybody else is too goddam short-sighted, right?'

Roberts smiled, readjusted his swags of ammunition, and said 'OK.' Soup Kemble's idea of a joke, five hundred yards of open country and he calls for a point.

All the action was concentrated north of the village. That meant the Rangers were seeing most of it and welcome. Roberts wiped away some sweat knowing it was too hot for war and—good Christ! there, two inches from his toe-cap, was a pressure-mine, and he'd almost, just by thinking an irrelevance, he'd almost ... By a miracle the platoons ahead had missed it. Some-one had buried the thing in a hurry: the hump was visible and the freshly disturbed earth showed dark against the surrounding dirt. Gribble threw him a marker, he planted it and then walked right on down the middle of the track.

As it happened, A company reached the village first. As it happened, all their infiltration tactics were wasted. They could have walked in singing 'Hail to the Chief' and weapons decorated for Xmas for all the resistance they met.

Like bored tourists they just wandered around, watching the last huts burning to nothing. The quad-60s had done a fine job on three mamasans and what looked like a mother with two children if you could put the bits together.

'I calculate,' Whitney Fletcher drawled, 'this little hoe-down should cost the US taxpayer around one hundred thousand dollars.'

Lieutenant Able Thompson nodded. Not a bad assessment, especially as Fletcher planned to be a company accountant some day.

'Hey fellers!' Something odd-sounding in Roberts' voice

15

brought most of the company running.

They crowded round the scene keeping much of their attention on Roberts at first. Definitely something in his voice, not a cry for help exactly, and the way he just stood there, uselessly, as though no-one in the world could have comforted him if that was what he needed.

Then they forgot Roberts or, at least, became like him, members of a collective paralysis that drew more and more men into a momentous circle, till the Viet Cong could have cut down maybe three or four hundred men, so stupidly concentrated in one small clearing.

What they were watching through the drifts of smoke was a thing they would watch for the rest of their lives. It would determine the rest of their lives, and, for some, it would be the last conscious memory.

A boy and a girl, the boy about twelve, the girl a little more maybe, were stooped, peasant style, as though cooking a meal or scooping rice out of a common bowl. But what impressed was an intensity, a great and silent dedication in their aspect that had to be about something less mundane.

Between them lay a child, naked, big-bellied, that once upon a time just now was around three years old. Its legs drawn up for protest against agony gone too far. Blood flowed from a gaping tear in the shoulder region where a .60 bullet had sheared away the arm.

And the children were striving, with a surgeon's deliberation, to fix it back on. The way youngsters in nice, tidy countries click one Lego block to another. They worked with quiet desperation to join sinew with sinew, cartilage to cartilage. And they wept silently because nothing seemed to be going right.

Might have been the last children left on earth; the soldiers, or whatever they were, the other side of a dream.

The moment happened for all of them. Nothing was to be the same, ever again.

Roberts and Marshall moved together. As if by instinct the one approached the boy, and the other, Marshall, went to the girl. For a second or two they stared down at the futile operation, then both stooped and, very slowly, lifted the children into their

16

arms. Gently, Marshall disengaged the dead child's limb from her fingers.

More men from companies B and C were crowding into the compound.

'*Không phải,*' the girl was muttering quietly, over and over.

Marshall swallowed a large piece of nothing, and wished to hell he didn't know the words. 'It's not right' in any language was too inadequate.

'*Phải-phải,*' he said softly, mechanically, but nothing was right.

The others waited, with a special kind of silence, while Roberts held the boy close and Marshall talked and talked, using all the Vietnamese he knew.

'You men! Get your asses outta heah. We have VC five, five! hundred yards north. Move!' An alien voice, reeking of high class Virginia tobacco—uncured.

'Oh now, Captain,' said Racowiczs, being about the most senior officer present and no-one else seeming disposed to say much. 'Oh now, Captain sir, I'd say Airborne and Rangers should have that pleasure since they're great pleasure-seekers.'

'That so?' Lacey swaggered a little just to show who was who, and his pearl handled revolvers thudded nice and easy against his thighs. He stalked round the protective circle for everyone to see the ear he, personally, had cut from a gook two days back, stuck neat and viewable in his combat jacket like a fraternity pin.

'Well allow me to tell you something, Lieutenant. I do not appreciate the way you keep discipline in yo' outfit and I now have enough evidence to put the whole bangshoot tribe on a charge and by hominy I——'

'Now didn't y'all know we all on a charge already, Captain sir? That's why we all is here.'

'I will not have you derogating ma rank, Lieutenant, and I'll tell y'all something else——'

But there was that about Racowiczs' stare had him marking time quite suddenly. One of those looks, held by a hair-trigger, that could go off in your face like a WP booby-trap hung from a jungle vine.

He glared from Racowiczs to the men around him, was about

to depart when he caught the picture of Roberts and Marshall, talking to ... to ... he couldn't believe his bright blue eyes.

'You men! What do you think you're doing with those fucken kids.' Pushing his way through the cordon.

Marshall let his gaze wander slowly round till he had it staring down into his superior's face. He took plenty of time to inspect the pint sized captain all over, trophy and all, then suddenly, as though he'd pulled a knife, the severed limb materialized under the officer's uptight nose.

'*Em bé dút tay,*' he announced, without emphasis.

Strangely the warrior, flaunting his flesh and blood trophy, looked sick at the stuff being waved in his face. He even took a step back.

'What in fuck's that supposed to mean?' he snarled.

'Means—"Baby's cut his finger" ... sir. And where I was dragged up we don't use your language in front of the children ... sir.'

'Funny man! You put that dink down and get right back to your platoon—yo' hear me!'

'It's right here ... sir.'

'OK then drop the kid—you too.' He turned on Roberts who seemed unaware of all the fuss going on around him.

'Aid and comfort, sir,' Roberts looked and sounded deadpan. 'I was told by my Saigon superiors I must win hearts and minds, hearts and minds. Yessir, that's what I was told. Right, fellers?'

Five hundred men present by now and they all nodded and smiled. This was the first confrontation with the enemy they could honestly admit to relishing.

All of which put Captain Lacey in a very delicate fix. Either he backed out and lost some more face which would leave nothing much to keep his helmet from off his shoulders, or he could practise a real Napoleonic gesture.

He thought rapidly back to the movie he'd seen sixteen times, the life (sic) story of his hero, General Tite Button; yes indeed, there was a man, a real man.

What would he have done in the circumstances? He took a few thoughtful paces towards a smouldering hooch then sashayed back through the still swirling smoke, planted himself squarely in front of Marshall.

18

'Put that kid down,' he fired, 'or I'll shoot it right out of your grip.' And there was a pearl-handled .45 in his hand, to back his words.

Houdini couldn't have done what Marshall suggested to him in low Vietnamese.

'Speak American dammit!'

'I said,' loud and clear, 'you do that, sir, and I'll snap off your head and push it up your ass to join the rest of your waste products ... sir.'

This got a round of applause.

Believe it, people were fighting like crazy not five hundred yards distant.

Racowiczs was watching very carefully.

'What's got into you, Roberts? Don't you know anything 'bout the enemy? These could be VC with a couppla grenades somewhere around. Turn your back and you're dead.'

'They could be just a couple of frightened kids, sir.'

Blind anger put Lacey beyond the reach of insults. Beside himself as he was he still failed to add up to a man.

'What you all going to do? You gonna motherlove 'em all the way from here to——?'

'Yessir, Captain, that's right. We're gonna motherlove 'em all the way from here to the good old USA. Right fellers?'

More of the men had drifted along, joining in the roar of approval. And that again, was how it all began. Back there were the birthpangs of an odyssey.

Why he'd said it, Private Ed Roberts would never know. The fact seemed to be just sitting there waiting to be picked up, like the two children. He looked beyond Lacey to where Racowiczs stood smiling easily as though he knew about it too.

Lacey rounded on the lieutenant. It was easier bullying a fellow officer. And safer.

'He's yo' responsibility, Lieutenant. You'd better get him in line, damn quick.'

'Well now, I don't rightly know, Captain. Nothing in regulations says an outfit can't adopt a couple of orphans if it's that way minded.'

Lacey's expression turned so mean it had to sum up for the onlookers what war, this war, was really about. Impotent rage,

the destructive, unreasoning hate of a spoiled child who wanted
—and couldn't get. Breathed like asthma, that meanness stuck
in his throat so hard. The ridiculous Colt hung useless at his
side. Needed a battery of quad-60s to shoot his way through
that much humanity.

'Well I'm gonna tell yo' good, Lieutenant, an' I want you all
to hear me good, everyone in companies A, B and C. I'm puttin'
in a request to the colonel—no slicks to return for take-out.
You're walkin' back to base, that's two days marching for every
motherfucken one of you. I'm gonna make you eat shit for this.'

Quick as a cotton-tail he darted forward and picked up the
tiny corpse by a leg, tossed it into a still burning godown.

An ugly kind of forward movement by the whole mob
checked at the click as Marshall shifted from safety to automatic
fire. The M16 held in one hand, Indian style, was aimed right
between Lacey's beautiful blue, close-set eyes.

For just long enough he was inspired, or prodded by his evil
genius. 'Go ahead, grunt. Shoot and be damned.'

They gave ground unwillingly as Roberts called 'Extra!' and
as Lacey strode through the gap to look for his RTO, the little
man from Arkansas was monkey-running into the hooch as
though he'd known for certain sure what Ed had called him
about.

Moments later he stumbled out holding the broken remains
with a world of tenderness.

'Medvac!' That was Marshall. He whispered reassurance or
maybe an explanation to the girl in his arms as Sims Littleton
came surging forward.

'Is she hurt, Marsh?'

'No, she's OK. It's the small one—the baby.'

Sims looked puzzled. 'But he's dead, Marsh.'

Marshall frowned, conscious that something big was happening, rolled his gaze around the circle of faces, serious, intent,
far from considerations of war and the humours of war. And he
saw that it was happening to them too. Just now they cared
only someone should do the right thing, any whichway to undo
the wrong thing—he understood they were counting on him
to fix things.

He took the dead child from Extra and passed it to Sims. 'I

want you to sew that limb back on, man.'

Bewilderment. 'Aw c'mon Marsh, we don't show funnies before a funeral.'

The coloured man pulled himself to a new height, spoke loud and clear.

'Sims is gonna stitch the boy's arm on so we can bury him decent. In Vietnam they have a respect for the dead like we used to have for the livin'. They got their own kind of Coney Island for one-way riders only they ain't goin' no place if something's missin'. They gotta be physically intact. Let's see one of 'em gets there, right?'

While the children gazed wide-eyed, forgetting their fear as natural curiosity took over, while five hundred or more silent men looked on, while Airborne and some Rangers got shot to hell in a distant square of the grid, while Cobras went in gunning and others came out dripping blood, Sims Littleton did what he could to tailor the child's spiritual homecoming.

And, as they buried it, PFC Ed Roberts, happening to look up, saw Major Halliday, almost merged with the smoke and the trees shadowing the compound. There could be nothing of expression visible at that distance, but, as he considered the lone figure, apart, and yet part of the scene, Roberts felt even more strongly, that moment was giving the future a new direction.

A gavel rapping harshly, like an AK47, confused him for a second. He jumped off a train of old thoughts to find Senator Winfield hammering the Chamber into silence.

It came quickly. No-one was anxious to waste time when history beckoned. There was too much to be written into the record and everyone present, even most people watching their TV screens, were aware of the fact in varying degrees.

No-one more so than Erwin D. Winfield, the distinguished senator for Nebraska, loaded with honours won in a long and impressive political career. He was supposed to belong to a party, but as Lippman once said, 'there are Republicans, Democrats and Winfield.' A shrewd verdict on the one-time presidential candidate who never made first base.

Most people forgot to hold it against him, he was too

21

valuable as self-appointed keeper of the nation's conscience: witness, FOR Carswell FOR ABM—AGAINST cutting military expenditure AGAINST Cooper Church amendment and so forth. In fact his voting record alone would have guaranteed progress free of suspicion. But he, at least, never forgot that single moment of humiliation and what it had meant in terms of living with himself in a *ménage à trois* with thwarted ambition.

He might have been content to act out the rest of his life as Majority Leader in the Senate. If the pinnacle's high enough, it serves to justify existence. But, interestingly, twenty years of that homespun philosophy left him utterly prepared for the unexpected.

When news broke on the first events of that never-to-be-forgotten day in March, it had taken Senator Winfield no more time to reach an 'agonized decision' than it takes to soft boil an egg.

It suffices to abbreviate his decision in these few words: 'My country needs me'.

History issued the meal ticket that could satisfy Winfield's appetite and wipe out the memory of that long ago derisory vote.

Something of his thinking showed in his masterly handling of the gavel. Something of his conviction that all America had its eyes on Winfield alone, ready to renew its faded belief in integrity, which was almost his second name in hotel-room politics, something of that underpinned his impressive showing of authority as he sat in the Vice-President's chair, hanging on to the moment labelled—expectation.

'I realize,' he began in a low key, 'that the eyes of America, indeed, of the whole world, are turned to this place as of now. Our enemies, no doubt, will view our meticulous scrutiny of the tragic and melancholy past, with exultation. Some of those countries we took to be our friends will dissemble even less their satisfaction that we must endure an aftermath transcending the condition of a temporary embarrassment.

'I must tell you that I am indifferent and impervious to the world's reaction whether it be sympathy, feigned or sincere, or triumph of any kind.

'This is a domestic tragedy. It is America's own cross; only

America can bear it and, ultimately, understand why it was required to shoulder it at all.

'I will say nothing more of a personal nature at this stage.'

He paused and looked slowly about him. That way the TV cameras took his clean cut features from ear to ear, left and right profile and a full frontal.

'I have been charged, by the Congress of the United States, to assume the functions, executive powers and all attributes pertaining to the office of the presidency; I have taken the oath to uphold the Constitution according to the obligation imposed upon the presidency.

'I will do so.'

'Winfield for President?' *UPI* whispered.

AP was about to ask how you lose a one-horse race then remembered the place was bugged thicker than Watergate.

New York Times passed a note to the *Tribune*. 'Another body found in Madison Avenue.'

'My first duty,' Winfield continued, 'is formally to call the Senate into full committee to investigate the causes of a catastrophe which even now is not fully documented, not wholly understood, and by no means explained.

'I make a pledge to you, the American people, that this committee will not end its sittings until every last piece of evidence has been unearthed, until every last remnant of conspiracy has been rooted out.'

While the *ex officio* President rolled out his programme, the TV cameras ranged over the Chamber on a pre-arranged schedule. America heard his ringing phrases against a backdrop of bloodstains, of shattered windows left to tell their story, of chipped marble walls, and a ceiling laced with bullet holes.

It was dramatic, but somehow not as effective as it was supposed to be.

'In order effectively and efficiently to discharge its sacred obligations, I have decreed this committee will observe the minimum of formalities.

'Further, witnesses may be required to appear before us at any time and with minimum notification. There will be no right of legal representation and by order of the Emergency Committee the Fifth Amendment is suspended until further

23

notice. Any witness who nevertheless refuses to testify will be in contempt and subject to a gaol sentence to be determined by the Joint Emergency Committee.'

Came a movement, perceptible as a fugitive breath of wind, through the close packed Chamber, and it went its way into every nook and cranny of the country; a soundless stirring of millions made uneasily aware that nothing was sacred anymore.

Those bastards sure had something to answer for.

So thought the *Tribune*. But his reaction had to do with professional jealousy and frustration. Another day such an announcement would have had them all stampeding to file their lead stories. Now they just sat there and listened because what could you do with a comparative after a superlative? By paradox Halliday had made the big news too small. Noting reactions, the stances, the salient facts was about all they could do with the inevitable.

Winfield elasticated the moment belonging to him and to him alone; rearranged the papers on his desk, conscious that his every move was being recorded for posterity, unconscious of the fact that history throws up many Winfields who owe a greater debt to tragedy and disaster than they would care to admit.

'You ran away, Roberts, you said you did.'

'You're confusing my words. I said "I ran, I just ran". I meant I ran into a firing position. You don't jump out of a truck and stand there firing, that draws the enemy's fire on what you're trying to protect, you run *away* from it, zig-zag towards the enemy. Do I have to tell a military man?'

'But you were not firing, Roberts. When you headed for that Marine block you were not firing. Don't you realize that?' Words, smooth as poppy oil.

'That's not true.'

'They left you to get killed, Roberts.'

'I knew what I was doing.'

'And knowing they'd left you, you decided you wanted nothing more to do with it.'

'I never stopped firing till the gun jammed and you damn well know it.'

24

'Your M16 was carefully examined. It fired easily, there was no jamming.'

'You must think I'm stupid.'

'It still held rounds, you know that?'

'And how about a white flag of surrender, you forgot I was waving a white flag!'

'I'll work on it. Let's be honest about this, Ed. You jumped out of that truck and something happened back of your mind. You *lost* your ability, your intention to fire another shot. You realized at some crucial moment, the enormity of what you were doing and you ran, telling yourself "I want no further part of it". Isn't that right?'

'I know what I intended to do, Doctor Splitbrain. I was gonna kill those sons of bitches because they were in our way, defending the right of crap like you to engineer my mind any way you want. You know it, I know it, so why bother?'

'Because I have to convince *you*, Ed, that you were sick in your mind. You're the one that matters. I have to convince America that you suffered a spontaneous recovery, greater than St Paul's conversion; that you broke out and ran, preferring surrender to more dishonour than you could carry.'

'Who set you up as a goddam arbiter of my mind?'

'The US Government, Roberts. But if it hadn't, I'd still be glad to convince you of your error and by God I'm going to do just that. Now let's start right out again, shall we?

'When you saw Halliday hit you decided to quit and you leaped out of the truck——'

'I was mad! If they got Halliday the whole thing was finished.'

The uniformed mind smiled. 'You were mad. We now have that for the record. We're beginning to get somewhere, Roberts.'

Roberts frowned, looked more tired than he knew or cared to admit. The session had been on-going for three hours already.

'We've got plenty of time, Roberts. No-one expects a dunghill to look like a rose without a whole lot of trying. But if America needs a miracle, why then, I'll see she gets one.'

'Why not call the President, Doc? He'll roger that.'

The doctor, psychiatrist, or whatever the Pentagon said he was supposed to be, lost his friendly expression, or it was raped

25

maybe, by the meanest grimace Roberts could remember since the last days of Captain Lacey.

'Colonel Gorton has testified to this committee that three full companies of infantry with Ranger and some Airborne support were transported to the An Loc sector from Firebase Four.

'His evidence shows that these companies were considered to be unreliable, indisciplined and, in the opinion of S 2, hostile to the aims legitimately pursued in South East Asia *before* the search and destroy mission on which they were engaged that day.

'You will recall his account of the message from Captain Lacey, "the only worthwhile officer in the whole outfit" to quote his words, requesting permission over Halliday's head, to discipline the unit by marching it thirty-eight miles back to base.

'Colonel Gorton gave that permission.

'It may be that, in the course of our investigation, we shall learn whether Captain Lacey, by his action, signed his own death warrant.'

Companies A, B and C withdrew from the village and threaded their way east through the jungle without too much strain. Typically, Major Halliday himself was far out in front taking point. Isolated, dangerous work. To be in the lead was to invite the quiet drop by a VC armed with a length of vine. By a quirk of logic you were dead almost before it happened.

They ate C-rations and fed the children as they marched. And not for one moment did they give a damn that they were in extended line, deep in Viet Cong territory most of the way, open to every X Y Z ambush the enemy cared to set up. Whether it was because of the children or because a decision was in the making no-one, perhaps not even Halliday, could have said.

They just walked, without resting. There was nowhere in that thick secondary growth to ground arms, so they pushed on. The army records don't have much to say about that march, except that it happened.

Back at Firebase Four they got word of a new assignment. Almost the last combat troops left in Vietnam, they were to be

26

flown to Cambodia. Something about harassing a Viet Cong concentration somewhere near the junction of the rivers Se San and Mekong.

'What for?' Fletcher wanted to know.

Lieutenant Benner shrugged up to his ears. How could there be a reason for a damn fool mission like that? If they really were expected to liaise with a bastard like Do Cao Tri and his killers it must be part of Foxwell's spoiled-baby plan to give the VC a last good kick in the teeth.

'In which case,' Private Whitney Fletcher announced, 'I don't want no part of it.'

'Me too,' said Lieutenant Benner.

Actually, it represented the Saigon Command's solution to an almost intractable problem. What to do with three companies with a body count so low, either they were militarily anaemic or, as Gorton later testified, they were 'inimical to the stated aims of the Government in prosecution of the war'.

At any rate they were reduced to virtual impotency in the new position since the Viet Cong left them entirely to their own devices. This was made possible by the fact that there were practically no VC in the area anyway.

They had time to look about them, to think too much, to debate their situation during the long, boring hours and first days of sheer inactivity, ignoring the everlasting B-52s droning overhead on another arc-light mission or waiting for the choppers to lift in supplies when they happened to remember.

Mostly they took care of the kids.

Over the radio they caught some of the noises that were being made about that peace; the peace that passeth every intelligent body's understanding.

Colonel Gorton's testimony before the Emergency Committee of Investigation.

Senator Maskelyne of Ohio questioning. 'Colonel, was it army policy to inject unreliable personnel into areas where they could be least troublesome to the overall programme?'

'I wouldn't say that. Apart from the detail that we didn't have a sizable programme outstanding as of that time, we wouldn't anticipate a problem of disaffection measured in hundreds, so I'd say no, we didn't have a policy.'

'But you had some way of dealing with individual trouble-makers, even a dozen dissidents?'

'Certainly. Every army has its methods.'

'It never occurred to you or your superiors that the equivalent of a battalion could act in this way?'

'There was no precedent for it.'

'In the light of subsequent events would you have an opinion as to what happened to these men?'

'After Saigon?'

'No—I'm talking now about the Cambodian posting.'

'I don't think there's much doubt these men were exposed in some way to Communist influence for the whole time they spent in the Se San area.'

'We're talking here of five hundred and forty men, Colonel.'

'If we assume they were hit by a kind of corporate insanity I don't think numbers need affect the assumption. They just blew their minds collectively. There's no other explanation.'

'Thank you, Colonel.'

Gorton had to be right on one point. Something did happen to those companies in the long, punishing weeks spent on the Mekong. In the beginning it concerned the officers on that very first night in Cambodia. After hacking out a makeshift perimeter, siting tents and establishing outposts within the surrounding razor-wire defences, Halliday, Lacey, Racowiczs, Thompson and the other officers sat in relaxed mood round a small fire outside the command post. The coffee tasted good for once.

Relaxed, or chewing at their silence, just enjoying the heat of coffee mugs in their hands, or listening to Seth somewhere near, giving the news of the times in his own way. Seth was A company's minstrel, the only man who rated a gun-bearer so he could carry his guitar.

Every day's end he would take it in hand and sing the news in a haunting blues style that snagged the emotions every so often, wrapped up the day for them all in a way that made it easier to remember.

'Someone should tell him to button up,' Lacey said. His brother officers looked in each other's general direction. Benner was thinking: the moonlight's beautiful and Lacey has a knack of debasing the beautiful simply by opening his mouth.

'You want to go and tell him?' Major Halliday suggested.

'Why should I? You're in command.'

'That's exactly why I'm not going to tell him.'

'He's subversive, downright subversive. You know he sings that crap just about every night and it's—counterproductive.'

'Ho-ho-ho,' Lieutenant Able Thompson, prone on the ground, laughed at the stars in what he took to be an undertone.

'What's tickling your ass?' Lacey snapped. 'You think it's funny for nigras to knock down everything we set up and stand for?'

'What else can you do with it?' someone said.

'I think it's natural.' Able Thompson, normally hot-tempered was keeping as casual as he knew how. 'They're not fighting for any little old USA, Captain.'

Racowiczs pointed his empty pipe at Thompson. 'Right,' he agreed.

'They're just imitating,' Thompson explained.

'Right,' Racowiczs jabbed his pipe again.

'What's that supposed to mean?'

'Anything you care to make of it, Captain.' A lordling's tone of voice, useful for dealing with peasants.

'Well I'm intending to put it in my report when we get back. This nigger-nursin' has to stop.'

'Everything has to stop, every damned thing, right Lacey? Everything that isn't you and your Georgia Wallace coon-shit.'

Relaxation went another way as tension, never far distant, returned. The difference between blank shot and a live round.

The handful of officers stirred, kept a careful eye on the only man that mattered just then. Maybe the gods passed round the message: this is of epoch-making importance that Haliday, the quietest officer in the Third Infantry, was on his feet, standing over Lacey, a gleam in his eye that took nothing from the fire burning nearby, but was internal, illuminating, all suddenly, his deepest being.

'Someone told me, Lacey, you carried your Ku Klux hood around wherever you go; is that right?'

'That's my business, Major.' But the snap had gone out of his voice and Lacey sounded no more than querulous.

'Where is it?'

'I told you——'

'Get your pack open or I'll do it for you!'

Lacey had no choice; not the way Halliday was looking. A way not even the rest of the officers could remember in the worst fighting moments.

Madness, Benner tagged it later. Messianic, was Able Thompson's impression. Lacey found it indescribable so he fumbled in his haversack and drew out the pointed relic from home sweet home, a neat little hood worked by his mammy's own hands, a cute little headpiece he'd worn on so many night patrols in the Georgia hills.

Halliday stared at it as though trying to work out why it should mean more than itself.

'Silk,' he said, almost incredulously. 'That must look good among the wool hats.' It seemed to slip out of Lacey's grasp as Halliday continued. 'Here's something to sing about, Boston. How the Ku Klux rode high and walked tall in Vietnam.'

Before Lacey could move, the hood was jerked into the fire. Impassively they watched Lacey, incoherent with rage, playing demon dip to get back his precious rag. Unbelievingly they watched Halliday hurl himself forward to grip the captain's right hand as it paltered with the flames.

He whispered, low and intense. 'I remember you, Captain, the man who cuts off a VC's ear while he's still dying.' Then loudly. 'OK Lacey, ordeal by fire if that's how you prefer. I say it remains. If you've got Ku Klux courage to stay in it longer, it's yours.'

The officers tensed, unaware of their men edging closer to watch a novel kind of challenge. The smart ones were already taking bets.

To his credit Lacey held till their flesh began to smell of bad cooking, then he screamed and broke away, mouthing obscenities.

Shame and rage sent him stumbling out into the darkness,

and some said it was Marshall who took off after him. Somebody must have, because no-one saw Lacey again.

Rear-Admiral Flugzeuger, former commander of the US carrier, *Carolina*, and one of its few survivors. Part of his testimony to the Emergency Committee.

'At that time our instructions were to take off all military hardware surplus to the requirements of the Saigon government.'

'Can you specify the material?'

'Fifty Chinooks, and a last minute intake of crates—about a hundred maybe.'

'Did you have reason to comment on this merchandise?'

'In what way?'

'I mean the Chinooks could be assumed, but the crates contained material, arms, ammunition—explosive, RTs and so forth, already promised to our Vietnamese ally.'

'We had no way of knowing what the crates contained.'

'You had no manifest?'

'Our documentation merely referred to crated war material. The Chinooks were identifiable of course.'

Senator Wythenshaw passed a sheet of paper to the rear-admiral.

'Did you ever see this document before?'

The naval man examined it doubtfully. 'Can't say I have.'

'Why not?'

'It has to do with matters dealt with by a lower officer.'

'But you know what it is?'

'Oh yes, it's a routine army form listing supplies to be shipped on behalf of the ordnance department.'

'That's correct, Admiral. Do you recognize the countersignature?'

'Why yes, it plainly identifies Colonel Massey—I believe he was in charge of the surplus arms and equipment situation.'

'Do you recognize the top signature?'

'I can't read that, it's illegible.'

'Yes, as you say, it's illegible. Let's move on a bit, Admiral. You were ready to sail on the night of March 4th, is that right?'

'Yes.'

'Two hours before preparing to weigh anchor the *Carolina* was standing in the approach roads to Saigon harbour?'

'That is so.'

'Were you expecting passengers, officials of any kind?'

'No.'

'But number two gangway was lowered.'

'Only for the convenience of the pilot.'

'When did you first become aware that something was wrong?'

'Lieutenant Coleherne came into the operations room and informed me a craft of some kind had come alongside and a considerable number of men appeared to be coming aboard. I asked what he meant by a considerable number and he replied, "About fifty". He mentioned that they were armed.'

'How did you respond?'

'I think I made some joke about GIs who couldn't wait to get out of the war.'

'In other words you refused to take this lieutenant's information seriously?'

'Who would have?'

'I'm asking you, Admiral.'

'I was in no position to go either way. One assumes a junior officer doesn't play that kind of joke at any time, so I suppose I was momentarily confused.'

'Did you have time to act on his information?'

'Not at all. I was about to send the staff captain to investigate when, as I estimate the number, a dozen armed men burst into the room.'

'How long would it take a man familiar with the ship to go from the gangway to the control tower, Admiral?'

'He might do it in two minutes.'

'And someone who was not cognisant of a large carrier's layout?'

'Much longer than two minutes.'

'Was it your impression these men arrived soon after the lieutenant?'

'Very soon after.'

'What do you deduce from that at this distance in time?'

'Only that someone on board ship was ready to help these men gain their objective.'

'Who was leading them?'
'A man I took to be a major in the United States Army.'
'What were his opening words, Admiral?'
'He said, "All of you, put up your hands".'

But that was old, old history, all of three months ago. No, the admiral did not remember Roberts, but Roberts had been there, right behind Halliday, the night they hi-jacked the US carrier *Carolina*, the pride of South Eastern Command's Seventh Fleet. It had more strikes to its credit than almost all the other carriers put together. A real sassy little number; nice, tight ship with some of the meanest, deadliest fliers in the service who saw the whole operation as a love affair between them and their F100s. And now, the fun was over; they were on their way home to make swoopy hand movements for starry eyed gals and stripey-eyed moms, showing how they'd shot the crap out of those Red mealie-bugs in Haiphong.

And, ho-hum, here we are again, Ed. Stuffed Shirts Inc. and Ivy League distaste rearing its ugly head all over some more. Just look at the way that admiral without a ship is looking at you.

But Canada won't give 'em back. That Prime Minister, or whatever they call him, is AOK. Roberts' thoughts leaped around like antic goats as the Senate rambled on, unfolding a tale of woe. One moment he was reliving the incredible days on *Carolina*; next, he was back in the Cambodian jungle hunting and training with the fellers, or helping to bring up the two orphans with approximately five hundred daddies.

Each day a couple of GIs took their turn, trying to teach the children a little English. Marshall stood by to help with the Vietnamese part of it.

Extra looked bewildered came his spell. 'What do I tell 'em?'

He gazed blankly at Thu ba and Thu hai seated grave and solemn in the centre of the compound. They had two rickety chairs and two splintery desks lifted from some bombed-off village on the river's edge.

Sometimes a number of the other men sat in on lesson time

33

when they were free. It could degenerate into a comedy show when someone like Extra took class.

'Just tell 'em anything you want, Extra,' Marshall drawled. 'Just so they get used to hearin' the language. It's a beginning.'

Easier said than done. Extra was no pedant. Sensing his difficulty the children began to giggle. His was a droll kind of face, pointed and worried, almost clown-like. And, in the fashion of a clown he'd prompted a twinkle in their solemn eyes, enough to explode pent-up laughter the moment he did something funny.

'Come on, Professor, tell 'em how you got a Xerox degree from Harvard,' someone piped up.

'Shut up.' Extra felt acutely embarrassed.

The way it slid out of his mouth struck the children as funny. They giggled and he felt very pleased with himself.

'Uh—suppose I tell 'em what we are?'

'They know what we are,' Marshall reminded him.

'Poor little sheep who've lost their way,' a member of the associate teaching staff suggested.

'Why don't you guys take a walk, I'm teachin'.'

'OK Extra, tell 'em what we are,' Marshall said.

Extra swept his arm around the compound, then pointed to himself. 'American—we are American soldiers. You understand?'

'Chúng tôi là lính Mỹ,' Marshall explained to the bewildered faces. 'Ông hiêu Không?'

They nodded brightly and began giggling again, which had Extra a little anxious.

'Hey Marsh, did you tell 'em right?'

'Sure, they understand.'

'Well what's so funny?' After a moment's thought he looked vaguely about him, then spoke more slowly, unlike himself. 'Yeah, I guess it is funny.'

Supplementary from Colonel Gorton's HQ TX/7/721. To Major Halliday. A company's request to take two war orphans, Thu ba and Thu hai, on combat duty negatived. The children will be handed over to the appropriate agency immediately, repeat, immediately.

Ed Roberts remembered that day well. Not only because of Extra playing teacher like someone out of a burlesque show, but because it disguised yet another beginning, out of context with the working day, but all of a piece with the future.

The mail had come clattering in with rations, PX stores and a collection of newspapers that about represented every state in the Union.

Not even the interminable bombing missions brooming overhead could penetrate the siesta style silence draped over the compound. Wherever there was shade men crouched or stretched, reading the news from home. Scenically it recalled a bad ambush, made in Hollywood, defenders cut down where they stood, dropping into comfortable attitudes of death.

Many were reading about themselves, one way or another.

'I'm sorry Joe, I wouldn't have it this way for the world, but you said to be completely honest with each other and I figured you meant what you said.

'I paid the quarter's rent and there's still six weeks to go. Your Mom said she'd take care of your stereo equipment.

'I guess we were too young to know what war really means....'

'So I'm telling her, why don't you wait and open your big fat mouth when Harold goes off to fight for Democratsy. You never heard a woman yakking like that Bertha, right in Schultz's Supermart she's standing between me and the canned beans telling *me* she envies me on account of you're fightin Communism—and who else like hell I said. I told her, right there in Schultz's, my spouse was just too damned ignorant to know how to dodge the draft is all. And you know what the bitch said: It's that kind of ignorance is what makes America great. At the top of her sick-provoking voice!'

Some got laughter, some got tears, a lot remained indifferent. One or two were moved to protest, simply by turning over and going back to a sleep that excludes all. Except for one GI who got to his feet, pale and shaking with a discernible anger.

'Goddam you,' he muttered, 'goddam you.' Quite suddenly he shouted to nobody in particular: 'I've had enough of this fucken war!'

Evoking a faint ripple of applause as everyone within earshot turned dramatic critic. Most of them had tried that line at different times and in various ways, but for sheer intensity, Private Klinger from Detroit had them all, in a manner of speaking, glancing at their programmes.

Lieutenant Thompson had an eye on his paper and one on Klinger. An outburst like that could so easily be the beginning of an out of hand situation. The last berserker in his outfit had gone running into the jungle forever.

Sergeant Kemble ambled a little nearer to the storm centre as Klinger looked wildly at the faces dotted around him. They were interested enough because Klinger was the kind of man who'd sooner throw a punch than talk above three consecutive words.

'Fellers, I'm gonna read you this letter—I'm gonna let you hear how one American bitchofabitch feels about this war. Grab this.

' "Well son, it looks like Foxwell's got those gooks real jammed up for you in old Hanoi. I tell you I went on my knees when I heard what he did to that Commie nest of hornets. Guess you must've heard how our B-52s flew a thousand missions and blew the hell outta Redsville. It kind of makes up for having to leave Vietnam. Reckon you must feel the same. I'm real proud of you son. And so is Pop. He says to tell you he's put your name down for the local Veterans Against Communism League." '

Klinger looked up, all truculence melted into sweat, and said, in a strange voice that sounded like all the moms of America rolled into one: 'And four more pages of that palpitating shit.'

'What's different?' said PFC Comaggio. 'We all have to swallow it this or that way. Mine I get with Balsamella. You should hear my old lady. She's appropriated a couple of thousand dollars for a marble statue in the Lakeside Resting Grounds

36

for when I get killed.' He fingered the coke-filled cross hanging next to his identity tag as he spoke.

'That's what I mean!' Viciously, as though, in his rage, he couldn't clearly see what he meant; could only guess at it. He simply repeated the words, for the comfort they gave: 'That's what I mean.'

'What exactly do you mean, Private?'

That was Halliday asking. When he wanted to know something you had to search around in your mind for a respectable answer.

So Klinger tried hard. 'Well, sir. Like—does anyone back home have any conception what this is all about? I mean do they care?'

Halliday studied him for a moment, reflectively, as if Klinger was part of some decision, some grinding conclusion which only now began to make sense....

Halliday's biography is now a part of America's history, and researching students will major in their thousands, devoting a mountain of theses to his psycho-pathological condition; Halliday and the Rejection Principle, the Regressive Personality Under Fire. Biography be damned. Who wants to tell a straight story about a premeditating murderer, a traitor and besmircher of the one true flag?

They knew he'd served ten years or more in the army, but how explain that he no longer believed in it because he saw clearly that it had subverted the political system and become its own master in the process? How explain that it was a part of the world he had no further use for, or belief in?

At forty he knew he'd seen everything. It had taken Vietnam to open his eyes wide to the limits of astonishment, and it did nothing for his peace of mind to discover he was a necessary part of a corroding process.

For him the truth had become a fierce realization: a man, licensed to kill so long as it was far out, right away from the Statue of Liberty. Preferably somewhere you couldn't put your hand on your heart and swear your enemy was human.

But he wasn't alone in his thoughts as he once had been. Vietnam had done that much for Halliday. Like has a knack of attracting like. When he got back from the army hospital

37

at Zama he'd been glad to take temporary command of the toughest personnel in the entire US presence.

Excepting the few hard-hats, they were just a bunch of boys, not particularly American, humans who still hadn't lost the universal touch; they hated the army, hated their rôle in it, hated the officers and ultimately, had reacted in the only way they knew how. Violently.

Knifings, even shoot-outs in the steamier alleys of Saigon. Desertion, insubordination, total lack of discipline; anything disrespectful to the current *mores* of army thinking you could put a name to, they'd tried it.

There were so many of these misfits that some chairborne champ at headquarters had conceived the beautiful notion of forming them into an assault battalion, a kind of hellcat élite that could be sent express anywhere in Vietnam where the fighting was meanest, and maybe they'd get their asses kicked so bad some sense of conformity might penetrate to their heads; alternatively they could get themselves wiped out in a Dien Bien Phu situation and Old Glory would flutter a little stronger in a big, windy sigh of relief from Saigon and Pentagon.

But companies A, B and C were clean contrary. As a unit they just refused to die, and sometimes they didn't even agree to fight. When they had to, they fought well, like tigers in a wild-life reserve resenting the belligerency of tourists poking cameras in their direction. Almost to a man they stayed plain ornery, cussed as mules, the despair of genocidal killers like Lacey. Who were less likely to stay alive than the Viet Cong if they protested too much.

So they'd survived, to the very end of the Involvement, and in spite of extensions beyond the normal tour of duty, which was illegal; but who in hell and Saigon had ever cared about legality?

And they owed their survival to Halliday; not because he was the world's greatest expert in paddyfield warfare, but because he'd seen, soon enough, what his superiors were aiming at, and with a quiet desperation, bringing flexibility to a fine art, he'd fought to keep his men out of that kind of trouble.

Every man in the three companies knew it. And if every other grunt in Vietnam had known as much, and fought under

38

his supreme command, the US might just have won that war.

Able Thompson, commanding B company, once put it in some kind of 78mm shell. 'Someone made him piece by piece, friend. He never came off an assembly line.'

His junior officers, mostly short term, were cast in a similar mould. They came out shinier, unmarked by all the years Halliday had seen, but no less in sympathy with what he'd learned by experience. College men, passing through or dropping out, some had joined the army in a what-the-hell show of bravado, one or two had even followed the Flag with a deep down desire to give the American system one last chance to justify itself.

Most of their reasons had long since lost validity as they followed their disillusionment beyond the gates of hell (which, as every slouch quickly discovers, lead out of any US army base to the halls of Montezuma and the shores of Tripoli di dum di dah) and grown more long-haired in the process than the men under their command. A little more subtly perhaps, as befits officers and gentlemen, wipe your mouth before you speak to me and so forth.

Back to Halliday.

'You're asking me questions, Klinger. You really want me to answer them?'

'They're good questions, Major. You know that,' Marshall called, answering for Klinger.

Halliday turned, regarded Marshall for a long moment, then surveyed, one by one, his men; every manjack had that tense, expectant regard he'd seen so often. They wanted him to say something, but he still couldn't be sure what it was exactly.

They seemed to divine the thing lurking back of his mind and that couldn't be right since it had to do with monstrous possibilities he hardly dared admit to himself. Remnant conditioning still persuaded him they were Americans first, disgruntled GIs with a human flavour second. For the moment he ducked the issue, kidding himself his first duty had to do with their survival.

'Well then, if they're good questions, the right answers won't be far off.'

You bought time with that kind of response. They knew as

39

much and guessed the major, who seldom ducked anything, from bullets to minutes, must be going through a lot of travail if he needed to haggle with the clock for a decision. Knew he'd give the right answer when he was good and ready.

He walked away with his preoccupation and they returned to their letters and whatever.

Later in the day he heard one of them call to his buddy. 'You know what it says here? Some female in Florida just traded her baby for a Chevrolet.'

'Well what do y'know?'

And who puts it into people's minds to say the wrong thing at the right time? His pace slowed to the tempo of his thoughts. A snatch of small town gossip could do so much? Trigger off deep, or was it cheap, emotions? Babies traded for automobiles—what's Hecuba to me?

But it took his problem where it belonged; out of Vietnam and back to America.

Where such things could happen.

And they were defending the right of the free world to allow such things to happen.

He returned to the officers' tent deeply troubled by his apparent involvement in things that essentially were his concern; superficially, were none of his godamned business.

'Something on your mind, Major?' Able Thompson noticed everything.

'Klinger's on his mind.' Benner was sitting on an ammunition box drawing complicated mazes so he could find his way out of them.

Racowiczs and Mellors were deep in a chess game. Some of the others were standing by with advice.

'Klinger—maybe.' Halliday surveyed the game with a tactical eye. 'You're in trouble, Black.'

'That's because Mellors insists on playing chess like it was poker. Everybody's happy except Klinger?' Racowiczs wondered.

'Nobody's happy, just contented in a confused kind of way.'

'The best anyone can hope for,' Mellors bequeathed.

'Do they know we're going home after this assignment?' Benner asked.

Halliday drew a long breath. 'Time enough when we finish with it.'

'If we finish,' Benner pointed out. 'Three months is one hell of a long time.'

'The way I'm feeling I could stay here forever.' Racowiczs had a moustache that must have been Zapata's second-best long since.

'What you afraid of, Jan?' Mellors.

'Your king's bishop and that kind of peace, I guess. No, it's more than that. This damned heat does nothing for the thought process.'

'I'll roger that—check!'

Racowiczs sat back and it was plain the chess-game had been forgotten long before. The others shifted their mental attitude to accommodate the something he had on his mind.

'Klinger doesn't know; and I only know what I'd do if I knew how. I'd cure the American people of an obsession—and I don't know how because I don't see clearly what is the obsession.

'No, I don't much want to go back. To America? OK. Let's be fair, I don't think there are many places in the world I do want to go to. There's a bad smell hanging over most of it. So what's the prospect? Go home—shoot the shit, great to be back, uh now where did I last hang my hat in the rat-run? Yes ma'am I surely will marry your daughter because if I don't, how can I tell my kids I was a great guy in Vietnam? And if I don't have kids what a dirty way to make sure they escape the draft for the next little line-out. All that copulation and no population; is that patriotic I ask you?'

'You're talking about a way of life—so how do you change it?' Mellors wanted to know.

'I don't accept it's a way of life, that's what I'm saying. *This* is a way of life—who's responsible? Did you go down on your bended knees and pray for it? I didn't.'

'So,' Mellors persisted, 'the question remains: How do you change it?'

'Violently.'

Instinctively they looked to Halliday.

'What kind did you have in mind, Jan?'

'There's only one kind they're really scared of, the only kind they'll slap down harder than Mafia ... democratic violence.'

They broke off to watch Thu ba and Thu hai playing a variant of baseball with a handful of GIs. The kids were laughing as though nothing had conspired to wipe out their lives, nothing had forced them to begin all over again.

As he watched them running around, lithe and almost carefree, Halliday caught a fleeting glimpse of a vision, a scanty, subliminal impression of a haggard column of men, headed by two children carrying a flag on which, emblazoned like a battle honour, was a word.

And the word was 'Love'.

The 707 swooped in for a touch-down on runway three. From every window heads were craning for a view of America.

It didn't look so exciting at that. California was beautiful at fifteen thousand feet, but as you dropped level with the mountains there was little to see except broad highways and the rectangular buildings paraded around the air base. Lots of shining white concrete—but at least it was American concrete.

'Whoo goshamighty we're home! If I hadn't been watching I'd say America came up to meet us—guess it must've been *vice versa*. Well come on, Joe, the folks are down there waiting for us. Gotta put a smile on, feller.'

Joe was blind, but he smiled to please Chuck, the irrepressible Chuck who'd kept him going through some dark days somewhere outside Hanoi.

'What can you see, Hawkeye?'

'Well, I see a whole lot of pretty nurses—why is it a pretty nurse makes me feel so ill? And what have we here? A couple of hot dog stands, I guess that's to make us feel homey. Er—we're just slewing round to taxi in, and Jeez! they got a—hey fellers —they got a whole bale of red carpet run right up to the stop-off —you see that? And TV cameras and—like we were heroes.'

'Yeah!'

Loud and clear. Man, the way Sergeant Willis mouthed that one word equated with an ice-cube dropped down a doll's house chimney. The chatter died away and the medics nursemaiding the returned POWs glanced at each other with meaning.

'Ah come on, Sarge. Maybe POW doesn't spell POW! but

42

no-one's sore with you because you didn't make it the way you planned. Jesus, someone had to get captured. You should see his expression, Joe; he ain't looked like anything else these last three years.'

'*Cho câm máu lai!*'

Chuck glanced across the aisle. A tall, thin boy from Missouri sat staring straight ahead. He wore an idiot's grin, betrayed no sense of occasion; lost, irretrievably, in an old memory of pain and haemorrhage.

'Hey, Medic! You'd better give Stevens his shot. He's excited and it ain't good for him.'

'*Cho câm máu lai!*'

'Well come on. He can keep this up for hours.'

The plane had come to rest. As the jets whined down to nothing the passengers were meant to hear an air force band too-rooting 'Dixie', or some such antiquated crap. It was conditional. Supposed to make them feel good and back in the fold.

But all the sixty-five men could hear was the ex-ranger, his voice monotonous and on a rising note, endlessly repeating '*Cho câm máu lai!*'

'Medic!'

'OK soldier—cool it.'

One of the medical aids hurried along the aisle with a hypo. The man from Missouri seemed not to notice as it bit into his vein.

'What's he yakking about anyway?' An indifferent kind of question.

'Pressure mine—got a leg blown off on patrol. Couppla VC found him just in time. Last thing he remembers is one of 'em saying, "Stop the bleeding". Now he can't say anything else— ain't that a wonder? Look Joe, I mean, those nurses look real handsome. I sure wish I was temporarily dying.'

Everyone was standing, ready to make contact with that good old American soil baking under a Californian sun, white as a governor demonstrating his teeth. The excitement was intense but somehow—handicapped. None moved with that easy assurance to be expected in men of their age. They were like senior citizens preparing to step off the bus for a picnic or a day by the sea.

43

'Hold it fellers. Just relax and set back in your seats a moment.'

The thinned faces creased into anxiety, looked questioningly at each other and at the quiet men in rear of the plane who hadn't spoken much to anyone on the flight from Hawaii.

Heads turned and followed the speaker's smooth progress up to the front of the cabin. He looked genial enough as he called for their attention, but it was push-button geniality.

The man from the Pentagon even smiled a little.

'Now you'll all understand, a great deal has happened in the little old world since you were last in it.' This got an uncomfortable titter from those nearest him.

'What I'm trying to do is briefly to fill you in on one or two immediate problems.

'Now, most of you have folks out there and they're going to be real proud of their sons, husbands and so on. When you go down that gangway some of the kids are gonna be seeing Pop for the first time. It's first impressions that count, so I want you to step out smart and cheerful like you'd just landed on the moon. You're all looking great in your new outfits, so do 'em credit.

'And just one other thing. You're going to have to fight your way through the Press and TV's out there too. I don't have to tell you they're meaner than a bunch of gooks——'

'Could I have that again, sir?'

The marshal looked sharply down the seat rows and identified the voice. It had to be from the young man with one half of his face scarred a livid red. Corporal Jim Patmore from Vermont, a quiet type who'd said nothing very much to any of his travelling companions, and not a great deal more in the last two and a half years. Those who knew him from the camp days looked surprised.

'Why certainly, Corporal. I was saying the gooks couldn't be worse than some of those newshounds.'

'That's what I thought you said, sir. And I'd be obliged if you'd strike out "gooks" and maybe refer to them as North Vietnamese or something like that.'

A silence bent only to the windbreaking strains of the tara-boom band just swinging into 'The Land of Stars and Stripes'.

44

The geniality was gone, as if maybe he'd pushed another button. Cut informality, intro steely expression, pan vision over whole scene, demand submission through lips gripped tight.

It worked. That is, they all seemed cowed into a line of conduct. A few of the obstinate ones kept their eyes on the Pentagnome, but most wavered and looked down or around.

'Well,' reflectively, 'I'm sorry if I offended your friends, Corporal. Er—what did you say your name was?'

'I didn't, sir. But it's Patmore, James.'

'OK Jim. I like your spirit. Yessir, I like your spirit—but we have to hustle it because the folks are waiting. Now just remember, be nice and easy when the Press come gunning for you. Oh I almost forgot—I suppose you know what to say?'

They looked puzzled. How the hell should they know what to say? 'It's great to be home, wouldn't that do?' someone asked.

'Well now, that's perfectly natural in its way, but how about something with a little zing, something peppy like "America's the finest country in the whole world and I never stopped telling the—the North Vietnamese jailors".'

'They weren't jailors, sir. They were military guards.'

'Or maybe "I never knew till now how much *Democracy* meant to me" you know? Something your kids'll quote to *their* kids. How the first words my daddy spoke were heard throughout America. Because fellers, what you say will be heard all over Stateside. You read me?'

Some of them mumbled a reply, enough to put the whipped cream smile back in place. He clapped his hands, country-style like MC Cornpone.

'OK fellers, go to it. Have yourselves a real good time. It's all on a grateful country.'

But like senior citizens who climb back on the bus at the day's end, the ex-POWs got heavily to their feet, fumbling for their personal effects and avoiding each other's eyes.

What America saw on TV as the cameras swooped in to lock on the open doorway was a long file of shambling, drooping, hobbling has-beens who would have been dead long ago but for Foxwell's stupendous triumph over the Communists.

While millions shook their heads between commercials, while

45

tears blinded the eyes of shocked relatives standing as near as they were allowed, while sixty-five hostages to their own misfortune threaded like a slow dance of Death along the blood-red carpet, the marshal was having a quiet word with his expressionless deputy, in which time he never once took eyes off Patmore, James, Corporal.

But that was then and this is now. Ed Roberts still stands between the guards, listening with half an ear to the run-down of events as far as they'd been chronicled. The heat in the Chamber was intense, a mixture of TV lights and body heat creating a heady brew that had him dizzy and sweating profusely, as were the book-ends.

Through Winfield's drone he could hear laughter, children's laughter. He peered through a shimmering mist that had settled between him and the crowded room, then closed his eyes and shook his head slightly. This was an adults' world, there couldn't be any children ... simply, the malarial touch that he'd never quite shrugged off. Must account for the radio buzzing in his ears.

'Waco Charley and heed me all you guys out there wherever you may be. Twenty-two hundred hours Saigon time and what's your pleasure fellers? Got a real great line-up for inspection tonight—*tôi nay*—that's Vietnamese for "tonight" I give you it for free. PFC Wilbur Alright bringing you all the best in big A American entertainment. Yessir we aim to please fellers so lock 'n'load and POW! for the big hits like don't you all go getting skunked on beer till you hear—Springsteen! "Blinded by the Light" Laura Nylo by special request Biff Rose singing "Garbage" I kid you not so what do y'mean is that all? You think Wilbur Alright is some kinda slouch well all right, how about this? Pete Roberts, Aunt Jesus, Fat Katz and a whole lot more I could tell of ready to turn you on but first off fellers I got a hot line all the way to Stateside. Yessir from Hollywood LA your favourite comedian and mine—believe me he's so good though he's so old—come on in and talk to the guys: *Joe "Poface" Duffy!*'

'Hi guys, guess you all thought I was alive huh? Well anyone

46

can make a mistake and I apologize but seriously I thought you oughtta know I saw the President last night and he said "Joe, if you can make the boys laugh I'll award you the Congressional Medal of Honour". "That's great, Mr President," I said, "So what would I get if I made *you* laugh?" "Well Joe, you'd get a long report from Caressinger on my reaction." But seriously fellers I just want you to know he's proud of you all. He—he doesn't say it, but he looks it whenever the boys out there come into the conversation which is most of the time. And I know he'd want me to say how grateful we all are for whatever you're doing every one of you, in defence of that freedom others don't have—and we know all about.'

'Turn that mind-deforming punk off!' someone called out of the darkness. A hand reached out and put Poface into someone else's limbo. The natural silence seemed not only profound but grateful.

'Proud?'

Pause.

'Whatever we're doin'.'

Pause.

'Right now I'm scratching my ass. What's the country comin' to when it's proud to know where your goddam finger is?'

'Yeah,' another voice, heavy with sleep. 'I was dreamin' of a girl I laid in Cholon three months back. I guess it goes to show my country needs me.'

'What you going to do when you get DEROS, Cal?'

'Straight to Frisco—college.'

'Berkeley?'

'You must be kidding. Anyway I said "Frisco", rat-head. There's a new college opened in a little room off Harry's Street. I'm gonna take my diploma in "How to beat the RAP".'

'How's that?'

'The Responsible American People.'

'Save me a place.'

'Me, I'm just gonna be an ole ex-warhorse.'

'So?'

'So I put myself out to grass.'

That got more chuckles than Poface Duffy.

'Like a saying they have in that little old country that went

47

to market. "The world's going to pot".'

'I sure could use my share right now.'

All the officers were gathered in the large tent that served as a command post and meeting-house. No-one was doing anything very military. Reading, writing, that kind of stuff. The youngest lieutenant, Collins, was actually knitting, which was a measure of the mess the outfit had got itself into. A junior officer in Benning would have been hanged with his own skein of wool.

Able Thompson, glad to be back in the warmth of the CP, had just finished his tour of the outposts, not that anyone ever bothered them, but he liked to be sure everyone was comfortable.

He gazed round at the fellers and wondered how so much peace could exist in such primitive conditions. Then he noticed something that gave him a curiously pleasant shock. No-one was wearing his hair at the regulation length. Collins had brown locks down to his collar, or where his collar might have been if he'd been wearing a vest.

He glanced at the major who was reading. Good Christ! The man hadn't shaved in days. In fact, there was five o'clock shadow all over the place. If the colonel should drop in for inspection—not very likely. The colonel had a reputation for keeping well out of trouble.

What the hell. Another two weeks and it wouldn't matter a monkey's.

The tarpaulin lifted and the RTO stuck his head through. 'I've got the colonel on the line, sir.'

Halliday heaved himself up and picked his way through the bodies to the 'Radio-room'. 'Wonder what the bastard wants this time.'

The other men grinned.

'Halliday?'

'Sir.'

'We're pulling you guys out in ten days. The war's over—as good as.'

'It always was.'

'What's that?'

'I said, "Do we lift off or are we to march back, sir?"'

48

'The slicks'll take you off—you'll be notified.'

'Oh good.'

'One other thing, Halliday. I want more action out of your people. My information is the area is lousy with VC. We need something big, make the folks back home feel it was all worthwhile.'

'Wasn't it, sir?'

'Wasn't it what?'

'Worthwhile.'

A long pause. 'You've had damn near three months to clean up the situation in your sector.'

'We have combat training every day——'

'Fug your combat training! I'm talking about missions. There is not one mission in your reports, not a single body count, the whole US air presence at your service and you didn't call for a single air strike. What kind of a war is that?'

'What kind did you want, sir?'

'I want action. I want results. Now you get your men off their asses first light tomorrow and you go out looking.'

'What for?'

'The enemy.'

'But there isn't one. We've looked under every stone. I've even had my men dive in the river just in case some of those crafty gooks had grown fins to swim up the Mekong. Nothing.'

An even longer pause. 'Major, I have a note of our conversation on tape, and I'm warning you I'll use it to bust you right back to buck private if I don't get satisfaction out of your last combat reports. A search and destroy mission every day *and* a body count. I don't care how you get it—is that understood?'

'*Quos vult perdere*, Colonel.'

'And none of your pidgin Vietnamese, speak American, dammit.'

'OK. How about Mickey Mouse?'

'I'm ordering you for the last time——'

'Thanks, Colonel. Now why don't you fuck off like a good little uniform, it's past your bed-time.'

Halliday cut off and winked at Roberts, who was smiling broadly as though he'd just eaten a good meal.

'I wouldn't mind a recording of that one myself, Major.'

49

Halliday grinned and tried to get back into the main tent. Tried, because every one of the dozen officers was crowded unashamedly round the hanging flap-door to eavesdrop.

They'd been right behind him all the time.

And what he read in their expressions was confirmation of his own too-long delayed decision. Some kind of mystical union between minds? Or the primeval drawing together of the herd against triceratops?

Whatever held them in bond at that moment needed no words. But, because they were humans, with an alcoholic's need to communicate, there had to be words too.

'I wonder what's Vietnamese for burning one's boats,' Racowiczs pondered as they made way for Halliday.

'What happens now, Major?' Benner looked happy but sounded serious. He liked things to be cut and dried.

'What happens is—we return to America.'

'And then?' Able Thompson prompted.

'We return as a unit—and we run for the President and anyone else we can find responsible.'

Putting it right on the line like that, it seemed the natural, the only thing to do. But the enormity of Halliday's theme evoked at least one whistle of astonishment. Just like that. Back to the USA and get Foxwell. While one or two of them wondered if they could match up to the design, Racowiczs was already being practical.

'Where do we start?'

'With the men, Lieutenant. We have to be sure how many are prepared to go along—too few won't be enough.'

'I don't think you'll have any problem,' Benner said.

Captain Sweetman wasn't too sure but then he was never too sure of anything—on principle. He had an intellectual's approach to every problem that required an intricate blue-print, convoluted enough to get him off the ground and into airy realms of speculation. As it happened he could fly which made his choice of the infantry that much more inexplicable.

'You'll need a programme, Major. I mean, these guys'll go all the way with you, but it has to be specific, spelt out, or they'll fall apart.'

'There's nothing in the programme they don't already know

about. Funnily enough, Captain, I think they got there before I did.'

Sweetman looked a little puzzled. Watched the major cross to the opening from which he gazed out at the tented compound bathed in brilliant moonlight. Behind him were a number of shadowed faces, tension, eagerness, anticipation drawn into sharp focus by the glare of a single lamp. He turned back to them at last.

'They know,' he said, 'that what happened out here is unforgivable, that by no standard of logical necessity known to man can the kind of filth we've been handing out be justified. We haven't been fighting for a beautiful ideal. We just happen to be the poor slobs committed to supporting the system, and the system is manifestly rotten. It must be—or we'd have won this war.

'We bulldozed the South Viets into believing our way was better—we were going to hand them something bigger than the TVA. But take a good look around this country and tell me what else you see besides craters and Pepsi cans.'

'Isn't it possible we can make too much of the Pepsi cans?' Benner asked.

Halliday's negative was loaded with a concentrated vehemence none of them had seen or heard until now. 'No! How many thousands spilled their guts to keep Communism out of this country? But Pepsi gets the concession for the whole of Russia, and they toast the deal in Moscow.... No, Benner, you can't make too much of downgraded principles.

'We've killed needlessly, heedlessly; everything that wasn't American we destroyed. We stripped the land bare to give the Daughters of the Revolution a corporate orgasm at sight of so much nudity.

'And now the creeps are working on the Constitution back in Washington, another kind of corruption, another kind of Vietnam. What do I have to tell you you don't already know?

'If that's what you want, if any of you can put your hand on your heart and say "I go along with it" then you'd better say so right now. Because actually, even if I'm on my own, I'm going back, and I'm going to get Foxwell and any other Prussian

51

I can lay my hands on. By my reckoning, someone's got to pay.'

The wind never rustles a single blade of grass. And how each man arrived at his decision is unimportant. Inconsequential too that it took little time to arrive. They had all been travelling towards it at varying degrees of motion, some headlong, like Racowiczs, Thompson; a few haltingly, Benner, Sweetman, who needed intellectually to be convinced of actions they could emotionally accept as necessary.

The die was cast, and that same night Halliday sketched out a plan of action.

By the time of the two o'clock adjournment Winfield had only just laid out the framework on which the conspiracy had to be stretched.

The *New York Times* described his opening speech as lucid, the *Chicago Tribune* dubbed it Ciceronian and the *Christian Science Monitor* doubted if it lived up to the occasion, but it was generally agreed that Winfield had gone beyond his brief in the most subtle way possible. His veiled hint of the need for a stronger Executive with less inhibited powers of control and surveillance over every aspect of public life, cast a shadow no bigger than a senator's hand over the future of a great and free country. No-one dared to editorialize on the similarity between his kind of Executive and a Praesidium.

Winfield made his way to the lobby in a cloud of security men. The Press was nowhere and, in fact, the lobby had been entirely cleared five minutes before adjournment. One agent walked ahead with a metal detector, sweeping the senator's path with a housewife's care.

Winfield got to his office eventually and settled down to a little routine business before thinking about a desktop lunch. There were various orders to be signatured, and a run through of the almost daily Reparations Committee report. This dealt with the mounting cost of the affair in terms of private property damaged and destroyed.

He had some difficulty in digesting their latest assessment. Was it possible that a few men—— but it hadn't been a few men, there had been hundreds—the lofty brow darkened as one figure led to another. It must never be known that there had been thousands, not hundreds but thousands, of letters actually supporting or excusing, condoning and even applauding Halliday's diabolical enterprise.

The FBI and SIS were checking every single one; that was his consolation. He picked up a letter received that very morning, frowned again as he read the contents.

Dear Senator, I feel you ought to know that not all of us have indulged in the orgy of hate which you seem so anxious to foster in the wake of this melancholy affair, unless your TV appearance in which you answered questions fed by Jack Jacobson is not to be taken seriously.

If one remembers the Indians, the Mexicans and the Philippinos, America does not have so much to be proud of that it can afford to feed more hostages to Baal.

As a retired schoolteacher that is my first thought in a world where one has tried, without much success, to distinguish between justice and legalized hate.

I believe that what happened was a catastrophe no less natural than an earthquake or a tidal wave. We don't condemn God for these disasters. We have to set to and build something better on the ruins. It's all we have a right to do.

These men reacted naturally to an unnatural situation. Perhaps we should thank them for what they've done *for* us, not vilify them as though they did something *to* us. Sadly yours, Ms Eleanor J. Cartwright.

The senator tore the letter to shreds, slowly, as if it had metamorphosed into a little grey spinster from Jamesburg, New Jersey.

'Stupid liberal bitch.' He noted her name and address in the book just as his secretary came through on the intercom.

'I have Senator Feeny for you.'

'Good, send him in.'

That was nice; that was precisely what Winfield needed to activate his digestive process. And if he couldn't tear Eleanor J. Cartwright apart then by God he could do a job on Feeny. That mealy-mouthed son of a—— Abruptly he took himself

53

in hand. Why waste epithets on the air? He felt positively impatient to meet America's number one liberal in private session.

Feeny had a frank, boyish expression that could only enhance his quota of considerable good looks. It belied his forty-five well-kept years, reflected pretty accurately the composition of his followers. These made up the so-called intellectual segment of the population which had the classic disadvantage of being smart because it was well-heeled, well-heeled because it was smart.

The Eastern Intellectual Élite was no myth, it just happened not to be intellectual. Money could buy the means to a well-informed mind but that didn't prove it could go any further.

The Republicans and the genuine intellectuals, whoever they were, agreed only on that point. Even the hippies would have had no difficulty in nodding concurrence.

But these people, typified by their golden hero, had power, and they had money, and it gratified the egos they sunned on countless patios and alongside a multitude of swimming pools, to be accounted some kind of force in the land. For years these vociferous ones had urged others into outraged protest against the Vietnam situation. Like good staff officers they'd waged war against war from poolside headquarters far in the rear of the actual front line.

They knew all the words to express their disenchantment with official policy, but they had no conception of where the logic of their opposition should lead them, or if they did know, they would hope to see the incitement of the opposition stop at decent limits. The sincerity of their motives was soiled by the fact that, deep down, they knew the reactionaries would always be able to deal with an out-of-hand situation.

So now, with the war that never was fading into a peace that never could be, they had just begun to hail their 'victory' when Halliday erupted with a force that had them gasping. The stones he dropped into a thousand placid swimming pools from Hyannis to Atlantic City sent them all struggling to change out of their costumes before the reaction saw how damp they'd gotten.

They must be seen, and quickly, to have nothing to do with

54

this adventurer, or they would be in danger of losing their privilege of polite dissent. Unthinkable to be tarred with the same brush by an irrational majority, and so it became a categorical imperative to make their position quite clear.

That was what Feeny's visitation was all about. Winfield knew as much and the knowledge gave him such satisfaction that he actually smiled when the senior senator for Massachusetts entered his office with that well publicized stride, so redolent of youthful big A get up and go.

'I never thought to see us shaking hands in this life, Senator.' Amiable, but it looked bad because Winfield made no move to hold out his hand.

'Sit down, Senator, and tell me what I can do for you.'

'Thank you.' Feeny, usually so voluble was already having trouble with his equanimity. He guessed it must be too obvious to Winfield why he was there. 'Thought you made a great job of the run-down, Senator.'

Winfield's exuberant laugh said much about positions of strength.

'Well, I thought so too. But coming from you I guess I don't need have any doubts. Now you didn't call to indulge in a little harmless flattery, did you, Senator?'

Feeny grinned sheepishly. In certain Georgetown circles it was considered to be his greatest asset.

'No, frankly not. Essentially I felt you ought to know that among certain sectors of the community you have unqualified support for whatever measures you see fit to take——'

'No matter what?'

The question, abruptly put, took Feeny off guard. He still hadn't mastered the art of non-reaction. 'I'd say that would depend.'

'On?'

'Well, the extent of the conspiracy—if there was one.'

'You don't think there is?' Gently, but loaded with implication.

'We—that is, I wonder if it isn't an isolated event without——'

'Overtones? Is that the word you're looking for, Senator?'

'That would about fit, I guess.'

'Perhaps undercurrents might do as well.'

Winfield gazed reflectively out the window for some time. Constitution Avenue still looked a mess. 'Suppose we agree on overtones?'

'Certainly, I don't see why not.'

'And suppose I tell you evidence exists and will be presented at the hearings confirming that overtones do exist?'

'Then I'd have to accept that.'

'Yes—and you'd further accept, I take it, that overtones or undercurrents, what you will, must imply a moral support for Halliday's actions?'

'That would be a logical concomitant of the situation——'

'Therefore we can presuppose that moral support stems from —certain sectors of the community?'

Feeny stirred uneasily: the movement of a drugged butterfly which sees the pin's approach. 'I don't think we need carry it that far.'

'Don't you, Senator?' Winfield paused long enough to consider the small pile of shredded paper on his desk pad. 'Did you approve of my run-down in total, or only parts of it?'

'I—approved of the line.'

'Well let me spell it out, so we have no misconceptions on our side-plates.

'When I said I would spare no effort to bring to heel the recalcitrants riddling our country I meant it. Because it's those recalcitrants who created the climate in which Halliday and his bunch of hoodlums were enabled to flourish.'

Iron-jawed, Winfield waited for Feeny's response. It was a moment of hang-fire that would have enormous repercussions, not only on Feeny's future hopes *vis-à-vis* the presidential candidacy, not to mention his moral leadership of liberal America, but on America itself.

Small wonder Feeny sweated through a lightning and agonized reappraisal of his personal standpoint. But first he had to save as much of his beautiful face as he could.

'Is this a vendetta you have in mind—the kind that subserves personal ambition?'

Winfield glanced at the address carefully written into his notebook. 'Why not bring it right into the open?'

'Do I need to?'

'No—I suspect we understand one another. Let's just say, I'll be happy to have you run against me when the time comes.'

Feeny coloured at the scarcely veiled insult. 'Why not? Maybe by then the country will've had enough of witch-hunters.'

'Was there anything else you wanted to talk about, Senator?'

'Yes—that boy, Ed Roberts. He's supposed to have deserted from Halliday of his own free will. At the very least he could be given a chair for the duration of the——'

'He killed American women and children. Waded in American blood. What should I do—comfort the rest of his miserable life?'

'He passed out during——'

'He passed out. So I adjourned the proceedings to get him on his feet again—do you think Halliday had as much humanity in him as we show for that killer?'

'It was never conclusively established that Roberts actually killed.'

'You must have been a cussed Attorney General in your State. Roberts is a murdering bastard, and he's going to suffer for as long as we can keep him going. But first, I'm going to make his living presence mean something to the American people. They'll see his shame, his infamy, day after day, watch his reaction close-up as he listens to the whole saga clinically examined—a chair....'

The senator's voice dropped to that familiar, low note that had dramatized many Congressional hearings. 'He tried, with all the others, to operate on America without an anaesthetic, Senator. Well now, America's going to operate on him—and he'll have to stand up to it, the way America did.

'Now if you'll excuse me, I'll get back to work, assuming I have your full support in the difficult days to come.'

Five hundred men were hunkered up in the clearing, packed tight and in varying stages of undress. Marshall had the little girl on his knee in the front row. Thu hai was off somewhere trying to fly a kite Sims Littleton had fixed up for him out of an old first aid pack.

Except for the never-ending roar of high-flying B-52s there was more or less silence. The officers stood around, smoking and chatting with little groups of their men. Not a gun in sight.

57

For the fiftieth time the VC could have taken them apart.

The major ducked out of the broken down tent that was headquarters. Bare-headed, almost bearded, lacking any sign of rank, he might have been a guerilla leader shaping up to a briefing.

He began hesitantly, too much aware of what he was about to say. Not that he doubted the validity of his dream, but he couldn't dismiss the fear that it might disintegrate in face of a hostile reaction. Could not believe he had nothing to worry about.

'They tell me I'm cursed with the worst outfit in the whole of south-east Asia.'

Most of them managed not to look too proud.

'Personally, I'm satisfied. An officer only gets what he's worth, so that makes me worthless too.

'What it really means is that I—you—we do not believe in this war and never have.'

'Right!' Gribble shouted.

'The reason we're worthless is because we tried to fight a clean war. We took the trouble to identify an enemy, and because we were soldiers we killed him if we could.

'But that's not good enough for our superiors. They say "Go out and get a body count we can be proud of—no matter how".

'I said No in the beginning and last night I said No to Colonel Gorton at the end.'

There was a murmur of approval.

'So, at the end of the day, we've proved exactly nothing. There is no more democracy in Vietnam when we leave than when we arrived. All we did was infect a whole people with an imported virus.

'And the biggest, ugliest lesson we taught them was that life is a disposable plastic container, to be used and thrown away.

'We salved the American conscience by equating disposability with Eastern fatalism. You know, life is cheap, all those teeming millions, what's a mamasan more or less? Their lives mean nothing to them, why should they mean something to us?

'*Our* teeming millions long ago accepted they were consumer products, to be used and thrown on the trash heap when they outlived their usefulness.

58

'The Vietnamese saw life differently. They took it as a gift, shared it with the family and gratefully accepted it as a package deal with built-in imperfections *no-one*, not Communists, not USAID, could do very much about.

'That was once upon a time. We helped change all that. We told them, in our arrogance, they had no right to handle their own problems. We brought the rubber stamp of our soft option civilization and stamped all over theirs the word "Democracy".

'Someone—a writer—once said "They committed atrocities that had everybody throwing up at Nuremburg", but who wrote the book, wringing his hands but sighing with relief because our atrocities were different?

'Tell it to a peasant spilling his guts in a ditch.

'We were the enemy.

'Just now the enemy killed a thousand women and children and maybe a couple of soldiers too in a place called Hanoi—how many of us knew where the hell Hanoi was five years ago?

'Conclusion—and I'm wasting no words on this—the American people voted in those who made it possible; the American people are responsible for the blood on our hands.

'I'm returning to the United States with my fellow officers and we're going to demonstrate to the American people what this war was really like. If we die fighting it'll be within sight of the Capitol, because our last mission in this campaign is to reach Foxwell and his elegant creeps, bring them to trial and judgment for what they did to the Vietnamese, to us and to the ideals of better men who didn't need to phone-tap their way to power.

'If you're with us, we'll be glad to have your company.'

Even the most pessimistic of those behind him, which would mean Sweetman and moody Lieutenant Wilde, looked optimistic at the howl of delight that spiralled up out of the crowd.

'Maybe they don't understand,' Sweetman shouted above the racket.

Racowiczs grinned. 'Maybe you don't know your ass from your elbow, Lieutenant.'

'One can make out a case for most things,' Sweetman retorted, but he sounded more pleased than he knew.

The GIs crowded round Halliday as if he'd just annunciated the first Coming of the Chase Manhattan or something. They wanted to get close enough to give a personal assurance that they'd be in there pitching. More than ever they felt a pride in their worthlessness, as if a band of tramps and vagabonds—black and white—had set out on a corrupted crusade, to be told that, after all, the meek did have a right to inherit the earth.

They grabbed at the purpose. It had materialized under their noses and it looked right. They didn't have to go back to Mom's suffocating arms, or hi-jack a plane to keep the memories burning, or shriek themselves awake at night, or shoot up a liquor store to get that old, gladiatorial feeling.

They knew, deep down, they were cheering their own death warrant; but no-one was asking them to sign anything. And they were cheering their freedom to choose.... It was total; not a single negative response. Something even the most optimistic of the officers, men like Racowiczs and Able Thompson, had thought improbable.

As five hundred and thirty-seven pages turned that day Major Halliday went straight to the problems of planning the impossible.

It was no ordinary council of war. Every man, from Halliday down to young Cooper, the latest replacement, sat in on the discussion. To his own amazement the major detailed an operation he'd hardly begun to consider consciously.

The plan had a Napoleonic simplicity, was adopted with negligible modifications. They were left with little to do but train and wait for lift-off and nurse the hope there would be no last-minute change of plans for them or the US Carrier *Carolina*.

'OK Roberts, let's roll it again. You're saying that better than five hundred men read nothing but the army paper when it was available, newspapers mailed from home and a few Westerns some of the guys might have been carrying?'

'That's right.'

'So how do you account for the seventy-four copies of Mao-tse Tung's Thinkout found on the bodies?'

Roberts had to open his eyes long enough to look from

Colonel Milton's smile to the microphone nearby. 'How do *you* account for them?'

'Oh I don't have to, that's your job.'

'OK, then I'd say it must be the right time of year for planting thoughts.'

'That's not very smart, Roberts. We don't seem to be getting through today. I'm half-inclined to let 'em try that new drug. They say it works wonders on rats. What do you say to the fact that copies of the Berkeley Committee's leaflets were also found in those men's pockets?'

'I think it proved they could read.'

'I'd suggest it shows they were subverted.'

'That's right.'

The officer looked pleased and a little surprised. 'You agree, well that's fine.'

'They were subverted by corporational propaganda first then realized their mistake. That's what you call conversion fall-out.'

'Too clever, Roberts. I can strike that from the recording. Now I'll tell you what, you've had three weeks in this place and I think you're suffering from—well let's say—you need a change. After all it's been nothing but us ever since we started, and if the truth were known, I'm a little bored myself. At least I have TV and the papers, and I can talk to people, but you don't have anything but a bright little light to watch—yessir that's kind of hard.

'So I've fixed you a little surprise, Roberts.'

The man inside the uniform rose heavily and walked towards the door, Roberts eyeing him all the way.

'I've got someone outside you'll be mighty glad to see.'

And suddenly, standing in the doorway, there was Marion; his kid sister. Only she seemed different, grown up, like a butter-fly out of its chrysalis. He half rose, tears pricking his eyes, and nothing they had done or could do to him would top this.

It was humiliating, meeting the one person you'd ever had time to love, in a padded cell, holding up the sack-like pyjama trousers with one hand because they oh so much didn't want you to die your own way instead of theirs.

'Hullo, Ed.' She tried to smile, and he almost failed to keep the tears back. While the door closed softly behind them and someone saying, 'I guess you two must have a lot to talk about.'

Fortified by lunch and the memory of how he'd handled Feeny induced in Senator Winfield a post-prandial *joie-de-vivre* that had him back-slapping a few of his senatorial colleagues as he made his grand entrance down the centre aisle. A sense of delicacy kept him from entering by the Vice-President's door. And a sense of timing.

The moment wasn't opportune for that kind of performance.

He waved to a friend or two in the distinguished persons' gallery, noted the Russian ambassador's presence and gallantly retrieved a Hershey bar accidentally knocked from the clerk's desk. *AP* swore to the *Detroit News* the distinguished senator had winked at the pressmen which meant either he would have some delicacy for them at the five o'clock briefing, or he was having trouble with that right eye again. *UPI*, the optimist, settled for a delicacy.

The session was under way.

Colonel Gorton was called and everyone craned forward to see the man who had been kept incommunicado for so long.

Fifty, perhaps, with what once might have been a Florida complexion, but the tan had worn down to something less attractive. The eyes were steely if faintly rusted and his bearing, though military enough, showed signs of strain. The mouth was thin, the only part of him that hadn't changed.

No-one missed the fact that he scowled at Ed Roberts, standing close by.

After the oath-taking and petty preliminaries Winfield came to the point.

'Colonel, I shall want to take you through the happenings in Saigon, point by point, but I must tell you that my colleagues are at liberty to claim the Floor at any time if they have questions pertinent to the hearings.'

'I understand, Senator.'

'Fine. Now on the particular date we have in mind, you were ordered to call in those units still operating in an area with a map reference of 25/28?'

'That is correct.'

'Was there something special about this area?'

'Very. It marked a terminal point of the Ho Chi Minh trail.'

'So you and your superiors had good reason, based on intelligence presumably, to feel that three companies could be of exceptional value in that sector?'

'Certainly. Strategically it was important we continue to destroy men and material coming from the North.'

'I understand. The reason I ask, Colonel, is that we seem to have a conflict of evidence about this. Some people doubted the Vietcong were operating so far south at that late stage of the war.'

'I can only say they were misinformed. The Communists never stopped sending munitions and reinforcements downtrail up to and beyond the peace settlement.'

'So you would give no credence to the theory that these particular companies were sent to the area because they were trouble-makers?'

The colonel hesitated, desperately trying to remember the details of a briefing that had put him through the wringer more times than he could count.

'Shall I repeat the question, Colonel?'

'That won't be necessary, sir. I simply—I want to be as precise as I know how on this.'

'I appreciate that, Colonel.'

'They *were* trouble-makers—yes. Very few of them had escaped disciplinary action of one kind or another. In my opinion they were almost incapable of accepting the peculiar demands made on every soldier. Their behaviour, especially in the rest and recreation centres—even in hospital—was deplorable. They fought men from other units, anybody—knife fights, fists—some of them were real tigers.'

'The kind of men you would designate anti-social in peace-time?' Winfield wondered.

'Undoubtedly.'

'And these misfits were returned to Saigon March the seventh; is that correct, Colonel?'

'Yes, it is.'

'You had a debriefing session with Halliday on the eighth?'

'I did.'

'Can you inform the Senate Committee what was said at this meeting?'

Colonel Gorton cleared his throat and thought back via his subsequent conversations at the Pentagon.

'Come in Halliday, sit down.'

Halliday closed the door and let his attention wander on a reconnaisance of Gorton's command post. One big room, light and airy, conditioned, part of a large apartment not too far from the embassy. Some very nice furnishing, pastel shades for the walls at the limits of which high-piled carpets lapped. Colour TV. And a battery of stereo equipment too. He remembered the colonel was fond of Sousa and suchlike.

He shrugged and wandered over to the couch, well away from one severe looking chair standing obsequiously before a magnificent custom built, teakwood desk.

Gorton glanced up from some paperwork and began a conversation with the vacant chair, then he shifted focus, frowned, again started to say something, but it was no use. He just had to stare till the right muscles reactivated his jaw.

Halliday was studying a pair of panties he'd found peeping from behind a cushion.

'What do you think you're doing?'

Halliday laid them aside. Smiled. 'I was just doing a body count.'

'Why are you here at all in that condition?'

Halliday surveyed his filthy combat outfit then scratched reflectively at a badly stubbled chin. 'I had a few things to do, and then again, I needed some sleep, and, well, you know how it is, Colonel. Somehow I just didn't seem to have the time to clean up before I got your summons.'

'What kind of example is that to your men?' Gorton snapped, conscious of his own, immaculate appearance.

'I think they're a little tired of examples, they want the real thing—whatever that is.'

Gorton appeared to soften a fraction. 'You always did talk in riddles. I know how it is, all those weeks out there. It takes time to reorientate.'

'Or reoccidentate.'

64

'And you were never less than sharp, Halliday. I had great hopes once—but that was once. Now I'd say you were just crocked.'

'Yessir, I guess the war got too much for me.'

'Well, that's how it goes. Now about this report—I want you to make out a fresh one.'

'I thought I did a job with that one.'

'I told you, I want results, even if they're only paper results.'

'Is that what we've come to?'

'I'm asking you to do this for the good of your country——'

'Will my country smell any better because I forge out a report?'

'No-one's asking you to forge anything. Just indulge in a little honest exaggeration.'

Halliday regarded the battered helmet dangling in his hand. 'What we haven't done to the English language.'

'I'll give you five—five days to think it over, Halliday. That's almost all the time you have in Vietnam.'

'I appreciate that, Colonel. And do I have orders for transit?'

'You'll be notified of flight schedules in due course. Meantime, have all personnel check in their arms, ammunition and other combat material on time.'

'I don't see a schedule posted for that.'

'That's right. Some bastard tore it down last night. It'll be back on the Divisional Bulletin board before tomorrow.'

'Oh good.'

'And Halliday——'

'Sir?'

'Tread carefully. Don't make things worse for yourself.'

'I'm not sure I understand, Colonel.'

'Your record's gone from pretty good to lousy. Some things can be forgiven, I can even overlook your intemperate behaviour to me; but when you return Stateside, you'll be back in the army.'

'Oh yes, now I follow. Will that be all, Colonel?'

'No! for Chrissakes stop smiling at that underwear and go.'

Things were moving better than according to plan. He, personally, was tearing off the orders dealing with the hand-in

65

of weapons and the other military hardware. The orders were always back on the board at the end of the day, but post-dated by a further twenty-four hours.

In the hustle and bustle of moving house no-one noticed or had the least grounds for suspicion that Halliday was playing for more than trick or treat.

Further, he now knew he had the right number of days to fix things. Every last detail stuck in his brain like pins to a pincushion, each one pricked with insistence to be dealt with.

For instance, don't forget you have an eight o'clock rendezvous with four matelots from the *Carolina*, tonight. That's important.

Only one fear nagged. The real possibility that any one—and it needed no more—of the five hundred and thirty-seven men sharing his intrigue, could blow their minds at the last minute, thought of what was stored, like a terrible dream, in suspended animation, at the bottom of the deep-freeze.

But a man can't stand at the edge of a minefield for ever. He has three courses: to go round, go over or go under. Halliday went on over, towards an important element in his plan of campaign.

He drove out to what used to be Saigon's biggest watchdog; the unbelievable base at Long Binh, looking these days as if it were bleeding to death. Not a khaki coloured corpuscle in sight.

Nothing stirred his memory so he took the jeep through a full turn and headed back out of the gates and on to incredibility.

Ho Nai junk yard.

If Long Binh bled to death it surely spilled its guts into this vast compound.

As far as the eye could see and further, rusting refrigerators, office furniture, mountains of steel shell casings, rows of armoured personnel carriers, acre upon acre of trucks, jeeps, cars, even fire-engines.

It was, he concluded, as though a whole consumer society had taken a good look at itself—and vomited.

Even as he tried, one more time, to encompass the meaning of that vast graveyard filled with the dead artifacts of a dying civilization, another funeral cortège was inching through the

66

gates: truck-loads of lockers, TV sets, typewriters and interior sprung mattresses—you name it. A South Vietnamese solemnly directed the procession to an alley carved out of two lines of trackless tanks.

'Can I help you?' An American, probably on the civilian staff, had wandered over, and was standing at his side. Halliday needed time to restructure his thoughts after that full frontal exposure of mammoth obsolescence.

'Pretty impressive,' he managed.

'You could say so.' A half proud, half ashamed response. Like, it's all American, but that's all.

Halliday assumed he was an auctioneer out of retirement for the duration. He puffed hard on an obscene-looking black cigar between phrases.

'Three million dollars a year ... clear profit. Guess we have to get some return outta this war.'

'I guess we do. Would you know where I can find Sergeant Trabs?'

'Trabs! Well now, I should just say I do. You don't forget a guy with a handle that twisted. Anyways, he's near the last enlisted man left out here. You'll find him——' he had to stop for the benefit of a cough that went with the cigar, then tried again, '... you'll find him ... over in "Information", that tourist caravan right ahead—used to be General Cumberland's field HQ.'

Before Halliday had taken six paces over rough ground carpeted with nuts and bolts the cigar stopped puffing.

'Hey!'

Halliday turned back.

'The caravan's for sale too, if you're interested.'

It was worth a brief smile before he continued on his way.

'Major! for Chrissakes, am I seeing things or is this Doomsday?'

A look of sheer joy on Trabs' countenance, which was as ugly as his name, brought a hatful of memories flooding back. They'd seen out a lot of the war together.

'I heard you just got back. Was gonna look you up tonight. You're looking great, Major.'

A homely face, the battered physiognomy of a veteran who'd

67

seen too much of war from Korea on. Now he was reduced to the nothing status of an information clerk. Halliday knew why.

'Good to see you, Joe.'

They paused long enough to start cigarettes.

'You been doing this kind of thing long?'

'Too long,' Trabs grimaced his disgust. 'I've seen fifty-seven varieties of greed and avarice come through that door and walk out satisfied.'

'Philosophy of the junk-yard.'

'Philosophy—now if that comes in five gallon cans I can fix you a consignment.'

'Can we be overheard?'

The sergeant looked serious all suddenly. 'No chance, Major. You in trouble?'

Another glance at the officer's almost neglected appearance had him worried, brought out the paternal streak as always.

Halliday shook his head, smiling. 'You'd have me in diapers if I blinked long enough.'

But Trabs was old enough to be no-one's fool. 'Something's on your mind.'

'What kind of authority do you deal around here?'

Trabs spread his arms wide. 'Limitless. In fact, discounting Colonel Massey, I'd say without modesty I *am* the US Army Disposal of Surplus Goods Department.'

That was cheerful news. 'Some title—you've come a long way, Joe.'

'Yeah—well—I had no option—after what happened.'

He avoided the major's eye knowing he hadn't forgotten what few people would remember. How Trabs had taken an Arvin MP apart for shooting a captured VC because he'd stumbled through sheer exhaustion. They'd given him psychiatry and a desk job for that, losing Halliday the best sergeant he ever had.

'Forget it, Joe. Won't be long now.'

'That's the problem. What comes after what won't be long? Crap! I'm talkin' about me, let's turn it around.'

'I could do with some help.'

'Like I said.'

Halliday hesitated before taking a sheet of paper from his

pocket. 'I need this stuff, Joe. I want it in less than a week, and it's got to be shipped by the carrier lying out of Saigon harbour.'

Joe frowned at the totally unexpected, took the sheet of paper and ran his eye over it. Then he looked up, pursed his lips to whistle; but nothing happened. Astonishment somehow rendered him helpless. Only, it gave way to an expression Halliday couldn't quite identify, something not unlike smouldering dislike.

'I said it was dangerous,' he prompted.

'Dangerous! You gonna set up as an arms dealer or something?'

'No.'

Trabs fumbled at the problem a while longer, then his eyes slowly lit up. 'I've got it. You're gonna start another war. Something with a little more class maybe?'

Halliday had no choice. He would have to put Trabs in the very foreground of the picture and trust to luck and what he thought he knew about the man before laying the last of his fears to rest.

When he'd finished, the NCO still continued to stare. And it was all admiration, growing and growing like a sunflower blooming out of control.

'For Chrissakes,' he said at last, and in a dreamy tone of voice; then because it didn't seem adequate, he said it again.

'Well, Joe?'

'Why didn't we do it before? When I think—when I think of all those fucken civilians——' he almost snapped to attention as though to shake off an attack of creeping lethargy. 'I'll have that stuff—every single item—on board the *Carolina* in four days. Massey won't know a thing. I can get his signature to a whole pack of release forms without even having 'em filled.'

'Is that important?'

'Without a release form the ship wouldn't take delivery— it has to have the equivalent of a manifest.'

Halliday nodded. 'OK I'll leave it all in your hands, Joe.'

'You can count on it; and you didn't have to have doubts.'

'I doubted asking you to take a chance.'

'What have we been doing all this time?'

'This is different, Joe. The enemy is us.'

69

Trabs looked around him, as though searching for a mislaid argument. 'When that mortar chip near took off Collins' leg—you remember? Da Nang—there were just the three of us. Collins was an OK bastard, you liked him, but you didn't stop to think whether you should hack away that leg and tie off or he was dead, right? A part of Collins had to die—so now the rest of him is hopping around like a two-year-old. So where do we rendezvous?'

'What?'

'I said where do I muster for jump-off?'

'I—can't ask you to——'

'Now listen, you can't do a damn fool thing like this without having an experienced damn fool along with you. Well just let me finish. What've I got to lose? The wife took off with the mailman because I wrote her too regularly and also I soiled the honour of my uniform—her stinking words not mine. My son says I'm a killer and he's got long hair to prove it. I'm forty-five, Major, I made a bad decision in the days when kids didn't wear long hair, so why shouldn't I have the right to—maybe show I know how to do right—after what we've done; or is this some adolescent barbecue while the old man stays home and watches TV?'

'The boys'll be glad to see you, Joe. When I find the right spot for take-off I'll let you know.'

It seemed to be all Trabs needed to make him look happy. 'Good to be in business again, Major.'

Halliday smiled too. 'Good to have you with us, Sergeant.'

They saluted *pro forma*, for old time's sake.

Winfield played around with a few papers on his desk as a sign of preoccupation following Gorton's account of his meeting with Halliday.

'So it would be true to say, Colonel, that Halliday showed himself to be slovenly, insubordinate and the very antithesis of everything one would expect from a United States army officer?'

'Undoubtedly.'

'Could almost have been another man.'

'I had difficulty in recognizing the Halliday I'd once known.'

'That's very interesting. Now as I understand it, you made no effort to discipline him at that time?'

'There was no point or opportunity. By then the machinery hardly existed for initiating summary proceedings. In any event, I knew he'd be required to answer for his conduct on returning to the United States.'

'But you were prepared to make recommendations concerning his conduct?'

'It was my duty as his commanding officer to do so.'

'Thank you, Colonel. Now we've heard something about the Communist literature found on these men. I'd like to touch on another aspect of the same issue.'

Winfield leaned forward and low-keyed his next question. 'Isn't it a fact that more—toxic—material was found?'

'Yes it is.'

'Do you have any notion what it could be?'

'Underground papers. Published on the West Coast mostly.'

'Underground papers.' Winfield stayed his hand long enough to let this sink deep. 'Do you have a copy of any of these— underground papers?'

'Only a personal copy—the one I found in my Saigon quarters.'

Gorton held it up so the cameras could get a good view.

'What, basically, was the message, Colonel?'

'One item here advises GIs, and I quote—"Don't desert. Go to Vietnam and kill your commanding officer".'

Again the indrawn breath, like a weird vacuum cleaner, sweeping the Continent; the sound of a nation anxious to keep itself clean.

But Winfield hadn't finished. He grabbed a whole fistful of papers and literally flourished them above his head while some memory processes in that Chamber went shrieking into reverse for better than twenty years.

'That's right, Colonel. And I have a whole bunch of the same disgusting filth right here in my hand. "Movement for a Democratic Military", "The Fort Lewis Press", "Bulletins from the Order of Maximillian", "The Home Front", "The True Enemy" and dozens more. Every one aimed at the seduction of serving men from their sacred duty to defend the Constitution, to aid their country in its greatest need. I have the names of seventy-

71

three of these ink-filled dissidents, those wordy traitors who, ultimately, must bear a large part of the responsibility for this, the greatest tragedy in our long history.'

Once more, the dramatic forward thrust, and his attention narrowing, this time to one man. Again, as though by instinct, the cameras panned to frame Senator Feeny in a geometrical trap. The eyes of America were upon him and he could not escape.

'I say to you, to everyone present in this Chamber still reeking with unholy memories, is there a single senator who can condone, can find mitigation, can respond with a particle of sympathy for the perpetrators of blasphemies fouling these— shreds—which not the meanest tramp would use to cleanse himself!'

Naturally all eyes had shifted to Feeny, if only to avoid that merciless gaze from the rostrum, if only to off-load the burden of responsibility to more obvious shoulders. To his credit, Feeny remained impassive, brilliantly oblivious, as it seemed, to the fact that the full force of Winfield's pyrotechnics were focused on him. He might have won the contest if Winfield hadn't known when to play an ace.

'Did I hear the distinguished senator for Massachusetts?'

Feeny started visibly, frowned and made the mistake of looking around him; found himself staring at a blank wall of coagulated hostility.

He made the further mistake of stammering some kind of reply.

'What's that, Senator? I'm afraid I don't hear you.'

'I—I know of no-one in this Chamber who would quarrel with your interpretation of the facts, Mr Chairman.'

'Thank you, Senator.'

Meanwhile, long ago, or not so long since, depending on how much one's personal sense of time lags behind the cosmic acceleration, three GIs were threading their way through the five and ten piaster stalls in a crowded Saigon thoroughfare.

Half game and half deadly serious this business of negotiating a street filled with dynamic hawkers, displaying, suggesting, cajoling or just threatening with a smile. The GIs: one was Seth

72

alias Boston Chronicle, another was Seth's buddy whose name nobody could remember so they called him Buddy most times. Once in a while, when he was stoned, like now, he would stop being diminutive and rebel.

'Got me a name, dammit. Everybody got a name since Adam.'

'Well go on, Adam, what's your name?' Seth or someone would ask.

'In my condition, rat-head, what am I supposed to know?'

So they called him Buddy.

The third member of the trio was Extra, so it was interesting to see the two tiny soldiers flanking six feet three of Seth as they moved through the street of a thousand twitters.

'Hey Seth, there's Harry's Bar. We was thrown out of Harry's nine months back, remember?' Buddy was a sentimentalist.

'That's right. Harry's Chinese but his liquor was OK.'

'I'd say Buddy's had enough, Boston. We don't wanna get into any trouble now, do we?'

'Ain't no trouble. Just a quick flick of the wrist and back to base, OK?'

'If you say so, Boston. Maybe tomato juice for Buddy, huh? He's stoned out of his mind.'

'Button your ass, Extra, I know what I'm doing.' But spoken like a man with teeth turned to rubber.

They turned him around and pushed him in the right direction. Entering the bar they found it was just as they'd known it from way back. Crowded though. Some of the faces they knew but there was little opportunity to talk because the drinks appeared like magic. Harry, a one-time professional conjuror, ran a good number.

Eventually Buddy and Extra found seats at the counter and Seth wandered over to a small table from which he could keep an eye on both of them. He was minstrel enough to prefer avoiding trouble, but they could magnetize to a brawl at the droop of an eyelid.

Some kind of civilian sat opposite, his back to the bar. A sharp dresser in a casual fashion so far as Boston could tell. The greyish head was nodding gently at its glass like one of those plastic ducks with a thirst. It straightened up suddenly and Seth was made aware of features so refined there had to be some

73

mistake. Then he noticed the fine lines running like Indian trails all over the Fauntleroy face. So many, it suggested a net, woven of dissipation, trapping that face forever.

The eyes were clear enough, even striking in their way. They took in the GI and the guitar at his side.

'You play that thing?' A thick but cultured voice.

'That's right, man.' For Chrissakes what else could you do with a guitar?

'You know why I came here?'

But Boston was busy watching his companions. Extra showed signs of arguing with a burly top sergeant.

'How's that again?'

'I came here to get away from it all. I had no idea—the misery.'

'Uh-huh.'

'You think we're indifferent, don't you? but some of us care.'

'Well that's nice.'

'I mean it, soldier. I've been right up to the DMZ and I've seen everything, all that suffering; and the haunting question —how does one live with oneself?'

Extra was raising his voice just a teeny bit too much for Boston's peace of mind.

'Excuse me.' He got up and pushed his way through the crowd to just behind Extra's ear. 'Extra.'

'Uh hello Seth. I was just tellin' this non-com punk——'

'Shut up.' Quietly.

'Sure, anything you say, Boston.'

Boston returned to his seat.

'How is one going to tell them—back home?'

'I'm sorry?'

'What we've done to this country.'

'Yeah. It's tragic.'

'D'you know who I am?'

Boston shrugged but grinned politely enough. The man could have been a Daughter of the Revolution in male drag for all he cared. And what makes anyone feel so important they have to ask a question like that?

But Boston was good-natured and he tried the first name he thought of. 'Richard Burton?'

74

'Are you kidding? Do I look like an actor?'

'What does an actor look like? I'm sorry, I have no idea who you look like.'

The semi-drunk laughed bitterly. 'There are those who say I look like me.'

'Yeah?—well, I guess that solves a lot of problems.'

'And creates a few.'

'That's life, man. Extra! The sergeant is trying very hard to be nice to you. Reciprocate.'

'Anything you say, Boston.'

'I'm J. B. Baxter.'

'Seth Hardacre, most people call me Boston. Pleasetameet-cha.'

His howdy grin faded as he watched Baxter's face screwing up like something doubtful was crawling around his crotch. That's how Boston saw it. How was he supposed to know it betokened a sense of betrayal? that the world, not to mention its wife, should fail to recognize——

'I wrote *The First Calvary in America.*'

'Really? You must be a writer. Extra! cool it. I heard of it, all about the Civil War——'

'Calvary.'

'That so? Then I must've missed it.'

'What you'd call a best-seller. Quarter of a million copies.'

'That's great; you can stop writing and settle down.'

He was trying hard to be kind, but it was difficult. Nothing he said seemed to make the man happy. Finish your beer and go.

'I can't stop you being funny if that's how you feel.' A resigned voice, loaded with *weltschmaltz.* 'After all, you're the man with the gun.'

Boston looked his puzzlement. 'I told you, it's just a fucken guitar. And who's being funny? I'm fascinated, I really am. I mean what's out here when you could be—you could be back home reading a good book?'

'I needed to suffer—don't you understand that?'

This time Boston really turned into the statue of astonishment.

'You could'a joined the fucken army and suffered for free,

man. I mean—air fares, hotel and dry-cleaning bills—it makes suffering expensive for just one.'

'You're really putting me on, Private.'

'No I mean it.' Boston, being the simple kind of man he was, did indeed mean what he said, whereas the Baxters of this world only suspect that they think they mean what they say.

'You know what bugs me? The fact that decent men, like you, come out here and do this to people just because they're told to. That's what really makes me unhappy.'

For the first time, Boston took both eyes off his friends and studied the well-manicured face drooping over its Bourbon. A faint touch of expensive after-shave lotion tickled his nasal passages and for some odd reason it reminded him of civilian street. Lotions, deodorants—no rat could afford to run and sweat without preparations. Boston was too full of other emotions to show his anger.

'I'm real sorry we disappoint you, Mr Baxter. And I wouldn't have mentioned it if you hadn't brought up the subject. Ever since this damn war got started maybe a dozen writers a year come swooping in—usually between Tet and the Spring offensives—it must be the suffering season. They all go out looking—sometimes, if they lucky, they find a dead body, and they shoot back to Saigon clutching their asses because war is so ... they come seven thousand miles just to prove to themselves people get killed in war.

'So what do they do? They sit around Saigon and suffer; they really work at it, Mr Baxter. They sit slumped over their booze and yak about the dirt, the disease, the dead and the decency implied they had to bring with 'em, because there's none out here even on the black market.

'They tell any ear they can find, "I can't live with myself after what I've seen". But you know what they really doin', Mr Baxter? Just rehearsing all those fine phrases they gonna put in the eighty-seventh fucken book written about 'Nam.

'Now I'm gonna give you a phrase to put in your next heart-render. Every war is a funeral and people of your cut are the professional mourners. Excuse me, Mr Baxter, I think my friend just got thrown out the door.'

* * *

76

Mechanically she shifted her chair, tried to shift it, the way one does, but it was clamped tight to the floor. She nudged the table surreptitiously. That too seemed to be anchored. Over Ed's shoulder she could see the bed; more obviously fixed. There was nothing else in that room bounded by its rubberized walls. Even the floor gave an inch to the pressure of her foot.

She hardly needed time to take in what there was and why it should be like that. Yet she could only stare, uncomprehendingly, at the wasted figure that was her brother, trying so hard to smile, but having so much difficulty.

'Great to see you, Marion. My, but you're a real grown-up lady now. Come a long way in a year.'

'Eighteen months.'

'That long? well it shows; time certainly flies.'

But he couldn't bear to be looked at like that. The nakedness of her emotions made nonsense of the care with which he'd concealed his own.

Horror, pity, shame—it was all there in her eyes, so that, for the first time, he could picture himself in his situation as plainly as if he'd been given a mirror. It had been bearable before, when he could deal adequately, practising a rule of thumb philosophy that had to do with self-discipline, objectivity, meticulous remembrance of what it had all been about.

Other memories helped; the way of the Arvins when they captured a suspect VC. What they could do to a man to break faith—his faith. What those guys could endure, the hair-raising stoicism with which they died—believing.

He had time to think because Marion, poor kid, didn't know what to say.

The big brother you'd always looked up to, sitting in the bogie hole like a pile of cold ... he tried not to mind the silence. And it was good just to look and look at someone you loved.

'Ed, they told me I mustn't mention about—about...' she faltered, as though the words to describe their diabolical escapade hadn't been coined yet.

'That's OK, Marion. Plenty else to talk about—college, your latest date...'

How could she tell him no-one wanted to know? Or that she didn't mind? 'Did you get my letters?'

77

'I'm not supposed to read.' He smiled to make it sound better.

'So you didn't know about Mom.'

He shook his head, half guessing the fact.

'She took the car, and just drove. She ... I didn't have to identify—Aunt Josie took care of all that.'

'She just—drove ...'

'Why yes, she's dead.'

And he had to ask: 'Because of me?'

Marion looked away, not wanting him to feel it was some kind of accusation: 'Because of the neighbours.'

It would have been so easy to say, what kind of a mother is that? Maybe the son's a no-good bastard who betrayed his country and all the rest; but to walk out on Marion, leaving her completely alone ... Another auto accident, just like Dad in '66—then, it was depression, because nothing seemed to be working out anymore. So jump in the car, accelerate to beyond the point of life tolerance and pow! The American way of escape.

He couldn't grieve even if he'd wanted to; not for himself certainly, never for the ex-parent, and maybe not so very much for Marion. What had she lost that she'd ever really had? It takes more than one to make a generation gap.

But she was on her own. He was as good as dead, could do nothing to help her? And not being able to help is a kind of death.

The problem dragged him down to the deepest level of depression, and for a while, the thing he feared most, happened. Marion was left alone.

She stretched out a hand tentatively, to comfort his misery. 'Ed, it's OK. I'm with Aunt Josie and I'm—very happy. You know how considerate she is—and she's kind. Ed, she wants you to know——'

Roberts looked up sharply: 'OK I know! She thinks I'm a bastard,' at the same time trying to convey in dumbshow what he really meant. They'd be running tapes on the conversation.

She seemed to understand. 'Why yes, that's right, she thinks you are—but—but she wants you to know she'll take good care of me for—Dad's sake.'

'Well, that's something in her favour.' He brightened a little.

'How's the history course? I know you were doing fine in history.'

'I still like it. Ed——'

'And there was something else you like doing—Jeez my memory's shot to pieces—now what was it? Poetry, that's it— you still write poetry?'

'Not so much, so many other things——'

'They're not important, not like poetry.' He grew strangely excited. 'Listen, Marion, you keep writing poems like the ones you sent me in Vietnam. Why, d'you know, I used to read 'em aloud to the fellers and they were really impressed.'

She looked pleased, and a lot of things, their surroundings and those funny pyjamas Ed was wearing, got forgotten as she listened and contemplated the enthusiasm suddenly lighting up a face so inlaid with shadows.

'You mean that?'

'Sure I mean it. Marion, the world's full of lousy words, like it's full of lousy people, but words can be good like people can be good. Words are meaningful, and if you can use 'em for good then my God use 'em. Anybody can major in history, science, economics, anything you like, but it doesn't make 'em better people and it can even make 'em worse.

'But poetry; I tell you, one Emily Dickinson is worth a thousand college professors, a million politicians—we need more Emily Dickinsons is all. So don't you stop writing, Marion Roberts, and the major would say the same thing. He thought you were damned good.'

'He did?'

'Heard me reading 'em out one night.'

Which reminded her of the here and now of things and the reasons why nothing was as it should be.

'He meant a lot to you, Ed.'

'Anybody worthwhile means a lot to me and that includes my sister. OK?'

She had time to smile before the door was opened, bringing the blind half-way down between them.

'OK Miss Roberts.'

Neither one looked for the owner of the voice.

He leaned across the table, kissed her gently on the forehead the way he always used to back home when he tucked her up for the night. 'Always believe it—we did the right thing,' he whispered.

Marion nodded and, as though satisfied by the words and the contact, she managed to walk away from him without too much emotion moistening her eyes.

'And don't forget—keep writing!'

But the door closed on the small, trim figure leaving him with the hours. And the hours. And the hours.

Halliday found the bar he wanted, deep down an alley in the harbour area of Saigon. To reach it was, in its way, an act of bravery. The waterfront of any city is a doubtful proposition at night, but Saigon's riverside takes some beating.

A bar is a bar and a brothel is a brothel; whichever and wherever, you could be taking your life in both hands. But there were facets peculiar to Saigon's low-life no-one ever heard about in backgrounders and briefing sessions.

Like the prostitute who robbed and killed fifteen servicemen and took every last cent they had. She was doing very nicely till the police finally took an interest and discovered she was a man with a wardrobe full of *au dais*.

Every other shanty was a junky's Tiffany. From heroin to paint-stripper there was nothing you could not buy unless the Honda squad got to you before you got to Tiffany's. Vietnamese veterans mostly, making a living as best they could with a limb, even two limbs, missing. Individually they were useless, but a bunch of them bearing down on a nightwalker, if he was stupid enough to go solo in certain localities, could be an ever-lasting experience. They operated with a single-minded fiend-ishness from which there was no escape, as though the war had gone to their heads and the world turned into one big Vietcong.

Legend had it they were gentlemanly; would cut out your heart and lift your pocket-book with a gently murmured *dù'ng sọ*. But by then it was too late to be afraid, and you would be left, fighting to live, as they roared off into the darkness on their infernal Japanese machines.

Majors in those parts were rare of course, and with their kind of spending power no less welcome for that. But Halliday's luck held and he found the right place at the right time.

Four negro sailors were draped over the tiny bar. They knew enough to go in packs on the far side of old Saigon. The biggest of them stopped in mid-sentence as Halliday entered, a smile of genuine admiration creasing his face.

'Man, you sure got some gut walkin' lonesome through that shit.'

'I took a short cut.'

The sailor laughed and his companions, more uncertain about things, joined in.

'Ain't gonna name no names, Major, till I know where you heading. Just a precaution and no offence, huh?'

Halliday nodded.

'This here's the major I tol' you 'bout, Clarence. Shake 'em by the hand and we'll see how it rolls.' One after the other gave him the dap and he accepted it—why not? So they accepted him straightaway.

The spokesman studied him with a faint air of astonishment. 'Now my brother Franklin, he's OK, says you run a good outfit and you OK. Man, he worships you like he was some kinda Jim Crow. I says he'll grow up soon enough but if he says right then I say right.'

'That's fine. So now all I want is some information.'

'Sure. Have a beer, Major.'

Lukewarm machine oil, but one had to be sociable.

'What can I tell you?'

'Any possible change in your sailing schedule?'

'Ain't no strain on ma intelligence. No change, we go-go on twenty-two hundred hours, Tuesday night.' He looked round for confirmation. The others nodded sombrely.

'Up through the China Sea and across the Pacific?'

Franklin's brother looked surprised. 'Man, is there another way?'

'Suppose you went south, through the Indian Ocean, round the Cape and up into the Atlantic?'

This seemed to worry Franklin's brother. The others, taking their cue from him, looked worried too. 'You should be askin' Rear A'miral Hackenfucker, like I mean, I'm just a shit-shoveller, man. I dunno my East from my Ast—how 'bout you, Clary?'

Clary shrugged up to his ears. 'Personally, talkin' bout ships makes me sea-sick,' he offered.

'What's the *Carolina*'s range?'

'Round the world damn near if it has to,' said Franklin's brother.

'That's if you got the oiler with it too, man,' the third sailor explained.

'Like I mean what's flushin' man? You just a hero marryin' the heroin? I mean if the price is green enough I and ma colleagues would be elevated to help you slip it aboard.'

'You'll take on a pilot—so a gangway's lowered?'

'Tha's right.'

'Can you be at the head of the gangway at twenty-two hundred?'

'That wouldn't be difficult. I got the port watch like ma friends here.'

'What's your specialty?'

'I'm in the armoury, right in the shit'n'shells, man.'

Halliday looked pleased. It was worth the effort of finishing his beer. 'Fine. I'll see you then.'

Bewilderment.

'When?' That was Franklin's brother.

'On the gangway, twenty-two hundred.'

The gravel-voiced sailor's astonishment grew indescribable. 'I never heard we shippin' personnel.'

'In that case don't tell anybody.'

And he was gone.

They stared in the direction of his disappearance for some bemused moments. Then Seaman First Class Jones finished the sediment clogging his machine oil before returning a definitive verdict.

'Man, this war sure put an ass-full on the white man's burden.'

Clarence laughed with the rest of them, but stuck at the top note of a falsetto cackle. 'You know, Zulu, I never did figure out that old snakeshit they always pushin' in the third grade. I mean, what *was* the white man's burden, man?'

'Why that's self-evident, Mr Bones. The white man's burden is the white man....'

* * *

82

'You've still got time, Roberts. Just examine your feelings about that day. Face them. Admit that you ran because you just couldn't go along with Halliday and his mobsters.'

'I did what I had to—they had to get through—I cleared the way.'

'You think you did. That isn't you talking, you realize that, Ed? Did you ever hear tell of the Devil? Well I never used to believe in him myself. What should a psychiatrist be doing with that medieval crap when he has a whole deck of labels any which one he can pin on a man to show why he acted this or that way?

'But I saw the light when this thing happened, Ed. I had to admit to phenomena I hadn't recognized since I was a kid to Sunday school. We lose so much as we grow up, Ed. All the qualities we took for granted at our mothers' knees, good and evil, virtue and vice and yes, God and the Devil. Why I'd even come to doubt the existence of God, would you believe it?

'Now, I *know* he's around. He's gotten through to me at last. It's as if he had a personal message for me: "Colonel J. Wordsworth Milton of the US Army Medical Corps (Psychiatric Division), you can't escape facts. I am a fact. Therefore you cannot escape me." Well I guess I just put up my hands, Ed, and I surrendered. But that didn't mean I had to demean myself, or lose my intelligence. I saw that God really allows one to think, and what's better, he's even ready to put beautiful thoughts into one's head. It seemed as if he'd been telling me, "Psychiatry's fine, Colonel, but probing a mind isn't the same as loving it. When you can do both then you'll know as much as I do about your fellow-men."

'And he was right as always, Ed. I came to see that a man isn't responsible for what he does. He's driven by nothing more low down than the Devil. I don't have to tell you he's walked pretty tall in this country lately.

'I'm trying to explain, Ed. You don't have to blame yourself for what you did. The Devil was in it right from the start— you didn't have a chance. So when you get up on that stand you only have to tell them how it was that day, how you threw down your gun like it was demon bait and ran to keep

83

your soul out of the Devil's clutch; because that's how it was, Ed, believe me.'

'And if I don't?'

'Well now, I couldn't guarantee your sister's inviolability....'

Chuck Willens just wasn't the same boy in Ann Arbor as the man he'd become in camp five somewhere in Ha Nam province. The first selfish flush of youth had vanished on the day he was captured and he'd bought his time to grow thoughtful at a painfully high price, learning more about responsibility to his fellow-men in ten days at camp five than he'd discovered in as many months of army service.

First despair had given way to forced optimism, for Joe's sake, then well on the way to blindness and badly needing help. Nothing much: horsing around, playing the fool in words to raise the ghost of a smile on a face already haunted by the darkness to come.

These self-conscious antics had developed into a genuine cheerfulness and a real concern for others. Odd, because he'd never wanted to help anyone in his life. Not selfishness exactly, but simple ignorance of the fact that people anywhere, anytime, might deserve help.

But he came to it and stayed with it. His first thought when they returned to America was for his blind friend as they were going their separate ways from the air base.

'I'll come and get you when they check you out of hospital, Joe. And you'll come back to my place. OK?'

Because Joe had nurtured his brand of kindness too. Had spent all that time in the camp talking about his folks and so convincingly that not till the last moment, when Chuck looked around and asked; 'Where are your folks, Joe?' that PFC Joe Rideout had to admit at last, all those letters, the little parcels, came from the people at the orphanage. Mom and Pop, why they'd seemed so real you could have reached out in the dark and touched them....

So he returned to Ann Arbor in some confusion of mind. The neighbours dropped by and said 'Hullo, Chuck, good to have you back', and even the mayor called with a crate of lager and to say how proud he was of all their boys. The 'all' had

84

hurt, because it said as clear as a bell: now don't you go thinking we mind you got caught—that can happen to anyone—
we're mighty proud of you just as if you'd gotten yourself
killed.

But there comes a time when the back-slapping has to stop
and euphoria goes down the drain along with the water from
the dirty dishes on which you'd eaten a celebration dinner. The
ugliness of second thoughts, of tiny hesitations in the conversation grown sluggish, and the remembered glances flickering
signals between folks.

'Well, Chuck, guess you'll be lookin' around for something
to do soon.' Pop, the auto-worker, who'd given most of his life
to Ford's and four years to Europe. Now he spent the balding
years taking what he could get in recompense. A supervisory
little big-shot now and a union convenor, he was doing pretty
well as the world goes and he could dress Mom like a queen
in hard times to prove it.

'Plenty of time, Pop. I've got my back pay, army savings and
a pension, I'll look around when I get tired of too much freedom.'

'Well, don't set around too long, it can be unhealthy at your
age. I put the colour portable in your room; Mom thought you
might like it.'

'Thanks, Pop.'

They kept their voices to the lowest level as Mom was sitting
before the monstrance with her fading square eyes glued to a
re-heat of an old chain programme: 'The Loves Ride Again'.

For some reason Chuck didn't mention Joe, though he'd been
back of his thoughts all day, and how they could easily accommodate him now Pop had had the extension built in rear of the
house.

It happened to be Veterans' Club night. He'd never known
his father miss it since he was knee-high.

'See you around, Chuck.'

'Sure, Pop. Have fun.'

Typical Tuesday evening, and the fucken clock couldn't have
stirred a hand all that time. He didn't know whether to smile
or blubber quietly so as not to disturb the Old Lady at her
devotions.

Nothing much occurred except a police siren wailed from

one end of the avenue to the other, and Mom sat back instead of forward for the commercial.

Ooh wah-wah. Bermer's Bread. Ooh wah-wah. Bermer's Golden Brown Bread. Ooh wah-wah!
Heap big slice with heaps of butter.
Ooh wah-wah—BERMERS!

The kids playing Injuns with cute little feathered head dresses jumped back into the loaf and the picture faded.

'I think I'll grab an early night, Mom.'

'OK Chuck, good to have you home, son.'

He bent over and kissed her while she eased a slipper off her aching foot. Now why should that make him thoughtful?

And the loud noises that were supposed to mean so much? Chuck! Oh my darling baby! Ooh wah-wah, Chuck! It's been so long! They'd all faded too, like the commercial....

He sat down on the bed and thought he was looking at the familiar objects: bats, football helmets, pennons, the Grouper badges, and he felt—how did he feel? Like an actor on a stage full of properties that had nothing to do with him, only with the part he was playing. Those damned noises off: 'Chuck! Great to have you home!' they had nothing to do with him either, because now, he remembered, it had all been said in front of a fistful of cameras at the local TV station.

The folks had made it sound real good and convincing because they'd had better than three years to rehearse. And so the noises came out right on cue—like Injuns jumping out of a loaf of bread.

Slowly he looked up and caught at his astonished reflection in the mirror on the chest of drawers.

Just—like—they—were supposed to....

This time, and at last, he wept; for himself, for Joe, for all the others who'd come back from reality, only to take their places in some ancient, non-stop movie.

This time, the first in many a long day, the one-armed veteran out of Vietnam had real difficulty getting out of his clothes, and into bed.

* * *

The spot Halliday chose for jump-off was a long way out of Saigon to where even the waterside shanties petered out as though baffled by the everlasting inlets.

One of which, the largest in the area, was choked with APBs, ancient LSTs, APLs or 'apples' and the tangos long since abandoned by the Riverine Brigade.

He requisitioned a truck from the base and drove most of his officers down to the road by-passing Cholon. They were supposed to be having a night on the Town.

A moonlit scene, romantic in its way, excluding the redundant hulks. The silence was a blessing broken only by obscure, watery noises that might have been Vietcong moving up to investigate, but were, they hoped, no more than water-rats on a search and destroy mission in the muddy waters.

'Does any of us know how to drive these things?' Racowiczs sounded awed to extinction.

'Sergeant Dayson was with the river brigade till we got him,' Halliday said.

'That's so,' the lieutenant agreed. 'When I think of it we have a very motley crew on the payroll.'

'We need all the motley we can get,' Benner reminded.

'How about fuel?' That was Thompson.

'That LST over left is loaded with all we need.'

'Well, I suppose we should be grateful to someone.'

'You can be. Trabs arranged everything. He even had two Vietnamese technicians come down and check the engines.'

'Trabs, I might have known.'

'How do we tell which craft are ours, Major?' Sweetman asked.

'Anything splashed with white paint belongs to us.'

'Then we're set to go.' There was relief in Benner's voice.

'Twenty-two hundred tomorrow. The tide'll be right and the weather report says the weather holds.'

'Suppose it doesn't?' Mellors knew he was no seaman.

'Then we'll all be seasick. Let's get back to base and go over the contingency plans once more.'

The solid black shadows of eight men moved away from the silvery mudbanks and gave the silence back to the water-rats.

*   *   *

The men stayed on base most nights. Very few cared to taste the dubious delights of Saigon after dark. They were sick of the place, preferred the rugged austerity of the almost deserted barracks where you could, at the least, drink a beer in peace and even take in a movie if you felt so inclined. But mostly they moved back into the dormitories and made of them some kind of home where they could lie around, play card games, shoot craps, read or just talk. More than anything else, they talked.

For these were the men of companies A, B and C, and it was widely held by all who had contact or commerce with them, that for sheer staying power they had mouths that beat all. They never said much on combat missions, words take too long when life seems too short, but off-duty they simply never stopped.

Like tonight, their last full night in Vietnam.

'I sure hope your moose is taking good care of the children, Extra.' Gribble, stretched out on a top bunk was supposedly reading a paper-back.

'How many more times do I have to tell you—she is not my moose.'

Extra was very sensitive on that point, as Gribble well knew. He happened to believe it was degrading to a lady, referring to her as a moose, and he'd hardly changed two words with any Vietnamese woman let alone taken one for a mistress.

Gribble's little needle had to do with the woman Marshall and Extra had arranged with to take care of the orphans while they were on base. Every man had chipped in a dollar for their maintenance; enough to keep the woman's tongue from wagging and some over to help her start in the laundering business she hankered after. A war widow with six children of her own, she needed a lot more than Thieu was allowing her to keep seven from going hungry.

'You know,' said Private Jackson who chewed gum perpetually, and so viciously they called him Alligator, 'I'm still wondering if we're doin' the right thing, takin' em back home. Imagine they go to school and someone says "those kids ain't white enough to sit next to my angels and they got funny eyes",

88

so the angels start callin' em Martians—I mean, Vietnam has a smell they can recognize.'

Marshall leaned over his bunk. 'You're forgetting Alligator, we ain't takin' 'em to America, we just passing through, remember? We aim to get where they can grow up straight.'

'But suppose something happens to 'em? Like I mean, suppose we don't get through?'

Most of the men nearby stopped whatever they were doing and fell silent. It was defeatist talk of a kind and, until now, the question of failure had never really entered their minds. With Halliday in charge why should it? Still, it was possible, they couldn't deny that.

'We ain't gonna fail, Jackson. Get that into your head, you and the rest. We ain't gonna fail because some things are *ordained*.'

'What's that mean, Marsh?'

Marshall shifted to a more comfortable position and considered his bare feet for which he had a positive liking. 'It means, like you throw a stone up in the air, ain't no way for it to go to but down again, that's the natural law, Extra. Like it's natural you so goddam stupid.'

'That's what I like about Marsh—he says what he thinks,' Extra explained proudly.

'I still find it kinda hard to believe we're really goin' to do what—what we're goin' to do,' Sims Littleton sounded apologetic.

'What's difficult?' Whitney Fletcher asked. 'They wanted Americans to be Americans in Vietnam right? So we go home and we'll be Americans in America—it's perfectly logical.'

'Maybe he knows what he's talking about,' Extra suggested, then went back to playing the Vietnam War Game with Private Meadlo.

'I still have four reserve counters to my credit, Meadlo. You have not taken the replacement factor into account.'

'I don't have to, rat-head. My VC just captured all your goddam cities. That means total withdrawal of all American forces, so what about your four fucken reserve counters?'

'One of them happens to be Caressinger, wise guy, so I'm still in with a chance.'

Everybody in the dormitory had different ideas about what Extra could do with his mere Caressinger.

Further evidence of Rear-Admiral Flugzeuger, given before the Emergency Committee.

'He told you to put up your hands. What was your reaction to this, Admiral?'

'I told him to go to hell, and what did he think he was playing at?'

'Yes?'

'He said, "We stopped playing at twenty-two hundred hours". He then told me the ship had been occupied, operations room, communications centre, every strategic point on the carrier. I told him he had to be joking whereupon he took me at gunpoint over the whole ship. There were armed men everywhere.'

'How about your people?'

'I learned later that about one hundred twenty members of the crew had defected to the extent that they were obeying his orders and giving technical assistance denied by my officers.'

'Was this an ethnic division?'

'With possible exceptions they were all coloured men.'

'I see. What happened then?'

'He told me I was to shape a new course and signal the *Hyannis* to do likewise.'

'Did he give you a destination?'

'No more than that I was to make for the Eastern seaboard of the United States.'

'You were originally bound for San Diego?'

'That is correct.'

'Did you ask what purpose he had in all this?'

'Not immediately. Frankly I was too confused. I made certain conventional responses, tried to reason with him, warned him he couldn't hope to get away with it.'

'How did he answer that?'

'He ignored it. Told me quite calmly, that if I, personally, didn't give the orders, he would shoot my junior officers, one by one and at two minute intervals, until I complied.'

'No doubt you formed an opinion as to his state of mind?'

'Again, not immediately. I debated any number of explanations, all of which got mixed up in the process: that he and his men were under the influence of narcotics, that they were victims of a collective psychosis, or it was just a freak-out that had gotten out of hand.'

'And you hoped that any one of these conditions would diminish to a point where you could regain control of the situation?'

'That was my expectation.'

'Did you personally give instructions to change the course?'

'Yes.'

'What did the change mean in effect?'

'That we were to head for Singapore and negotiate the Straits of Malacca.'

'Normally you would communicate your instructions to the navigation officer?'

'That is so.'

'Would it have been possible to redirect the ship?'

'Not at all. One or two of the coloured hands had enough rudimentary navigational knowledge to prevent that. In any event I was too closely watched.'

'So, effectively, you had no further command of the *Carolina*?'

'Not then or for the duration of the voyage.'

'Was there any point on that voyage, Admiral, when you or your officers could conceivably have contacted the outside world in the hope of obtaining assistance?'

'Halliday had given orders that most of the radio and tele-communications systems be destroyed. I understand a specialist seaman advised him on the minimum equipment required for routine international communications at sea.'

'Thank you, Admiral.'

He was wading through swamp water. That's right. Three hours of bugs and leeches, and stop-overs just long enough to peel off as many as you could find. Three hours at port arms is a real drag. The arm goes numb and the heat makes you want to sleep, sleep, sleep man. And I'm tired of staring at Corporal Pulbright, visible only from the ass up and the 'funny' on his helmet: 'Like Jesus said, get me off the fucken hook!'.

He'd smiled over it once, but that must've been years ago.

Now, Pulbright was deep down in his craw on account of that grenade launcher poking over a mountain of shoulder and threatening his face at every unscheduled stop.

It all had to be done in silence, that was the beauty of the beast. They slurped delicately through the shit aiming not to play 'Jingle Bells' for the edification of the VC. 'Wrap band-aids round what you can, fellers,' the sergeant advised, but there was always some item ready to ring out the good news, 'Lock'n'load, pyjama boys, the Yanks are coming with Irving Berlin at point.' Oh dear oh my, where was I?

That's right, we're nearly at the jungle's edge, and then's the time to chatter, just the teeth, nothing else. Who wants to talk even if the opportunity presents itself? Pulbright's a comforting sight really—he never flips no matter what we take, and we've taken maximum in this.

My first week of war.

Was it possible? A whole week of combat, and I'm still in it. Rugged.

Oh Jackson it's a sorry story. Three elephants in a week and I'm heading for dandruff but that's no ticket for dust-off. These leeches now. I could make out a case for pernicious anaemia....

If I meet a Viet Cong face to face I'm gonna tell him I don' wanna die man. How about you? And all the time we'll be injecting each other with bullets, that's life-saving for someone. I must mean infecting, that's death-dealing—oh come on, come on! I know what's coming. Let's get to the last reel and forget all this phoney crap like I saw a movie once, a line of grunts wading through paddy water, carbines above their heads. I could have been dreaming of the future it's so like the fucken present. That's right, uptight officer, like Walters, uptight sergeant, like Trebisco—very well acted, but they shouldn't do it. Makes you kinda feel you oughta be right there fighting your way through Hollywood. Those lips, man, so tight they remind me of something: the sweat, the agony, the fatigue—like it's a bull on his forty-seventh cow. Never mind. You walk out of the cinema and there you go, man, headfirst into the mud—but when's the goddam finale?

Pulbright is heaving himself out of the water.

You should be so anxious for sequels, necrognome! This is

the end, right here or hereabouts. Lift up and feel that good eastern mud pulling you back as though what's the hurry, something has to get you. Well there's the guy behind me, mud, I'd love to stay longer, because any greenhorn knows you don't get Vietcong chicom mines in a paddy-field—that's strictly for the rice, macrobiotic!

Oh Christ I don't want to do this because in ten minutes I'll know I never should have and that's not the philosophy of despair. Fuck philosophy and despair, to save time. It's the song of the elephant. I am dead because I should not have done this. Please give me another chance. Absolution, shit! I need further education, I need to learn how not to die. Please, ma'am, where do I buy a diploma so I can graduate *cum* lots of *laude* in the Faculty of Resurrection?

Will you please stop pushing, Tango. Don't say it, don't even whisper it, just throw a glance at him over your shoulder, eyes popping like a brace of grenades. If looks could kill, Tango you're a dead man.

That fucken nigger! I love him like he was my own brother but his impatience is wearing my nerves thinner than used bargain G-strings. He *likes* this fucken war. Why do you like this war, Tango? I ask him twice a day. Well I tell you, soul cousin, back home you get kinda screwed up with honkies saying how black meat has no nourishment, like its human nature to feed off each other's hog-fat, but we got no black-eyed protein and they has white protein man.

I know it.

Yeah tha's right, soul cousin, you know it. So I join the army and I get me a gun and I fight for honky's right to call me shit, right? Only I ain't killin' no VC, soul cousin. Every time I pull a trigger I'm aimin' at a honky so now I eat regular, sleep soft of nights and I ain't screwed up no more, right?

Tango deserves his war but I wish he wasn't butting my ass to get outta this slop.

We've got to *what*! They must think I'm Alice Cooper in Disneyland. A hundred fifty yards to that mean-looking cloud of trees which looks like it's on the horizon and I ain't running across no open country to reach no horizon.

One hundred US army personnel, what's the word Webster?

93

—silhouetted?—on the sky-line so this PFC is having bowel trouble due to the evidence of his eyes. A fine time to go into liquidation. They could've lifted us across this terror firmer. What the shit are choppers for?

We're standing around, believe it, while Cogswell confers with his Benning Babies, every one a chip off the old Spock.

'Shall we canter, trot or gallop, Lieutenant?'

'I'd say a canter in extended order, sir.'

Permission to speak, sir. Well, Private? May I suggest we grow fucken wings and fly back or they do say there's a coin operated travel agent in Saigon who can fix these things.

Day-dreams, Private. No-one's listening—you're talking to yourself as you never did before because how else drown out the sound of your own screams yet to come?

So walk easy and watch the ground. If the VC aim to set us up in the forest they won't muss around on the approach run.

Unpredictable is the word, Tango. It was on the tip of my tongue that day, but watching the ground drove it clean out of my mind.

Tango on the left, one of the M60 carriers with Con Connolly, a real pain in the ass, and right was Pulbright, watching the ground, be it noted.

And I'm just an average American boy in the middle, steaming under a Vietnamese sun as I go my way suckin' a salt pill like I'm told. That's right, Mom, at last I'm doing what I'm told. What's that?

'Now don't you go getting your clothes all dirtied. Your father has to work himself sick for every single cent for every single item, you just mind that. And don't go too far from the house, it ain't safe. And don't you and your friends make too much racket d'you hear? your father's had a hard night at the plant and—watch where you're going for heaven's sake.'

And that's the answer. Have to tell someone if we get back out of this. Tango maybe, or General Cumberland. I have the perfect solution to this war, sir—any war. We draft the parents. All those wise words they spewed over their kids to make 'em do right. Why all we need is Mom and Pop behind each of us, telling us what to do and we could rumble those dirty, neighbourhood kids right back to Hanoi.

94

Where would we be without Mom and Pop?

Anywhere but this fucken country——

A scream from the right of the line.

Oh Christ he'd listened hard and carefully, knew for sure it wasn't him, not this time.

Every man froze, forgot the enemy, their collective gaze on Private Simpson in the second platoon.

EOD forward, someone calls.

Two men come running then stop as if they'd been hit. But it wasn't that at all. They had to back off, everyone had to, giving Simpson plenty of air. It was all they could give him.

Poor bastard had activated a pressure release mine and, Simpson or Sampson, he was an elephant.

The rest walked on while the helpless GI screamed, pleaded and cursed in a long quadraphonic wail that got inside their defences because he was to their fear as the receiver is to the transmitter.

But one at least had to look back, head wrenched around by nothing more than horrified fascination. Which way would he choose? Make a run for it and hope? Stay, and hang on to the precious seconds, but suffer death ten times over in the mind?

The man in the middle, racking his brains to find a soft option for Simpson. There was none. Maybe the Good Samaritan knew an answer. Maybe he'd never heard of Bouncing Betties.

'You go on like your head's talkin' to your ass, soul cousin, and you gonna end up likewise,' Tango called.

So he swivelled his eyes back to the ground at his boots' end and didn't even jump when the thing went off as they reached the forest's edge.

'He don' need no dust-off,' Tango said. 'Bebe sure gives a bad trip—like she spreads it around man.'

Naturally Tango is talking softly to himself. Any words will do to patch holes in ragged feelings.

But infernos come in several flavours and this one hardly scorched their egos.

They were fifty yards into the secondary growth when a point scurried back and reported a figure slipping away deep into the forest.

'That's a dummy,' Cogswell said, as though it signified noth-

95

ing. The men clustering around looked at each other.

'OK men, let's go.'

'Which way, sir?'

'Why straight ahead.'

'You must be kidding, it's a set-up plain as mud on your ass,' the trooper sounded incredulous.

'I said, "straight ahead".'

Everyone knew Cogswell didn't care any more. He'd blown his mind long since.

There was grumbling, but no real attempt to disobey orders. GHQ failed to see the significance in the fact that Private Average was no more serious in his insubordination than he was in fighting the war. Both attitudes betrayed unaligned conditioned reflexes.

'We're done man, I can feel it in my urine, we're fucked.' Tango muttering, audibly this time. 'Sure could use a fix this everlasting minute—hey, soul cousin, you got——?'

Tango's last request granted as a shot dug deep between the eyes. It was a fix of a kind.

All hell let go and pulled out the dampers instantaneously. The man in the middle just stood there stupidly, watching branches fly off the trees in every direction. It was magical, might have been a show put on for his unique benefit.

'Willens! get your head down and——' Pulbright began. Then a flash hit him full frontal and Pulbright had lost the whole left side of his face and he was down on his hands and knees as if he was looking for it. Willens hit the ground as a PFC squirmed to his side.

'It's a fucken X!' he screamed through the din. Willens stared at him blankly.

An X type ambush is the lowest form of strife known to man. There's no way out. You can't go any lower than that.

The RTO crouched close to Cogswell who surveyed the scene with the greatest possible interest. Fortunately the platoon leaders were on top of their jobs.

Willens, firing on automatic, saw Sergeant Zeckler tear the horn from Cogswell's grasp.

'24 this is 51 Adams. We're being hit—RPGs and mortars— Williams get that M60 goin'.'

'51/24 Roger that. Please give your location.'
'24/51. No time, will give you visual.'
'51. Roger.'

Zeckler unhitched the smoke bombs from his webbing and hurled two before they cut him down. A severed artery pumping blood over a radio pack does it no good. The RTO continued as best he could, wiping off blood and moving away to somewhere dry.

'Battalion strength.' Lieutenant Biggs bawled at the second platoon sergeant manning an M6o.

'51/24. We have visual. Coming right in.'

But a mortar shell stole the good news, the radio and the RTO who ceased to exist on the very last word.

The Cobras did more harm than good. They came in right on target and shot the area to ribbons. But the regular units of North Viets had already pulled back at first sight of the smoke signal.

The VC, knowing they had to die, stayed on, a mere dozen men, firing like madmen to let the Americans think they were still close in.

By the time someone tried to rectify the situation it was all over. The US army took seventy-nine killed and wounded that day, many of them gunned down by their own people. Willens was one of seven unaccounted for.

A medic slumped on top of him, shot through the back as he tried to cope with the shattered arm. His last act of mercy, the weight of a lifeless body staunching the bloodflow.

The screams he'd been waiting for came at last. The world expanded into one gargantuan cry of pain and, as strange men came running, shouting 'Bác si Mau lên!' the world collapsed and Willens remembered nothing more till Pop stood over him, shaking him by his good arm.

'Chuck, for Chrissakes, what hit you? It's two in the morning, son.'

Chuck opened his eyes wider than his mouth, still rounded to the shape of a scream.

He looked at the unfamiliar face balanced above the familiar dressing-gown with its chequered pattern he remembered so well and there, over his father's shoulder he could see Mom's anxious face peering puffily in at the door, as though it might just be a bad break in transmission and normal viewing would be restored as soon as possible.

'I—I'm sorry, Pop. I—must've had a bad dream.'

The old man looked at him strangely. 'Does this happen often?'

'It never happened before.'

'Well,' a long pause, 'you try and get a grip on yourself, son. It's a peaceable neighbourhood and we can't go gettin' the folks next door all worked up on account of our personal problems. Besides, you damn near scared Mom outta her wits. It ain't good for her, now is it?'

He made some show of putting the rumpled bed-clothes in order, but his lips were set in a line that had to do with highly personal dissatisfaction. If this was how it was going to be, well...

'Now you get yourself some sleep and don't—don't let things prey on your mind so. Tomorrow's another day, you just remember that.'

He watched the man he called Pop cross the room and switch off the light. A faint 'Goodnight, son' emanated from someone blessed with the name of 'mother'.

Chuck fell into a light, uneasy sleep, still clutching the six inches of stump in case the fear and the pain came gushing out once more and disturbed the neighbours.

Every ship in every navy of every major country of the world is required to radio its position daily. This is known as a respectable fix.

Naturally the high command wants to be apprised of where everything is or how does it move its little counters around the board without spoiling the game? So, when, after some hours, the US Navy Communications Center did not receive its quota of coded signals bounced back off the US navy satellite it began to get worried.

More precious time was wasted in arguing about the satellite which must have fouled up. But then it occurred, they were not getting signals by ancient radio systems either.

Puzzlement gave way to mild consternation.

They appeared to have 'lost' the *Carolina* and the *Hyannis*.
What was to be done?

And what had happened?

Could the Reds have crept quietly up in the night and forged another Tonkin resolution?

Sunk without trace.

The awful possibility tarnished a lot of gold brass in those endless hours of speculation.

Speculation was all they dared allow themselves. The disappearance of two ships could not be contemplated. Like what is a clutch of admirals supposed to *do* in the circumstances? To mutilate a phrase, this is not war, but it's ridiculous.

The Achilles heel of any junta is fear of being made to look ridiculous. How could they openly announce to the world: 'Ahem, I'm sorry to have to announce that we appear to have lost two of our ships'? The Kremlignomes would rupture their Politbureaux laughing and then offer to help look for them.

For the time being even the White House mustn't know. Foxwell was sufficiently steamed up about the San Diego mutiny not to need extra fuelling.

But they did send frantic coded messages to Saigon, top secret, asking US Ambassador Brinker whether Admiral Flugzeuger had *said* anything when he attended a dinner party given in his honour the night before sailing.

'No,' Brinker coded back, 'Flugzeuger only mentioned how pleased he was with his handicap now he'd sunk holes on the flight deck for putt practice.'

Holes! The brass-hats stared at each other in disbelief. Normally, and if Flugzeuger had been where he should have been, they'd have smiled indulgently. Merry Quipsies and a happy New Year—what else are carriers for eh, Admiral? Heh-heh-heh.

But taken along with his sudden disappearance Flugzeuger's holes began to look significant, even sinister. Could this be some kind of freak-out with special reference to war-weary mariners?

A council was held to consider the problem, but nothing came of it except they decided to sit on their hands and trust to necessity.

After all, as one admiral put it, 'He'd just *have* to radio for fresh golf balls sooner or later.'

Daytimes the off-duty men would pack into a recreation room and sweat through an hour of lectures on free-style tactics or one of them, from Halliday through to buck private, might give an impromptu talk, a kind of run-down on the reasons why they were doing the unthinkable.

One day they crowded in to hear Corporal Broken Cloud, a young Indian who'd managed somehow to retain, in the words of a lady sociologist, 'a physiognomical connection with his aboriginality'. The high cheek bones, the carved mouth, a timeless gaze that had taken a tribe over the top of a world on ice and down to the promise of a land not yet named for California.

His bearing rated as proud, not US army ramrod proud, but the natural kind belonging to the man with a long and tragic heritage. If Americanization showed, it was in the slight air of bashfulness with which he faced his audience.

Halliday introduced him and the men gave him a big hand.

He began hesitantly.

'We all know why we're here, why we're all here, but it's good to have a chance for each one to explain why he is here.

'Perhaps it is true I am treacherous—how can I defend myself against what I do not understand, against a charge made by the dead?

'In 1878 General Sherman ordered the complete extermination of the Modoc Indians because, he said, treachery is inherent in the Indian character. Maybe I should have told my draft board.'

That got an appreciative laugh, but Corporal Broken Cloud remained unsmiling. Quite suddenly he cut across their laughter.

'1848: One hundred thousand Indians in California—the year of the Gold Rush.

'1859: Thirty thousand Indians in California.

'1900: Fifteen thousand Indians in California.

'1971: Private Broken Cloud is sent to Vietnam!

'Do *I* need to tell you why I am here?

'Don't apply your Western style evaluations to the Indian character. The Indian knows nothing of revenge, nothing of historical necessity, of Bible-trading eyes for eyes, tooth for tooth like vultures haggling in a slaughter-house.

'He has even forgotten the meaning of natural justice which is a different thing. Today he is reduced to grubbing around for the means of survival, living off Federal hand-outs to cover his poverty in a land of manufactured plenty.

'I could find no work. I could not eat except the bread of my parents. I joined the army like they tell me and said, this at least is conditional survival.

'I will tell you some more of the things I am here for.

'In that time of Massacre at Wounded Knee, 1890, four days after your Christmas, the US Seventh Cavalry slaughtered hundreds of Sioux men, women and children. They ran like frightened cattle and could not escape. Women, heavy with child, were shot through the belly, small boys hid and were told "Come out it's safe", and then they were butchered.

'For that, Western man invented historical necessity.

'We know only of history; our history. It is not the same as your history. Hollywood has taken care of your history.

'I will tell you the words of Red Cloud: "You have taken the wealth of our country and called it your own and we have none. We are starving today. The majority rules. They have depopulated this country of Indians, they have taken the horse population, they have taken everything we have and we are starving. We are in need. We are in dire need..."

'I will tell you the words of Dewy Beard: "They knew I was wounded. I was shot in the leg and I fell. They knew I was wounded and helpless. Then they came and shot me again, in the breast."

'This is some of the history of the Big Foot, and I am proud to know it all by heart. For every word of the Bible you can quote to me, I can quote you back. You tell me he said "Suffer little children" and I tell you straight back "Wounded Knee, 1890".

'My history—your laws. If you want I can tell you, it's here, locked in my heart, all that has been done to my people: The Gros Ventres, the Yuma, the Menominees, the Shawnees,

Piegans, I can tell you a story for every raindrop in a shower how the White Man's laws plundered with words finer than feathers.

'It is so. What the white man cannot understand, he kills. His religion, his politics, his morals—everything must be accepted at the point of a gun. If not, he will use death as the ultimate argument.

'The Baker Massacre, Sand Creek, Wounded Knee or My Lai —what difference? The white man has learned nothing.

'I will give you testimony of soldiers at the massacre in Sand Creek Colorado and see what you can recognize.'

He told them of things done that no film ever showed out of consideration for white housewives' feelings.

How Colonel Chivington, a Methodist minister, slaughtered the Cheyennes under Black Kettle and the Arapahoes under Left Hand.

Women cut to pieces, scalped, their brains sliding out of smashed skulls like porridge out of an upturned saucepan. The children—troopers using a small child for target practice. The private parts of women cut out and draped over saddle-bows, on sticks, or worn like cockades in the hat on the journey back. The woman, violated both ways by two men, before they drove sabres through what they'd just violated.

Broken Cloud finished in deep silence.

'This is my history. And ever since, we have prayed to the Great Father. Please, please don't send your Son. After what we have suffered in the name of your Nephew, we will manage.

'I am soiled. To an Indian this is a terrible thing. For I have trespassed on the hunting grounds of my brothers in Vietnam. That I should have done this thing—to have killed men who wanted nothing of me. I am no longer Indian, but a true half-breed. That is my punishment.

'I shall return to America and do what has to be done, not because I am in love with the shedding of blood—but we have a saying which is deep in my understanding at this time: The setting of the fiery sun is the promise of its return.'

The Indian GI looked about him as though trapped by a dream in which nothing figures. A last remnant of a great people, whittled down from a tall tree to a bundle of kindling—that he should be standing in the womb of this monster devoted to death, special delivery; a bitchmother from the Badlands, giving birth every so often to tiny winged demons who cried 'whoopee' with every good strike they made. Broken Cloud stood like a hunter lost in the birchwood forest, could not see the trees for the wood and the tears in his eyes.

The session broke up in silence. What could be said? But by the set of the men's expressions Halliday knew he'd made the right decision.

The dream was emerging into daylight and reality.

In a crowded ship with its full carrier complement and five hundred or more troops sharing the limited space, there had to be some inconvenience. Broadly, the guests took care of security and, as far as possible, Halliday left the officers to run the ship after their own fashion.

There were many key points requiring an armed guard. On the bridge, in the communications centre, the engine rooms or wherever, he had men posted for four hour periods with weapons on 'automatic'. Each detail had a personal intercom radio pack connecting with Halliday's command post in a lower decks canteen. The armouries were under stronger guard since any attempted counter-move must depend on gaining the weapon stocks. Everything seemed to be under control as of that moment.

Halliday returned to the CP with Racowiczs and they fought their way through to a table in the corner. It was some command post. GIs all over the place, loud conversation and strong coffee.

Racowiczs looked at the scene doubtfully. 'In an emergency, Major, we could be in some trouble. Shouldn't we have a more secluded CP?'

They were wedged pretty tightly at their table and Racowiczs seemed to have a point. Two coloured GIs were arguing quietly in the opposite seats only inches from his face.

Halliday ordered coffee and then considered the question. 'Suppose we were secluded, and they rushed us. We might just get ourselves captured, held as hostages—and that's the finish. Here we're surrounded by never less than fifty of our own—

why throw away an advantage in numbers?'

Racowiczs conceded and was about to mention Broken Cloud's performance when a large, familiar-looking sailor pushed through the log-jam of tables, chairs and bodies and close-eyed Halliday's opposite neighbour.

'Hey, soul-brother, I gotta chew some fat with your number one—how we gonna manage like can I sit in your lap? Man, I'd hate for to get a good-lookin' feller like you a bad name.'

The GI's smile was a one-off carving in ivory. 'Zulu, how come you ain't a preacher with all that sweet talk? I tell you, Major, give him five minutes lonely with Foxwell and he'd have him convictious he was just an ol' anaemic nigger from Talahasee.'

He left his seat and Zulu roughed him by the shoulder before squeezing his bulk in across from the major. Almost immediately he grew serious. 'Major, when we met that night, how was I supposed to know what was goin' on? One word and I could've got a couppla hundred guys workin' solid for your outfit right from countdown.'

'I appreciate that, Zulu. But you did enough—I just needed information——'

'Enough! Just because you in the army don't mean you know how it all is in the navy, man. Like it's just a segregated Alcatrazville, ain't no place to get away from those cruds bawlin' y'out watch on and watch off.'

He leaned in to emphasize his words. 'You know we have one dead and a couppla wounded every *week*? It's cops and robbers, man—and they got more cops than we got robbers.'

Halliday stirred his coffee, said nothing.

'I mean look, Major—what you gonna do is what we *wanna* do.'

Zulu and Racowiczs waited and watched for some kind of response. Eyes lowered as though he contemplated no bigger problem than the sweetness of coffee.

'We shouldn't refuse help, Major,' Racowiczs prompted.

Halliday raised his eyes to their level. 'What kind of help?'

Zulu looked from one to the other, perplexity and the beginnings of anger folded up his otherwise good-natured face. 'What d'you mean, what kinda help? Manpower! You gonna hit 'em you need manpower. We got explosives experts, we got sharp-shooters, we got a whole lot of mean bastards itchin' to prove they got diplomas for Damage. What you lookin' for—dancing girls?'

'We're not demonstrating Black Power, Zulu.' Quietly. Zulu already had his head down with an angry rejoinder. 'Let me finish. I've got two-fifty negroes, almost three hundred whites, that's about right. What we're out to prove has nothing to do with white supremacy or black power. Personally I don't approve of either.

'What we're doing connects with people. There'll be a lot of killing—at the end of it we lose. Right away they'll look for a scapegoat and when they've finished counting they'll shout "That's it! Five-fifty niggers and only three hundred white men". By their logic that means there's only one enemy within —the blacks, Black Power—and they won't stop till they've got every last one of you, one way or another.

'If I was a liberal, Zulu, I'd say come right in, be my guest. But that's not looking any farther than the white man's salvation. Your moral support and even your advice I'll take, but it has to end there—for your sakes.'

Franklin's brother stared at Halliday for quite some time. He seemed to be trying to say something but the words had trouble existing. Eventually he glanced at Racowiczs before fixing his gaze on the crowded scene.

'Five minutes back, Major, I'd have cut my throat before I'd have said this thing, but just for once I'd take a chance on being a white man if I had to.'

Again he leaned forward confidentially. 'Me and the boys, we been keepin' our ears to the ground. Hear tell the fliers aim to break out of their quarters around o-two hours in the mornin' come whatever. They're ready to pay a high price, Major.'

'What have they got?'

'A few .45s that we know. If you need help——'

'Thanks, Zulu. We'll manage.'

Zulu, big as his name, grinned, then laughed aloud, as though some incongruous thought had tickled his ribs; still laughing he went back to his duties.

Racowiczs lit a cigarette, stared at it pensively. 'You must have taken a long time working this thing out, Major.'

An officer's cabin had been requisitioned for the children's use and it seemed to be filled with nothing but books, all the books Marshall and Extra could lay hands on in Saigon. Though what a volume entitled *The Economic Reconditioning of South Vietnam* by Albert Dreistein, was supposed to do for them was anybody's guess.

Extra, as usual, looked worried. 'Shouldn't they oughta have toys, Marsh? Children need toys.'

'Only one thing they need and that ain't toys, Extra. American infants have so many toys they bored to their ears, didn't you know that?'

'But toys are natural for children,' Extra persisted.

'Nope. Five hundred million dollars a year says toys is natural for kids. It's an industry is all; children don't make a profit. Toys is what children make for themselves. Back in Alabama I knew a little boy could spend a week makin' little animals outta used chewin' gum. And there was sticks to whittle and trees to climb and I just never had the time to be bored.'

'Must've had somethin', Marsh. I did.'

'I can imagine. Well, I had a guitar for one Christmas. "That's for music", my daddy said. Then I had a big blackboard —"That's to draw anythin' in the world you want," he tol' me.'

'Sounds quite a guy.'

'My daddy was blinded in Korea, but he could see pretty good.'

So the children had a couple of sensible uncles and five hundred stupid uncles who were always dropping by for a game and a fractured conversation. Almost every one of them would bring a candy bar till the canteen ran out. Then, scarcity being what it is, the sensible uncles would sell the stuff back to the stupid uncles at twice the price they'd paid, so they could hand them out all over again.

It was good for the children to have Marsh and Extra standing between them and overwhelming generosity. And because they were watched over with love the children forgot to be worried by their strange surroundings, the unusual circumstances; even remembrance of that day in the village, when the skies split wide open and took away everything they had, shaded into vague and puzzled recollection, as when old and familiar objects get gently pushed out of sight way up in the attic.

'This has gone far enough!' Admiral Hackenschmidt pounded his fist on the polished hardwood table, then rubbed it surreptitiously where no-one could see. When he started hurting himself he was angry indeed. All the other admirals—full, vice and rear—their caps sitting neatly on the table before them, coughed a little or shifted from one side of their below-decks to the other. Something big was brewing or why else the hurriedly convened meeting?

It could only mean, horror of horrors, somebody was going to have to *tell* somebody. That could predicate a few heads joining the gold braided caps gracing the table. They stared moodily but with love at their headgear.

'We've heard nothing for three days. The NOS has so far failed to pick 'em up and for all I know they could be steaming around Lake Michigan.'

The Chief of Naval Communications hastened to reassure. 'That's impossible, Admiral. They simply haven't had time to——'

'I am trying to lighten the atmosphere, Wicksteed,' Hackenschmidt said, slowly, and Wicksteed smiled obligingly.

'It's no damn laughing matter! Do you realize we are accountable for these ships? We dispose of the finest communications network in the world and we don't even know what's happened to the biggest ship in the United States navy's Seventh Fleet.'

'We need a response, Admiral. There hasn't been a single signal out of the *Carolina* since she weighed anchor.'

'To hell with a response! We have to find that ship, and the *Hyannis*.'

At this breaking point a junior officer entered with nice, nautical precision, breathlessly requesting permission to speak.

'Proceed, Lieutenant.'

'The naval station in Singapore has just notified in standard code that a fishing smack yesterday reported the *USS Carolina*

107

proceeding west at speed through the Malacca Straits, sir.'

Hackenschmidt stared at the beardless youth with the wide-eyed expression of a zombie who isn't feeling too good. Admiral Groover, in charge of Navy Shore Installations, kindly dismissed the lieutenant before Hackenschmidt's reaction could seriously impair his morale.

'What are they doing in the Indian Ocean?' Hackenschmidt, trance-like, asked the lieutenant, who was no longer there.

The others were looking grave. There just didn't seem to be any explanation. One of their number, noted for his freaky sense of humour, wanted to suggest, 'maybe they got lost', but calculated if they couldn't find a yard-arm to hang him from, everyone was in a mood to build one; so he kept silent and looked grave too.

'A fishing smack. A fucken smishing fack has to be the first bastard to find our ship, and we got a billion dollars of hardware up there supposed to pick needles out of——'

The unfairness of life, the enormity of its potential to play funny, funny games with a serious, dedicated admiral, almost unhinged his mind as it threatened to disturb his diction.

What in God's name was to be done?

They spent the rest of the watch working out what should be said, and by, and to whom.

'Come in, Patmore, sit down, be with you in a moment.'

Corporal Patmore did so. But he kept his eyes on the forage cap gripped in his hands. He had no curiosity about the surroundings or the officer seated behind a desk studying some kind of report—his, most like.

Hell, what was there to be curious about? It was just a room: four walls, a door and window, office furniture and that character crouched behind the desk. There always was. Ever since he could remember, there'd been some crud behind a desk: the doctor, teachers, draft board heisters. Has to be something separating somebody from nobody.

The POW camp had been a real vacation in at least that respect. Not a desk in sight. Even the commandant used nothing more than a deal table.

His depression deepened as he tacked a rider to his thoughts.

Someone behind a desk always wants something from the man on the other side.

What now?

He missed seeing the major look up and spend time studying him as though he was a mis-dated perpetual calendar.

'I've been reading your psychiatric report, Corporal. You're in pretty good shape.'

'Yessir.'

'But I'd like to know a little more about how you view the North Vietnamese.'

'I've been here three days, sir, and I believe I have a leave entitlement.'

'You'll get it, Corporal.'

'Almost all the other guys have signed off; what's so special about me?'

'Nothing of consequence, Corporal. It's just that Intelligence wants no slip-ups like we had over Korea and——'

'I filled out the questionnaire like everybody else. It took me a whole day. I stated on my oath—no brainwashing.'

The psychognome smiled ruefully. 'I know how you feel. They're living in the past. Times have changed, but some of the smarter ones know it. That's why I have to ask you——'

'What, for God's sake? I definitely told everything I know.'

'...why I have to ask you how it is you have so much respect for the North Vietnamese Communists.'

Patmore breathed tightly, so as not to betray the quickening tempo of mixed-up emotions, doubled the tension of his grip on the cap the way a drowning man grasps the straw tighter.

It all came back to the plane ride, and what he'd objected to. They'd slid over his outburst for that moment but it had been remembered, recorded, and acted on.

He should have kept his mouth shut; but that had been Patmore's lifelong trouble. He was incapable of dissimulation in a world where the easy smile, the cant words and phrases, disposable as a plastic container, were forms of currency with which you paid your way through life. Patmore was never so poor as to carry that kind of small change in his pockets. Even so, he felt he could do with a little right now, just enough to buy his way out of there.

The grey eyes, usually so clear, grew hazy, as though unused to circumspection.

'This has to do with what I said on the plane, right?'

The major nodded with a deliberation that left the ball in Patmore's court.

'OK, I just happened to be dealt with by North Vietnamese nationals. I resented the reference to "gooks"; what's so kinky about that?'

'The NVA was also an enemy.'

'For Chrissakes! what are we? Kids, that we gotta fight the enemy *and* call him names?'

'It's a question of degree, Corporal. You can't defeat the enemy unless you go all the way.'

Patmore was careful not to point out that they hadn't defeated the enemy. Instead, 'I owe my life to what he'd call a "gook".'

The medicine man raised his eyebrows at the seemingly minor revelation. 'So you feel grateful?'

Patmore bit his lip very slightly. 'What am I supposed to feel?'

'Let's put it another way. Gratitude is a concession; it weakens your position *vis-à-vis* the party evoking it. From the particular to the general you're softened up to the extent that you can look around you and say, "Hey, this system's not so bad. It's got a lot going for it." Back of your mind, you're accepting what you see because if it wasn't for one small part of it you'd be dead which means you wouldn't be seeing anything at all.'

Patmore took the measure of the major's sophistry and tried hard not to appear sickened by it. 'Major, I am a complex human being; which in my book means I can hate an ideal, respect the man who holds to it and be glad if he saves my life while I'm trying to take his. I can even find something to commend in his system if it looks worthwhile, but that doesn't mean I won't fight like hell in the first place to prevent it being rammed down someone else's throat if he doesn't want it.'

'Corporal——'

'Wait a minute. That's what I was told this war was all about. Nobody told me I had to go out there and pin my ideals on other people's hats. No-one told me I was just a camouflaged salesman promoting Coca-Cola to people who never asked for it in the first place.'

'I think it would be better if——'

'Nobody had to condition me. I've got eyes to do the job. One time I was near Quynh Lap, I saw the leper hospital there, two thousand patients—imagine how it looked after thirty bombing attacks in two days. But they were only "gooks", right?'

'Corporal, what kind of a case do you suppose you're making out for yourself?'

Patmore leaned forward, his fears forgotten; he no longer cared what those on the other side of the desk thought. Fortunately he still had a rugged independence of mind which might just carry him through the difficult days ahead.

'If I tell you a single person out there has to save for two years before he can buy a bicycle—what does it mean to you, with maybe two cars and TV in the bathroom? That's why we didn't win.'

'And is that the good news you'll be spreading in the outside world, Corporal?'

The two men stared at each other for as long as it takes the vulture to swoop on possibilities. The soul surgeon spoke first, concluding with all that needed to be said for the time being.

'When you reach it?'

The flight crew quarters had two ways in and out, midships. These were bisected by a corridor running fore and aft. The bulkhead doors, three and six, were normally closed and guarded as were the other exit points connecting with B deck. If an attack were intended it had to come from a concerted rush at one level which meant either or both of the bulkheads.

Halliday had M6os set up to cover each one. He took charge of number three, Racowiczs had the other.

All they had to do was wait.

Zulu and his friends had heard right. At exactly two in the morning, the fliers forced the doors and appeared in the entrances looking as though it was way past their feeding time. Most of them were in flying gear. To a Vietnamese peasant at the wrong end of their napalm rockets they might just have looked intimidating in that Batman get-up.

They were badly hampered by the fact that only two could squeeze through at one time. The first to appear on Halliday's side certainly looked fierce enough, masked, as he was, by heavy duty goggles. He brandished a .45 and came storming out with all the fury and invective to be expected from one of his kind.

'You, white nigger! Get outta my fucken way or I'll blow you apart. You don't do this to Big Batman and get away with it.'

Now that was a coincidence. Batman.

'You'd better go back to your belfry, Fledermaus,' Halliday suggested. 'We're not defenceless Viet women and children so you'll need some really smart bombs under your armpits to back up your big mouth.'

'Why you——' Batman had ten yards to go, had covered half of it as Halliday stepped aside and the M60 opened up. Just a brief burst, long enough to bat the eyelid and take the eardrums by storm in that confined steel-lined space.

Big B disintegrated. No other word for it. The man behind him was caught in the side-effects and died instantly. In battle-field language there was stew all over the place.

Their comrades, jamming the entrance, looked shocked, all cowed suddenly, because their style of courage had to do with romantically zooming in on anything they fancied and maybe getting themselves shot out of the sky in a *Gotterdammerung* blaze of glory.

But this was nasty.

I mean, people getting splashed all over the walls right under one's nose. And there was blood and—and stuff everywhere. One man wiped some guts from his goggles and looked sick.

'You!' Halliday barked.

The green hero seemed bewildered. 'Me?'

'Catch!' He threw him a bucket and mop. 'Get some water and wipe your friend off the deck!'

Pukka top-sahib contempt in his voice as he walked off leaving the guard to watch over the remnant opposition. The GIs didn't even bother to call in the .45s. Nobody showed signs of waving one, much less using it.

Racowiczs reported no trouble from his side. They'd backed off as soon as they caught sight of the M6o.

*   *   *

The middle phase begins with the event which partially unlocked the mystery without actually pushing it into the open.

Halliday had been advised by some of the knowledgeable hands to take on fuel and supplies from the *USS Hyannis*, a day's sailing in the rear. This would be necessary if they were to make their objective as one unit.

He gave orders for reduced speed and calculated for a rendezvous off the Cocos Islands. The insurgents aboard *Hyannis* were informed and requested to report back briefly if there were people aboard who could make the necessary course corrections. Able Thompson radioed 'No problem'.

On March 12th the two ships hove to within hailing distance of each other on a dead calm sea. Some humorist on the *Carolina* ran up the B flag; and the transfer of men, including six of the *Hyannis*' crew members, supplies including napalm and explosive packs, and fuel, took place without too much trouble.

The tanker's radio equipment was left intact. All else apart, the news would have to break some time.

This operation took place about eighteen hours after the Chief of Naval Staff advised the Defence Secretary of events as he understood them.

I have to inform you that two operative units of the US Navy, the *USS Carolina* and *Hyannis*, are no longer responsive to our control.

We have received no communication of any kind since these ships left Vietnamese waters at approximately twenty-two hundred hours Saturday March 4th.

We are integrating all resources in order to ascertain what exactly has happened. It is, of course, impossible for two ships of their size to have disappeared without trace.

113

Be assured I will keep you apprised of all developments.

'What for?' the Secretary asked himself. He read the communication marked 'Most Secret' and being a very busy man he naturally put it to one side. For heaven's sake! he was concerned with defence, not the recovery of lost property.

Winfield very much wanted to know about that.

'Admiral Hackenschmidt, you've heard Admiral Flugzeuger describe how he found himself in dire straits——'

'Malacca Straits——'

Winfield killed the reaction with his gavel. 'The time is hardly propitious for levity. The admiral obviously misheard.' He returned his attention to the discomfited mariner. 'Plainly, a critical situation existed at command level on the *Carolina*?'

'That was our impression.'

'Let's just have yours, Admiral.'

'Yes, it was my impression.'

'Then why, in a potentially dangerous situation, did you wait so many hours before informing the Defence Secretary of the crisis?'

'There was no identifiable motivation,' Hackenschmidt explained, 'that could preclude the event from remaining situational.'

'You mean you had no idea what Flugzeuger was up to?'

'That's right.'

'Let's move on to Defence Secretary Melville's acknowledgement. Can you tell the Senate how he expressed himself on this?'

'Certainly. He was brief and to the point. "Thank you for your communication. Please keep me informed."'

'Did it occur to anyone at top level that these two ships might have been the targets of Russian submarines?'

'Our information was that no Russian units were operating in those waters at that time.'

'Would the Defence Secretary know that?'

'Certainly, he's fully informed on enemy dispositions.'

'Would it be true to say that, during this period of—indecision, you were completely unaware that three infantry units had defected in Saigon?'

'Absolutely, we had no information on this.'

'If you had known about it would the two events have connected in your mind?'

'Not at all.'

'So there is no foundation for the view held in some quarters that closer liaison between the two service departments might have prevented the disaster *ab initio*?'

'*Ab* what?'

'From the outset.'

'Quite definitely not.'

'But the situation changed dramatically on the following day?'

'Indeed it did.'

'Christ!'

The exclamation came so plosive that one of the gold braids actually looked over his shoulder. Hackenschmidt seldom took the name of the Lord High Admiral in vain. Something was obviously wrong, all over again. In true naval fashion the collective unconscious decided on silence.

Hackenschmidt looked up from the scrap of paper in his hand. His normally ruddy complexion—for why else did they nickname him the Red Admiral?—had been infiltrated by a more ambiguous hue not unlike the colour of sea-sickness.

'*Hyannis* has radioed that she and the *Carolina* were boarded by an uncertifiable number of armed American troops just before sailing time. *Hyannis* reports she was occupied by ...' he looked back at the print-out to verify his disbelief, '... by fifty GIs commanded by a lieutenant. As of now, the *Carolina* has taken on fuel and the *Hyannis*' boarding party and is heading SSW, presumably to round the Cape.'

There followed a long, long silence; so protracted indeed that it badly got on Hackenschmidt's nerves.

'Why doesn't somebody say something?' he shouted.

Cutting right across intense inner speculation as to which head would roll first. They responded by coughing, exchanging glances and shifting around in their seats to prove they were capable of action at bottom.

Wicksteed was, as usual, the only man to oblige. 'Well if that doesn't beat everything.'

'Wicksteed, I am still waiting for the problematical day when you say something that will fill me with pride.' He glared around at the assembled officers. 'Has anybody anything he wishes to add?'

Admiral Clarke, in charge of Naval Strategy Co-ordination, gave a slow and characteristically reasoned opinion. 'It seems to me, Admiral, we're faced with a problem not entirely within our competence to deal. From a minor, though unusual, localized issue it has now developed into a crisis determinable only under direction from the Government.'

A fair assessment of the situation going beyond the limited comprehension of the majority, including Hackenschmidt who managed to look hurt and bewildered in equal parts.

'Now look, George, are you saying the navy can't handle this?'

'That's right. For the very good reason we don't know what we're handling.'

'But if it's an internal issue——'

'I said it was minor and local to start with. Now the US army is involved. What are we supposed to do, chase after the *Carolina* and threaten to blow her out of the water unless she surrenders? If you want to take that responsibility without consulting the Administration go ahead, but I'll be the first to dissociate.'

Hackenschmidt looked badly harassed. He could handle the Reds if he had to because they were tangible assets, but he was all ends up when it came to intangible liabilities.

'I had hoped we could keep it in the family.' Harassed and petulant. 'Don't any of you have some conception of what this could do to our credibility in the eyes of the world? The pride of the Seventh Fleet captured by American troops—it's laughable.'

'That,' said Clarke obdurately, 'is precisely what it is not. A hi-jacking can happen to anybody, anywhere, ask the captain of the *Kronstadt*. Nobody found that amusing. This is a problem which needs co-ordination at the highest level and I can add nothing at this stage that would be meaningful.'

So, at four o'clock that same afternoon, the contents of the White House Press room were jolted into watchfulness by a series of hurried arrivals and departures.

The usual presidential aides were as restless as exotic butterflies and equally uncommunicative. The Chief of Naval Staff followed in the wake of Defence Secretary Melville and barked 'no comment' before anyone could frame a question. But when the great Doctor Caressinger himself was summoned from the West Wing to join these arrivals in the Oval Office their curiosity knew no bounds.

Hastily, the accredited reporters compared notes and found that not a single international crisis was upstanding as of that moment, yet clearly some matter of considerable importance was in the making.

No guidebook could do anything with Foxwell's careful conception of the Oval Office except to state that it was, in its own right, a very beautiful room. Outside that brief note to the tourist, it existed only to subserve Foxwell's belief that it was the veriest focal point of power, which power further resided in the inmost being of Foxwell.

Small men had been known to cringe in Foxwell's presence. Smarter men got round the problem by carefully avoiding his eye.

'Oh, he's so good and kind,' Mrs Dusterling, the head housekeeper, once confined to a ladies' magazine. 'And he's so considerate of the staff.'

But what did any of the domestics have that he wanted? Furniture polish?

Of the three men summoned to that office on the day in question, two would face the discussion with a degree of equanimity. Defence Secretary Melville could be relied on to do whatever he was told to do and Caressinger trod his personal tightrope simply by laying it on the floor.

But Hackenschmidt had never met the President except in social circumstances and this was hardly a time for smiles and congratulations on the latest naval airstrikes against Communists in Cambodia. To make matters worse, Hackenschmidt had the illogical feeling that all of this was somehow his fault.

He regained a little of his composure when Foxwell smiled affably on introduction, but lost most of it as the last aide closed the door on the four men and Foxwell glanced up sharply from his position behind the desk.

'What's your assessment of this affair, Admiral?'

Hackenschmidt cleared his throat and covered his feelings by looking alert and on top of his job, which was how he got it in the first place.

'Well, Mr President, my feeling as of now, is that this is some kind of horse-play which has gone sour. I don't think it has any serious implications.'

Foxwell was not President of the United States for nothing. He leaned forward with a show of polite interest. 'I've also been wondering about the serious implications, Admiral. It seems I'm not alone on that. Suppose you did think the incident had overtones, could you spell them out?'

Hackenschmidt literally looked to the professional politicians for help, but they knew enough to find the room very interesting. Caressinger stared at the ceiling while Melville slowly vacuum-cleaned the carpet with his toe-cap.

This was nothing like the Naval Committee.

'Er—the difficulty as I understand it, Mr President, has to do with lack of intelligence.'

'That's a little ambiguous.'

'I mean lack of information. We simply have a situation in which a wild bunch appears to be on drugs.'

'I don't think that quite meets my question, Admiral.'

He turned to Melville. 'James?' and indeed, the Defence Secretary had the comfortable air of a butler who knows how to time his appearance when he's called.

Nature had been liberal with Melville. He seemed to be rotund in every part of his anatomy. Many people found this reassuring; as though a stout Defence Secretary could, personally, screen them against ICBMs.

'The admiral may be correct, Mr President, but the fact remains that five hundred GIs on the rampage suggests something more than a drug festival.'

The President frowned, a special kind of darkness matching perfectly the ever present hint of a five o'clock shadow. 'What, for example?'

Melville shrugged with a strange, inflationary movement, as if he'd blown himself up a little, then thought better of it. 'Who knows? Right now they could be feeling very ashamed of themselves. Like kids who burn down a house and have no notion how to call the fire department.'

'Is that how you see it, Herman?' the President demanded.

The heavy duty countenance detached its gaze from the ceiling and concentrated sombrely on the First Man. The gaze from behind those spectacles suggested a profound intellect but his worst enemies knew it went deeper than that.

'In this type of situation, where nobody knows sufficient of factual value, the admiral's intuition may be more dependable than his speculation.'

He paused, but no-one, not even Foxwell, made an attempt to interrupt. 'Unconsciously he thinks in terms of serious implications; the mere fact that he verbalizes them suggests he's glanced at the possibility. You have the same uneasy feeling in that direction too, Mr President, and I have to confess to misgivings myself.' Again he paused, but Foxwell, having nothing to say, motioned him to continue.

'This, of course, doesn't get us any further because we simply do not know what their purpose can be. The more one looks at it, the less likely it seems that five hundred men could have done this thing purely for the joy of it.'

'Can't we put any sort of name to it?' Foxwell sounded impatient. Caressinger was almost too good at taking a situation apart.

'I don't think we should even begin to predict the probable sequence of events. We have to get those men off that carrier and returned home for special investigation.'

'How do we do that?' Hackenschmidt queried, inadvertently.

Caressinger gave him a civilian's look. 'You're the expert in offensive operations, Admiral.'

'Against an enemy,' the top mariner pointed out.

'There, you see,' Caressinger turned his gaze on the President, 'those serious implications surface once more. Admiral Hackenschmidt is ready to assume these so ashamed men will resist arrest.'

'I don't see why not,' Secretary Melville allowed. 'Our information from Saigon states these units to be some of the toughest in the army—they have a notorious record of indiscipline.'

'Then we're talking already about mutiny, piracy and for all I know, murder,' the good doctor argued. 'After all, it's possible the *Carolina* resisted the hi-jack.'

The President rose quite suddenly, enforced a break in the discussion by turning away to stare out the window at the Rose Garden. It was a characteristic action, a kind of calculated, controlled piece of violence which few could interpret satisfactorily. Some said, a pause for reflection, others diagnosed impatience. Cynics settled for dramatic effect; very few guessed at a mind deeply disturbed....

'This has been going on long enough, and I must tell you, Admiral, I should have been kept informed from the outset. Time has been wasted. As of now I expect you to act with energy and dispatch.

'You have only one objective, to regain control of the *Carolina* and have the men responsible for this outrage placed under close arrest. What units do you have in that area?'

'The nearest would be a missile carrier at Cape Town, the *Ladybird*, Mr President. She's on a goodwill visit.'

'Then have her intercept at the earliest opportunity.'

For this once the admiral stood firmly on his own two feet. 'And if they resist attempts to board her, Mr President?'

All three men watched the presidential brow darken, all three knew what obstacles meant to Foxwell, all three knew as one that he had it on the tip of his tongue to blurt out: 'Have her blown out of the water!' but practical politics and the need to repair his shattering image had to be taken into account and he merely replied, 'In that unlikely event, have her shadowed until they fetch up somewhere and grow tired of their game.'

'Very good, Mr President.'

Hackenschmidt relaxed, missing the faint signal given to indicate his dismissal.

'Thank you for coming, Admiral.'

'Oh—er, my pleasure, Mr President.'

Foxwell watched him right out of the room with that speculative look at least one of those remaining knew so well. The longer he remained in a ruminative posture the worse it boded for the newly departed. Watching Foxwell, Caressinger wondered how long it lasted for him these days.

Appreciably later Foxwell brought his attention back to another aspect of the problem.

'Those damned brass-hats, they're all the same, no matter which branch of the services you take. They're like pitchforks with a single prong, think they can handle any situation alone.'

'How could they know, Mr President?'

'That question is the logical sequel to a disaster, Melville. Men in positions of responsibility must make it their business to...' Unaccountably he tailed off and then pulled himself together as he remembered, not only who he was, but that he still was.

'A little more co-operation between them and we might have known that much more and so acted that much quicker. We now have to consider how best to handle the situation in terms of informing the nation. James!'

The Defence Secretary regarded the backs of his hands. Maybe the Supreme Biophysiological Manufacturer relented when it came to creating Melville's extremities. His hands were as slim and beautifully proportioned as those of a girl.

'I would advise unhesitatingly, "No Comment".'

'Herman?'

'I would say "no comment" is a good servant but a bad master. To begin with, the Russians will have monitored all signals coming from the *Hyannis*. By now they'll have some idea of what happened. On past performance they'll wait to see how we react. If we do nothing that will be as eloquent as if we had spoken. They may then disseminate what information they have in such form as would make our silence untenable. A guarded announcement from our side neutralizes that possibility.'

'And makes us look ridiculous in the eyes of the world.'

Caressinger's personal pinnacle was in some remote world of his own. Almost visibly he would make the descent charged with such intensity of thought as to appear in distilled words like the outpourings of a heavy-eyed oracle.

'I do not think the world is amused any more at this kind of escapade, call it what you will. The boundaries of lawfully exercised power become more and more clearly defined, which definition throws into sinister relief the unauthorized and illegal powersnatch, whether it be the seizure of diplomats for political purposes or the hi-jacking of a passenger plane for any reason at all.

'Anyone concerned with the maintaining of law and order, from a housewife in Milwaukee to the Party Secretary in Moscow, will find nothing laughable in this situation. It could be a case of "us today—you tomorrow".'

And that was why Foxwell leaned so heavily on Doctor Caressinger and on his executives not at all. They kept him in power; Caressinger confirmed it.

'Well, James?' the presidential tones betrayed a touch of pride.

'If Herman is right, it's not as much a question, do we call a press conference, as how do we deliver?'

'No!' Caressinger was unusually vehement on this. 'A press conference does half the scare-mongers' dirty work for them. All we need is a simple statement of fact—let it filter out without fuss.'

'I don't think Geoff can handle this now,' Foxwell said.

Herman didn't think the President's Press Secretary could handle anything at any time but let the thought stay on deposit.

'Suppose I just give them a line on my way out—casually?'

The President almost smiled. 'That sounds about the style.'

He drew the yellow legal pad towards him and between them they shaped a brief statement to be delivered by the doctor.

And so the world learned officially that an 'unquantified' number of US troops had hi-jacked the *USS Carolina* in Vietnamese waters and were now cruising around the Indian Ocean on a drunken tour as if everything had been arranged by American Express.

That was the impression they meant to give; but the media, predictably, smelt a rat dressed up to look like Mickey Mouse. For the moment the Press confined itself to stark announcements in late extra editions of the evening papers. By the morrow editors would have had opportunity to mull over the news and make of it what they could in time for the cornflakes hour.

Reporters were sent to the White House for 'clarification' but they got nowhere, which was about where they expected to get. Radio stations beamed the news in brief flashes and even the newscasters read what was put before them with a hint of puzzlement. Puzzlement, in fact, summed up the national reaction. Why should our boys do a thing like that? developed into a Federal question.

No-one mentioned the word 'mutiny' till NBC's Jack Awkright 'Line-Up' show on TV that same evening. One of the shrewdest commentators on the All American scene gave the event number one billing and further justified his reputation as the Devil's Legman.

'I guess everybody knows what's meant by a pretty kettle of fish, but whoever saw one? Actually it defies description and has one groping for a clue to its purpose.

'To exemplify, I have an evening headline here: "Viet Veterans Bum Ride on *Carolina*", and the account goes on to leave a lot of questions unanswered.

'Like what happened to five hundred GIs gone AWOL in Vietnam? It doesn't suggest a shipping spree if a whole battalion of defectors make their own plans to wind down our commitments.

'Of course if a carrier is smooching around the Indian Ocean when it should be somewhere in the Pacific, the authorities can't be expected to know what's back of the runaways' collective mind. In fact, no-one would be the wiser at this point if the satellite ship *Hyannis* hadn't got left behind.

'Now there are many ways of looking at this thing and I'd like to go along with official thinking—just an ornery escapade, no question of mutiny, leave 'em alone and they'll come home, dragging their tails between their legs. But, I have to ask myself: Why was nothing forthcoming from Saigon for over four days to explain the virtual disappearance of five hundred men—with their arms?

'Why was it so easy for these men to appropriate the ship?

123

One gets the impression they were practically piped aboard. Which poses questions about the navy, especially if you think back to the rumpus involving an executive officer and a dozen ratings now languishing in the San Diego brig on a mutiny charge.

'The admiral reported at that time: "I run a tight ship, a happy ship". It seems as if the troops got the word. Let's hope they're looking for happiness—but supposing they aren't?

'Stay focused for further developments.'

The day after Awkright sent the first delicious shudder down the spines of the Mid-American faithful, a young man in denims and jump boots threw his grip out on to the highway and dropped down after it.

He watched the bus pull back into the mainstream and sighed with relief. It was good to be out of a planned congestion that reminded too much of chopper assault trips, everyone hunched up ready to go-go-go.

The blue sky gave promise of a fine day and the air was so Spring-soft you could damn near stroke it. Gazing around him at the rolling countryside Chuck caught his first glimpse of freedom's true meaning.

How could he not—standing at the great divide, between the natural order of things and the freeway—free? All those cars streaming in and out of someplace. How could that be freedom? You obeyed the controls, the road regulations, the cops, the road itself and your personal satisfaction quotient, the steering wheel replacing the mother's breast. The poor bastards were slave to everything Corporational America could throw at them. He broke off his reverie, took another look at the scrap of paper in his hand, picked up his grip and started walking.

About half a mile along Highway Ninety he came to the filling station mentioned in the directions. It was set back a little from the road, nestling into the side of a low, wooded hill. Might have been an old village store at one time it looked so homely. A verandah, believe it, but no rocking-chair.

He crossed the forecourt and climbed a trio of wooden steps to the glass-fronted door, wiped it clean and peered through. Certainly must have been a store once, about the time people

124

ate real food. There were brown painted shelves and drawers, mostly stocked with cans of oil, car lotions and all those other carriage cosmetics without which no self-respecting vehicle could survive the light of day.

Somebody responded to his tapping. Just a voice out of nowhere demanding: 'Who's there?'

'Excuse me!' he called back.

Moments later a heavy figure appeared, taking its time by way of sizing up the visitation. The door was unlocked, reluctantly, it was opened, reluctantly, and Chuck saw right away how dirty the door glass had been.

The man was about fifty maybe, leery-eyed and no cleaner than the place behind him, not much hair slicked down over his scalp, with motor oil most like, plenty of which was spattered over his monkey-jacket. The shirt was unmentionable.

In fact, the only clean thing about him was the .38 gleaming unwaveringly in his hand.

'Never heard y'drive in,' he made of it a powerful accusation.

'That figures,' Chuck tried to smile. 'I walked here. These boots don't knock like an Oldsmobile.'

The proprietor's eyes flickered downwards then up again. 'That's what bothers me,' he said. 'I like to hear what's comin'. Best suppose you just turn around and keep walkin' or I might have difficulty promisin' anything.'

'Now look man, all I want is some information.'

'I've heard about it. On your way.'

Chuck stared incredulously, he had to work at believing it was happening. The constant roar of traffic helped a little. But he had to find out why—why this?

'What kind of a menace do you imagine a one-armed man is?'

'How should I know? Maybe there's a two-handed sidekick hangin' around outta my visibility. You're wearing out my patience, friend.'

'Friend! Listen—I'm a Vietnam veteran——'

The man laughed, or made an ugly sound, which was which. 'They're the worst. Now move.'

The sun still shone as brightly as before but the sky had clouded over. That didn't make sense either. Not giving the gunman another look he turned full round and went his way.

Luckily a car was just turning in for gas or whatever and the driver had no particular inhibitions about pointing out the way Chuck needed to go. Not that he made it sound friendly, eyes seeming to frisk the traveller as he clipped out the directions.

Chuck thanked the patrolman and headed towards the lane that would take him through a pinewood, out alongside a field or two and 'straight ahead down the dirt-track'.

He didn't look over his shoulder, didn't have to. Knew the cop was still standing there, a thumb jammed in his gun-belt, the other reflectively razoring his chin.

He'd almost forgotten the incident when he came on the orphanage with its neat, well-trimmed lawns, and flowers—he'd seldom seen that many actually growing. Somewhere he could hear a choir of children singing fit to bust and very nearly drowning out the Warblers and Bobolinks. Trees everywhere. He stared up and around as though it was all something quite new, beyond any previous experience. It was just beautiful.

No-one could have told him how hard he was working at it, as a kind of therapy; the need for heartsease after the ugliness of so many things.

'Can I help you?'

He was gazing up at the great house with its balcony running right round the second floor level, supported all the way by slender white pillars. Then another floor above with a whole row of tall, timber-frame windows through which smoky white curtains tried to escape on the back of a light breeze.

Had been so busy looking at everything Chuck missed the tall, grey-haired stranger coming up behind him.

'Can I help you?' he repeated.

'Oh—er—I certainly hope so. I'm looking for Joe Rideout. Bayside Orphanage.'

The stranger smiled and held out a hand. 'You must be *the* Chuck Willens Joe told me about. Glad to have you with us. I'm Superintendent Gaythorne, most people call me Harry.'

It was hard not to like him straight off. He might have been fifty or a little more, but without lines climbing down from nostril lobes to beyond the mouth's corners like everybody had

these days, as if it marked their entry into a stressful meno-
pause. He used language gracefully, not as a kind of verbal
shorthand for time saving; moved slowly, not with dignity so
much as deliberation. Everything, in short, was confirmed that
Chuck had ever heard about him from Joe.

'Let me take that. I hope you mean to stay with us a while.
We have a guest bunkhouse at the back of the main building.'

'I'd be glad to.'

'I'll take your bag over and meantime, if you take this path
to the right, just follow it along the side of the house, then go
left and you'll find Joe in the nursery.'

'In the nursery?'

Gaythorne laughed. 'Don't worry, he hasn't regressed. Go and
see for yourself.'

So the sun hadn't really gone behind the clouds after all.

Sure enough there was Joe in the greenhouse which looked
big enough to accommodate the New York Philharmonic.
Plants everywhere, everything imaginable. Not many actual
flowers though.

Joe was alone.

What should he do: call or knock? It seemed important to
do the right thing. For all he was wearing a visor cap and an
old lumber-jacket there was something about the lone figure,
hands carefully feeling through a large seed-tray that put Chuck
in mind of a priest he'd once seen in a church. There was this
guy at the altar making strange passes by candlelight while he
looked on, uncomprehending, but glad to be out of the cloud-
burst.

Joe solved the small problem by turning his head. 'That
you, Harry?'

'It's me, Joe.'

Well they fairly ran at each other over those crazy duck-
boards. Nothing too emotional, like, 'Well I'll be', 'You old
son of an AK47', 'For Chrissakes!' Just a holding on and
Chuck saying quietly, 'Man it's good to see you', as though
thirty-five years had passed since they last went their ways.

Joe just smiled. 'Let's look at you, Chuck,' and ran his hands
with a thistledown touch over Chuck's face. 'You're growin' a
beard, man—and your hair's over the ears. And—and your

127

cheeks are wet as if—Chuck ... you OK?'

All shipping in the Indian Ocean had been alerted. The *USS Ladybird* could never have located the runaway carrier all by herself. Indian Oceans are very big places if you happen to be looking for something that doesn't particularly want to be found.

A Japanese tanker, the kind that's half-way there before it starts out, was the first to get a visual and she promptly radioed her position.

The missile carrier's captain calculated a day's hard sailing before he could cross the *Carolina*'s almighty bows.

Meantime, and aboard the aircraft carrier, Halliday continued his daily briefing sessions. Plenty of questions were still being raised and answered, but all the real problems had been solved.

'Major,' Benner was speaking, 'we haven't tackled the transport question in any detail. Do you have any ideas on that?'

'The Ford will provide,' Racowiczs intoned.

Halliday laughed with the other men scattered around the table. Lieutenant Jesse Stoker, the quietest and the only coloured officer in the unit, shifted in his seat, a sure sign he would say something in his usual quiet fashion.

'I don't see that's a problem. The US is lousy with transport. We just grab whatever's to hand, right, Major?'

Halliday nodded. 'As we want it, when we want it. I have some reserve ideas on that but it depends on the situation when we land.'

Racowiczs wondered what kind of resistance they could expect. Halliday hadn't given it much thought.

'Nothing of consequence to begin; they'll build up to it slowly. As we get closer to him it'll get worse.'

'I have a feeling we'll be eliminated long before then,' Wilde said. But he didn't sound too bothered by the possibility. Maybe because his father had made a million dollars as a mortician in Kansas City. 'Son, I owe everything I have to the best coronarys in town.'

'That's what we joined the army for, remember?' Racowiczs pointed his filthy pipe at Wilde for emphasis. 'I once heard a

128

colonel at RTC telling his chicken-feed "It is the bounden duty of every soldier to allow himself to be wiped out if the situation demands". How about that for life insurance?'

'You really mean what you said about the statue, Major?' Jesse Stoker enquired.

'Why not? Liberty is suffering from an incurable disease. We might as well put it out of its misery. OK, I think we've got enough to be going on with for tonight's session. Let's break it up if no-one has any questions.'

Eventually he was left alone. They knew him well enough to sense his mood which every so often forced on him the need for solitude.

The time scale bothered him; the simple act of waiting was a factor he hadn't taken into account. The men seemed reasonably relaxed, but he had to face the possibility that the accumulating days would act like a subtle drogue, braking their determination to go through with it.

He had no remorse about what he intended to do, but ... responsibility for his men was at the very core of his being. Not something to be shrugged off with the insouciance of a colonel haranguing a shelf-row of canned beef.

There was something else too, deeper even than his concern about the venture, and yet a part of it. An item that would find no place in all the histories and biographies; intangible, because it must surely belong forever to only two people— Hilda, the girl he'd married when it had seemed almost too late.

It wasn't that he'd reached forty without a thought for women, or had been so in love with the army that nothing else could share his affections. There had been conquests, those unsatisfactory liaisons which fall into place with death-like inevitability and then, two people, back to back, walking away from each other, not even bothering to hate enough to turn back and fire the shot that ends all.

Then, and yes, it can happen to Major Weltschmerz, you see her across the crowded room, or better still, you walk, lonely as a cloud, along a beach, let's say—near Salem—and she's sitting there, looking out to sea, hair streaming in the ocean breeze, and it becomes indeed an enchanted evening.

Conversation between two strangers who've known each other all their lives, flowing like a freshet of spring water. Not love at first sight, but a slow awakening, delicate as the evening primrose risen to the night. It had meant a lot of things to them both ... but he'd had that much longer to know it.

Only, one should be prepared for the unexpected in any relationship. She had loved in spite of the obstacle and that's dangerous. Not the years between them—she was little more than half his age when they met—but religion. What was worse, Salem Massachusetts religion, was still a forcer of destiny, even in a highly plasticated society.

Perhaps not religion as such, he'd decided during one of his many post-mortems. She had too much humanity to interpret her faith with a parent's unyielding rigidity. They hadn't objected to a soldier for a son-in-law, but were shocked by his refusal to admit he served God in the profession of arms. He was no longer acceptable; no more was Hilda who'd done very badly for herself by marrying a mercenary.

What they had going for them was stronger than that kind of ostracism. They could even survive a year of officers' quarters in Fort Calvados, and the officers' wives, and the morning coffee sessions, not to mention those junky little social evenings which almost teetered on the brink of a double meaning. They'd survived by ignoring the whole thing.

In fact, as she neared the finale of pregnancy, Halliday had all but decided to throw in his hand and look for something better in the wide world. If it was to be a son, he had no great wish for him to be proud of a soldier father.

Then he got his posting: Vietnam, three days before the baby was due.

She was lying in bed in a private room of the hospital. Looked very peaceful, incredibly beautiful. He figured, she has to know sometime, so he told her. In seven days' time it would be too late. He couldn't know it was already too late. That's the really corny thing about fate. It never lets on.

Fumbling the explanation, but gently, like a man giving a girl her first experience. But it still hurt, and he watched the first cloud shadowing their happiness.

'And you're going?'

130

Between remorse and puzzlement he could only reply: 'What else can I do?'

'Do you believe in this war, John?'

The one question that had lain dormant in their acre of contentment, the dragon's tooth, not sown but buried against the day.

'I'm going because that's what I'm trained for.' He wanted to say 'No-one is an absolute master of destiny. The options are narrowing for the individual. So we all have to do things we don't want to do.' But she'd only smile at that.

'They're killing women and children, John. Pregnant women. Do we have discriminating bombs?'

'Don't make it harder for me. After all, I'm not a flier. Most times I'll be looking the enemy in the eye.' How many bitter smiles he'd shed over those words while waiting in the dark.

'Soldiers burn down villages, John. "Zippo" it's called, isn't it? Do you belong in that kind of—confusion?'

He tried not to sound angry, knowing his anger had to do with her gentleness that couldn't conceive of him—'You're judging me before the event. Trust me to fight the war the way I believe in it—helping people to help themselves, to defend themselves.'

It sounded fine, like bits discarded from the Gettysburg Address, but three months later he was burning villages with the best of them. Not because he believed in that noble war of prehistoric memory ... but to dull his despair.

Halliday knew he'd go, but didn't know she'd die in childbirth, taking his son that never was with her, defending to the last a logical conclusion, her right to protest at man's inhumanity to man.

'There was no reason, Major. No complications of any kind.'

The surgeon's brow was puckered into alternate lines of incredulity and anxiety. If Halliday cared to make out a case for negligence it could badly dent his no claims bonus. But the bereaved knew there was a reason, knew what that reason was, and it had nothing to do with obstetrics.

He spent the next two years doing penance in his own way. After ten months he almost got what he wanted.

A two hundred pound chicom mine hurled him out of the

131

war and across to Zama, one of four major hospital bases in Japan. Only it wasn't as simple as that. Three stop-overs with the medics performing holding operations all the way. The last stage by chopper and they had him out before the rotor-blades had fluttered to a stop. He'd lost so much blood they had to top him up with five units, right there on the pad. The leg was just one stinking mess.

But he survived. Left the ICU ten days later, graduating to the medical ward. And when, a month after, he announced he was going back, even the hard-nosed commandant took a double look at his medical profile and seriously considered a transfer to the psychiatric division.

'You can DEROS any time you want, you realize that, Major?'

'Yessir, but I think I'll go back.'

'You're working pretty hard at physical therapy. Think you'll make it?'

'I'm not sure I'm qualified to give an opinion on that.'

'I mean you don't have to kill yourself trying.'

'I'll make it.'

The medicine man had looked at him so hard, and the question was so blatantly obvious that Halliday felt obliged to answer.

'What else is there?'

'The birds, the bees, flowers and a respectable pension——'

'I mean there's a war on wherever you go. Why not stick with the one you know?'

Halliday made it back to Vietnam, found himself in command of three companies with a loss factor of around twenty per cent which he reduced to three and, in the process, turned into an even better soldier than he'd been before.

But he never came near to death again, however hard he tried. Death gets kind of shamefaced when it meets a success.

As evening fell, the day guards would get some rest while the others came to. Take a shower, eat some, stroll on the flight deck, then down to the hangars for a session with Halliday.

Later, reading, singing, karate demonstrations, a dozen poker games, there were even educational groups in which specialists

132

gave impromptu lectures on their particular skills. Plenty of talk; mostly a kind of verbalized unarmed combat.

Private Henry Hands, coloured, trash collector. Educated to sixth grade. Born in South Carolina. Versus: Private Golden D. Baker, coloured, unemployed. Completed ninth grade. Born in Washington. Sergeant Thomas Lincoln and PFC Abraham Dexter holding the ring.

'Is that what you want, man? Is that what you *really* want? Movin' trash for seventy-five rix per week after week after week?'

Baker rolled his eyes; was leaning so heavily on Hands because he couldn't believe his ears. Hands looked bashful but defended as best he could.

'I didn' say I wanted to go back to it. I jus' said it ain't a bad livin', man.'

'Bad! Hunkin' white men's trash for seventy-five ain't *bad*! Man, the Vietcong sure shot the shit outta your self-respect.'

Lincoln gently pointed out: 'He said he didn't want to go back to it, Golden.'

'I heard what he said. I also heard like how he said—wistful as a buncha June roses climbin' up his member. I tell you, Mr Hands, you deeply disgust me.'

'Go right on, Golden, you may depend upon my tol'rance on account of I'd slit you ear to ear if I was ain't in th'company of gentility.'

'You got an unhealthy mind, Henry and I'll tell y'why, Mr Meatball, fashioned in the likeness of my Aunt Harriet's ass. Your name is Hands, right? and Hands is ante-bellum, which is Caesarean for "cold war".'

'Screw off with your ante-bellum, Private Golden. And you should be ashamed to talk that way 'bout your Aunt Harriet when you don't have brain enough to plug up her private embarrassment.'

Dexter tried to take personalities out of the argument. 'So what's ante-bellum about Hands, Golden?'

Scorn, spreading visibly. 'Well I declare! and you a college-educated nigger inaccessible to a simple matter of fact like that. Ante-bellum—before the Civil War, rat-head. You sell a nigger into slavery maybe don' have no name—so call him

133

Hands. Ain't no use payin' good greens for a nigger with no hands, those he's gotta have, so, christen him right there on the block. "I hereby name this nigger 'Hands'." Sure 'nough, next Sunday the preacher tells everyone "I hereby baptize this nigger 'Hands'." Oh baby, tha's a real honkey legacy you got there.'

This troubled Hands badly. While the others talked and argued over his head, he sat hunched up in his personal bit of the world and thought about it. Then, as though he'd struck a match to peer into the darkness, a light glimmered in his eyes, grew brighter as he leapt to his feet.

'Hear me, soul brothers—I got the word!'

All he needed was a chorus, and that never had been a problem.

'Roll it, Henry!'

'This is a good thing we're doin'!'

'Yeah!'

'We ain't black and we ain't white!'

'Right!'

'We jus' for shovin' around!'

'Say it!'

'You do this, boy—you go here, boy. Sweepin' up, cleaning out, hosin' down, what've we got!'

'What'll we get!'

'We gonna do the shovin'! We gonna show 'em what shovin' *means*!'

'Right!'

'They say, gotta have two cars, two deep-freeze, two TVs, two asses, two o' fucken everythin'—who gotta have it man!'

'Mr and Mrs Whitey, trash-can!'

'Tha's right—everywhichway they got freedom like they say, you poor white trash! and you nigger shit—you go on out'n fight for *our* freedom to tell you that's your job not ours. We high-class maggot breeders don' know 'bout trash, but lordy we know Communists is trash, 'cos they ain't white, is red.

'So grab a gun now, nigger, put on that tiger suit, white trash, and go get your Fed'ral Relief in Nam. Go on now and clean up for us good, 'cos we too busy bein' decent Americans—you murderin' bastards with what we heard you doin' to those poor

134

little kids out there but don' you stop pullin' th'trigger y'hear me? 'cos it's for Americah you evil-smellin' polecats. What you wanna go doin' that mean thing for? Burnin' people's houses down that way?'

'Keep it rollin', man!'

'Don' y'know there's laws 'gainst what you doin'?'

'Hallelujah!'

'I declare, if'n it wasn't for you doin' all this terrible thing 'cos y'all love Democracy, homicides, we'd string y'up on Main Street!

'I tell you, soul brothers, I finished bein' a nigger, I done bein' a hired killer, now on I'm gonna be a whole time man 'stead of a part-time American, an' my name ain't Hands from now on to Kingdom never come, I'm just a Man!'

While they yelled and cheered, the new Man, breathing hard from so much exertion, brought himself slowly back to earth.

The *Ladybird* knifed across *Carolina*'s bows somewhere off Port Elizabeth. Her commander immediately radioed his position and put the ship close in alongside. No question of a boarding party at that speed.

For the first time the *Carolina* broke her long silence. The exchanges read as follows.

USS Ladybird to *USS Carolina*. You are ordered to heave to immediately.

USS Carolina to *USS Ladybird*. What is your authority?

Ladybird: You will comply by order of the United States Government.

Carolina: Negative.

Ladybird: Confirm your statement.

Carolina: Negative. Repeat, negative.

Grim-visaged as Ahab, Captain Hart turned to his executive officer. 'What in hell's going on over there?'

The subordinate officer kept his glasses focused on the carrier as he spoke. 'God knows. But I'd sure like to see the look on the President's face when he gets this in his in-tray.'

* * *

There's safety in numbers. That's to say, not one of the top White House aides cared to face Foxwell with this bombshell.

Only one thing to be done. Someone, who didn't like Caressinger, dropped it on his desk while his back was turned in the men's room. After all, he headed the NSC so who was better qualified to take delivery?

But Caressinger was nobody's fool. He knew that the man who brings bad news is the first to be shot. Recent events had proved that. So he contacted Helderman, Foxwell's most trusted fixer, and Bob Muntsch who paved the way for most of Foxwell's daily progress, aside from letting the occasional Mr Anonymous in at the presidential tradesmen's entrance.

Helderman came straight over to Caressinger's office in the West Wing. Muntsch came out of curiosity—the only way the doctor could hook him.

Muntsch, youthful looking but greying, one of Foxwell's oldest political associates, came bustling in, looking, as always, for trouble. Some said it was his main function, that in place of brains, he had a radar scanning device implanted and paid for by surplus funds from the Creep Company. Certainly, if there was trouble he knew about it—sometimes even before it had happened.

'What's wrong, Herman?'

He glanced from Caressinger standing by his desk, unusual in itself—he never stood when he could sit—to Helderman who wasn't standing anywhere, just pacing agitatedly from one spot to another, his face white as sickness.

'We just heard from the *Ladybird*.'

'Well?'

'The *Carolina* refuses to stop or be boarded.'

Muntsch stared. He couldn't be astonished because he just didn't understand. Caressinger had to spell it out for him.

'But that's impossible.'

'Impossible maybe. It's happened!' Helderman snapped. Each step he took seemed to add another implication.

'You're talking about mutiny, Herman,' Muntsch accused.

The spectacles flashed briefly but the mild brown eyes told Muntsch nothing. That voice, weighed down with gravitas—

'That's right, Bob'—and irony.

'But why?'

Caressinger gestured impatiently. 'I don't think it's productive to assign motives right now. Let's take this one step at a time.'

Suddenly, both men were glad to have Caressinger on their side.

'OK. What's the first step?' Helderman.

'We have to face the President with it.'

'We?' Muntsch went wary all at once, realizing too late, the trap had been sprung.

'The three of us.' Firmly.

'I don't see that. You got the message.'

'It predicates a hundred possibilities. I can't cope with that number.'

The two aides glanced at each other, with badly concealed satisfaction. Caressinger admitting to inadequacy. Things must be very serious. Muntsch tried a touch of humour.

'For a moment I thought you wanted us to hold your hand, Herman.'

'The President is going to want action on this right away. He'll need all the options spelled out from whoever's on the spot. There isn't even time to call an emergency Cabinet conference.'

Helderman ran a hand through carefully barbered hair. 'Are you positive you're not making a mountain out of a molehill on this?'

The good doctor smiled, but somehow he managed to keep the humour to himself. 'Who's talking about mountains? But doesn't it bother you when a molehill moves and refuses to stop?'

Foxwell's appointments secretary was furious. 'I don't care how urgent it is, Bob, the President has to see Sweeney at five. You set it up yourself, remember? All that crap about apple-pie relations with ALO. You took six weeks to sell him the idea and now——'

Caressinger thrust himself forward to confrontation distance with Petersen. 'Bill, you will please tell the President we are here to discuss a matter involving national security.'

Which had to clinch the argument, except that Petersen felt he deserved the last word. 'Sometimes I think the hot line runs between the wrong people.'

'I never doubted it,' the good doctor replied, with not a trace of facetiousness.

At 5.01, immediately after the departure of the grim-faced Chilean ambassador, the three men ushered themselves into Foxwell's office.

As the Congressional hearing was to learn much later—from official tapes—Caressinger presented the information to Foxwell in the following words.

'I have to report to you, Mr President, that I am in receipt of the following information, presumably from the Joint Chiefs of Staff bureau just twenty minutes ago.'

His two companions, usually relaxed enough to sit without invitation, hovered as close to the sofas and chairs lining the walls as they could get. The President was shooting from the hip more frequently these days.

A full minute's silence followed disclosure. They waited for the typical Foxwell gesture, a sign manual making bad news official. Hands covering his face, finger-tips digging into his eyes as though to eject tiredness by forcible means. The question came like a whip-crack.

'Why didn't I get this direct?'

Caressinger's shrug was in his voice. 'I imagine some people prefer not to be involved in target practice.'

Foxwell almost smiled, or the five o'clock shadow lifted a little. 'So they got you to do it. They should pick on little guys when they want to outsmart someone.' Matter-of-fact. No question of flattery.

'Well, gentlemen. How do we view this? Still a minor, local difficulty? Dave?'

'I wish I could tell you, Mr President. It simply doesn't make sense.'

'Bob?'

Muntsch tried unconsciously, unsuccessfully to echo Caressinger's massive self-assurance. 'I'd say it was a protest, Mr President. A spectacular protest, but I couldn't say what

138

purpose it's supposed to serve. It could, of course, take the heat off certain problems. . . .'

A darkening brow, the expression of a gunslinger being asked to make do with a catapult. He turned to Caressinger, and the eyes of both men transmitted an identical message: this is something big, but what? Caressinger added a postscript. I'll try and explain, but it's speculative, it has to be.

'The whole thing is concerted. That much is certain. Assault craft abandoned, Colonel Gorton's statement to our investigators, how two Vietnamese children are involved makes absolutely no sense.

'As Bob says, there has to be a purpose. From the positioning we have they clearly intend to round the Cape; that means they're heading for the Eastern seaboard.'

'I realize that,' the President, drily.

'But why? Why don't they head across the Pacific? They must have an objective, there's no other conclusion. My guess would be . . . New York, in the first instance.'

'What does that gain them?' Helderman demanded.

Caressinger hesitated. Not once had he taken his eyes from the sombre-suited man before him, not since he'd started to speak. 'Whatever they plan to do will not be pleasant,' he said.

Foxwell stayed eye to eye with Caressinger for most of the subsequent silence, then lowered his gaze and turned to the window. It left no doubt in the doctor's mind. This time the movement had to do with masking his struggle to force violent emotion into compliance. But even a man with Caressinger's microscopic insight can make mistakes.

Another creature turned back from that window. Marginally it connected with the office of President; basically it was the man who'd served his country so well in the fearful 'fifties.

What they saw both astonished and frightened. It was as if the latent beast had fed on wormwood for so many years before learning to live the part of a domesticated animal. But always the fear of exposure from any direction, threatening to rip off that façade of qualified benignity, showing him for the power-crazed being he was.

Muntsch would describe that unguarded moment to his wife in impressionistic terms. 'He looked so like the last man the

First Lady wouldn't have recognized him.'

'We have to kill this thing.' Quietly, like the scraping of claws on a tree in darkness. 'This is concomitant with everything that's gone before. The increasing violence of the age. A senator shot in broad daylight. A whole string of hi-jackings. Gun battles in our cities, a bunch of hoodlums led by intellectual malcontents declaring war on our society. I tell you, this has to stop.'

He turned to Muntsch. 'I want you to arrange a five minute spot on all networks. For tonight.'

'Tonight?'

'That's what I said. Dave, get the Senate and House Majority leaders here at the earliest. Tell Petersen to cancel all forward engagements for this day. Herman, I want you personally to handle the agenda for an emergency Cabinet meeting, say nine o'clock.'

'Certainly; if I might ask——'

'When I've finished you may. Have the Attorney-General particularly informed. Your question?'

'The purpose of the meeting, Mr President?'

'It almost speaks for itself, doesn't it? Legislation to be fielded for the immediate re-introduction of a Federal death penalty.'

No-one spoke or moved. Three at least of those present felt the chill spreading through an office that had thrown up so many chilling moments, as though history had the power to freeze solid at the mere drop of a President's utterance.

Perhaps Caressinger recognized the associative idea. He was the first to find his voice. 'In the present political climate?' he ventured. Caressinger! Venturing!

'F... the political climate!' To spare sensibilities the word in full used by Foxwell is omitted, there are many people who refuse to believe a President of such moral integrity capable of profanities.

'The Hill does not represent the political climate. Blowing hot and cold does not constitute a climate. Out there,' he pointed melodramatically at the Rose Garden, 'to all points of the compass is what we're concerned with. Simple decent people who have a right to protection from within as well as without. A hard-working, God-fearing majority who ask for nothing better than to be left in peace to plough their acre, get on with the job of living, raising a family, taking in a ball game without having to move around in fear of their lives. *I* represent those people. I know them. I've had enough and I say they have too.'

Who heckled *Der Meisterschmalzer* at Nuremberg? No-one felt like arguing. It took courage, not to deny the words, but to cross the man.

Except that Caressinger stayed after the others had departed.

'Just one or two details, Mr President.'

'I'll try not to begrudge you the time, Herman.' Part joky, mostly serious.

'The Press.'

Foxwell took a deep breath, and not for the first time—especially in those trying last months—felt gratitude that he had this man at his side. His nod was a safe conduct to continue.

'It's a question of timing. If there's a press release now, people will automatically connect it with your appearance on prime time later. You know what an excavator like Awkright can make of that.'

'Don't ask me to change my mind on the announcement, Herman.'

'Any more than you would ask me to exceed my brief, Mr President.'

Another reminder of the too recent past. Caressinger knew, by Foxwell's reaction, that he'd not been as circumspect as his reputation allowed. He hurried on to smudge the mistake.

'It's a question of releasing too little information to keep the two facts from being associated.'

'For example?'

'A simple statement that the *Carolina* is proceeding to base under escort.'

'That's hardly an important part of the truth.'

Caressinger spread his hands with the air of a priest making a cut-price deal with the Devil. 'Do we have to tell them everything?'

Marshall was occupied tucking into bed the little girl.

By common consent he and Extra had taken on the main duty

of caring for them in the best way they knew how. Most of the men were little more than kids themselves, but they grasped instinctively that a smile and a candy bar were not enough. The children needed a rough approximation to parents who knew how to give twenty-four hours of love and a sense of security and continuity on the way.

The soldiers adapted to their rôle as naturally as bees to nectar. It helped that Marshall could spin their language a little, and between them they had Thu hai and Thu ba chattering in English like intelligent six year olds a week away from America. Daytimes, they worked in a flight operations room, Marsh chalking up simplicities on the vistavision blackboard.

He'd just finished reading the girl an article from an old *Harper's* magazine. Her brother was already asleep.

'How's she gonna understand that, Marsh?'

'She ain't; it just gives her the feel of the language is all.'

Now it was time for lights-out.

'OK young lady, let's try it one more time: *Quý—danh là gì?*'

'*Tôi tên là Thu hai,*' but her eyes twinkled wickedly just above the blanket line.

'Aw come on now, mutton-head.'

'My—name—is Thu hai.'

'That's better. How about an apology: *Tôi tiêc?*'

'I am—sorry.'

'*Phài, Duoc.* And how do we say *"Hân-hanh gặp ông"?*'

'Glad to meet you.'

'Solid! Glad to meet you too.'

And Marshall's eyes lit up with an expression some teachers could use apart from worshipping status hewn in their own image. But some afterthought made him grow serious beyond his years. 'Don't never forget your own language, little lady—forgot mine near two hundred years back—it's all you brought with you. We took everything else, wouldn't wanna take that too.'

Thu hai had stopped smiling too; not understanding, she grew worried. '*Tôi không hiêu.*'

'You don' need to understand, yet awhile.'

'*Súc-cù-là?*' she enquired, hopefully.

He straightened up and frowned like an ogre. 'Chocolate—at this time of night? You've gotta be kidding. Now you get to sleep like your sensible brother. Gonna say your prayer the way Extra told you? Prayer?'

She hooked on to the word and puckered her brow with the effort of remembrance. Haltingly, like a snatch of birdsong, she recalled—'Love one another.'

'Tha's right, you've got it honey!'

He turned at the door—'*Mai nhé, Thu hai.*'

'*Mai nhé*, Marsh.'

. . . then switched off the light.

Time to go through the last full evening programme. Everybody who could be spared from guard duty was gathered in the ship's cinema which accommodated the numbers in air-conditioned comfort.

Halliday opened the session. 'You'll be glad to know the missile carrier is still with us. I have to assume concern at government level for our continued safety.'

They appreciated this, but he was quick to detect the finest thread of nervousness in their laughter. He glanced at the officers each side of him before continuing.

'Two items on the agenda tonight.

'First, we have no wish, at the moment of landing, or indeed at any time, to act in any superior capacity whatever. From now on we will be fellow soldiers undistinguished by insignia of rank. We would ask you to vote on that.'

They didn't have to. There was silence for a spell, then, almost as one, they cheered fit to unbalance the guidance systems of the missile carrier downwind. The last baulk had been knocked away, the grand design was set for launching.

When he could make himself heard: 'Does anybody have a question?'

One man, an oldish negro sergeant, you could tell by the knife scars he'd seen a lot of action since Korea, stood up slowly.

'Yessir, Major, I'd like to know somethin'.'

'Go ahead, Ezra.'

Ezra Hannibal scratched his head first, just to show how bemusing it all seemed, the pace at which democracy was travelling. 'Well I ain't no talker, but it's like this. Gonna be a whole lot o' fightin' come gangway time and we *used* to bein' led, man. How we gonna make out runnin' around doin' our natural thing? Like I mean, how's anyone gonna do somethin' when nobody's tellin' him to do nothin'?'

'You've been following the basic forward planning, Ezra?'

'Sure thing. That don' trouble me none.'

'Fine, then do what you did in Nam. The colonel says "You go in and clean up that area so it shines like a button." What did you do, Ezra?'

'Well like I went in and did it, man.'

'You didn't say "Yessir Colonel and won't you come along with me"?'

'Never thought to ask him.'

'You want me to hold your hand, Ezra?'

That got a big laugh and Ezra subsided grinning a little sheepishly.

'What I'm telling Ezra,' Halliday continued, 'is what I'm telling all of you. Each of us is on his own but working in a common cause. People only take orders because they don't know what they're doing, don't much care what they're doing. The officer class exists to give orders not to prove the necessity of beating the enemy, but to show that in war, as well as in peace, one small part of the system can still keep the majority, the crowd, the hoi-polloi—YOU, in subjection!

'Don't doubt that when the time comes you'll know what to do.'

The motion was carried, as they say, *nem con.*

'If anyone has doubts about this mission we have a last chance to deny or confirm them. I've nominated former Lieutenant Able Thompson to play devil's advocate so put your questions and don't pull any punches. If he can't ride them, we have no cause.'

Halliday had his fair share of novel ideas; kept their minds ticking over by any means he knew. Made them think and think again to beat a process of conditioning that required men to be less than themselves or how do you get them committing acts of bestiality?

Able Thompson got to his feet looking a little self-conscious.

An amiable giant, all of six feet four, he had that easy-going air of a man who'd proved himself on the football field and what more was there? A brain of real quality to begin with. One doesn't major in philosophy without having a lot of grey matter going for him. A good officer, intelligent; he was also the man most of the unit had taken its problems to in the war.

'OK fellers, first question.'

No-one wanted to be the first in a minority of six maybe seven 'don't knows', but eventually someone back of the crowd spoke up.

'Lieutenant—er—Able—my problem is simple. First off I thought, sure! let's show those sons of bitches what it's all about. Then I get this insidious feeling. It's my country I'm doin' this thing to, it's my flesh and blood I'm threat'nin'. So how do I match what I think with what I feel?'

'That's a good, basic question, Selmer. Let's see what I can do for you.'

Bearded as a patriarch, by God, Able looked competent enough to deal with the national debt that moment. He paused long enough to find the right words and between man and men hung an intense silence underscored by the hum of ship's engines no-one heard anymore.

'What are we going to do to America that America hasn't done to us? Let's take a look at the record. And while I'm talking, just remember one word.

'Watergate.

'We gave the world mass-produced automobiles. Go anywhere and they'll show you statistics for road-deaths that make Vietnam look like nothing.

'We fashioned the assembly line and called it a path for progress. What have we got?

'Death, mutilation, cripples, environmental dangers, they're acceptable, hardly anyone complains—can that be right? But if we can accept all this with a shrug in the States, who cares if kids roast to cinders in a Vietnam village?

'What kind of freedom were we supposed to be defending? The freedom of corrupt politicians to monkey with the democratic system? The freedom of millions to watch one kind of violence—or any kind—on twenty-four hour TV?

'When those vigilantes went gunning for a hippy commune in Wyoming, killed two men, badly injured a pregnant woman and beat up the rest, was that what we were doing: defending their right to deny others the freedom to live as they choose?

'Nobody stepped in and said "That's enough". Foxwell yacks about "law and order" but where was the law in that commune? Right there Mister Magoo, on the side of violence, hatred, *fear* of anything or anybody different.

'Don't any of you kid yourselves fascism got sea-sick crossing the Atlantic.

'Concept for today—ours is a violence-oriented society. Yet oddly, most of the process is illusional. I mean, it depends basically on the unconscious assimilation and imitation of the shit fed to the *mensch* by every TV network in the country. The kids who hang themselves are only extreme examples of Traumatic Viewing, death by visual poisoning is the better half of a living death.

'So, paradoxically, America doesn't really know what violence is, it flirts with it, sure, particularly in the plush driving seat of an automobile, like it flirts with welfare relief, health programmes, integration, crime. They're problems we dicker with but no-one tries to solve. Why not? Because all these things provide the framework for a power structure which would be meaningless if someone really found solutions like they work at getting to the moon.

'Our war-cry is simple: Keep America clean and peaceful. We don't want the reality of total war in our own back gardens. We don't want blood flowing in our swimming pools, but splash all the tomato ketchup you like over our films and TV.

'America never fled from reality. She ignored it.

'Well, our purpose is to face America round, if only for a few hours. We have to demonstrate that a society condoning what was done to Vietnam is a sick society. Watergate won't cure it, Watergate only explains it.

'So where do we stand in all this? If you like, we're the ultimate sickness, the virus returning to its host, Americans doing to America the inconceivable.'

That looked to be about it. But another voice raised itself above the general buzz of appreciation.

'Fine, Able, and I agree with all you say. Ain't nothing to argue there. But suppose you're in there gunning and you turn a corner and come face to face with an old lady who says "Hullo, son". What you gonna do then?'

Thompson hardly stopped to consider the question. He was taking a letter from his pocket almost before the questioner could add a query sign.

'I got this around the time they were shooting the hell out of us at Quam Trai. "The mail has to get through", Wells Fargo Foxwell decreed. Well I got mine and this one I kept. Maybe destiny decreed something too, that I should reserve it for nowabouts.

'Quote: "My dearest boy, I'm writing this extra letter to tell you how that horrible protest meeting ended just now. They actually allowed the committee to congregate in Sundown Park, but I heard that was so the authorities could take snapshots of the ring-leaders.

'"When I thought of what you were suffering over there for our sakes I felt I just had to go along and make my point. There was the usual bunch of liberals marching around town and I saw Mr and Mrs Flamsteed in the line with my own eyes, actually wheeling their junior in a baby carriage, as if a child in its wisdom wouldn't know a bad cause from an American one. I assure you, I cross the road rather than pass their house as of now.

'"Well, I encouraged myself and I followed in the wake of the rag-tag and bobtails and you wouldn't believe it but they had a legless veteran up ahead in a wheelchair.

'"There was a whole lot of Red-coloured talk in Sundown and you'd have thought our country was run by a bunch of Mafia men the way they talked of dear Mr Foxwell and his loyal White House colleagues.

'"Luckily there were some gentlemen in the crowd who took exception to what was being said and they spoke up for the Administration.

'"Then they called on the legless wonder to say his little piece, carefully prepared by A. N. Other no doubt, and when he finished by saying he thought our boys should just pull out and leave their officers to do the dirty work, I promise you I saw red. I never did such a thing in my life before but somehow your mother found herself on that platform telling that so-called veteran a few things about himself he never knew before. With a beard and hair to his shoulders he just couldn't have been anything but a jalopy casualty and I told him so.

'"He just stared at me then said, through the microphone he was holding: 'Ma'am, whoever gave you the notion a womb is just another name for a shell-case?'

'"Imagine it, using that kind of language in a community where one is not unknown. Thinking of you out there and what you were going through, I clean forgot I was a lady and I slapped his face I was so angry. There was uproar as you can imagine and they hustled me off that platform without delay. But I just know everyone was on my side and quite a number of very civilized acquaintances have dropped by to say how much they approve of what I did.

'"I thought you'd like to know, my dear, we too have our moments of suffering because of this dreadful war; but no matter, *coûte que coûte*, as your grandmother used to say, I shall defend you from your enemies in this country as you defend us from our foes in Vietnam. And don't believe all you hear about the Watergate affair. Mr Killjohn says it's obviously a Communist conspiracy and everyone knows he's the best lawyer in town.

'"Jewella Parsons is looking prettier than dogwood and constantly asks about you.

'"Your ... ever ... loving ... mother."

'Unquote.'

Slowly, Able Thompson looked up and waited for comment. There was no comment.

He ended by saying, not loud but clearly, deliberately: 'If my mother stood before me at this moment and I had an M16 in my hand, I'd cut her down sooner than look at her.

'Any more questions?'

There he was again, black-jowled, black, crispy hair, eyes black, sombre-visaged as Death with a healthy appetite. He sat immediately under a portrait of Washington—I do not tell a lie—at the specially sited desk on which a casually placed

148

framed picture of his three claims to membership of the human race were carefully aimed at y-o-u.

There exuded from America's first President a fugitive hint of disapproval, a down-turn of the mouth suggesting that he hanged not in company of his own choosing.

Was this what we fought for?

Foxwell down below faced the blaze of light without batting an eyelid. He could rest easy, knowing there could never be enough of it to light the innermost workings of that stone maze designated his mind.

'I want to talk to you tonight about our country; about what is happening to it despite its strength and its progress.

'I realize that we cannot pursue those ideals without changing the face of America, without upheavals that may seem at times to be threatening those cherished ideals. We cannot go forward without treading on a few toes, but if that is what is happening, it's logical to assume that certain people are facing the wrong way, their backs to the future.

'These individuals are against progress; they are the dissidents, the subversives, the agitators who will strive, by any and every means, to thwart the aspirations of people like you, the silent majority.

'My duty is to that majority. First and foremost I am required by my sacred oath, to employ every means contributable to your contentment, to your welfare, to your safety.

'And because the issues which integrate our society are so complex, the actions of these trouble-makers are that much more dangerous. It isn't only the drug-pushers, the hoodlums, who at least stick to their own infested areas; if anything the threat comes from something bigger, more basically insidious to our good way of life.

'I refer to the professional wreckers, the urban guerillas and dedicated outcasts, men and women who seek to dismantle the social framework for their own unfathomable ends.

'Therefore, to deal with these enemies of society, I am proposing to introduce Federal legislation to restore the death penalty for all those who seek to subvert America, whether it be through the perniciousness of narcotics or the more deadly insidiousness of imported political ideas.

'I intend to treat this matter as one of extreme urgency, and I know I have the support of all loyal and decent Americans.

'God bless you. And goodnight.'

Next day the newspapers would analyse, speculate to the bottom of the back page on Foxwell's statement; most of them would get their sums wrong and lack of space permits only one shrewd comment on the reaction.

'America nodded its head in agreement—slowly.'

A storm takes time to break. The *Carolina* was still four days steaming distance away and the American people waited with monumental indifference for nothing very much to happen.

If an interviewer had taken his tape machine onto the streets of any city whatever and asked Mr Everyman what he thought about the strange case of the runaway aircraft carrier, he might have got a shrug for his pains or the puzzled reaction of Mrs Average who positively knows that such things don't run away. Before bustling into the nearby Safeway she might have added that, well, there's some mighty funny things happen and who knows, maybe the Martians got it like they almost captured New York once?

Thanks to Caressinger, carefully controlled releases to the Press kept the temperature down on that one and allowed it to rise on the Capital Punishment debate, which is as pogie bait to the masses as caviare is to the general.

One man at least was preoccupied by both issues.

The continuing silence from the *Carolina* was wearing Foxwell down. Almost hourly they kept him informed of its latest position, almost perceptibly he deteriorated in the light of his fears. Orders began to stream from the White House at the rate of panic; even more significant, they were being countermanded before they got to the front door, so to say.

Animal instinct was doing for Foxwell what no amount of intellectual theorizing could do for Caressinger or any other member of the palace guard. Foxwell knew, arguably was the only man in America who knew, what the *Carolina* episode portended. He couldn't believe it with his head, but the stomach never lies or why did the Romans grope in the entrails of birds for a glimpse of the future?

Like everyone else Foxwell had to wait and see. For the time being he could call his stomach a liar and act positively on the matter nearest his heart. Like calling his Cabinet to discuss the Capital Punishment proposal.

Attorney-General Kleinsach was for it. Called it the greatest issue since the New Deal. Kleinsach, young, ambitious and un-scrupulous, was made for the concept of capital punishment. And he knew the emotive doctrine of *sus.per coll.* could take the heat out of a lot of things...

Secretary of State Willbro was cautious but favourable and Secretary for Defence Melville thought the idea had a lot going for it. The lesser lights like Postmaster Bryce and Joe Ashton of HEW found it difficult to raise objections because everybody knew about the going price of retaining office.

But no real joy shone in the Cabinet Office on that partic-ular evening. Most of those present divined that in some way, America was taking a step backwards and it escaped no-one's attention that Caressinger stayed in wraps throughout the session, saying not a word. He must have known that critical analysis never yet went the distance with Sugar Ray Nemesis. Foxwell missed nothing. When the dismal conference broke up forty minutes later he asked Caressinger to stay behind.

Only a tightening of lips or an extra firm hold on document cases betrayed how the others felt about this. Outwardly they treated Caressinger with the deference one reserves for an *éminence grise*, but beneath exteriors smoother than sharkskin was something of what a copperhead must be thinking when a man crosses its path.

'You didn't say much, Herman,' Foxwell observed as the door closed on the last of them.

'I said nothing, Mr President.' He was busily polishing his glasses.

'What's worrying you? Afraid I might take us back into Vietnam?'

'After all the trouble we had?'

Foxwell laughed bitterly. 'One trouble more or less, what's the difference? The way those yellow bastards are infiltrating I'd have every excuse.'

Caressinger, knowing about the commerce between the White

House and Pentagon on limited nuclear warfare, looked more worried than he might have allowed if he hadn't been so tired. Working for Foxwell made a mess of one's stamina.

'You would lose credibility, I don't have to tell you, Mr President.'

Foxwell almost snarled. 'What credibility? When was I ever considered to be "credible"? How many years have I had to endure a stinking press committed to eroding my "credibility"? Listen, Caressinger, I've made an important decision. They talk of my hesitation, well I'm finished with that. They tried to crucify me over Watergate, well I can try for resurrection.

'The American people elected me because they believe in me —not the liberals, not the media—they trust in my judgment. I shall continue to act in their best interests and if that means smashing the North Viets or nuking the Russians or executing a few thousand worthless criminals then by God I'll do it!'

'Your judgment, Mr President?' Slowly, with care, 'Or your intuition?'

Foxwell narrowed his gaze. Had a shrewd idea what the doctor was getting at, but didn't particularly want it spelled out. 'Do you really doubt I have my finger on their pulse?'

'I'm not in a position to comment on that, Mr President. It's only that I wonder——'

'You're not the kind of man who wonders, Herman. Put it on the line. I don't shoot the opposition if it's basically on my side.'

Caressinger smiled bleakly. 'That's good news. What disturbs me is that you've said nothing about the *Carolina* for some time.'

The frown and a tightening of the jaw muscles showed clearly how a single word can work a man over. As casually as he could manage: 'Well?'

'This question of the death penalty; does it relate to your fears for the American people, or to your fear of something else?'

This time silence lasted for a snatch of eternity. Both men could hear the screaming of birds, a recording amplified throughout the White House grounds to scare off troublesome starlings and one or two ghosts from the past maybe; an eerie sound, making the room silence more profound, more sinister.

'I—think that's all we'd better say on the subject,' Foxwell said.

To speak in metaphor, Caressinger picked up his tight-rope from the floor, coiling it as he went. He saw the day approaching when he must find another use for that rope, but for the moment he was too tired to care.

They were strolling through the vineyards not far distant from the orphanage. Fine country is the Finger Lakes district, where long blue bones of water stretch south and take the sting out of winter thereabouts.

Spring was skittish as a girl this year and everything locked within the trees, below ground, from vines to wayside plants, cried out for release. Here and there the green broke cover without so much as a by-your-leave.

Something to be savoured in silence. They rambled on, enjoying in their own ways the peace and beauty of it all. Chuck seeing and marvelling, Joe unseeing but smiling a little as though— what the hell, there were advantages in just being able to feel the things he'd known all his young life.

They left the vineyards behind and broke into the outskirts of a wood that sloped up to a fine view of the Owasco on one side, the Cayuga on the other, pointing to the heart of Ithaca.

Last year's tangle of undergrowth made for slow going but Chuck soon realized his friend needed no help getting through.

'You must be kidding. I mean they actually produce champagne around here?'

Joe laughed. 'California isn't the only state in the Union. We used to go and help out at harvest time, you know, gathering grapes.'

'Sounds like fun.'

'It's beautiful country. Hold it, there's a fallen log just ahead of us.'

'That's right.'

'Let's stop off and have a cigarette.'

No hesitation. He walked straight to it and sat.

They smoked for a while and listened to the everlasting cry of the killdeer.

'Harry used to bring the children up here come fine weather
—still does. Brings a book and reads 'em a story. Sometimes he'd
say "I don't have the strength to carry a book today. I think
I'll just tell one out of my head." I always thought they were
better.'

'You used to quote Shakespeare in the camp. You get that
through him?'

'Anything worth knowing we get from Harry.'

'He's quite a guy.'

'Better.' Joe was positive. 'He's a good human.'

Chuck watched him feeling the ground at his end of the log.
'That's it, there they are. See down there?'

'Funny lookin'.'

'Funny! They're beautiful, even if they are parasites.'

'They're white: is that natural?'

'You sound like a segregationist with a pigmentation complex.
Indian Pipes or *Monotropa uniflora* if you prefer—it lacks
chlorophyll.'

'I still think they look funny.'

'OK, but don't blame 'em. See right ahead of us, there's a red
spruce sort of kissing the ground. I used to climb it like it was a
ladder ... when I was a child.'

'Great.' But Chuck Willens kept searching for some fact else
scratching the back of his mind. Too small to reach, a tiny
unimportance that might or might not surface ...

'My favourite time of the year,' Joe was saying. ' "Right on
the edge of spring," Harry tells the children. "If the world
started the year with spring it'd be a happier place." I believe
it.'

That was it! The reiteration of one word had got through
at last and Chuck held on firmly, for it was a small thing and
could so easily slip through his fingers.

'Joe, since I been here I never heard you or anybody talk of
anything but children, like I mean, most people talk about
kids.'

Joe Rideout almost looked at him. 'That's right. Most people
do. Parents especially, and teachers I believe. Harry has a
theory; what you don't value overmuch you don't give much
of a name to. It's a simple comparison—a child—that's a beauti-

ful word. A kid...' he shrugged and left it at that.

Half a paradox. One boy crying inside for what he had never
—experienced. There's selfishness implied in hankering after
what you never sought for and never knew you'd lost; but it's
allowed any man to regret an unknown state of being. More
than vaguely he felt the aridity within; the last and, very nearly,
the only legacy of childhood.

'What're you thinking about, Chuck?'

Willens pulled himself together, started to move his left hand
to throw back the long strands of brown hair crowding his face.
He didn't make that mistake often. 'Oh, I was just thinking, you
haven't missed a lot—not having regular parents and all that
jazz.' He laughed a touch bitterly. 'When I think I almost wept
at the air base thinking you didn't have anyone. But you were
crying too.'

'Sure, I was so happy I'd be seeing Harry and Jane again. Let's
go.'

Chuck watched the 'parentally deprived', physically handicapped veteran striding ahead as though he had eyes all over
the place.

'You lucky bastard,' he mentioned with feeling, and the tears
that almost welled were for himself. 'Thank God.'

Kill-dee ... kill-dee the eternal bird notes of the killdeer
sounded nothing like 'Amen'.

*   *   *

The storm has to break sometime. Sooner or later the *Carolina*
had to make landfall. She'd set a course that brought them all
to the Ambrose Light, just about where the New Jersey
sandspit indicates the harbour entrance. By now, of course, a
whole flotilla of US naval craft was in watchful, puzzled
attendance.

What in the name of Nimitz did they think they were doing?

Halliday watched the harbour launch chugging across to
come up alongside the near stationary carrier. The gangway
had been stepped out and the pilot, looking less than usually
bored, made a spectacular leap and came smartly topside to
face the bearded officer.

He stared at him, at the other officers standing around in casual attitudes, and tipped back his tiny black hat to show every inch of his disbelief.

'What the hell's goin' on here?' With a knife that Brooklyn accent could be cut.

'You're the pilot?'

'So I'm the pilot, what's the difference? To you I could be the Kaiser——'

'Just take us into the Hudson, I'll let you know when we get there.'

'You'll let *me*——' the pilot's eyes bulged. No-one had ever spoken to His Pilotship that way in the whole of his very important career. 'Now look, wise ass. I don' know you from nothin' and what you're doin' I have not the slightest desire to be acquainted—all I got is orders from the US Government to get you into the Upper Bay, that's all I gotta do.'

'Then what?'

'I told you already, how should I know? Now suppose you just take me to the admiral of this——'

'He's confined to his cabin.'

'He's—what?' Astonishment could go no further. The pilot, as he would testify at the Preliminary Investigation, could not believe his ears. He said it so many times to anybody who would listen that his hearing did, in fact, deteriorate, and he had to buy an aid and six sessions with a psychiatrist before he could face the truth.

'Boy, you're in trouble,' as he followed the major to the bridge. 'Lockin' up admirals and heistin' their means of support; I mean you're really in trouble, you got that?'

Some consolation. A calm sea and one hundred per cent visibility made his job that much easier and they were soon passing under the whipcord span of the Verrazano-Narrows bridge linking Staten Island with the Brooklyn sprawl.

At this point a great deal of confusion developed. Naturally enough, since the authorities still had no real conception of what they were up against.

Radioed messages had bounced off the *Carolina* like so many peas hitting a tank. Before they reached the bridge helicopters were circling just clear of the flight deck, using powerful loud hailers to question, threaten and command. They received nothing in the way of reply.

At one time some romantic had suggested a massed landing by police and air force choppers but the observation loaches radioed back to forget it. Halliday hadn't spread the fifty Chinooks over the flight deck for visual effect.

Nothing baffled and infuriated the authorities more—by now a lot of authorities were involved and busily cancelling each other out—than the absolute silence maintained by the mystery ship. If someone doesn't respond when you communicate, you have a problem. It's terrible when nobody will talk with you; makes you feel you're not wanted.

The fiction that the *Carolina* was under escort could no longer serve. Foxwell, who'd remained at his desk through the night, studied the inflowing reports and issued the following brief statement.

At six hundred hours this morning the *USS Carolina* entered the Upper Bay of the Hudson river. Repeated messages delivered by all possible means have evoked no response. What these men have in mind it is impossible to say. As a minimum precaution I have ordered partial evacuation of the Hudson and East River waterfronts.

And that, officially, was the chapter heading of an incredible page in the incredible history of one of the world's most incredible countries.

As the *Carolina* passed under the Verrazano, PA helicopters from West Thirtieth Street and their downtown heliport were lifting off for observation duties. All river police were assigned for the same purpose. All city police were ordered to report for duty. By which time the silent carrier was sliding past the US quarantine station.

The news media, sensing something bigger than the *Carolina* looming on their doorstep, began a major coverage that would stretch their resources to breaking point.

There was an atmosphere of water-carnival as launches filled with reporters and cameramen began to pull out into the bay. Night workers at the New York *Daily News* plant forgot the need for a good day's sleep and crowded the windows of their riverside frontage to watch the news literally sailing past Brooklyn.

Early-bird commuters yawned over their first cup of coffee until they caught the flashes on low-tuned transistors. They sat up, called their sleeping families, called the neighbours, friends, anybody.

Something big was happening.

Automatically they switched on their TV sets but there was only continuous studio news until the major networks could get their visual systems on target.

In the beginning was the Word and it actually beat the Picture to it that day.

'Your CBS reporter is now directly over the *Carolina*. The whole flight deck is covered with Chinook helicopters and I'd say they've been deliberately spaced to keep anything from landing.

'There are soldiers in combat uniform on the flight deck— maybe fifty or so—and I can see a few crew members as we go in not fifty feet above. No signs of feverish activity, in fact nothing out of the ordinary is happening.

'All around the ship is a small armada of launches and more are heading out from the East River mouth. The missile carrier *Ladybird* has dropped back to about a mile beyond the Verrazano bridge.

'I can see the Staten Island ferry lumbering across the *Carolina*'s massive bows, bound for Manhattan just as if nothing in the whole, wide world is happening; and on the face of things, nothing is. Just a carrier coming in to harbour, but the wrong harbour. Everyone is asking: What next?

'We're circling to come in behind her. To our left a small boat pulls out from Sandy Hook Pilots' pier. It's one of their men who's bringing in the *Carolina*, the only man in New York who knows exactly what the situation is out there.

'Right ahead of us is Manhattan, it's looking beautiful, just beautiful in the clear morning air. No haze anywhere to obscure this drama which has to have a climax somewhere, sometime.

'We're coming up on her port side. Passing the AP Line, the American Dock Co., the US Coast Guard Base, the US

Gypsum Co. and right ahead of us the huge US Naval Supply Depot, a tremendous complex thrusting out into the bay from Bayonne.

'Even at this early hour of the morning one can see hundreds of people standing at every possible vantage point.

'There goes a PA helicopter, loud-hailing the carrier "You are ordered to heave to," the same message repeated over and over. No response at all.

'They must have built Manhattan knowing this moment would come. Every building up there has a grandstand view of a mystery that threatens to rival that of the *Marie-Celeste*—but right now I have some news for you.

'The *Carolina* is slowing down, the pride of the US Seventh Fleet is slowing down, and it looks as if—I think she's respond-ing at last to orders from PA and Naval authorities. I think it's all over, this thing is ending not with a bang but a whimper.'

In fact, the *Carolina* was responding to nothing but Halliday's order to slow down, and for a quite different, utterly out-rageous reason.

Lieutenant Sweetman had done his loach training at Fort Rucker and then said to hell with it, I'll transfer. PFC Lucas had served an apprenticeship with the Bell Helicopter Company before drafting into the army so he knew a lot about helicopters and could even fly one, which was Halliday's good fortune.

There were a couple of KOWA OH 58s aboard the carrier and these, Lucas advised, would serve their purpose better. Chinooks made heavy weather if you didn't have a lot of flying time behind you. Lucas had given them an overhaul with the help of some friendly naval mechanics. They were all set to go.

Each loach carried enough explosive to sink the *Carolina*.

They waited on the flight deck while Halliday, up in the radio room, prepared to send out a message that was to circle the world quicker than Ariel.

'OK, Ed, what do we have up there?'

His RTO grinned. 'You can take your pick, John. They've even got the White House plugged in.'

'I'll talk to Foxwell another time.'

'There's New York PA, the navy, the coastguards—police

department—or I can fix you a nice line with CBS. They'd welcome a puff.'

'Fine, let's give 'em one.'

'*USS Carolina* calling CBS/3. Receiving?'

'CBS/3/*Carolina*. Roger.'

'OK. We have a message.'

'Roger. Go ahead *Carolina*.'

'The message reads—— We are bringing Vietnam to the American people.'

A long pause.

'CBS/3/*USS Carolina*, please confirm. Repeat, please confirm.'

Halliday was happy to oblige.

'My God!' the man in the helicopter stared down at the carrier glinting ominously in the light of the newly risen sun. For some time he could find nothing else worth saying. He was not alone. Within seconds plenty of other people got the message, and stared at it no less blankly. Including Foxwell.

He turned to Caressinger. 'Did you hear that?'

Caressinger nodded slowly. 'Yes, I heard.'

'What are they trying to do?' A kind of implosive outburst, but sending the days of tension flying in all directions like pellets from a Claymore. 'For Christ's sake what—are—they—trying to do!'

'Mr President——'

'Don't give me soft syllables, Herman. I want words cast in iron, in steel! Tell me what it's about.'

Let the observer leave compassion at the front door at that moment, he might still have found reason to pity Foxwell. Maybe not someone from the *Washington Post* or a discarded member of his own staff; but someone like Joe or Chuck Willens, someone who knew what suffering was all about, could lecture to the Faculty of Apathetics on the true meaning of mental anguish.

But there was only Caressinger.

'Mr President, you have just one course of action. There are no options. You must use everything at your command to destroy these men.'

Foxwell broke from the grip of a strange reverie, but the faraway gaze remained, seeing through and long beyond the

160

good doctor. His expression having to do with Death and the crushing of beetles in one's hand.

'I know what I have to do.' Can a voice be haggard? 'What I need to know is, why?' Almost to the point of inaudibility.

No-one else but Caressinger had the courage to give him his answer. 'They wish to lay the spoils of defeat at your door, Mr President.'

The same blank gaze and a long, indrawn breath told its own story.

'Got everything right?'

'Sure thing, Major,' Sweetman turned to Lucas. 'Be my guest.'

Lucas grinned. 'I'll race you over.' Their four companions were already piled aboard.

Halliday said, 'We'll have you covered all the way.'

Sweetman, nervous as hell, climbed in. 'That's good news. I'll try and die happy.'

Halliday and the others retreated and stood watching as the rooky pilots made contact and spun the blades into an increasing whirl of activity.

Both men were sweating a little as they gave the main rotors power. Suppose, for example, the anti-torque propeller didn't respond with an equal number of rpms? And who lives to tell the tale of dissymmetry when articulating rotor hubs get as temperamental as an opera star and twice as mean? Sweetman remembered all over again why he'd quit the flying course first time round.

But, they both lifted off in fine style, tried out their minimal forward speeds across the flight deck and, thus encouraged, they accelerated and veered away to the left heading for Liberty Island not two hundred yards away.

By the time their skids touched the forecourt below the Statue CBS and ABC were over the *Carolina* with a first relay of camera crews. Telephotography was ready to take America right into the action.

Meantime the morning listeners were plugged firmly to their radios *and* watching TV studio newscasters so as not to miss a thing.

'Two light helicopters have just taken off from the carrier's flight deck. Both are carrying army personnel, that much we can see. We're now some way off having been ordered back by police loaches buzzing around like angry bees.

'And through all the confusion, one question must be occurring to everyone in New York, in the United States and eventually to the whole world: What was the meaning of that message from the *Carolina*? Let me repeat those words which have a sinister and, possibly, an historic ring, "We are bringing Vietnam to the American people".

'Speculation must continue until this thing dies a death or erupts into action of some kind, and here we have it!

'The helicopters from renegade *Carolina* have landed on Liberty Island!'

The six men leapt to the ground, began tugging at the explosives' packs under the still whirring blades. Six hundred pounds of H and E and if that didn't do it—nothing would.

Sweetman, Lucas and two more of the party ferried the stuff up to the base while the others rounded up the open-mouthed members of the custodial staff who promptly accepted the invitation to climb aboard mainly because it was too early in the morning to argue with M16s and anyway they might just be having bad dreams.

They shot the locks off the door leading to the base interior. Straightway began packing the stuff in centre for maximum all-round effect then laid a five minute fuse.

'OK fellers, let's blow before she does,' Sweetman called and they ran to gain the helicopters. A little more sweat as the pilots gunned their engines. Three minutes to go but at least they had lift-off.

Two minutes twenty seconds to go and they were almost over the carrier.

'Jesus! What does he think he's doing?' one of the party yelled.

Sweetman glanced over his shoulder. An army helicopter was swooping in to land on the very same LZ. 'Somebody should've told him,' but his words weren't exactly weighted with concern.

'That's what I call taking a liberty,' Lucas suggested.

'Or getting one.' That was Gribble.

One minute left as they bumped down onto the deck. Lucas busted a skid but otherwise the whole thing had gone the way it was planned all of three weeks back.

Most of the men were topside gazing across to the monumental symbol of freedom that had barred the way to America for so long.

No more helicopters were landing, the others hovered around like blue-bottles inspecting a carcass that had gone rotten beyond the point of decency.

They saw three figures jump out of the army 'copter and walk cautiously towards the base.

Ten seconds . . .

'The two loaches are back on *Carolina*'s deck. What they were up to on Liberty Island is anybody's guess, maybe some kind of symbolic gesture. . . . An army helicopter has just landed in the forecourt close to the statue and presumably . . . Christ Almighty. Jesus Christ!'

A first agonized cry from the heart to brand the mind of America with foreknowledge of what this was all about. Nothing could have underlined Halliday's cryptic message more effectively.

While the country blanched in face of that terrible cry, the professional fought to overcome the mere man, and succeeded in an almost poignant moment that would long be remembered with the echoes of that fearful explosion.

'Ladies and gentlemen, I have to apologize, but we have witnessed a phenomenon beyond any man's power to describe in adequate terms. These men, soldiers returned from Vietnam, have just now blown the Statue of Liberty to a shamble of stone. The whole base, dynamited, blew apart and brought down that universally famed symbol of freedom . . . we're flying closer to a maelstrom of dust mushrooming over the remains. I can see great blocks of stone—a fragment of the torch, the observation platform itself, I can see a chunk of it still in motion, as though a landslide of gigantic dimensions is rolling its last stone over a self-composed tomb—it—it is, without any

163

doubt, the most terrible spectacle I have ever witnessed.'

Hundreds of silent, grim-faced men stood on the deck of a ship made for death and destruction, stared impassively at the downfallen monolith. They too had seen terrible things and were used to it.

'*L'état, c'est moi,*' said Louis the Mouth. If, conceivably, there is a grain of truth in an absurdity, then Foxwell the Escapologist could as well declare '*Les États-Unis, c'est moi*'. The difference between the two? Foxwell really believed it.

Thus, America stood in the ante-room of the Oval Office that day. Stood shaken and disbelieving before the TV console watching—in vivid Disneycolour—the CBS scoop of the disaster.

He had heard long since of course, but hearing was not strictly believing. Caressinger, more intellectually exercised by observing the effect of calculated destruction on the observer, was watching Foxwell closely, scientifically.

A worthwhile effort, to plot the course of disintegration in one who had kept so much of himself secret. Easy enough, in the context of normality, to talk of the capable politician, the breadth of his vision, the depth of his compassion for the poor, the underprivileged and so forth; but where *do* the flies go in wintertime?

He liked nothing of what he saw, not because Foxwell was President, for which he, Caressinger, held shares in culpable responsibility, but because at that moment Foxwell was indeed the United States writ small.

Information, or facts swollen to uselessness poured in the whole time. Aides came and went importantly delivering nothing; for what could minions tell Foxwell and his number two more than they had lately witnessed?

A meeting of the 'Washington Special Actions Group' had been arranged. Caressinger in the Chair, the Undersecretary of State, the Deputy Secretary of Defence, the Chairman of the Joint Chiefs of Staff and CIA's Director. Foxwell was to join the meeting later and prime himself with the results of their deliberations. But a hitch developed; the kind that makes a moment of high drama look like a vaudeville act playing the

Carnegie Hall. Nikos Papadopolous showed up. Which altered everything.

The opinion of the Senate about Nikos is quotable, apposite and enough: 'The less said about Papadopolous the better'.

The fact remained, he *was* the Vice-President of the United States. The fact also remained, he'd woken up after Inauguration Day realizing V-Ps were chosen to play shadow to the light. This, he had stormed at his wife and seven children, was not what he had fought for all these years, playing dishwasher to the head waiter. 'In Greece I coulda been a colonel!'

Consequently, when crises developed, as sometimes happened, he would pace around his lair in the Old Senate Office Building and wait for the phone to ring. It seldom, if ever, did.

This time he hadn't waited. His enormous frame, on which hung an undeniably rejectable personality, shouldered its way through any attempt at the polite brush-off, though confusion was such he had little trouble reaching the centre of things.

Caressinger was in the Oval Office with Foxwell just before the meeting was due to begin, when Papadopolous literally intruded. Another small indication of how the day was beginning to degenerate.

'Mr President, I have to see you right away. This is sheer urgency!'

'Take a hold of yourself, Nik.' Foxwell's contempt showed worse than two inches of shirt-cuff.

'You realize what's going on out there? This is civil war, Mr President.'

In spite of his fierce anguish Foxwell managed a grimace that only just missed the connection with mirth. 'Everything's under control, Nik.'

'Because Caressinger's here? This needs something better than poker-playing with gooks.'

'Don't demean yourself more than you have to, Nik.' The something in his voice, the tone a dog-breeder allows a mongrel, made Papadopolous think a mite longer before he spoke again, and this time he sounded deferential.

'I don't have to remind you, Mr President, in a state of

165

emergency the Vice-President is entitled to a voice in the matter of decision making.'

Foxwell studied his side-kick in a way that did nothing for Papadopolous' peace of mind. 'Very well. Herman, the Vice-President and I will attend the meeting. Will you let Bob and the others know?'

'Certainly, Mr President.'

Extracts of Minutes of the NSC meeting transcribed and given in evidence to the Senate Emergency Committee sitting for the purpose *in camera*.

'I have decided to be present at this meeting from the outset, gentlemen. It seems important that, until the emergency is resolved, I be fully acquainted not only with decisions made but also your immediate thinking on this matter. The Vice-President feels he should contribute to the debate and I suggest that is both reasonable and a tribute to his loyalty. I shall therefore ask the Vice-President to make known his opinion. Niki?'

And that, Caressinger told his *alter ego*, is what being a consummate politician is all about. How to get a man on the rack simply by asking him to stretch out.

Watching Papadopolous' discomfiture gave him no great satisfaction; he could almost sympathize with a man who knew nothing from nothing, only wore the trappings of power which were—precisely—a trap. Cruel fate. To be chosen for high position for the sole purpose of being left in ignorance.

And here he was, facing a group of men who knew all that could be known...

'Gentlemen, I have to say I do not believe this is a simple case of mutiny. There's a more sinister import, that I firmly believe—have done ever since the *Carolina* went missing.' Pause for effect. 'We are faced with a Communist conspiracy.'

Forgetting the weakness of his position Papadopolous had vaulted, booted and spurred, onto his favourite hobby horse.

'It is my considered opinion,' he concluded with a sizable helping of triumph, 'that the men on board the *Carolina* are Veetnamese guerillas, holding the crew hostage....'

The others kept eyes firmly on the glasses of water and ashtrays set before them. It might have been a Convention of Morticians at table embarrassed by some body saying Grace.

'Thank you for your views, Mr Vice-President. Naturally they'll be taken into account. I'll call and let you know the result of our deliberations.'

Papadopolous blinked at the President then discovered that no-one else was looking at him either. Except Caressinger whose owl-like gaze stayed on him, as it had done throughout. Sympathy yes, but he didn't want the Vice-President to harbour any illusions.

'Certainly, Mr President. I—thank you. I'll be glad to...'

He left the room without another word.

'Now gentlemen, let's proceed. Fouchay, I'd like to know what steps you've taken and how you see the ball-game developing.'

The *gauleiter* of the CIA narrowed his gaze at the wall ahead of him. That was how he regarded everything. Nothing was beneath his suspicion. Not anyone in the room, behind their façades, not anything in it, behind the picture-frames. And if all was clean he knew how to soil things a little. He showed like a strange gardener in an alien world where seeds could germinate, just by thinking about them. Viridian and virulent were the plants he tended, and their roots spread far...

'We have a complete list of all the men involved.' A lazy, self-indulgent voice. 'In collaboration with the FBI we have background reports plus a rundown in depth on each and every family involved. This information is being computerized as of now and should yield useful categorizations. Surveillance has been arranged of course. No problems there.

'From the Agency standpoint we need to decide how we can best use the situation as a back-up to broader considerations. Out of evil some good maybe.'

'In what way?' the President demanded.

'I don't think we can make a lot of mileage out of the Communist theory. I mean GIs being subverted by Red doctrines. That's what everybody will expect but it's really just more of the same.'

'A lot more,' the Deputy Defence Secretary pointed out.

'Perhaps so. But my feeling is the American people need a

change. If we play it for what I think it is, the action of a disgruntled bunch of trigger-happy but atypical GIs then it shouldn't be difficult to tie in with the campaign for law and order. We need that campaign and I don't need to spell out why....

'So we have a situation ready to hand. People are going to say, if this is what can happen, let's go along with the man who's ready to stop it by any means. As of now, Mr President, you could demand legislation for summary executions and the Hill wouldn't dare cast a contrary vote.'

Caressinger listened carefully to one man telling another exactly what he wanted to know.

'Thank you, Paul. Any further thoughts on that, Howard?'

The Deputy Defence Secretary cleared his throat, a habit little men have: rehearsing to make the right noises. 'I'd go along with what Paul says and maybe something else follows in the global context. These fellows may do a few million dollars' worth of damage but that can be ironed out. We can build another Statue of Liberty, twice the size of the one they've destroyed.

'That fact by itself puts the nation on your side. Nobody likes to see the death of a symbol. The iconoclast is the lowest form of traitor because essentially he's destroying the visual aspect of popular mythology.

'Better still, and I'm sure Paul is cognisant of this: the rest of the world won't so much take comfort from our misfortune as grow leery of a similar situation developing within their own borders.

'What I'm postulating is that any spectacular act of violence in one country immediately arouses the repressive instinct in others. Naturally that couldn't happen in America because there's no repression—period. But if the Communist countries profit from our experience by introducing even more stringent measures, then eventually their dissidents could blow the system apart like an unstable element bottled up with uranium.'

'And so do our work for us,' Paul Fouchay nodded appreciatively. 'I like that, Howard. I really do.'

So did Foxwell. He smiled just enough to make the Deputy

Secretary feel he could relax—cautiously.

'General?'

General Booth, the pin-up of the armed forces, the man who'd never lost a battle because he'd never fought any, not outside the Pentagon, turned his Valentino profile in Foxwell's direction.

'I have to admit, Howard's reasoning is attractive. If you go along with that, Mr President, it becomes a question of how far we let these criminals proceed before they can get out of hand.'

'A controlled containment?' Foxwell suggested.

'That's what I'm aiming for. We have the National Guard on standby as well as regular units of course. If the whole New York City police force can do a good job that should pin them down until we choose to really move in. No-one in America is going to cry into their beer when we do—and afterwards—the field is yours, Mr President.'

The Undersecretary of State saw no reason to disagree. But then he never did.

'Herman?' But Foxwell wasn't looking at him, only calling by name. Caressinger's sensors were acting particularly delicate that morning.

'I think perhaps we have forgotten this Major Halliday's message, Mr President.'

As though someone had switched off the light. But Caressinger, still sure of himself in an uncertain world, still more confident in the superiority of intellect over reptilian cunning, pushed forward like a man holding a guttery candle in a dark cellar full of inexplicable noises.

'He says he has brought Vietnam to the American people. Now I do not know if he is an iconoclast posing as an idealist or an idealist masquerading as an iconoclast. But if my intuition serves me well I would say he is the latter. In which case he might easily do irreparable damage to the nation in a ratio determined by——'

'With five hundred men?' Foxwell interjected.

'. . . the period of containment. Physically no, but I would say the national psyche has taken as much of a battering as it can stand. Any interior assault on the values of that society might well force it into a reconsideration of its values.'

'That doesn't quite add up,' the general said, not because he'd evaluated the doctor's analysis which he didn't fully understand anyway, but he was anxious to let Foxwell know he was on the right side.

Caressinger gestured impatiently. 'Whether it adds up or not, one thing is clear: an event ten thousand miles from this country, and another not far from this room, had it searching its conscience in a manner never known before. If those men return and do what they threaten, a lot of people might feel a need to resume that search.'

'Therefore?' Foxwell snapped.

'Therefore, Mr President, I consider it imperative you exercise your prerogative as head of the armed forces and hit them with everything you have at your disposal—immediately.'

It looked as though Caressinger had won yet again. His appeal to the power vested in Caesar was unanswerable except in one particular. The others remembered what Caressinger had forgotten or no longer cared to think about: Foxwell's toxic ambition to be commemorated as a great president, a supreme political strategist timing his actions to reap the maximum personal advantage. That meant moving when *he* was ready, not simply operating in response to the renegades in old style action/reaction ploys culled from a dog-eared book of manoeuvres.

'I see your point, Herman, and I'm sure you speak in all sincerity—you want what's best for America. We all do. But I think you underestimate the judgment of the American people. They're not Germanic in the sense they blindly follow their leader no matter what. I'd say the national psyche is in good shape, essentially it knows what's good for America.

'I like to think I have an idea too.

'This man *is* an iconoclast, don't let's make any mistake about that. What kind of idealism could perpetrate what he's done already? He has to be eliminated, all of them, we agree on that. But the consensus of opinion, if I'm not in error on this, says he must pay our price first. We have the right to capitalize on his iniquities and that doesn't necessarily mean killing them all in one big *blitzkrieg*.

'On the whole I think we'll play it my way.'

He rose from his chair with that characteristic, but not very nice, motion of a jack-knife. The others got to their feet too.

'I shall want hourly briefings from all your departments till further notice. And it may be necessary to convene a further meeting tonight, gentlemen.'

They left in quick succession and Caressinger, as always, was last to go. He hesitated, but the President seemed immediately absorbed in a document left by the Undersecretary. As he opened the door Foxwell glanced up.

'By the way, Herman, you might remember for future reference. Halliday is not to be designated "Major". As of now Halliday can be regarded as *persona non grata* with the human race.'

The grey eminence looked a little greyer, half-blinked and replied with his customary deference. 'I understand, Mr President.'

INTERLUDE

Now, it might surprise you folks to know that deep in the heartlands of North Carolina is a little itty-bitty of o-o-old Vietnam. Yessir, the country of the Nam Viets as they were called all of twenty-five hundred years ago. And who knows, friend, but what Communism wasn't raisin' its ugly ol' yeller-head even then some 'cos the Chinese was busy pushin' those poor ol' Nam Viets clear across the RED River. Can you beat that? Why, hist'ry's jus' gettin' instanter all th'time.

Like I was about to say, Carolina N's as purty as the moon in June and that ain't State's secret. Nossir! and what is furthermore, it has its positively own piece of Vietnam real estate, wanna match me a dollar? Got a sayin' up here like Texas talks but we mean it in Carolina N.

Let you into a little secret and it don' obligate none. I'm Sergeant F. O. Grunt—Francis Oswald just to correct mistaken impressions—and I was born'n'raised on my daddy's hog farm not twenty miles yonder as the pig flies (tha's a little local joke you can read in our family Bible, friend).

Well, I'm in the Marine Corps and I couldn't be prouder if Goldwater, my daddy's primary hog, had snuffled up the Durham Rose in th'all comers class.

Now I don' have to inform you 'bout Camp Lejeune down on the New River, 'cos just about everyone knows it's the biggest Marine Corps base ever was. And this is where I put the pork in the beans 'cos it's right in Camp Lejeune you'll find that little bit of ol' Vietnam I told y'bout.

Why even the ground you walk on comes from Vietnam. We had C130s bringing dirt all that way jus' to make it apple-pie

173

real. We got the cutest little paddy-field you ever did see, the boys really did a job on it, you can take it from ol' Triplestripes, and there's plants and things flown all the way from Vin Binh. We got the finest jungle you ever saw outside Hollywood, and it's near all plastic. Sometimes, when my squad's crappin' up the routine and I gotta whip their asses—beggin' y'pardon ma'am—I tell 'em you go on out to that ol' jungle now and wash it down good so I c'n see every ol' leaf shinin' like a general's button.

Then there's the village right slap in the middle of this green delight with all the hooches like they should be and a Buddhist temple too—look inside for surprises—you'll find ice-cream, Cokes and hot dogs on sale with a monk all purty in saffron to serve your needs, just drop your offerin' in his genuine beggin' bowl. Even got a real, live cemetery like you see in 'Nam.

Now you may wonder, why all this in the good ol' USA when ain't there enough Vietnam in the world already for landsakes? And I have to concur, folks. But it's all on account of helpin' the boys learn the conditions out there, see what I mean? Makes it easy on the mind if you got a preview of comin' attractions.

Like you'll see an innocent ol' man goin' along in his white robes and when you lift up his skirts and he's wearin' army issue jump boots why you just *know* he's doin' business with the big, bad Vietcong.

Or you see an ol' Pepsi can lyin' on the ground and you pick it up thinkin' how come that ol' Pepsi can lyin' here? and zonk! why pick up my face if it ain't a WP grenade.

When that mean ol' jungle's booby-trapped as a Christmas tree I declare you gotta learn to walk smart. Now we're the Marines and we can bite the top clean off a whiskey jar but we don' aim to throw everything in the hog-trough. So we use itty-bitty charges in th'booby-traps, just enough to take out an eye or make a superficial hole so a man'll always know he warn't smart enough to be a leatherneck.

Like I say, we got a real nice set-up. But now we're windin' down out there the commandant figures we don't need it anymore. So tonight we're gonna have a real hoe-down to which all you good folks from Richmond through Durham and every place else is right welcome to attend, when the Marines will present their very own Gran' Ol' Opry, *The Fall of Khoaca-Khola*, with real live napalm packs for the spectaculoso zippo finale.

So roll up, folks. Get your tickets here for positively the one and only performance. See the peasants plantin' rice in the paddy-field. Take a peek at the seductive village beauties—in their sexy *au-dais*. See the interrogation of the treacherous headman, Yu Winh. Don't miss the daring exploits of the gook disguised as a Buddhist monk. Thrill to the sudden meeting of a GI and the headman's daughter, Nhot Nhow. Yes folks, all the drama, all the pathos, the tragedy and the treachery will be on show tomorrow night. And if you care to participate why jus' bring your own matches and help make it a zippo you won't ever forget.

THEY JUST PUSHED the Chinooks clear off the deck and there they still lie at the bottom of the bay. Halliday ordered up the Skyhawks while the aerial observers, still recovering from the shock of what had been done to Liberty, shook their heads in mute wonder. What, one bemused CBS man asked of his equally bemused listeners, could they possibly be up to now?

Hadn't they done enough? There couldn't be a more effective way to make their point. So they've made it....

One thing needs to be affirmed. Much has been said and written subsequently to show that Halliday and his men took a kind of fiendish delight in everything they did.

Nothing could be further from the truth.

They behaved no differently from any unit on a search and destroy mission in Vietnam. As the colonels never stopped telling them: 'It's a job that has to be done.'

With the coloured sailors who were helping out it was another matter. When they saw old Lady Liberty disintegrate like a poverty programme, they went wild. Halliday could have ordered them to jump into the Bay and they'd have queued for the privilege. Almost before the *Carolina* was under way again they had those Skyhawks up on deck and the rockets primed ready to fire.

Twenty sets of missiles were ranged on both sides of the ship. For a week a special task force had taken instruction from the armourers on how to discharge the things, though they were still complaining they could do a better job.

The first salvo from the port side slammed into the Baltimore and Ohio piers. Something exploded as the first rocket struck and a great column of fire and smoke made the shape of things to come....

And as the armourers rushed to fit more rockets America erupted and, one might say, went mad with fright and anticipation.

The CBS man aloft said 'Jesus Christ!' again but by then everybody was saying it. ABC was operating from Pan Am and the Empire State and people sat trance-like watching destruction sail up the Hudson. It was—unbelievable.

'A fantastic experience,' a Woolworth Building maintenance man was to admit later. 'Well like I had a grandstand view. This one ship sailing along, firing salvos at regular intervals. I saw the whole thing till they got parallel with Chambers Street. By then there was so much smoke and stuff we just lost the action.'

'How did it look down below?' the interviewer asked.

'Well that was the funny part. All that shooting and noise and yet right up here you felt kinda remote, you know? Like you're in a 'plane and you look down maybe and see people sprawling and fire tenders and police trying to clear the buildings. It was fantastic—it really was.'

'You saw a lot of casualties?'

'I'd say not, it was still early in the morning, long before the rush or there'd have been a massacre—no, I think casualties were minimal at the beginning.'

'You were there when the Woolworth was hit?'

'That's right, it took a missile on the fifteenth. Place just rocked. That was one time me and my buddies felt really scared y'know?'

'What else did you see, Frank?'

'Well, like I said, the smoke and all, but they hit Saint Paul's Chapel, the Chase Manhattan—we saw that—the Stock Exchange took a ricochet and someone said Washington on the first Inaugural site got badly splintered, but I couldn't say I saw that. There were so many rumours flying around, I didn't find out till later most of 'em were true.'

Most of them. No witness, no imaginative observer of events needed to take up embroidery. It was all there in essence so strong you had to dilute your impressions by adding 'That's

178

what I saw happen, but I could be wrong.'

The pall of smoke began to thicken on both sides of the Hudson. A light north-westerly nudged it across the river mouth, obligingly putting the carrier into semi-obscurity and increasing the chaos in the Manhattan area almost as far as Canal Street.

A US coastguard base at Battery Park reported a small boat putting off from the *Carolina* but nothing was done about it. A lot of communications got lost in the confusion that day. There was no co-ordinated police action and anyway, no-one was disposed to believe it.

Sergeant Soup Kemble and Benner were part of a forty man mission on that particular assignment. Each and all carried a forty pound explosive charge with a 'suicide' fuse, which meant you left the luggage and ran for your train.

They tied up a few piers down from the Hoboken Ferry terminal, released the men from Liberty Island and proceeded literally to take over the tip of Manhattan. For thirty-eight minutes they worked to a carefully pre-arranged schedule. All the places mentioned by the maintenance man were targeted plus the Federal Reserve Bank, Trinity Church, the American Stock Exchange at Trinity Square, and others.

The whole inner city rocked under the impact of a dozen hundred-fifty pound explosions. Damage from blast and resulting fires according to later reports was incalculable and it's still an open question whether the old Exchange can survive the structural damage.

Loss of life on that occasion was minimal. A police patrol opened fire on one group but was cut down to nothing and all units were back on the *Carolina* two minutes ahead of schedule.

'Frank Lester, CBS, reporting: The *Carolina* is on the move again. And over Wall Street the smoke rises like mushrooms.

'We have reports that the United Fruit Co. wharves are burning fiercely. Unconfirmed news just in gives one cargo ship ablaze on the Standard Fruit and Steamship Co. property and that has to be wrong since their piers are over on the East River just above Brooklyn Bridge, but if there's confusion at this time it's not to be wondered at.

'This is like a war one might dream up in a nightmare. This

enigma, disguised as a steel-plated Nemesis, draws slowly up the Hudson and seemingly nobody can do a thing to stop it.

'And we have firing again. It's closer—it's coming closer. You can hear the whoosh of missiles as they rip into piers, ships, buildings at point-blank range. There's a flash, and another—and—my God! the whole waterfront is going up in flames!

'... yes I have that. I have news that the Baltimore and Ohio complex is ablaze and out of control. We're getting a whole stream of reports up here: Hoboken is hit, the AP Lines pier, even Central Railroad of New Jersey—these rockets are penetrating beyond the waterfront.

'And still it goes on. This is beyond belief, past anyone's comprehension, these things are slamming into warehouse after warehouse, cranes are toppling, Zim Israel is hit, an Israeli ship has been fired, Holland America Norwegian American Line rocketed—they can only be a mile distant from where we stand at this moment.

'I've just been handed a public announcement. May I have your attention, this is of the greatest importance. Mayor Lindsay has issued the following decree. Immediate, repeat, immediate evacuation of the whole West Side from the Battery tunnel to the Lincoln tunnel. All A shelters to be opened to the public. All high buildings to be evacuated as of now. Please take note: all bridges between the Bronx and Manhattan Island will be closed to incoming traffic. Please stay off the approach roads to the following: Queensboro, Williamsburg, Manhattan, Brooklyn and George Washington. These bridges are no longer accepting incoming traffic.

'These tunnels are also closed, I repeat, closed, to incoming traffic: Lincoln, Holland, Brooklyn Battery and Queens Midtown.

'This message will be repeated at fifteen minute intervals. You are requested to stay tuned for further public announcements.'

Reeled! New York staggered under the shock.

A cloudless blue sky and the sun, at last giving a promise to spring, had metamorphosed into a strange and local kind of hell, an amphitheatre of fire and brimstone throwing up black billows and white plumes; strange because this hell was without a roof.

Ambulances were rushing the first batch of casualties through panic-stricken streets to the hospitals. People of every or no degree were running or wandering in all directions. Except the drug-outs and Rosie—the white hot evangelist who'd been predicting this kind of pay-out for years on her Broadway and Forty-fifth Street pitch. But even her leathery cry 'Repent ye, repent ye, the Kingdom of God is at Hand!' drowned in the everlasting wail of police, fire and ambulance sirens. No-one stopped to argue. No-one could deny the qualified darkness draping itself over the city.

Whichever way you turned this was infinitely worse than the day the Martians invaded. After all, this was happening. Wasn't it?

There would be the usual crop of incredible stories in the days to come; but nothing could generate more wonderment than that intangible happening, subtle as memory; an air of Mardi Gras that took root here and there in this fantastic city.

In places it wasn't so subtle as that. Not dancing in the streets, but kind of, an air of liberation from who cared what, as though, when the chips were down, this was what a lot of people had been waiting for—they actually wanted a piece of the action. It was their city dammit and if it had to happen, like getting bull-dozed out of your tenement—OK roll it.

Not dancing in the streets exactly...

Like around Pete's Backyard on West Tenth which took a rocket though no-one can figure how, so they opened for macro-biotic breakfasts and did great business. Bleeker Street got hit too and a woman died of heart failure in an apartment house—everybody gathered around and got friendly. It was like very old times and no wonder the Buddhists came leaping around as if it were firecrackers for Buddha's birthday.

Why not be cheerful? If it's a funny way to die let's have fun.

So, while the armourers sweated at clipping in the fire-crackers, and five hundred grim-visaged veterans headed by a man with binoculars, studied the carnage, New York, or some parts of it directly in the line of fire, was not exactly *en fête*....

*   *   *

181

Mrs Cratowski debouched from her dumb-bell apartment back of Forty-second and called down the stairwell. 'Mrs Pinos! Consuela!' she managed to stretch the Christian name to four syllables.

'What is it, Mrs Cratowski?'

'You heard the news?'

'Why should I hear the news? I can practically see it, and I have a cracked ceiling. You think I should send the kids to school today?'

'What else can you do with 'em?'

'I think it is serious.'

'You can bet on that. My husband says it's the Russians.'

'I don't mind anything so long as it is not the Chinese. This city's overcrowded already.'

'If you're goin' round to Schmulz will you fetch me a quart of milk?'

'I go in five minutes.'

Joe Valacchi had a *New York Times* reporter for fare during the first hours of that morning.

Fred Olsen's assignment demanded courage, persistence and paid up life insurance in that order. It meant going where the action was; not paddling in the aftermath but swimming in the Styx at flood-tide. There were many Olsens that day, father-confessors to catastrophe, recording on-the-spot eye-witness accounts which would provide humble footnotes to history in years to come.

He began with Joe as soon as he and three portable recorders were safely stowed in the cab.

'What's your opinion, Joe?' Olsen knew the man.

Joe waved a hand. 'My opinion is you ain't told me where to go.'

'Just take me where it's hottest.'

'This ain't no tank, man.'

'Well let's pretend it is.'

'OK. But I ain't goin' on the Miller Highway or West Side Elevated for Fort Knox. It's Demolition Day over there.'

'Right, just go as near as you can. Now how does it rate with you?'

182

'You heard the radio.' Joe pulled into Seventh Avenue and wondered about Houston Street.

'Well what do you suppose this guy Halliday is aiming to do?'

Joe gave a king-sized shrug. 'Like he said, this is what Vietnam's all about.'

'So what's he out to prove?'

Joe slewed towards the kerb-side as a fire-tender went screaming by. He decided against Houston Street, it was chaotic down there. He swung into Hudson Street and headed for the Wall Street area.

'Christ!' He slammed on the brakes narrowly avoiding collision with a wall of smoke that seemed not to be going anywhere. There was rubble and glass all over; strange, helmeted figures darted in and out of the gloom. A cop ran towards them waving his arms frantically. As he came closer they saw he was bleeding from a gash on his head, but it didn't seem to be bothering him.

'What the fuck do you think you're doin'? Get outta here!'

'Press, Mac.' Joe knew the officer.

'Well take it back to the cleaners, this area's prohibited.'

'You can say that again.' Joe looking less like a bored cabby who's seen all, gazed wonderingly about him.

'This is important, officer, a few words from you may not seem much, but they'll mean something to the future.'

Olsen had a knack of getting people to talk, mainly because he really believed their views and opinions counted. Who would argue otherwise?

The officer took a fresh look at the Stygian scene behind him, to where the fire-fighters were rushing around, paying out hose or looking for the source of screams. He felt tired suddenly, ran a hand over his face and stared stupidly at the dried blood flaking off.

'They hit this area twice. The first time wasn't so bad, just a few missiles of some kind. Then I heard they came in with explosives—you know why there's so much fire? Paper—paper! And the Chase Manhattan, torn apart like—like——'

'What's your feeling about it, Sergeant?'

'Feeling? What's one supposed to feel about a thing like this?

I get up, I go to work, I sign a few tickets and pull in a couppla junkies—what am I supposed to feel?'

'The men who are responsible,' Olsen suggested.

'Man, I hope they die the death. What they're doin' to America beats the Crucifiction. Now get the hell outta here, you're blockin' the tenders.'

They had no choice.

Joe turned, with some difficult, and cruised back along Hudson Street towards Fourteenth.

It was closing up to eight o'clock in the morning.

'What bugs me is, what's he gonna do next? I mean, he can't keep it up forever,' Joe said.

'Don't we have enough to think about with what he's doing now? Pull over, Joe, there's something interesting.'

Olsen, clutching his portable recorder, was out of the cab before it had stopped. Just ahead of him a city employee was calmly sweeping up yesterday's litter as though he'd never heard of the *Carolina* and one or two other items apropos.

'Do you have any comment on what's going on?' Olsen yelled above the Babel of explosions and sirens.

The coloured face turned his way belonged to a man in his fifties; a tired countenance, one that had seen too much without ever having enough, and now asked for nothing better than a long sleep for consolation.

'What kind of comment would you suggest?' he enquired politely, leaning on his broom and waiting, with a half smile for an answer.

Olsen felt unaccountably embarrassed. 'Well, I guess most people have a response to a situation if it's big enough.'

'This is big enough?' The street-sweeper smiled a lot more at this, let his one eye flicker over the microphone and Olsen's recorder. On the face of things he seemed to be perfectly at peace with himself, and the world.

'That's a mighty pretty toy you got there, mister. You wanna know what I think with you playin' that thing? Well, I wish so many times this good ol' land of liberty and punk equality and fraternity crap should drop beneath the sea that I'm just a little disappointed in the situation. Like I go home and mention "Ella May, I sure could use a steak", and she just sets me a plate

184

of ol' beans—well that keeps my guts quiet awhile but it don'
satisfy none.'

'You're glad?'

'I ain't glad. I ain't sorry. Jes' don' make no difference is all.
Now if you'll excuse me I got me a job to do.'

Olsen returned to the cab more slowly than he'd left it. Joe
Valacchi was smiling sardonically as though he knew already
the reason for the reporter's air of puzzlement.

'It doesn't bother him,' Olsen explained.

'What's he got to lose?' Joe pushed into first gear and
headed parallel with the *Carolina* towards Chelsea Park.

At about that time a score of missiles tore into the Transatlantic Terminal complex. Another salvo followed, and
another, leaving no salvage or survivors from the PA West
Thirty-second Street Heliport through to Furness, Withy and
Co.

This time the destruction was more spectacular and a lot of
people died. Hundreds more were injured. The West Side
Elevated highway was cut, a multi-storied car-park collapsed
and took fire, many rockets found a way to buildings at the very
heart of Manhattan.

Fires were spreading and becoming commonplace along the
waterfront. What else could be expected when many of the
missiles were packed with high-grade napalm?

And still they kept coming, with an effect that grew more
and more indescribable.

The prestigious *France* for example, blazing from stem to
stern. Most of the passengers were ashore; some members of
the crew died when the first rockets hit. About three hundred
longshoremen and customs officials, crowding the Cunard
terminal to see the fun, were wiped out where they stood. The
seriously injured died because there was no possibility of medical
aid. The ambulance situation already showed signs of
drought...

Olsen and Valacchi died when a chunk of masonry, torn off
by a missile, plummetted onto their cab crushing them both. By
then Olsen had almost two tapes filled with folk-history and
these survived.

Halliday had set up a battery of quad-6os on the flight deck.

His gunners took two of the coastguard observation loaches and three police helicopters. The media craft kept a healthy distance after that.

Essentially it was a clearing operation. They had to keep the authorities in the dark about intentions as far and as long as possible. There were several hours to go before they could move into the next and most important phase.

He had a dozen Skyhawks repositioned to fire obliquely downstream at both banks of the Hudson. Salvos were rationed to three missiles, each time alternately at four and five minutes. The bombardment would continue for another ten hours.

By now the *Carolina* was riding at anchor a little to the Weehauken side of the river, her engines worked at holding her steady against the ebb-tide and in a position that kept her field of fire relative to the Manhattan shore.

Most of his men went below decks to get some sleep.

'What do you think, Major?' Racowiczs was watching through the glasses as a missile exploded against the middle storeys of the Empire State.

'I think they'll keep their heads down till we're ready to move.' That was all.

Benner wanted to know why he was leaving the Furness Withy piers strictly alone. Halliday smiled for the first time that day.

'Because that happens to be our line of advance and retreat and no soldier worth the name cuts off his nose to spite someone else's face.'

He added nothing to the inexplicable so none of those around him rightly understood what he was getting at. But John Halliday looked so calm and imperturbable standing there, not anybody doubted he knew what he was talking about.

One of the ratings came hurrying along laughing fit to bust, wanted to know what they should do with the redundant pilot. 'Man, he's twittering like a budgie with St Vitus!'

'Lock him up for the time being,' Halliday said. 'We can make the dockside without his help.'

The White House switchboard has seventeen trunk lines, a score of female telephonists and a smaller number of men to handle the night work. Daily calls average around six thousand and can easily double that if things are going badly wrong.

The day they killed the Statue of Liberty another ten girls were drafted to dig their sisters out of an avalanche of incoming calls. No figures for these have been released at the time of writing.

All kinds of America had something to say about the situation, would have been flattered by the attention their calls received. The majority of the Press Secretary's staff had orders to monitor and summarize the prevailing mood of the country. Hour by hour it sweated at the mammoth task of reducing reaction to its lowest common denominator.

Foxwell was taking no chances.

Stunned America called.

'My name is Mr Hoober, that's right, would you please tell the President I am overwhelmed by this catastrophe...'

Mystified America dialled.

'Listen lady, you tell Foxwell I pay my taxes and I have a constitutional right to be told *exactly* what's goin' on!'

One of the Four Hundred condescended a word: 'This is Mrs Deidre Geldichabe speaking. Will you tell the dear President our sons are ready to defend our country to the last drop of the people's blood against these traitors. Will you also inform him we are forming a committee to provide relief funds?'

Mortified America chipped in.

'I only want to say, as a member of the silent majority, how much I sympathize with Mr President in his present ordeal which is so much worse than Watergate and I intend to remain in church on my bended knees and pray for God's mercy and his guidance for all Mr President's endeavours in this time of disaster.'

Long distance from San Francisco came the voice of America *sans* illusions: 'Bad trip huh? Like could you please tell me what's the acid this guy Halliday's using? If it ain't State's Secret I could use a couppla tabs.'

There was even a phone phreak who called to sympathize via Moscow.

Foxwell spent most of the early morning with various DD

187

officials, members of the Supreme Court—the four who mattered—Pentagon types and various members of his staff. Winfield called to pledge his unqualified support to any measures the President might deem necessary, as did the Speaker of the House, and there were numerous intriguing calls received between times. For example: the obliging boss of ALO.

'I appreciate your calling, Kelly. Can I count on your members?'

'Solid. We're right behind you, Mr President. You do what you have to. I can guarantee my boys.'

And the man who'd practically swung the vote single-handed to give Foxwell a coveted second term put his head right in the noose Mr President was preparing for him in the Labour Relations Board.

But all that had to do with future job satisfaction. Presently he could see little but grim realities filled no doubt with potential advantages, but tricky from a decision-making point of view.

Caressinger stayed in his tent most of the time, not sulking so much as re-programming his mind to cope with the possibility of a changed relationship.

When Foxwell announced his Press conference for noon without seeking Caressinger's advice as to the wisdom of so doing the good doctor reasoned that having other fish to fry is fine if you are not one of the fish.

Mrs Adams used to air the laundry in the East Room. A great deal else has happened in the intervening years, even Chinese wrestling as Teddy Roosevelt could testify. Now, on rare occasions, the most famous room in the White House is used to wash the grubby linen of the Foxwell Administration. The wheel has turned full circle.

When a President beckons, be he elected or suspected, the world comes running whatever its prejudices. Not that it leaves those behind. The Washington Press corps lugged theirs along as manfully as a platoon humping ammunition carriers through swamp country.

The room was packed ten minutes before the President appeared. The buzz of conversation hit a new note in volume and hysteria. Never had so many journalists been so fretful to get back to a TV set.

The *New York Times* made the only point worth mentioning to the *Post*. 'Observe, Charley, the number of mean-looking itchy-fingered muscle men lining the walls of this delightful boudoir.'

'I've observed,' said the *Post* drily. 'I have also been frisked so thoroughly by those guys I don't know why they don't just lay us on an ironing-board and run a steam-iron over——'

'Sign of the times, friend.'

'Gentlemen,' the pompous parroty voice of the Press Secretary, 'the President of the United States.'

And there he was indeed, striding to the lectern between George and Martha.

'Thanks to the Gemstones,' whispered the Chicago *Examiner* to his neighbour.

'Gentlemen, I've asked you to gather here today so that I may spell out my position and the position of the American people in face of this grave threat to our country.

'I think you know enough by now to appreciate that what we face is a lunatic group of ex-convicts who found their way into the army because things got too hot for them in their home-towns. Two hundred fifty of these men are coloured. I have names of three hundred twenty with a history of disruption from their earliest schooldays. Four hundred plus were in breach of army discipline at one or more periods of their service. The unit in which they last served on combat duty was almost entirely composed of malcontents. These, in essence, are the kind of men we have to deal with.

'There is, in any army, a criminal element which may be sufficiently fragmented for the duration but continues its former violent activities on demobilization. I emphasize I'm talking of a minority.

'In this case, unhappily for the nation, the anti-social element coalesced and operated almost independently of its higher officers through the agency of the one-time major, John Halliday. Circumstances conspired to place this man in an aggressive posture, the consequences of which are tragically obvious.

'Through you I wish to reassure the American people that I will not rest till I have brought this man and his bunch of killers to where they can do no further harm. Until I redeem this pledge I have no other cause.

'You may put your questions.'

The *New York Times* beat the others to the draw. 'Mr President, you say two hundred fifty of these—killers—are coloured. Could you say how many are white?'

As white as Foxwell digesting the subtlety of innuendo. 'About three hundred. I hope you don't think your question was too smart.'

Times looked innocent. 'I had no intention of being smart, Mr President. Just wanted to know how many are involved, that's all.'

His colleagues looked a little more cheerful. Hal never failed to make first base. The New Orleans *Chronicle* felt emboldened to try his hand.

'Mr President, we've had almost six hours of continuous bombardment. How much more life and property has to be destroyed before positive action is taken on this?'

'As far as possible we're persuading all non-essential civilians in the area to move over to the East Side. Members of the National Guard are standing by at their armouries and regular troops will be deployed when needed. But I do not intend to risk the life of a single American in a sustained assault on the *Carolina*.'

'How many *does* he intend to risk?' the Detroit *Examiner* mumbled to the Detroit *Examiner*.

'Isn't that taking a chance, Mr President?' the LA *Times* wondered.

'I don't think so. I would calculate some further damage, but given temporary evacuation of the area, a minimal loss of life.'

'Do you have figures of casualties sustained so far?' the *Christian Science Monitor* enquired.

'The situation is too confused to make reliable estimates meaningful, but I understand the number of injured on the New Jersey shore is around three hundred eighty.'

This stark fact provoked whistles of astonishment and some rapid scribbling.

'Are these acceptable figures, Mr President?' the quiet, serious voice belonged to Jerry Mansholt of the Boston *Herald*, one of the deadliest and most respected figures in American journalism.

The President took the question in his stride. Gave no sign of his true feelings at that moment. 'If you mean, can we rely on them, I can only repeat, these are the figures I've been given. If you intended to imply that they give me some kind of satisfaction then I'll gladly disabuse you of the notion.'

'I think the question is legitimate. As Commander-in-Chief of the US Armed Forces I assume you would take this factor into account whether the action is here or in Vietnam,' Mansholt persisted.

'I'll repeat, for your better understanding, there can be no question of rushing this ship until she has exhausted her missile capabilities. Sooner or later she has to run out of those things. That will be the time to put the cork in the bottle.'

'Isn't this degenerating into the slough of linguistic niceties, Mr President? If the ship had been Vietnamese would you have balanced the probabilities quite so carefully or just blown the ship out of the water?'

A long silence.

'I would remind you that almost two thousand loyal Americans are held hostage on that carrier.'

Mansholt pressed on with Tonkinese resolution. 'As I understand it Halliday has the deck lined with war planes. I don't see why our sophisticated weaponry shouldn't deal with them without endangering the crew members' lives below decks.'

'Are you the military correspondent for your paper?'

'No, I'm not. But one of your military aides is quoted as saying a few "smart" bombs could resolve the problem.'

Foxwell grasped the sides of the lectern, a sign, a betrayal in public, of inner tension. It was the grip of an anarchist, about to loose his hold, activating the bomb he had to throw.

He began quietly enough.

'I have the impression you gentlemen are insufficiently aware of the gravity of this situation. It extends far beyond the graphics we've all seen on television.

'There appears to me to be a common attitude among you, a

determination to interpret this tragedy as some kind of vindication for your corporate antipathy to our involvement in Vietnam, to those charged with handling it.

'I've learned to live with your animosity and I flatter myself I've risen above it at *all* times. If you feel that hostility because I put my country before a bunch of liberal defectives anxious to sell out at any price, if you prefer to echo those who can squeeze virtue out of the actions of traitors, that is your deep misfortune.

'But you had better understand this. When I say I have powers vested in me to take *any* action to destroy, not only the operative philosophers of anarchy, subversion and outright treason, but the philosophy itself, I am not uttering empty threats and I am not confining my strictures to the *Carolina* renegades. My actions will extend throughout society until all negative elements have been eliminated.

'I called this conference for two reasons. To give you the information you require to discharge your professional duties. Second, as you leave, you will be given subpoenas, signed by the Attorney-General and myself requiring you to appear at the Department of Justice for background checks in depth. The penalty for refusal to comply will not be light.

'From now on this country is going to have a clean press, a press it can be proud of, the press it deserves.'

The President, so to speak, dropped his laundry into the spin-dry machine and abruptly vacated the podium, leaving behind a stunned and, what was worse, a defeated silence.

The itchy-fingered creeps lining the walls kept a particular eye on Mansholt.

Zulu was giving Halliday technical aid on the missile situation. By two in the afternoon it became a matter of economics.

'Mr Halliday, I hate to tell you, but we running outta cream soda.'

'Four hours to go, Zulu.'

'Yeah, that's what bothers. Have to slow up the firin' rate some or we don't ain't gonna get there.'

'Any ideas?'

'Well now, I'd say forget the Weehauken shore, ain't nothin' to worry us there—maybe pop off a single every now and then just so they keep their heads down. And why not bring up the miniguns? Man, we can break every window in town that way.'

When the first shells began crashing through the windows of every building within range, including the Empire State, a lot of people died or were injured; spectators who just couldn't believe that this time they were actors.

That's what too much television does for one.

And it was a family size bullet skittering into the spacious office of I. M. Bloomberg that set in motion one of those comic diversions with which Destiny sometimes gets so screwed up from too much laughing.

I. M. Bloomberg, promotionally pronounced I'M Bloomberg, had spent most of the morning in a state of fright for which his surrounding collection of Jasper Johns, de Koonings and Gorkys did positively nothing. He'd had his stainless steel desk moved so that 'Teeth', a giant cast-iron sculpture of teeth by Windi Asshole, stood between him and the window.

Whenever there was a crisis—and what other times were there?—I'M Bloomberg instinctively defended his tangible assets with the maternal zeal of a lady puma. But this was something novel in the chequered career of the man who'd launched the upstage musical of the century, *Jesus—Son of Superstar*, his assets were now protecting *him*. Only a direct hit from a 103mm shell could have got through those teeth.

Thanks to Bloomberg, half of America was humming that catchy tune 'The Twelve Commandments'. Nobody actually liked it but it was compulsive, like an overdose of laxative. And who else but Bloomberg could have persuaded God to write the extras?

The success of *J.C.—Son of Superstar* was obviously comparative. You had to see the competition to find out how Audrey Tawdry they both were. Still and all, no denying Hovis Wesley was the nearest thing to J.C. since the Cancellation of the Second Coming.

The idea for the show and Hovis transpired 'synchronomously' as I'M Bloomberg explained to the bird from

Harper's. Always one to cut his cloth accordingly he told the 'Voice': 'I mean, like when I laid eyes on Hovis I nailed him —what else could I do?'

So Bloomberg, 'the Broadway Guerilla' as he was known in the business, because he was in and out faster than Guevara, and Hovis signed the Covenant for their mutual resurrection and held the feast of their assumptions at Sardi's.

For fourteen months the bearded honeymouth from Alabama had packed 'em to the exits and laid a few in the aisles including half the Season's débutantes who reasoned they must still be intacta theologically and notwithstanding. Bloomberg had a nice little spin-off industry going in religious statuettes of Hovis, that kind of thing.

But now there was a disturbing tendency for audiences to diminish in numbers and enthusiasm. Even the LP, *Hi Folks! I'm Jesus and I'd like Your Vote*, was slipping faster than gravy down the front legs of the league table.

And on top of everything, some crazy loon has to hi-jack the US navy and sail it up the Hudson shooting the crap out of everything in sight. Where was the justice in this world? It only needed one stray missile to enter the foyer of the Marion Ponds Theatre and he'd be back in his Miller Street subsidiary selling dog time to the TV commercials' agencies. True he'd won the Golden Bowl for the best performing pooch of the year but that was no goddam reason why he should have to eat out of it.

All of which is why that cannon shell smashing his plate glass view of the smoky Hudson did more than make Bloomberg duck behind Asshole's 'Teeth'. Shaking like Jello but otherwise unharmed, the crouching impresario had a vision. That's to say, his mind went to work on a promotional exploit that could keep him and Hovis in the religious revival racket for a long time to come. In two minutes flat he had the whole thing worked out to the last detail. (That is the first and only requirement for any 'visitation'.)

From his position on the floor he fumbled for the intercom. 'Miss Mooch, get me Hovis on the line.' 'Mr Bloomberg, they've smashed the windows!' 'Fuck the windows, just call Hovis for me.' 'But Mr Bloomberg, all the lines are jammed, I can't get a call through to anywhere.' 'So grab a cab and get him at the Dakota, he ain't gonna be anywhere but in bed this time of day.' 'But you told him to drop by this afternoon at three, Mr Bloomberg.' 'Then why didn't you say so!'

Half furious, half pleased with himself Bloomberg got off his knees and stared distastefully at 'Teeth'. It had cost him a pretty dollar which accounted for the love-hate relationship and he felt resentful in the knowledge that he was now under some kind of obligation. The damned thing had probably saved his life. There was glass all over the place. The only way he could contain his excitement was painstakingly to pick up all the pieces he could find and drop them in the Golden Bowl.

Ten minutes later Jesus Wesley arrived.

'Hi y'all, Deity, what can I do for you you cain't do for yourself?'

I'M Bloomberg blanched at sight of the beautiful face rising from the purple suit with its flared trouser bottoms. 'For Chrissake do I have to repeat myself endlessly? If you go on screwin' like a rabbit it's "Son of Dracula" or nothin'. And what kind of gear is that for the Messiah to be runnin' around in? Remember what the understudy said, "Blessed is they who got class, for they shall make a killin".'

Hovis looked southern sulky. 'Well now, that ain't nice, Bloo. 'Membered you said it was important so I threw on the first gear I could find and I had no end trouble getting here. Don't you have any conception what's goin' on out there?'

'What more d'you want? I just lost a window, am I supposed to die for my country? I been in the firin' line since ten this morning.'

'Well if you ain't gonna act conformable I'm goin' straight back to my little ol' apartment and you can whistle for me when that ol' curtain goes up tonight.'

'There won't *be* any show tonight, little ol' dumbhead. Didn't you hear Lindsay's latest? All places of entertainment closed till further notice.'

Hovis looked concerned. 'Jeez, Bloo, this must be serious.'

'Serious! Are they celebratin' the Fourth of July on the third of April out there? They're using bullets and rockets and the whole waterfront's on fire.'

'That's what I heard on the detour, but it's unbelievable.'

'Unbelievable!' He must've been so shagged he slept through it. I'M Bloomberg laughed bitterly at his reflection in the steel-topped desk. 'What did you figure all that smoke was—Indian signals?'

Luckily he remembered why he was so anxious for Hovis's company. 'Listen Hovis, I don't know whether this guy Halliday dropped out of heaven or came up the hard way but I've had a visitation tells me whichever way he's in Town is good for business.'

A fresh burst of firing in the not too distance brought Hovis round the desk so they were both staring at 'Teeth'.

'Why don't you get rid of that thing, Bloo?' son of Superstar enquired plaintively.

'Get rid of a denture that saved my life? You've gotta be kidding. Now grab this: while I was on my knees prayin' I had an inspiration. You know why I said to come over in the first place? to tell you I had intimations of fatality, the show is making noises like thrombosis; you may well look the colour of your goddamned suit, Hovis, but that was the situation as of two thirty-seven. So this Halliday then puts a bullet through my window—am I worried?'

'Not if you got insurance, Bloo.'

'Jesus Christ, how did you make it with that brain when he couldn't manage with twelve backers and a bunch of miracles?'

'I had you, Bloo.'

'That's right,' said the mollified one, 'and you should go down on your knees and worship my socks, 'cos I've dreamed up the greatest publicity stunt since Aimee Sempill MacPherson went for a bathe. This is gonna put 'em right back in our pockets.'

And, as though the sun had suddenly appeared, shining on his face alone, I'M Bloomberg told Hovis Christ, Son of Superstar, all about the mysteries involved in raising the dead...

Can anyone believe the earth is so big and fair that the smoke from an industrial stack or the oily pall over a battlefield simply cannot drift across all of it?

Once, a whole island disappeared, torn apart by a volcano. On the other side of the world the tide heard about it, lifted itself a few inches or so, and then subsided. As if nature could shrug indifferently at such catastrophe because that too is part of her being.

But times change. Nature takes note and gives due warning: little man, if I feel like committing a touch of *hara-kiri* once in a while, that's because I'm in control and exercising my right; but you have no control and very little right that I can see.

By a stroke of irony that, or something like it, was what Joe tried to explain as they were returning from their walk on that fateful morning.

They too were nowhere so deep in the outback that the wonders of telecommunication could not bring the smoke from the Hudson River billowing over every habitation in the Five Fingers region.

Harry was waiting for them on the porch. He looked not so cheerful as usual, or his deeper seriousness was that much nearer the surface.

'Have you heard the news?'

Somehow Chuck knew it had to be momentous.

'The *Carolina* arrived in New York Harbour this morning. They've dynamited the Statue of Liberty and they're sailing up the Hudson blasting everything in sight.'

He waited for their reaction, curious to see how they would take it.

Nothing for a while. The sightless eyes studied the scene he'd sketched, seemingly without recognition, then Joe smiled, very gently so as not to offend anyone present. And Chuck, his bearded face heavy with frowning, head inclined as though to catch the familiar sounds of what he too could not see. The frown lifted, and he also smiled, faintly, so as not to disturb sensibilities.

'If you want to see and hear it, they're televising of course. You know where to go.'

One TV set was provided for the orphanage staff and their friends. The children were never allowed to view till they got to sixteen. By then they were too intelligent to be interested.

They were starting in when Joe held back. 'What's your opinion, Harry?'

'All I can say right now is that I understand Major Halliday's message.'

197

'Halliday! I might've known.' Chuck's eyes lit up. 'You remember, Joe? Patmore said they used to fight to get into Halliday's outfit.'

'That's right—what was the message, Harry?'

' "We are bringing Vietnam to the American people." '

The two young veterans not only looked at each other, but they saw each other too. And not even Harry with his deep understanding of the human heart, could have defined their thoughts with certitude.

'OK Ed, let's go through this one more time. You had all these rockets going zoom, zoom, zoom—must've been a kinda nice feeling, huh?'

'I wasn't on the firing detail.'

'Oh that's right, I forgot. Well you must've been doing something while your buddies were loading and firing. Watching the hits? Wondering how many people got killed this or that time? You must've had some thoughts on what was happening.'

'I was asleep.'

Milton looked shocked. 'Asleep! You mean you could sleep through all that? Don't you know thirty-seven hundred civilians died in the rocket attacks alone? Better than six thousand injured—and you slept? Come on, Ed, you can tell me.'

'I tell you I slept. We all did. And I'll tell you why, little man. When we killed or were getting killed, when we were screaming in agony, when thousands died in Hanoi or a couple of kids flew in all directions in Xam Tho—I didn't hear New York was full of insomniacs. Did you lose any sleep? You fucken machine! Hypocrite! Poor Americans! Bleeding to death—I've gotta be sorry because people didn't want to know there were fifty-seven varieties of death? So we showed 'em. They must keep you down a Pentagon sewer, you bastard. You fucken star-striped bastard!'

The colonel sighed, more in sorrow than in anger. 'OK boys, move in, not too hard—then try the number two jacket and let's say, 300 mgm. of thorazine. See you later, Ed.'

I'M Bloomberg had it all worked out in one hour, no more. He fought his way through the telephonic log-jam to reach an aide near the President. The aide, a former showbiz whizz kid, had no difficulty persuading Foxwell this could be a great thing for national morale.

So, armed with presidential approval, Bloomberg gathered up his actors and made his way to the waterfront. CBS got word of what was afoot and gladly sent a mobile TV unit for coverage.

Somehow, Bloomberg had rustled up a coach into which he bundled Hovis Wesley, the All Male Apostles' Choir backing Hovis in the show, and the wardrobe mistress who'd just finished ironing their nightshirts, which was a minor bonus in I'M Bloomberg's plan of campaign.

The cordon of shell-shocked cops barring access to the waterfront from Forty-second to Fifty-first Street stared in red-eyed astonishment when the coach turned out of Tenth Avenue and came to a halt. As a white figure, with a beard and flowing mane, stepped delicately out of the exit door they simply lost all sense of the perils to which they were exposed and let their jaws sag beneath the strain of comprehension.

And what was that large, expensively dressed character with a head of skin glistening in the heat *doing* handing out a whole bunch of weirdies wearing sandals and night-dresses down to their ankles?

A beefy-looking sergeant glanced about him for moral support then moved slowly over to the group still clustering around the coach. The wardrobe mistress was fluttering from one to another with brush and comb, anxiously putting the finishing touches to a lot of hair.

Sergeant Murphy accosted Jesus Christ. 'Hallo, gay eyes. Ain't you supposed to be over at the Park-Miller?'

Hovis simpered and flashed his eyes prettily. 'Except ye be born again, wise guy, ye ain't no better'n hogshit.'

Murphy opened his mouth and shut it again. 'What's goin' on around here? What's this then, feller? Benefit night for a dikes' rap session? Now you just turn around and get the hell outta——'

'Not so fast, officer.' Bloomberg knew how to handle opposition. He'd been handling it all his life. 'We got special presidential permission to be right here. Don't you know who you're talking to?'

'Yeah! I'm talkin' to some punk who's askin' for his ass to get kicked if he don't——'

'This is Jesus Christ, Son of Superstar.'

Which dropped Murphy in his tracks better than one out of a .45. He looked from Hovis to the choir through to Bloomberg and returned in that order. From his eye's corner he could see his men were watching with interest. Something had to be said.

'Is that so? Well I'm Judas, and any time now I'm gonna betray the whole bunch of you to the lock-up if you ain't back in that bus in one minute, right?'

There was little of versicles and responses in the exchange. Both men were bawling above the wail of sirens, the shouts of nearby fire-fighters and the every now and then bursts of gun-fire. It looked as though Murphy might win the slanging match till the CBS unit came screeching to a skiddy stop on the wet road. The driver, young, unconcerned and chewing gum so it made your jaws ache to watch him, leaned out of his window.

'CBS, fellers, where's the action?'

Bloomberg looked scared but triumphant. More and more he regretted not bringing 'Teeth'. Things looked decidedly murky at the bottom of Forty-second.

Murphy hesitated, but as a burning apartment house close to the A shelter slowly collapsed, the mass of blazing wreckage spilling into the street, he gave in. There was plenty else to do. And if a bunch of kooks were dying to get killed that was their cold potatoes.

'I'll see you guys in the ice-house,' he said, turning away in disgust.

Between Forty-second and Fifty-first was one of the worst hit areas. Fires were out of control and moving inland towards Eleventh Avenue. If people were still trapped in the run-down apartment houses no-one would know about it till long after. In a real sense the CBS van and the coach following were running the gauntlet.

Twelfth Avenue was impassable; they tried a parallel up

Eleventh as far as de Witt Clinton Park and found breathing a little easier along Fifty-first. Turning back on themselves they discovered Twelfth was hardly damaged for a hundred yards back to the main holocaust. The Elevated on their right was smashed and cars were strewn about like Titans' litter, but somehow they managed to reach the first undamaged pier-head jutting into the Hudson. This belonged to the NY Sanitation Department and for some reason Bloomberg accepted it as an omen.

A few of the GIs were leaning over the ship's side on the open lower deck. They were simply waiting for phase two rather than watching the closing stages of phase one.

'Hey!' said one, peering through the smoke haze, 'you guys see what I see?'

Difficult not to. The *Carolina* had swung with the incoming tide to within fifty yards of the Manhattan shore.

'Jeez!' a second man exclaimed. 'The sanitation squad. They got new uniforms.'

'Maybe they aim to clean us up.'

'Somebody ought to tell the major. It could be a truce party,' the first soldier opined.

'Why would they be wearing nightshirts?' a fourth man wanted to know.

'Never mind, the CBS is trainin' cameras. I'll go tell the major.'

But Halliday and the former officers were already giving the shore party some scrutiny.

Racowiczs, leaning against the fuselage of one plane, was lost in amusement. 'What oh what do we have here?'

Jesse Stoker grinned. 'My guess is a Republican convention—man, they sure could use one.'

'I think,' said Halliday slowly, 'I think we are at the receiving end of a commercial.'

'Detergents,' Benner suggested.

'Wait a minute.' Thompson screwed up his eyes to see better. 'They're unfurling a banner—"Jesus—Son of Superstar".'

'No kidding! I watched it in Saigon till someone threw the TV out the window.' It came to Jesse in a flash. 'Oh now I remember, it was me.'

'Entertainment, at a time like this.' Racowiczs saw reason to shake his head.

'Or a slight case of conversion,' Jesse decided. 'As a good Beale Street Baptist I owe it to myself to duck.'

More men drifted up as the news spread. This sleazy phenomenon had to be seen. And, as the CBS men rolled their KCR cameras, highly amplified music went booming across the river.

Cut to the Twelve Apostles mouthing the words.

> Hey-hey-hey! He's with you all the way!
> Get down upon your knees ma friends and pray-
>   pray-pray!
> If you wanna go to heaven got no money for the
>   fare,
> Just climb upon his shoulders and he will carry
>   you there.
> Oh come, oh come, oh come to Jesus now!
> Jacey climbed a mountain—lookin' for the Lawd
> Cried 'Daddy, are you sure I'm doin' right by the
>   Word?'
> 'Doubt not, kid' The Lawd replied.
> 'Now this is gonna kill ya
> But it's time you died.'

Yay-yay-yay and ten more putrefuctup verses in this strain, all to the big beat thumping into the smoky void like a touch of wanker's doom. An incredible episode seen by millions, and if nobody believes *schmalz* is a staple of Mr Average's diet, then nobody is aware of the many thousand letters and phone calls received by CBS and the major newspaper offices next day from all parts of the sub-continent.

A museum devoted to the Day is already blue-printed and will contain the following letter, framed, from Mrs Sarah Ruckett of Kale County, Missouri to the Ed. *Missouri Examiner*.

Dear Editor, I felt I just had to write and say how beautiful that appeal by Christianity was to an undeserving bunch of murderers. I cannot believe they are Americans. And if I had not seen dear Hovis Wesley with my own eyes, begging those horrible men to stop their insanity, I would no longer believe in God. My faith was stretched to breaking point, but after what he did I know there has to be someone. It was so beautiful—just like the Bible—that heavenly music rising to the 'empyrean' (Tennyson) out of the smoke and all.

Jesus may be dead—but he will rise again and again while there is evil in this world and as long as there are good American boys like Hovis to take his place when 'he is gone where no-one can find him' (Otis Lamotte 1876).

Naturally, no-one mentioned the small miracle. When *Carolina* loosed off a single rocket it so unnerved the Apostles their mouths froze into a dozen round Os and the voices went on singing. That is what is known as a technological miracle.

Pan slowly across the *Carolina*, just to see how she's taking it, zoom into group on flight deck. That could be Halliday standing a little ahead of the others.

Mix to KCR Two as Hovis walks forward, microphone in hand. Check volume, keep strings playing BG.

Walk Number One Camera for CU Hovis.

Hovis raises his arms in big come-to-me gesture. Hold it.

Cut to *Carolina*.

Superimpose Hovis. Beautiful!

Fade *Carolina*. Volume adjustment.

Cue Hovis.

'Oh my brothers! I come to thee in peace...'

'He must think we're fucken Indians,' said soldier one to soldier two, who spits disgustedly into the harbour.

'...Whyfore dost thou bear arms against thy people? We are not strangers to ye. What are ye to us if not friends, Americans, countrymen! Give ear to what I have to say. Caesar is merciful to those who repent...'

'Who wrote this shit?' the CBS driver demanded.

'I did so why don't you just go scratch yourself,' I'M Bloomberg hissed. After that last rocket he was looking very pale and uninteresting.

'We are all your brothers even as the lilies in the field;

203

surrender yourselves to your Friend and ma Friend and he will grant you everlasting forgiveness...'

'And there, gentlemen,' said Halliday, his glasses still trained on the honeymouth from Alabama, 'you have in microcosm what threatens to make America no more than a rotten apple. Life is one big soap opera, Vietnam was a soap opera, Christianity is a soap opera.'

'It's all in the mind,' Racowiczs suggested.

'No, that's the pity of it, it's all in the eye of the camera, so you can believe without believing. I guess it's time to get rid of that illusion. Ed.'

Roberts handed the M16 to Halliday who sighted very, very carefully.

'...Now why don't you boys join with me in the Lord's Prayer? Nothin' like the old LP for makin' you feel knee-hi to Heaven.'

Halliday squeezed the trigger, gently.

'My father which art——'

And Jesus Wesley was dead before he hit the water, yea verily, a bullet clean through the heart.

'Christ!' said Bloomberg, then turned and ran as though 'Teeth' had animated suddenly to pursue him with evil intentions. It's possible I'M Bloomberg is still running. But that also he is accustomed to.

To do him justice, everybody else ran in harness, especially as Halliday shot the hand-camera from one man's grip.

Horrified America saw it played to the end thanks to cameraman two who kept his KRC going right through, but the men on the *Carolina* stared impassively at the body of Hovis Wesley bumping gently against the pier blocks.

'Rapid,' said soldier one.

'What did he expect—crucifixion?' soldier two wondered.

It was time to go below and get kitted up.

At 16.35 a napalm rocket hit the Bryant Park area at the Fifth Avenue intersection.

At 16.36 a hand reached into a black-velvet window at Tiffany's and removed six grammes of moon rock set in a platinum band. Asking price $250,000.

By 17.00 approximately six thousand National Guardsmen were assembled on the West Side of Central Park. Two thousand men of the Third air cavalry were on their way from Montgomery.

Precisely at 17.30 the *Carolina* began to edge towards the Furness Withy Line's piers.

The former officers watched and waited. There were no orders to give. Every man knew what he had to do.

Ten soldiers with portable acetylene cutting gear were ready to jump ashore. Behind them, two hundred GIs in full combat gear would disembark and fan out quick as silver, creating a defensive perimeter while the rest unloaded supplies.

The last salvos of rockets were touched off to keep the opposition quiet.

Halliday pointed a little to his left. 'Now d'you see why we left that area alone?'

'Makes it easier to get ashore,' Benner decided.

Halliday smiled. 'Take another look.'

Comprehension dawned. The simplicity of it was breathtaking, had been staring them in the face all that time. Who else but Halliday could find miracles and transform them into utilities?

'Solid,' Racowiczs' summary of their satisfaction.

'If that don't beat everything,' Jesse admitted.

At which point the *Carolina* crashed horrendously into Consolidated Edison's wharf and sideways on to the pier.

Like a giant step sideways for mankind—some of it.

'This is Tom Lester reporting for CBS New York City, at eighteen hundred hours.

'We continue our longest newscast of all time with up-dated details of what is already being referred to as America's worst nightmare.

'As the shadows lengthen the pall of smoke from Manhattan spreads and lies heavy over this stricken city. Fires started by missiles from berserking carrier *Carolina* still rage. Pockets of death and destruction are everywhere.

'Hardly one skyscraper in the line of fire escapes damage, ships are blazing on both shores of the Hudson. Casualties increase by the hour, not least because of influxing sightseers anxious to see with their own eyes what they no longer believe on their TV screens. Thousands are roaming the streets as though it was some kind of Roman holiday decreed by Nero himself. This in spite of Mayor Lindsay's repeated appeals to evacuate or stay home.

'All access to the Island is barred. We hear one operator from Atlantic City was turned back with six of his coaches packed with rubbernecks.

'Late this afternoon the President issued a special decree declaring rampaging Halliday and his confederates outlawed. This gives the whole civilian population power of life and death over these men.

'Meantime the net draws tighter; troops pour in from all sources. Police drafts are being rushed from many parts of New York State and New Jersey. Indications are that an assault will be mounted soon after dark.

'Hospitals report they can no longer deal with the increasing number of injured. Many of these are being shipped across the East River to hospitals in Queens and Brooklyn.

'A list of temporary posts for blood donors and volunteers to transport the injured will be given by all radio and TV stations every fifteen minutes.

'World reaction continues and is unvarying. "Horrifying", to quote France's President Pompidou. "Interesting but disturbing", from Communist leader Brezhnev. Prime Minister Heath reports "We must all look to our defences". The Queen of England sends a message of sympathy. In Tokyo Mr Tanaka speculated on the possibility this could be the first shot in a new trade war. Unconfirmed reports from Pekin suggest Chairman Mao is having second thoughts on the wisdom of preaching peoples' revolutions.

'Later bulletins will report on further world reaction, but in President Foxwell's words—this is America's own tragedy.

'The attack on financial nerve-centre, Wall Street, is reflected in world money marts. All indices show a downcurve in anticipation of protectionist measures believed inevitable in the post-crisis period. The dollar showed further weakness against most foreign currencies.

'One hundred fifty picked FBI agents are standing by to reinforce police cordons on the West Side where *Carolina* is presently holed up.

'Late news: the *Carolina* has moved in from her mid-stream position to the Transatlantic Terminal. What Halliday intends to do is anybody's guess, but time must surely be running out towards the hour of retribution.

'As darkness begins to fall over the burning city the whole world watches and wonders: what now?'

For ten years Foxwell stood in the ante-room, his attention welded to the TV which showed the announcer against a constantly changing background of filmed devastation.

A lonely, brooding figure, this President, flanked by aides who hardly dared breathe without a nod or some other sign for permission. A kind of updated Napoleon who had just lost Moscow and now watched from afar as it burned while his generals waited and remembered what they'd heard of Russian winters.

'Muntsch!'

The first of Foxwell's surviving top dogs stepped forward with Teutonic precision. Blue eyes, a blond rinse crew cut plus a lot of spring in his step made nonsense of Muntsch's fifty years. An interior sprung mind had kept him bounding up ladders and over obstacles since his Harvard days. In fact the two men had leaped around in politics for so long together they were practically interchangeable.

Of all the wheeler-dealers Muntsch was the veriest. For Foxwell he hired and fired, for Foxwell he intrigued and engineered, for Foxwell he penetrated, insinuated, incriminated; for himself, he licked the blood that dripped from the red meat of power.

When they conversed together in low tones no-one within hearing dared to eavesdrop.

'Mr President?'

'I want the decree of outlawry qualified. Whatever happens I want Halliday alive, you understand?'

Muntsch was a man who let his mind do his smiling for him. 'I understand, Mr President.'

'I'm depending on you to handle this. Don't bother about the FBI, I'll deal with that aspect.'

'Right.'

'Helderman!'

The other man moved up to take Muntsch's place. It was like watching a flight of upstart crows peeling off to attack an eagle.

'Mr President?'

'Get me Meyerbeer. I want him here in five minutes but not with a flourish of trumpets.'

'Very good, Mr President.' The rather more portly, almost comfortable, but not comforting, figure of his second oldest crony in deep waters went waddling about his errand with the assurance of one who never fails to get what someone else wants.

It happened in a nick of time. For some purgatorial moments he was, unusually, alone in the ante-room. In which period a still picture of the most hated man in America was flashed on the screen and Foxwell found himself trapped in that room with an illusion, while the newscaster babbled out uncomprehended facts freshly dug up by news agencies.

Something desperate happened in Foxwell's mind, something that had to do with a procession of ghosts from then till now. The statesmanlike calm claimed for him by his partisans appeared for what it was—a figment of PR imagination.

He stared at the face he most feared, striving to hold back blind forces seething within until the strain grew unbearable and, succumbing to the violence of the hour, he stepped forward and drove his fist into the face that was not.

Sobered a little by the pain of glass fragments driven into his knuckles he stared, almost stupidly, at the blood ...

'You ought to eat something.'

He swung round, wide-eyed with fear that someone, anyone, even or especially his own wife, should catch sight of his defencelessness at last.

For a long time they gazed at each other over the banquet tables, the Convention triumphs, the medal-giving ceremonies, the Inaugurals ... while he struggled to formulate a presidential reply.

'I'll have something in my office later. A formal dinner would be out of place tonight.'

'Yes, of course. I'll have Doctor Moxon come by and fix your hand.'

'Yes, thank you.'

'You gotta hand it to him,' said Soup Kemble, 'he knows what's good for the troops.' Rare praise from one of the toughest one-time NCOs in the US army. One of the smartest too. He wasn't tagged 'Soup' for nothing.

Once, when his platoon got itself bunkered near An Loc Fire Base, Kemble ran back to a supply dump, grabbed a carton of tins and returned to lob them at the Vietcong who were so puzzled they hauled off. The story spread as far as Japan how Kemble, short on grenades and ammunition had hurled cans of soup across the credibility gap.

Three months later he lost a stripe and three teeth in a bad brawl back at Khay Son's sergeants' mess.

As to the present. Whitney Fletcher was disposed to agree. 'You can't fault him on tactics—I've tried.'

Gribble looked happy as if nothing mattered anymore. 'I'm sure glad we're moving. My ass is still vibrating from those damned engines.'

'Yeah,' Soup was unhitching his M16. 'Now I know why all sailors are bananas. There goes the gangway. Safety catches off, fellers, I'll race you to America.'

Loaded like camels, the first two hundred invaders surged ashore, stumbled down the gangway, slipped down by a score of ropes, clawed their way down landing nets and fanned out to their defensive positions at the double while the detail with cutting equipment went to work on the dockside.

They met with no resistance.

The reasons for everyone's admiration were parked right there on Furness Withy's territory and in the street leading to it.

Eight giant Sea-Land container trucks and four of a smaller type were lined up ready to take loads from abandoned ships nearby. Halliday had solved his transport problem at a stroke.

The authorities never dreamed he meant to go anywhere.

They reasoned, disastrously, that he would put himself into a defensive posture from which they could dislodge him by attrition, starvation and sheer disenchantment with Fortune turned fickle. But Pentagonic jargon never was a substitute for the North Vietnamese philosophy of get up and go when all things are at hand to make the impossible possible.

Next to the Furness Withy piers was the New York sanitation terminal harbouring a couple of solid steel garbage trucks. He commandeered these too. Everything was grist to Halliday's mill.

While the ten cutters worked at shearing holes for gun-ports, front, back and sides of these vehicles, the rest of the men began unloading equipment, explosives, arms and ammuntion on to the quayside. Two small squads kept an eye on the unfriendly members of the crew, and a few mechanics did some work on the trucks' engines. A break-down in any one of them could ruin the plan.

Halliday was so occupied at this stage he almost forgot the men who'd made that day a lot more possible than it might have been; the coloured ratings who'd used up a lot of their black power to get those Skyhawks jacked up to the right elevation, taught his men to fire the missiles, loaded and re-loaded like cotton-balers on contract, had, in many other ways, committed themselves to the cause.

But, as he turned from shouting some advice to Racowiczs on the bustling pier Halliday noticed Franklin's brother, Zulu, standing on the lee of a discarded Skyhawk, gazing down at the activity below.

A forlorn aspect that marks the gregarious man caught out alone.

In the nature of things Halliday was bound to remember just then how much he owed Zulu and the others.

The seaman watched him approaching.

'All set to go, man?'

'A little business to finish first. Zulu, I appreciate it—we all do.'

'Wasn't nothin' man, we was glad to help out.'

'Why not jump ship while you can—just melt into the crowd?'

The negro looked contemptuous. 'Run? You know better'n that. They ain't ignorant when it comes to lookin' for people.' Zulu sketched the familiar salute. 'Black Power, man, that means runnin' ain't allowed outside the Olympics, right?'

'It's a good way of living to fight another day.'

'You just ain't cognisant 'bout the facts of life, Major. America's the land of opportunity, right? OK we got one opportunity—that's to die—and everyone gonna make sure we get it. But it takes time, man—*time*. Like it took time with the Indians.'

'Genocide?'

'Naw, tha's old crap. Ecocide, amigo. You know the logical conclusion of economy? From makin' do with less to makin' do with nothin'. You starve a man to death of all the things he needs: health, good grits, education, job satisfaction—you name it. That ain't murder, man, that's economy. Ask Foxwell, ask the Senate committees waggin' their asses when he barks.'

Halliday didn't have to think long. The decision wasn't that hard to make. 'How many of you?'

'In the deal? Better than two hundred, like I told you.'

'Grab yourselves guns and join us.'

That answering smile was no better than a facial drawl. 'Now you're puttin' me on, man.'

'I mean it.'

'I was sure hoping you didn't—tha's the trouble with honkies. You gotta sweat sympathy like I put sugar on ma grapefruit. We're rap with what you're doin' right? So no feelings. How d'you do what you're doin' *and* cry in your beer—did the cryin' first, right? So thanks but no thanks, Major. We got our own plans.'

'OK Zulu, tell the boys for me.'

'Sure.'

The last of the men were coming up from below decks. Among them Marshall and Extra carrying the children.

'Hey Marsh!' Zulu dug into his pocket, 'I saved these for the kids.' He produced a couple of crumpled Hershey bars and handed them to Extra.

Marshall nodded and grinned. 'Always thought you dipped your candy in acid, Zulu,' he confided.

Franklin's brother laughed like a gale but some thought

had him looking serious all suddenly. 'Take care of the kids, man.'

As they nodded and started down the gangway, Halliday and Zulu shook hands, and it seemed as though the rest might be silence, except the coloured man remembered what he most wanted to forget.

'Major!'

Halliday turned.

'Don' pay no mind to what I said 'bout honkies. Like I mean, I gotta admit, they's honkies and honkies.'

The major smiled enough to show he understood and went his way. One thing he could count on. His rear was secure.

Chuck, standing at the window, watched the children playing down below. He was thinking that's the way it always should be: laughter and happiness on green grass, because no-one, but no-one lets it last too long. Get up and go kids, eat up your education or you won't grow prosperous, and if you all do right by me—teacher, corporation president, Uncle Sam, governor, senator, representative, Flag, President—I got a nice little war brewin' up somewhere just for you to go and indicate your gratitude to all of us, I mean, to your country ... he felt the non-existent left hand bunching into a fist the way it used to when he was a kid, to keep from crying. Your country ... oh my country ...

Joe stood back of him in the TV room—the set was switched off. He just waited, head tilted slightly as though trying to hear what was going through Chuck's mind.

'I'm leaving a few things, Joe. Ain't gonna need 'em.'

'Sure. Anything you say.'

'I—I want you to promise me something if you can.' The one-armed veteran turned to face his friend. 'Don't ever leave this place, Joe. Stay with it. Harry tells me you could be assistant warden one day if you wanted ...'

'You make it sound important.'

'It's important. I don't have time to tell you why. I'm not even sure I know well enough to put words to it. But if you really know something you don't have to scratch around for explanations.'

A shadow rippled Joe's surface cheerfulness. 'Well, I suppose I don't have much choice at that.'

'You've got a choice. Stay or leave—just stay is all I'm saying.'

'OK, OK, man. When it comes to it I...' but one thought inevitably leads to another of the same kind. 'What are you going to do?'

'Do? You mean everybody has a future? OK, me I'm heading for New York.'

'New York! Are you crazy? You could get yourself killed.'

'I hear tell there's worse things.'

'But why?'

Chuck turned away. 'Just a feeling—that I ought to be there with 'em.'

'Chuck, you're a one-armed veteran, what the hell good can you do for them?'

'Why does everything need an explanation, let 'em know we're with 'em all the way, that's the least I can do ain't it?'

Joe sensed the feverish excitement, wisely left it at that.

They said their goodbyes and Harry drove Chuck to the nearest town where he could make a connection with the bus to New York.

One of the deeper meanings of friendship is perfect understanding that you're parting for the last time.

Meyerbeer was there on the deadline, his favourite habitat.

There are those in the CIA who do their job because they love America. Meyerbeer, deputy director of planning, was one of the few people who did what he had to do because what else is left to a psychopath?

Not that he pulled a trigger on anyone, though he'd done his share in the Dulles days; but he enjoyed the prospect of lousing up someone's life for its own beautiful sake—think of Torquemada crossed with a practical joker.

His was not called the Department of Dirty Tricks for nothing. With which some very fancy personalities have been involved, because of which some very fancy reputations lie deep frozen in the morgue.

But nowadays the grip seemed to be loosening. In spite of doing a job on the New Orleans assassination 'Plot', he'd made such a hash of the Chilean adventure, not to mention his piece of the Watergate affair that this surely must be his last chance.

Groomed, manicured and elegantly tailored, Meyerbeer could have passed for a British diplomat—exuded that air of absolute self-confidence not even his last two boobs could shake, much less efface. He even managed a smile as he entered the President's office; but it didn't last.

'Sit down, Meyerbeer.' The President, grim-faced, kept his eyes locked on to his satellite. The only man who could. Anyone who stared like that had to know all about Meyerbeer and they were dead. But not all Presidents or aspirants are Foxwells.

'What I have in mind admits of no mistake. This isn't a banana State fry-up or shaking the cap and bells under McGovern's nose. This has to do with retrieving our position—with our survival.

'Quite simply I want Halliday alive, the rest is being taken care of. Halliday must not die. I've given orders to that effect. The problem is—if he lives he can escape. There are plenty of cheapskate countries only too happy to give him asylum. Your job is to apprehend him by any and every means. Do you understand?'

'Yes I do, Mr President. Of course I would have to exceed my powers——'

'This is your authority.'

Foxwell pushed a signed sheet of paper across the desk. Meyerbeer noted that its contents gave him equal powers with the President before folding it slowly and putting it in an inside pocket.

'Is that all, sir?'

'No, I want your department to start work immediately, to formulate a background proving that Halliday is not only a Communist but a Russian.'

Meyerbeer swallowed his astonishment as best he could. Christ! Why wasn't Foxwell running his department?

'That—won't be easy, Mr President.'

'It'll be a lot easier than accepting an American could do this to America. Do you have any questions?'

'Er—no, Mr President.'
Somehow, Meyerbeer left the room.

'CBS news service brings you on-the-spot coverage from Mike Randall positioned on Forty-second and Tenth—Mike?'

'We've got action down here. Latest information shows five hundred GIs in full combat gear have debouched from the *Carolina*—we still have no word of the crew.

'It's an incredible scene here on Forty-second, duplicated on every approach to the waterfront. Everywhere I look there are regular units; National Guardsmen and a few police—for once the police are outnumbered. All this against a background of fire and devastation, a miniature picture of total war. Four ton trucks are pulling in close by as I speak. Scores of helmeted troops from the Sixth Armoured Cavalry are jumping down, you can hear the scrunch of heavy boots landing on the glass scattered everywhere.

'These men look tough and they mean business.

'Any time now they must be going in for the final kill and ... there's a lot of noise and confusion ahead of me as I look down on Forty-second Street, men are running towards us but I can't tell if ... there's a tremendous outbreak of gun-fire. Someone's yelling—take cover! Men are falling, you can hear them—we have continuous machine-gun fire and—my God! bullets are zipping into everything, men are being cut down all over and ...'

Mike Randall hadn't been hit. He'd tailed off because he just couldn't believe his eyes. Nor could the men who survived the onslaught. Those who had the nous to throw themselves behind the army vehicles were lucky, those who flattened anywhere were casualties.

This was Halliday's two pronged attack which, for timing, for perfect directional thrust, still has army tacticians brooding over the beauty of it.

His forward observers in the high deserted buildings flanking the elevated highway, could see the opposition clearly. They watched with open-mouthed wonder as the US army made the stupidest mistake possible, deploying on mainstreet intersections for everyone to see. In urban warfare side streets are the equivalent of communications and supply trenches and they feed men into position unseen.

Naturally when two garbage trucks roared at them from the river-side the Forty-second Street details were astonished, therefore confused and so, ready to panic. Likewise the army post at Thirty-fourth, which just refused to believe an attack would develop from that far east. It was an inferno down there and in fact the troops were hampered by fire-fighters even as high as Tenth.

Like armoured carriers the garbage trucks smashed their way through with guns blazing from every port.

The heavy MGs above the drivers' cabs did the worst execution. Nothing could stand up and live against their fire-power and all units in the two areas took one hundred eighty-three killed and wounded.

If the general in overall command had kept his head, drawing in enough troops to contain and counter-attack he might have regained the initiative. Might, if the link in communications hadn't been shot to pieces; might if the survivors hadn't been backing off from a last volley of CS gas grenades. In fact it was easier than picking cranberries in the New Jersey bogs.

Truck one arrowed towards the Grand Central Terminal below Pan Am. Truck two hit Broadway at the same time, turned left into the Avenue of the Americas and screeched to a halt in Greeley Square. Both areas seemed miraculously deserted, but the 'miracle' was a simple phone call made by Able Thompson from a deserted café on Twelfth Avenue. Police had closed the subways and station concourse an hour before on his advice that bombs had been planted. Pan Am and a few other buildings in the vicinities had been cleared.

So there were police, a few troops but no civilians in these places ...

Once again the general blundered. A platoon RTO at Macey's called HQ in Central Park to let him know what was happening. 'At least two platoons in a garbage truck, sir!' The four star didn't believe it because he wasn't smart enough to know that Mars is a god and to the gods all things are possible. That little miscalculation cost him ten minutes and gained Halliday's men the palm for audacity.

Six men stayed up top to give covering fire, the rest carried all the explosive packs they could handle and went straight down to the subway concourse. Each team had a watchdog with his M16 on automatic.

They immediately ran into a score of cops and some railway-men.

'Take your choice,' the point yelled. 'No time to argue; either get the hell out or be cut down!'

A few hands twitched, but a glance at those bearded and diabolically determined faces tipped the balance in favour of survival. .45s were no use against that kind of fire-power. None of them, then or later, doubted they'd have died if just one man had done something stupid.

The point watched them disappear up the stairway.

'OK fellers, let's go.'

To their right and overhead, the gas mains, electricity cables and steam pipes under Broadway. They placed the dynamite and gave it a fifteen minute fuse.

Back across the concourse, left and down a broad flight of steps to the Hudson tubes. More explosives packed against the ceiling above which a whole complex of electricity cables and switch-boxes, relay points and telephone cables. They gave it a five minute fuse.

Then up and out, back into the garbage truck and they were ferried a block away to Thirty-fourth Street close to the Sheraton-Atlantic Hotel. More trips to the subway with bigger hauls of explosives. Two journeys by each man put nearly a thousand pounds of material under the biggest power and light complex of all. The timing device was set for five minutes.

On the way out they met with some opposition. Personnel containers were coming hell for leather up Thirty-fourth Street summoned presumably by the refugees let out of the Thirty-second Street subway.

'OK troops, I'll handle it, you get back in the truck.'

As though he was out for some casual window shopping Soup Kemble moved to the middle of the street and without shift-ing the gum from one side of his mouth to the other he eased back the trigger, firing from the hip.

The short burst made icing sugar of the first personnel

carrier's windscreen and did the driver's face no great good. He swerved at sixty, mounted the sidewalk and smashed into the elegant frontage of the Sheraton. It left the twenty-five passengers in no shape to continue the struggle. The second PC, travelling at speed, tried to avoid hitting the first, got tangled with a parked car and shot rapidly across the street pitching on its side only yards from where Kemble was watching with a critic's eye.

The third and last truck acted a little smarter. It slowed at sight of the double disaster and the men began tumbling out in approved army fashion.

The nonchalant Kemble took a pin from the grenade in his webbing, *then* unhooked, then hurled it before hitting the ground himself. The explosion took the engine and triggered off the gas. He fired a short burst from where he lay, then, figuring it was time to go, leapt up and scampered back to where his comrades waited in the city truck.

'Plush,' Gribble confided.

Kemble disagreed. 'Those guys must've trained in night-school. I wouldn't have 'em in my army.'

The first explosion came ten seconds later followed by another—soon after, the thousand pound concentration blew beneath Thirty-fourth Street and plunged most of Manhattan in darkness.

In fact it was the biggest compound fracture New York had suffered since Wall Street crashed into the 'thirties.

Gimbel's frontage collapsed into the enormous crater and Greeley fell off his chair.

A city without power and communications is defenceless; an army, dependent on these things, is powerless.

But Halliday and his men were used to fighting in darkness, their RTs shot to pieces, the RTOs dead or dying. So number one group at the Pan Am reservation was not too worried, even though it was being hit by two companies and a group of FBI men set to guard the terminal.

It should have been a little more difficult than Thirty-fourth Street. Rows of army trucks were double parked to screen the now deserted Pan Am building.

Five hundred men were drawn up in defensive posture behind this barricade. It looked good but Halliday's men wondered how anyone could do something so stupid. They were blocking the entrance very nicely, right; but they also stood in the way of their own defence. And the truck drivers were still sitting in their cabs.

Broken Cloud and four other men ejected from their battlewagon and while the rest gave covering fire they ran a parallel line tossing W.Ps and regular grenades at the parked trucks till the whole double column was blazing from end to end. And why didn't they get hit by bullets or fragments of metal as some of the lorries blew apart? Because they used the line of cars parked on the other side of Forty-second as shields, dodging from one to the next, and that, General Cumberland, sir, is what is known as using local conditions to achieve an objective.

Faced with a blazing wall of fire the troops panicked. Instead of retreating into Pan Am itself, or even to the Grand Central Concourse, they streamed out at each end where they were cut down by the waiting men who sadly shook their heads. Like I mean, if you gonna defend America, you better do it with hearts *and* minds, man.

Twenty men humped forty pound packs of napalm and explosives *twice* through a side entrance opposite the Biltmore. They packed it into elevators and sent them up with four EODs to the Tenth Floor—alight here for the Savings Bank Life Insurance Fund. They set a five minute fuse and hopped into another lift going down. Meantime the others fanned through shops, restaurants and offices at street level napalming everything in sight. By the time the ordnance men stepped out of the lift, they'd finished.

One final burst of fire at the elegant lobby and they were out.

'Some Zippo,' a voice yelled as they hurled themselves into the garbage truck.

'Yeah!' said another briefly looking back at the flames already cracking the windows for escape, 'those places light up easier'n a Vietnamese hooch.'

It wanted four minutes to fall-down.

But they hadn't finished yet.

As the first city lights went they turned out of Forty-second into Fifth Avenue and headed for St Patrick's Cathedral.

'It belongs,' said Halliday during one of the *Carolina* sessions, 'to a man in funny clothes called a door-hinge, which is English for cardinal. This door-hinge has stated that the Vietnam war was a beautiful war, was a holy war. He has blessed the men who bombed the Vietnamese and told them "You are doing God's work". OK. If I misunderstand Christianity I apologize to his eminence the rusted door-hinge; but at school they told me to love my neighbour, they didn't say anything about loving him to death.

'It's not difficult to see why this holy mandrake had orgasms at the mention of Vietnam. It's one of his bastions. Every good, middle-class Vietnamese is Catholic so naturally papal business doctrine requires that every overseas investment be protected to the last drop of someone else's blood. This is the essence of a message conveyed from Rome to the then President who promptly escalated the war.

'Now let's be clear whom we're talking of. This door-hinge, drooling at the mouth about what we should be doing to human beings in a distant country, was, at the same time, christening in St Patrick's Cathedral the grandchild of none other than Kit "Tablet" dePressant.

'Of all people. Kit dePressant—the man who owns a piece of some of the best toupees in show-business, the man who said "I could buy New York if Lindsay didn't keep losin' the title deeds", the man who sends skin-divers to the bottom of the East River to anchor plastic wreaths over his more devout victims, the man who spends an hour a day in a St Patrick's confessional and one day a week hearing confessions in a blood spattered cellar, the man who's received by the Pope, the man who massacred a whole family in the Italian quarter because it got about poppa was saying "Kit's Evil".

'Evil! We've been fighting this stinking war so men like dePressant can stand up and say "This is my country, *mine*! And I got a gun to prove it. I got lieutenants, I got the Police Department, I got the attorneys, I even got Holy Pop *and* Junior on my side—punks!"

'DePressant, and men like him, bend a knee to their biggest alibi in St Patrick's and call it worship. It's a nose-running joke that ran too long. So we're going to hit St Patrick's because it's

220

part of a bad trip, part of America's sickness. We can't abolish it, but by God's indifference we can point the accusing finger.'*

There were just a few devouts kneeling before their pop saints in the candle-lit cathedral, praying God to lift his curse on their poor country. Three or four priests were chatting inside the entrance when the group burst in.

Smiles changed to expressions of astonishment shading rapidly into outrage as the tiger suits surged forward lugging explosives, napalm and heaven knows what intentions.

'What is this?' one of the priests stammered.

'Cosa Nostra, Jack. We're having a benefit night.' Buddy was the only one to stop for a chat. 'Now round up your fidelios and get 'em out fast. You got two minutes and then it's gonna be purgatory, OK? Move!'

They moved. Lifted up their skirts and scurried round the cathedral rounding up as many of the flock as they could find, not daring to approach the high altar where shadowy figures looked as though they were laying table for supper.

Everybody got out in time including the group who were back in the trash cart and bucketing down a darkened Fifty-first Street as it happened. The cathedral exploded and shook like a nervous wreck. Transubstantiating the high altar to a heap of rubble, but sacrilege went almost entirely unnoticed in the universal contemplation of a greater disaster.

No-one has given an adequate description of the fall of Pan Am; no-one believed such a cataclysm was possible.

Great slabs of facing flew from the tenth floor for half a mile, some of which devastated St Patrick's roof and steeples. The Rockefeller Centre was hit and even Carnegie Hall bears some scars.

Placing the charge at that predetermined height was the most lethal element in the affair. Under that enormous pressure the framework of girders buckled, it's believed, at the eighth or ninth floor and literally threw forward, perhaps only a few inches or so, the great steel and concrete structure which began, very slowly, to bend. Films show, as in slow motion, the doomed

---

* Halliday couldn't know that dePressant had third stake in a racket involving the smuggling of hard drugs from Vietnam in the caskets of KIAs returned to the States.

building gradually inclining towards Fifth Avenue; while those below, within range of its invisible but lengthening shadow, remained completely unaware of what was happening up there.

Once again a CBS reporter is credited with one of the few eye-witness accounts of the disaster. While cameramen filmed what they could of the scene he recorded impressions which would be heard by the Senate Investigating Committee and enshrined in the Foxwell Memorial Museum.

'We are speaking to you from the summit of New York, from the Empire State building at the heart of Manhattan.

'Almost all the lights are out on this beleaguered island. The situation has grown worse, confused, and we can only report what we see with our own eyes, though belief is another matter. To speak of this thing with feeling is becoming well nigh impossible. Death and destruction on a Richter scale dulls the senses and reduces man to automata.

'At six o'clock this evening the military authorities appeared to be in control, that much is known. Then, as darkness fell, it seems Halliday made two sorties in force, thrusting into the centre of Manhattan. These were not only unexpected, but obviously not enough was known about them. Nothing was done to seal them off from the main force. When eventually troops were rushed to Halliday's objectives it was too late.

'The first explosions plunged a large area of Manhattan into darkness and this has proved our greatest enemy. What light there is comes from burning vehicles, car headlights and buildings still blazing from the earlier attacks.

'At this moment of speaking we're looking towards Pan Am where the fighting has been most intense. Its façade shows pink in the light of fires at its base, these we assume to be army trucks fired by Halliday's raiders. It's a lurid, frightening light, a solid wall carved from Hell's antechamber.

'And there's ... you must have heard—good God! A fantastic irruption of sound and light, and pieces of ... somewhere on the twelfth level—fragments of the building are hurtling in all directions. We can feel the blast like a hot wind in our faces and the vibration is—terrifying. They've dynamited Pan Am. One can see flames leaping from floor to floor, glass is showering down from shattered windows. God help anybody caught in such a deadly rainfall.

'She ... what? yes—yes—she's moving! Great God in heaven, the whole gigantic structure is—is bending, it has to be unless my senses are reeling at the enormity of this—— Robert Friend nods confirmation, yes it really is shifting, sagging, it's going to fall! I simply don't—I—I apologize to those who may hear this but if you saw with my eyes what a terrible thing is occurring at this moment you would understand.

'Not that it should fall, but the manner of it. Slowly, but perceptibly it leans outwards as though even a monolith can be terrified of what it has to do.

'Do they know down there what's happening? Nothing in its path could live, nothing. Please God they know! And if you can believe me it's still inclining towards us, how long can it do this?

'I can—you can *hear* it! The grinding, wrenching sound of tortured steel, and a high whining note, as if it was coming alive, screaming with the first pangs of agony. Still it bends, must surely be seventy degrees off centre. A leaning tower, a leaning tower—but accelerating now, it's accelerating—burning—like the last year of the millennium rushing to meet us. It's going, listen to the noise! It's ...'

A leaning tower.

Crushing, maiming and crazing eighteen hundred civilians and military by its fall.

There was profound silence in the crowded Chamber as the tape-recording came to an end. An usher stepped forward to switch off the machine and the spell was broken.

Many of those present peeked at Ed Roberts to see what it had meant to him; but the callous bastard seemed ever to be locked in a world of his own.

Why not? Nobody was telling him anything. Like how they were still trying, three months later, to clear the devastated area of Park Avenue from Forty-second through to Thirty-fourth Street and beyond.

Winfield coughed and jerked his head sharply to relieve the tension. He was questioning General 'Wall-to-Wall' Jackson, operations commander in the New York area.

With pride Jackson had worn his reputation for being one of the meanest, *wehrmachtlich* generals since Tite Button—but that was long ago. In three months something had happened to him: the iron had rusted, the bully toughness had evaporated in face of toughness greater than his own. A man who had fouled mouth and mind by stating 'fifty per cent combat losses are acceptable if we're going to beat those gooks' found that nothing is acceptable when the gook turns out to be you.

'How did you handle the situation at that point, General?'

'I—had decided—that all possible outlets should be adequately sealed off.'

'I'm concerned with what happened at the point of attack.'

'Yes, I received a message from the company commander at Grand Central. His outfit was being attacked by—by Halliday's men.'

'Did he say how they got there?'

'Yes, he said they were operating from a city garbage truck.'

'What was your response?'

'I told him it was impossible.'

'As you told the RTO at Greeley Square?'

'...yes.'

'Did you expect these men to arrive in regular US army trucks?'

'No.'

'How did you expect them to move?'

'I had no reason to think they would move at all.'

'You were concerned only to fight some kind of containing action?'

'It was all I could do in the circumstances.'

'What were those "circumstances"?'

'I had received orders that Halliday was to be taken alive.'

'Are you saying this reduced your options?'

'It created a delicate situation.'

'You dared not push these active groups too far in case Halliday was among them?'

The general grasped eagerly at what appeared to be a let-out; but the Senate is not the Pentagon.

'That is correct, I had to consider the possibility.'

'Did you really think it conceivable that an officer of his

obvious capabilities, with sole responsibility for the whole diabolical operation, would risk his life in a *raiding* party?'

'The situation was abnormal, the conditions under which we were operating were abnormal.'

'More so than in Vietnam, General?'

Jackson looked down at his feet. There had to be an answer somewhere. 'I was also entitled to assume that any man capable of doing what Halliday did was abnormal.'

'Does your entitlement include the making of assumptions in a crisis situation?'

'I—it's necessary when intelligence of enemy intentions is zero.'

'But you *were* required to prevent hostile excursions?'

'Subject to the limitation I have indicated—yes I was.'

'How soon after learning of the Pan Am attack did you order reinforcements for the Forty-second Street units?'

There followed a long pause.

'It would have been ten minutes later.'

'So, after repeated calls from C company you sent three hundred men just about minutes before the explosion?'

'I—don't dispute that.'

'Do you dispute the fact that you ordered your men to go through Pan Am looking for the raiders because you *assumed* they must be using it as some kind of fire base?'

'That isn't so!'

'But all those men perished in the fall of Pan Am, General. And I have to put it to you that they died as a result of your completely false evaluation of the situation.'

'You have no grounds for making such an accusation!'

'I disagree. One of your own staff officers is prepared to testify that you did give such an order, that you gave it in a highly emotional state of mind, and in spite of advice from other senior officers present.'

Several reporters covering the Investigation were gathered in the makeshift basement canteen. They took a first sip of coffee and drew heavily on much needed cigarettes and still found no joy in their brief respite from the proceedings.

In the old days an adjournment meant exuberant conversation, swapping of self-perpetuating Washington gossip, the animated high spirits of boys let out of school.

The reasons why nobody was saying very much were sitting at another table. Poker-faced, taciturn reasons who simply didn't belong. They might say they were accredited representatives of the Chattanooga *Gazette*, but what if the *Gazette* folded in the mid-nineteenth century?

The journalists had their way of dealing with infiltrators. By arrangement a small group would gather in a corner and a whole crowd, acting as a buffer, would take tables around them. That way there could be some give and take of opinions or information, bearing in mind the room must be bugged to the eyebrows.

In such a plight as this the *New York Times*, the *Tribune* and the New Orleans *Dispatch* were holed up in their place and trying hard to stave off accumulative depression.

New Orleans had given up staving. 'The coffee gets lousier.'

The *Tribune* knew why. 'It's a deliberate campaign to contaminate the press.'

'I can believe it,' New Orleans promised.

The *Times* stayed deep in abstraction through which words came Sybylline—'Winfield should be in farming, the way he's harrowing the topsoil I'd say he's preparing a fresh crop.'

'He's certainly tearing the Pentagon apart,' New Orleans agreed.

'Wrong. Busting a few generals doesn't mean shredding the Pentagon mentality. Vacancies mean promotions equals gratitude to Winfield equals we'll do anything you say, Mr President.'

Chicago glanced at New Orleans who shrugged.

'Pleasant,' he suggested.

'He could be exaggerating,' Chicago sounded hopeful.

'*Are* you exaggerating, Tom?'

The *Times* looked unbelieving. 'The whole country under martial law, since three months—is that exaggeration?'

New Orleans flicked a nervous glance to where a couple of reporters with bulky .38 ball-points in their pockets sat watching without looking.

'The army's taken a caning, zero morale. I guess he had to give them something to do, justify their existence—Vietnam

—Halliday . . .' New Orleans tailed off, believing none of it.

'Whatever you think about Halliday, he was some soldier,' Chicago mentioned.

'Shut up!' low and intense. Tom was no longer lounging or just letting the words come.

'They took out Jackson Freeman of the *Post* yesterday, or maybe you forgot. He's in traction for a tenth of what you just said.'

'What's he shaping up to with Jackson?' the *Tribune* thought his question, any question, might help keep out the cold.

'Constructive treason.'

The *New York Times* finished his coffee, pushed back his chair as the bell sounded for reassembly.

Caressinger waited many hours in the West Wing office, his mood alternating from bag-packing to saving his country at the eleventh hour.

All he knew was what the transistor and TV coverage told him. No phone bell rang, not a leaf stirred. He, the NSC mandarin, the very ape of God, wise fool at the foot of a porcelain throne, he was being kept deliberately in darkness, and that simple fact wounded his colossal pride more than if he'd discovered dandruff in his beautifully waved hair.

Like all power-strivers Caressinger was basically insecure. But power is only the understudy to a prime need: to be believed in.

That was so important.

He failed miserably to understand how he'd exhausted his credibility with Foxwell; failed to comprehend that his master was tainted with the same disease, a kind of admin deficiency, insecurity, the need for someone to believe.

'The spoils of defeat.' He selected the rarest, most brilliant of his gaffes and examined it with a diamond cutter's care. Beautiful, flawless, injudicious, to say the least.

Unfortunately, even Caressingers are limited; paradoxically his brilliance was the limiting factor. To himself he insisted he'd spoken the truth. Halliday was laying the bitter fruits of defeat where he thought they belonged. He could not accept that he was no more than the victim of an epigram which he'd found

227

irresistible and Foxwell had not, simply because it laid an axe to the last of the stockade protecting his pathological insecurity.

Thus Caressinger was guilty of an error in judgment, of putting ego before meus, which is logical but dangerous. And, while the skies fell over Manhattan and anguished commentators spurred the rest of America to the very edge of hysteria, the grey eminence paced unseeing from one end of his luxury office to the other, deeply preoccupied with the supersessional problem concerning Herman Caressinger.

While shock waves passed over America and dust rose high from the demolition job on Pan Am (watch this space for an exciting new development, folks!), the flying garbage trucks returned without further incident to the night perimeter defence.

The main party of ten container lorries, drawn up in convoy and loaded with men and munitions, was ready to go. Number five contained Marsh, Extra, a couple of bunks for the children and the medical team.

'Casualties?' Halliday.

'None.'

'Any problems?'

'None.'

'OK let's get these loaded. We're thirty seconds behind schedule.'

Twelve men including Halliday, Trabs and Racowiczs worked quickly and in silence, loading the explosive, two tons of it, into the city trucks. Halliday was to drive leader with Trabs and Roberts riding shotgun for the next stage. A hundred yard gap would separate them from the first container truck and a hundred yards in rear of the last personnel carrier would be Racowiczs and his team.

No fumbling, no hesitation. Each man knew his job better than he knew himself. In war, knowing better is what counts, knowing better than the enemy what you're doing. Once he has an inkling you can tie a white flag to it and wave.

Strangely enough there was a man outside Halliday's circle who knew, with a desperate surge of intuition, what they had in mind. Caressinger knew all about the Ides of March, but nobody at the White House was even asking him the time of day.

It came to the good doctor in the finest moment of his career, at the very minute Halliday climbed into his truck and said, 'Right. Let's go.'

Their route took them along Twelfth Avenue to join the undamaged West Side Elevated or Route 9A and past the Edison Energy Control Centre. From jump-off to the Washington Bridge they met nothing worth the name of opposition.

As they turned on to the bridge Halliday accelerated violently, crashed a line of oil drums stretching across the approach. Shots were fired but continuous fire from the container trucks' side-ports destroyed enthusiasm. It was the same story on the far side of the bridge.

Thirty-four dead and wounded Guardsmen lay behind them as they gained the New Jersey shore. The captain never got home for breakfast.

They hurried on down to pick up the New Jersey Turnpike with a straight run of a couple of hours to Trenton or thereabouts.

Most of the men slept. 'Sleep when you can' they told them in Vietnam. It's valid anywhere.

The journey in itself is unimportant. By night a ride along the Turnpike is negligible. But when a call came through from the bridgehead survivors that a convoy of trucks had broken bounds the New Jersey police were alerted to watch all roads out of New York down there, particularly in the New Brunswick and Perth Amboy districts.

Which disgusted at least one patrol cop. 'What are we supposed to do, throw goofy balls at 'em?'

Eye-witness reports of their progress were beginning to pour in which should have simplified the authorities' problems somewhat. But they made stupid assumptions all the way. Like, we'll set up road blocks and hold them down because now they've finished hell-raising they're just a bunch of baddies on the run.

How could anyone but Caressinger know that Halliday was riding hard towards the second phase of a new apocalypse? Revelation had taken the road to Annapolis.

They got through the fifteenth, fourth and sixth districts without trouble. A few patrol cars paced them with marked lack of enthusiasm but a small demonstration of fire-power had them dropping to the rear as interested observers.

Representative Hoker was not the kind of Republican to take this sort of thing lying down. He was working late in his Camden office when news of the breakthrough came in; called the Governor right away who agreed it was time to stop these murderers and in quick time a couple of hundred National Guardsmen were assembled and hurriedly positioned on both sides of the Turnpike. Six lorries were parked across the convoy's path about two hundred yards further along.

'Don't forget, men,' a nervous young accountant pleaded, trying hard to keep his spectacles in place, 'just don't forget, the whites of their eyes are immaterial, open fire as soon as they're in sight.' And the helmet was much too big for him.

Halliday couldn't help seeing them first. They'd picked the wrong spot for an ambush or even a picnic. You must not see the enemy before he sees you or you won't get wiped out. It's commonsense—of course you don't start firing at the ambushers so soon either. You're not supposed to know they're there, and it could draw fire before you can figure out what to do with it.

So, Halliday kept up a cruising speed, counting the number of lorries—which still had their lights switched on, believe it—estimating the complement, how far they would be strung out along the road, then leaned back to talk through a hole in the cab wall. Kemble was in the rear compartment with a lot of explosives.

'Soup, I want flame-throwers hitting either side of the road the instant I accelerate till I slow down, OK?'

'Roger.'

And so it happened. Almost before a shot was fired the *flammenwerfers* opened up a withering stream of liquid fire for all of a hundred yards. The element of fire and surprise knocked fifty per cent of the NGs off their feet and sent the rest running hotfoot for Camden and other nice bits of the Delaware suburbs.

The rest of the convoy hardly knew about it, excepting a short delay while the garbage truck team drove the barricade off the road. That was all.

Pay no heed to rumours or report. One day the incident will

230

have its place in the projected Hall of Infamy in Arlington, and you will learn that the immemorable Battle of Camden was fit, that forty-seven men of the First Battalion Gloucesters and Camden County National Guard gave their lives gloriously in defence of their country.

There will be medals, photographs, citations and a charred flak jacket belonging to Private Harvey to prove it.

At this point it might be worth reflecting on the fact that a day of twenty-four hours had not yet passed since Halliday ran up, so to say, the skull and crossed bones.

We know what he achieved by way of national destruction to this point, but even Halliday would never discover that Lincoln's brother and his friends dumped Flugzeuger and the pilot ashore and blew up the *Carolina* in the biggest Kamikaze drop-out since world war two.

Fifteen hundred men died in an explosion that sounded the Last deafening Post to a stricken city. That was Black Power's contribution to the Great Exhibition of domestic warfare appliances for a consumer society that otherwise had everything.

Yes. An estimated five thousand killed or wounded in New York alone, but nobody can quote the figures for Vietnam.

It's hardly worth mentioning that in a nation of insomniacs he gave America a sleepless night. Even the dying waved away the last rites so they could stay to the end with their local TV or radio stations. Most would close their eyes to the breathless *Dies irae* of a newscaster.

The Senate remained in permanent session, dividing its time between futile discussion and television. All the lights were blazing in the offices of the Administration. Every government department stayed operational.

The Pentagon hummed with such intense activity the computers couldn't hear themselves print out.

CBS coverage was fantastic. With no interruption it fed material endlessly into the national network and scooped every competitor on the Halliday break-out.

A programme controller had a hunch that one-man teams should keep close to the perimeter in case Halliday planned to go. Two of the teams were snarled up in the Grand Central and Greeley Square thrust, two others missed him in the general confusion. Only Dave Barth was at the right spot when the convoy moved out and he tailed them all the way giving the only recorded commentary on the Camden ambush which reached the listeners via Annapolis at three in the morning.

He died in the centre of some fierce fighting in Washington.

*　　*　　*

Little is known of the President's movements in those last hours. It's believed he spent much of the time with various aides and government officials who later testified that he appeared to be calm and in control of the situation.

Bill Petersen, Foxwell's appointments' secretary, is the most reliable authority for the period.

Extracts from his day book read as follows:

10.20 pm　The President returns to the Oval Office from the West Wing. Studies the latest bunch of telegrams. Undersecretary of the Army Wilbert present.

10.30 pm　Call from New York. Confirmation of *Carolina* disaster.

10.40 pm　William Fauntleroy rings President who agrees America's top evangelist should go on the air to lead nation in prayer.

10.50 pm　Halliday reported to be down-route from Trenton. The President confers with General Dingle.

11.40 pm　The President confers with Senate Minority leader.

11.45 pm　Tom Crowley, chief of the secret service, calls on the President. He is anxious the Executive Protection Service be doubled as a precautionary measure.

11.52 pm　The White House doctor checks the President's pressure. No problem.

11.56 pm　Unconfirmed reports give Halliday breaking an army cordon on New Jersey Turnpike.

12.01 am　The President confers with Army General Counsel Coldstream. Later with General Kruppstadt,

232

Pentagon Chief of Army Operations Centre. The eleventh hour of God knows what seems to be striking—silently.

12.30 am The President has the ante-room cleared. Watches his friend, entertainer Riff Macluggan, speaking to the nation.

12.37 am Film star, Gore Spiller, long time friend of the President, rings to offer support.

Foxwell read the telegrams, rolled them into a ball and threw them across the room. Undersecretary Wilbert coughed, just in case the President had forgotten his presence.

'Demonstrations of support! I need information. We're supposed to have the finest communications system in the world and I can find no-one who can tell me *exactly* what's happening.'

Wilbert forebore to explain that the President was confusing communications with Intelligence, though he could sympathize with Foxwell's implied complaint that there was no-one left worth bugging.

'What kind of war can we hope to wage with the Soviet Union when we can't even deal with these bums in our own backyard?'

The Undersecretary carefully pointed out that he was in no position to give an answer to such a profound question.

'Then what are you here for?'

'You asked me to be present, Mr President.'

'Yes, I want you to stay in the vicinity, that's all.'

'Very good, Mr President.'

'I have a priority call from New York, Mayor Lindsay, Mr President.'

'I'll take it. Well?'

'I must inform you, Mr President, that the aircraft carrier *Carolina* blew up just half an hour ago. We had trouble getting through ... are you there, sir?'

Yes—and no. Foxwell replaced the receiver and sat for some time staring ahead of him. Then he got to his feet in a way that paid tribute to the brute force of destiny, crossed to look out of the window.

In the floodlit grounds he saw dark figures taking up positions behind the trees. But he could only think of old ghosts coming home to roost...

'A call from William Fauntleroy, Mr President.'
'Go ahead.'
'Mr President, I felt I had to call and let you know I feel and pray for you in this dark hour.'
'Thanks, Willy.'
'I wanted you to know that God works for America in the strangest ways.'
'I'm aware of that.'
'Do you suppose if I can get radio time, a prayer with the nation might help?'
'Whatever you think best, Willy.'
'Very good, Mr President. God bless you.'
The President replaced the receiver before adding, 'You stupid, curly-headed bastard.'

'My report, General, puts Halliday as far as Trenton *without* opposition. What do you have to say to that?'
Dingle moved his weight from one foot to the other. It was too bad, trying to throw all the blame for a catastrophe on his head when it hadn't happened yet.
'We're doing everything in our power, Mr President.' For Chrissake I could name a dozen four star generals with a better claim to your goddamned presidential disapproval. 'Our computer analysts are working intensively on the problem right now.' And I hope to God they know what they're talking about. 'We're confident they'll come up with a solution any minute.'
'Computer analysts! I want men in the field. Trained soldiers doing a soldier's job—what the hell do you people think this is, some kind of war game? Is that how you fought the Vietcong "evaluating" their strike potential on an IBM 600? Return to your command and have a division on the New Jersey Turnpike in an hour or I'll have you court-martialed for dereliction of duty, General.'
'But Mr President, you don't seem to appreciate that——'
'General, I'll remind you that you're not addressing the House Armed Services Committee, you are arguing with the Com-

mander-in-Chief of the US Armed Forces. Do you understand?'

'Yes, Mr President.'

'Then get out of here and do as I command!'

'Where are the kids?'

'They went to a party.'

He reacted more sharply than he knew. 'At a time like this?'

She continued to stare at the book on her lap. 'What else should they be doing?'

'Comforting you—if not me.'

'They're not children any more, to begin with.'

He watched her closely, frowned deeply at her words which always seemed to hover at the edge of a double meaning. Always.

'And to end with?'

She looked up then and stared him in the eye. Unwaveringly. Not many traces of her one-time beauty remained, but the hard edge to her voice was something new.

'To end with, Jason likes to think he'll handle his problems without invoking the death penalty or standing in front of the Lincoln Memorial trying to filch another man's courage.'

He digested this with no obvious sign that it left a bitter taste. 'I hope I have the rest of the family on my side.'

'Of course I am. They didn't marry you, I did.'

'What's the mood on the Hill, Sam? I'm not getting much down here.'

Sam Trimble raised those famous eye-brows in mild disbelief. 'Saw a few of your aides scouting around, Mr President.'

'They come back and tell me what they think I ought to hear. Does that do me any good?'

'I guess not, and I hoped those days were over. Well I'd say the Opposition is playing a little game of I-told-you-so. Right or wrong they see this situation as a watershed, not because of Halliday specifically, but it reinforces, in some mysterious way, their conviction that Presidents should never have monkeyed with their power. This is the inevitable result, so it takes a phenomenon like Halliday to stop the rot. "If the President had consulted with us more often this could never have happened" is about the burden of their song.'

'I hope you disillusioned them.'

'Oh they don't believe it any more than we do. They're just scratching around for any handle happens to fit their own little grindstone. Tell you what though, Erwin Winfield is acting a mite coy.'

'How do you mean?'

'Says the President must be given unqualified support in this hour of emergency, let's forget the past and pull together.'

'Calculated.'

'Oh yes, Mr President. You know Erwin, he wouldn't give a button off his shirt unless it was sewed on with elastic. My guess is, he's aiming for elder statesman status—there has to be one in every crisis.'

'He wants his day—every politician wants his day when it comes to it.'

And you should know, Sam whispered so that only Trimble heard. Aloud he said, 'I'd say he's looking for a term.'

'There's no harm in looking. Right now I'm more concerned to know how far I can——'

'They'll do anything you say, Mr President. For as long as it suits them.'

A thick-set character, Crowley, heavy but delicate in his movements. He carried the awesome responsibility of arranging security for Foxwell, the Vice-President and other high officials in the Administration.

'I hate to bother you at a time like this, Mr President, but it's important.'

'Then it's no bother. Go ahead, Steve.'

'Caressinger called me not ten minutes back, said it was imperative I increase surveillance on the White House. I told him I'd have to see you on that—I know how you feel about having the fellows round every corner.'

'Did he say why it was so important?'

Crowley started to shrug then remembered where he was. 'No he didn't say, Mr President, but he was adamant I should discuss it with you. I imagine he's thinking of the nuts a situa-

236

tion like this can throw up. Right now there's a demonstration on Pennsylvania Avenue about this or that. We're keeping an eye on it.'

'What are the police doing?'

'About the demo? Nothing that I know of, Mr President.'

'Have them crack down on it—hard!'

'Certainly, Mr President. And about the ESP build up?'

'As many as you think necessary.'

When Crowley left, Foxwell almost rang Caressinger. He badly wanted to know what was behind the doctor's thinking. Even though his own mind paltered with the realization that deep down he already knew.

And when he got the first garbled report on the Camden fiasco, he no longer had any doubts about Halliday's objective.

Army Counsel Coldstream was called in to clarify a constitutional problem. The khaki lawyer left as Chief of the Army Operations Centre for Washington Kruppstadt entered.

Foxwell was in no mood to mince words. 'The National Guard is unequal to the task of eliminating Halliday, General.'

And Kruppstadt wasn't anybody's man. 'I can't answer for the Governor's decision, but I'd say the regular forces are no better placed, Mr President.'

'What kind of defeatist talk is that?'

'If you want us to fight them to a standstill then say so. But don't tie our hands behind our backs by demanding *habeas corpus* for Halliday.'

'I want that man alive!'

'Then you'll have to accept the consequent limitations on our actions.'

'Have you "evaluated" his intentions?'

'I don't have to—he's obviously headed for Washington.'

'...for what purpose?'

'I'm an army general not a politician, Mr President.'

'Then what are your dispositions—General?'

'I have the Third Division to the north-east of the city, roughly on a line with Tacoma Park and Fairmount Heights. Men from Bolling Air Force Base and National Guard units are holding from Forest Heights to the boundary line on Penn Avenue.'

'All this for five hundred men...' there was wonderment in the presidential murmur.

'The Seventh Armoured is concentrated on Rock Creek Park and we're covering Arlington District with everything we can get.'

'That's a pretty tight ring.'

'After what happened to New York it could be a tight situation. With any other soldier I'd say hold every intersection on the Capitol Beltway north-east, but Halliday's unpredictable. He could as well sweep round and come from the south-west.'

'This—Halliday—how would you rate him, as a soldier?'

Kruppstadt had no doubts. 'I just wish he was on our side.'

'Thank you—that's all, General.'

'You still want Halliday alive?'

'The order stands.'

'As you wish, sir.'

'One more thing, General—all the units you mentioned; few of them served in Vietnam?'

Kruppstadt looked strangely at his Commander-in-Chief. 'You only set a thief to catch a thief when you're sure of your thief, Mr President.'

'Mr President, Mr Macluggan is about to appear.'

The aide spoke velvetly so as not to bruise what he took to be Foxwell's already battered feelings.

'What?'

'Mr Macluggan is speaking to the nation.'

'Oh, yes, have the ante-room cleared. And stop behaving like an undertaker.'

Foxwell rose from his chair sharply, noting the aide's watchful eye. Nobody was going to catch him dragging his feet however tired he might feel. He knew, yes he knew they were watching every twitch of his every muscle, storing details in their piggy-banks against the day when they could write all kinds of crap about the lonely individual bravely shouldering his burden just so they could make a fast buck with their everlasting 'Memoirs of the President', these little men with out-size pens.

He relaxed a fraction as the familiar, ravaged face of America's top balladeer spread all over the screen. No-one could say Macluggan had endorsed Foxwell's nomination, but it hadn't hurt to have him singing for him.

But the wizened little man wasn't singing right now. In fact he opened his big mouth mostly to talk these days; and while it could be embarrassing it made Middle Aged America love him, and therefore, Foxwell, just a little bit more. After all, people growing old together can do no wrong in each other's eyes.

'I gotta message for you, and this ain't no second class citizen talking. It's Riff Macluggan ya hear me!'

Dear off Riff, stoned again; but what's a little drink between old friends.

'I'm a full, red-blooded American citizen and I wanna tell ya this. The day of the liberal punks in this great country of ours is kaput. We're gonna help the finest President we ever had clean up America, and I mean clean up. No matter who, crummy students, hippies and yippies and a few people in high places, I name you no names, who'd sell their country for peanuts if they knew how.

'You gotta choose right now. Stars and Stripes or the Hammer and Sickle, there's no such flag as the Hammer and Stripes or the Stars and Sickle. Tha's what these punks would like to see flyin' over this country.'

Nice, Riff, nice.

'Well we're gonna stop the sell-out and I wanna tell the President, we're right behind you, feller. You do what you have to. Zap this stinkin' Halliday and his social perverts back into the dirt they came from.

'Confidentially this is what pollution's really all about. It ain't rivers full of acid or air full of smog; if these things help make America prosperous who's cryin'? *People* are the real pollution, people singin' "We Shall Overcome", people cryin' "Hands off Laos, Hands off every damned thing except Uncle Sam's throat"—believe it they'd strangle him if they could.

'All I gotta say is, let's get these people outta our hair then we can make America twice as great as she oughtta be.

'Now I'm gonna sing the President's favourite number as my tribute to a great guy.'

And he did. Against a string background, squeezing the last drop of embalming fluid out of an old Cole Porter number, this funny little man with a voice like sugared corn flakes actually sang and even stirred a few million coronarys that night.

Some people said it was pathetic. They were right. It was as pathetic as Christmas trees in a concentration camp.

But Riff's appearance made Foxwell feel a little better for the time being. It was good to have your friends doing a little back-slapping for you and your country at a time like this.

So he took the call from Oklahoma in a more cheerful frame of mind. There were some fine men in America and he was proud to know so many of them, men like Gore Spiller, ringing from his ranch near Lawton, in *Comanche* country.

'Mr President?' that slow-down drawl beloved of millions.

'How are you, Gore, good to hear you.'

'Oh I'm just fine, except for what I'm hearing, Mr President. I just saw Riff on TV and he put me in mind I could maybe do something for my country.'

'I appreciate that, Gore.'

'Well, how'd it be if I saddled up my plane and came on over and see this Halliday; go right on up and tell him stop playing soldiers?'

'Sounds dangerous, Gore. He didn't waste words on Wesley.'

'Guess a tenderfoot's one thing; but I think I could take care of myself, Mr President.'

'I wouldn't want to discourage you, Gore. Why not come over and we'll talk about it? I'll order you priority at the airport.'

'Much obliged, Mr President. Be right over.'

And that, Foxwell reminded himself once more, was the kind of man America was all about.

Nobody dared to tell him how some of America danced and sang in the street as news came through: the insurgents were crashing the Annapolis barricades and heading straight for Washington.

'Brethren—this is Deliverance Day! This is our people comin'

240

on in with the Good Lawd Jesus resurrected like a major in th'army of th'Lawd!'

'Hallelujah!'

One o'clock in the morning one-time member of the NAACP, Reverend Jefferson Lee, was still sweating in his Wylie Street pulpit made of coffin planks. Ever since they took out Luther King, Reverend Lee had all but lived in that pulpit, waiting, as he said, his turn to go over Jordan.

Lee had moved his sixty-one years away from the old NAACP ideals and nearer to the 'realism of violence'. But Lee was a naturally peaceable man who loved his people better than he loved their destruction, so he used his wisdom to resolve the dilemma. His words were like crumbs from a fire-eater's banquet, his sermons were God's own buck-shot right between the eyes, and at the end, if it ever came, you were so tuckered out congregationally and with participating you didn't have strength to shoot craps, much less cops.

But this time there was no holding the Wylie Street brethren and even ol' man Lee wasn't so sure he didn't see the dawn of a new era. The coroner said he'd let himself get carried away and in the light of what happened the good Reverend was signing up with Reaperman for the duration.

'He don' come sellin' life-insurance!'

'Yeah!'

'He don' come sellin' Pepsi-everlastin'!'

'Yeah!'

'He don' come sellin' love the Lawd thy dollar!'

'Yeah!'

'He don' come cryin' I'm a white man paint me black!'

'Yeah!'

'He don' say I love you niggers 'cos I'm scared white to do otherwise!'

'Yeah!'

'He come with a gun, man, like Jesus come with a sword and he say, "Whosoever believeth with me is just a human bein' and I'll shoot the crap out of any man who says ain't so!"'

'Hallelujah!'

The smoke, beginning to rise over Washington. Again.

They'd forgotten the despised enemy within: the coloureds, smarting under sophisticated injustices. Men, and women, without faith, hope or Federal relief who'd do more than rise up and sing and pray to the white man's Jesus.

Reports of looting were coming in from Euclid Street and Rhode Island Avenue. The same old story writ large. Reason enough for the police to look a little more square in the jaw.

It was going to be one of those nights.

First reports of the gathering storm reached the *Washington Post* newsroom by teletype at 1.15 am local time: ANNAPOLIS MARYLAND (UPI) HALLIDAY IS THROUGH BARRIER. BELIEVED HEADING WASHINGTON.

In fact, news was coming in from all quarters and so fast the staff could barely keep pace. Every available reporter and photographer was on assignment. All radio cars were patrolling the city streets, assessing the mood, reporting on every incident they could reach.

At Pennsylvania Avenue and Eighth Street intersection one journalist stopped his car to watch a crowd of around fifty men sitting on the sidewalk. Most of them were negroes and without exception they were dismally dressed. One man stood proudly holding a giant placard attached to a length of steel pipe: 'Welcome to Vietnam II from Vietnam I Veterans.'

There was something about the group, an air of waiting with purpose, that had the reporter ready to leave his car and go looking for an interview when three trucks filled with the 'Old Guard' out of Third Division came roaring to a halt close to where he was parked. Men in full combat gear jumped to the ground and surrounded the veterans who stayed motionless, staring dispassionately at the latest development.

A full blown captain with a weight problem stalked across the street and straddled the sidewalk, thumbs jammed in his webbing, helmet shadowing his eyes like Death hiding in shame.

'What do we have here, male voice choir from the Deaf Asylum—Blind? You better run fellers, Old Guard's ridin' again. Old Guard!'

His men teetered appreciatively.

'You,' he toed a negro with his boot. 'Know the penalty for being litter? What you doing here?'

'I shouldn't do that, man.' Quietly.

'Is that right now?' The captain cast a mock dumbfounded eye over his men. 'Well now, I declare, we got us a one-eyed joker and me thinking all this time he was just an ol' ace of spades.'

He toed him a little harder.

'I still advise you, don't,' the negro muttered.

'Well now I'm gonna give you some advice, trashman, you get your asses outta here—all of you—and don't let me see you again, right?'

'We're waitin' for Halliday,' someone said out of the semi-darkness. 'Can't you read English?'

'You're——?' the captain made no pretence of being astonished this time, looked from the placard to the group. 'How d'you know which way he's coming? You're in on the deal. Hey you guys, this is a bunch of Halliday's killers.'

'We're veterans, sonny boy.'

'Veterans!' the captain's voice got shriller as he rampaged among the implications. 'I'll show you a bunch of veterans. OK fellers, let 'em have it.'

Well now that wasn't sensible. Before he'd finished making speeches the veterans suddenly produced .38s and .45s and shot the troopers down eye-ball to eye-ball. Then they were on their feet grabbing M16s almost before they'd fallen from their owners' hands, turned them on the remainder and took out the whole unit, around sixty men.

They lost five killed and two wounded. Leaving four men to help the WIAs the rest grabbed all the bullets they could lay hands on and melted into the night.

How did that happen? Well one side worked in Vietnam, the other didn't. It's that simple.

The *Post* reporter was still radioing his account back to the office as the last of them disappeared.

It was the first of many such incidents. The enthusiasm was volatile, midwife to the violence bound to follow. Jefferson Lee was only the mouthpiece of unco-ordinated desires, the spokesman of frustration never far below the surface of a simmering city.

This time the police and military had orders to gun down any and every demonstration of support for Halliday, and it has to be said, they did a fine job in the name of law and order.

Police Chief Calhoun called personally at the *Post*'s offices and explained to the editor. 'I don't like having to do this, Frank, but I've got my orders. You print nothing of what your boys see this morning till it's vetted in the right quarters.'

'Right! We haven't had right quarters in six years.'

'I don't have time to argue, Frank. I'm just supposed to tell you what's the score. But I'll give you this much: Foxwell isn't scared of the Press any more. I know you're busy right now, Frank, but try and find time to tremble.'

'Stay tuned to your local station for up-to-the-second reports on the Halliday EVA. Six hours thirty minutes after shooting his way out of New York in garbage disposal trucks and containerized vehicles Hellfire Halliday and his five hundred warriors gunned a clear passage down the New Jersey Turnpike and are now reported to be on the Capitol Beltway. Informed sources predict an attempted break-in at any one of six points from Route 29 through to Baltimore-Washington Parkway. This does not take account of secondary main roads.

'The Cabin Guard plan shows signs of rapid up-dating. Troops continue to pour into the city. Two companies of the crack Military Police Battalion are latest arrivals. Among other units identified we have the Sixth Cavalry, the Hundred Seventy-first's Guard MP Battalion, units of the Sixth Infantry and paratroopers from North Carolina. The Ninety-first Combat Engineers are standing to in the Arlington district and the DC National Guard are reportedly mobilized to full strength.

'Overnight Washington has become an armed camp.

'There is no question—no question at all—Halliday plans to do in Washington what he has achieved so disastrously in New York. Latest reports from that stricken city tell of fires raging out of control, looting unchecked in what remains of Fifth Avenue. Three looters shot dead at the Metropolitan Museum of Modern Art. The city remains in almost total darkness while army engineers struggle to restore power and light.

'And now, Washington, one of the world's most beautiful capitals, holds its breath against the terrible possibility of such things happening here.

'In fact we have official assurance there is no cause for alarm or panic. The element of surprise no longer exists. The surrounding terrain lends itself to more intensive military operations and top men at the Pentagon are confident Halliday and company have two hours more off the hook at most.

'I have an official request: will all members of the National Guard who have not done so report to the Independence Avenue Armoury immediately. Repeat: immediately.

'All citizens are ordered to stay off the streets...'

Aside from the black community no-one needed to be ordered. Mr and Mrs America were too well conditioned by the box *populi* to be curious about realities outside their own homes.

Why roam around the streets looking for trouble when you can sit home and enjoy it in comfort with the ice-box clogged full of beer and ice-cream. Feet up for the greatest danger man of the century, Mrs Creamcake. The longer you watch history in the making the less you feel inclined to participate. No exercise involved. We want a nation of great, fat slobs; you also serve who only sit and put on weight.

The watchdogs of democracy know the score.

Already they'd seen military police beating up a score of niggers looking suspicious on H street. They'd actually watched the cops shoot a looter at the new pharmacy on Fairmont Street. They'd thrilled to the scene as cameras zoomed in on Dulles Airport with magnificent close-ups of huge C130s bringing in paratroopers from Fort Bragg. And what a beautiful panoramic sight all those trucks filled with red-blooded American boys high-tailing up Jefferson Davis Highway all the way from Fort Lee in Virginia.

Made you proud to belong, that it did. What's better than a demonstration of power with a capital POW? I mean, just take a look, Belladonna, see that long line of MP jeeps hurrying on down deserted Connecticut Avenue! They've got Military Police written all over their spare wheels lookin' like

Convention buttons—*that's* how I can tell.

'Hey Mom, they're settin' up an MG post right outside Kaufman's, that's only a block away.'

'Kaufman's! What's so special about his merchandise?'

Especially when they have machine-gun posts just about everywhere on the tourists' itinerary. Like outside the Pan American building, outside St John's corner of H and Sixteenth Streets, the Lincoln Memorial, even the Smithsonian. The National Archives, all Government buildings. They had so many they were looking for places to guard. So they chose the Waxworks Museum, the house where Lincoln died and Arlington cemetery—just in case.

And, being the military geniuses they were, the whole floodlighting system was switched on to illuminate old glory and improve television coverage.

As for the White House, it became virtually an armed camp.

The greatest concentration of available forces centred in an area bounded by Constitution Avenue, Fifteenth Street and Vermont Avenue, round New Hampshire Avenue, angling into the Washington Circle then down Twenty-third Street, past the State Department and back to Constitution Avenue.

Three thousand paratroopers held this area together with NG units, the Special Executives and three hundred MPs.

It should have been enough.

Foxwell thought so.

Fouchay and Muntsch, present in the Oval Office, watched the darkening figure draped over a map of Washington covering the desk.

There was no longer any pretence of formal coming and going. Aides scurried to and fro with *non sequitur* information, getting in each other's way for the privilege of figuring in this particular scrap of history.

The President seemed oblivious to the frenzied activity around him. Fouchay and Muntsch took it on themselves to provide makeshift buffers between his perturbed spirit and the clamour of the outside world.

Once, just twenty minutes before Halliday's reported appearance on the Beltway, he'd burst violently from his office headed for the Press quarters. There was hardly anyone present at the time; a UPI man and a couple of correspondents on standby.

'Get out!' he'd shouted. 'Get out of here!'

He returned to his desk with no other sign of a kink showing in a twisted psyche. If the aberration proved anything it was the hatred he felt for the media at that moment beyond even his hatred of the man who was crucifying America.

Fouchay and Muntsch shared anxiety, not because of his outburst—he was entitled to that when it came to scribblers—but his utter disregard for his personal safety was another matter.

Muntsch glanced at Fouchay who nodded.

'Mr President, might I have your attention?'

Foxwell took it with a frown. He preferred to signal his readiness to be disturbed.

'What is it?'

'We have helicopters standing by to move your family if you consider it necessary.'

'I do not so consider it. My son and daughter are at a party in Fairfax at this hour of crisis. And the First Lady is anxious to finish a novel she's reading right now.'

Fouchay muttered something about Mrs Foxwell's calm and cool nerve. That was the only time he saw the President smile; unless it was something else.

Muntsch blundered on with what had to be said. 'We also have a responsibility to your person, Mr President. The air raid bunker has every facility——'

Foxwell rounded with an almost snarl. 'What the hell are you talking about? This is not Berlin! We are not being invested by the Reds! I am in the capital of the United States of America! I am the President, and I will stay right here till this thing is through, is that understood?'

Perfectly.

A man who has waded through mud and blood to couple with power will never go back the way he came by invitation....

Food for thought. Halliday had not sustained a single casualty up to the moment of Foxwell's outburst. At which point in time he was studying the situation through his night binoculars from the Greenbelt area just above the Capitol Beltway on Route 201.

As far as his eye could see transport was moving in both directions, concentrating a dazzling ball of headlights at every intersection from the north at Highway Twenty-nine to the south-eastern District Heights.

'Trabs.'

'Major?'

'With so many men on the intersections any single one is badly in our way. We'll have to clear 'em. Ed, you have their codes and unit IDs?'

Roberts looked up from his radio pack. 'It's like you said, it never occurs to 'em we might cut in.'

'Fine, use the fourth routine, Trabs. Take Ed and a dozen of the boys, that should be enough. OK. You've got fifteen minutes.'

Trabs, Roberts and the rest of the section disappeared into the darkness. The others settled down to wait. Only the children still slept.

Boy scouts wouldn't have fallen for the fourth routine. But the opposition was operating at such a level of tension that a panic voice injected into the communications network could trigger the reaction Halliday looked for and got.

Trabs and company had ten minutes from the moment they hi-jacked the truck. No problem. A couple of bored-looking PFCs sat up and looked scared as they ground to a halt and found themselves hemmed in by GIs pointing guns in their direction exactly.

'Hey hold on, you guys, we ain't Halliday's men.'

'That's right, we are,' Trabs confirmed. 'Out.'

They were so scared they almost helped with the trussing, were carried to a clump of trees well off the highway and dumped. The truck streaked away and slowed for a U-turn just a hundred and fifty yards from Route One.

'Behind that low rise left—break for it!'

As they ran, Boston asked Trabs why go to the trouble. No-one could see them where they were.

'It'll mask the noise—they'll hear it but won't make out the direction. Right, this'll do. All set, Ed?'

'When you are, I'm tuned in.'

The men began firing, single shots to begin with, then changed to automatic, their M16s pointing up at the stars. The noise was deafening.

Ed Roberts got to work. 'All units on Red Bayou—attention. Red Bayou, this is General Havering, we are taking fire from Route One, repeat Route One. All units will converge on four-nine-five-one! We've got 'em!'

The boys gave it another two minutes while Roberts listened in to the snap, crackle, pop from the RT. Eventually he looked up bewondered. 'You wouldn't believe it,' he said.

'Sure sounded like a four star, you could'a fooled me.'

'That's funny. I was only imitating my fourth grade school teacher.'

'How did she miss the draft?' Gribble wondered.

They hurried back to the darkened lorry parked a little off the highway. With two minutes to spare they sat watching the stream of army trucks going hell for leather to where they weren't supposed to be.

'Someone's gonna get their ass defrosted for this,' Trabs sounded reasonably satisfied as he slipped into gear and drove at a sedate forty back to the 201 intersection.

Which they found deserted except for a three man posse of military police left behind to keep unauthorized traffic from going in and out. That's what is known as prudence.

Trabs slowed, stopped, and kept the engine running.

A beefy sergeant rested his boot on the step 'Where do you think you're goin', Mistress Poppins? All the action's over that way.'

'Is that so? Well we've got orders to go guard Dulles Airport.'

The sergeant laughed so much he had to take his foot off the truck. 'This guy must be the Unknown Soldier, he's takin' off to guard Dulles Airport.'

Everybody laughed including Trabs. Eventually the MP jerked a thumb in the opposite direction. 'It's over that way, ma'am.'

'Why thank you, sir. But first off me and my husband and twelve kids are gonna take a look at New York.'

Trabs kicked into gear viciously, knocked all three to the

ground before they could move as he backed, turned, weaved and drove back to where Halliday was waiting.

Not a word was spoken. It had worked—the fact was self-evident, because it was planned to work. Halliday took Trabs' place at the wheel. Trabs ran back to take over the garbage truck.

With lights dimmed they roared away down to the intersection, waited for a large gap in the traffic and then hustled across the Beltway.

Clear all the way down the Bladensburg Road the convoy sped, past smart houses filled with smart occupants crouched in front of wall-to-wall television with the reason for it all not fifty yards distant. Across South Dakota Avenue, skirting the National Arboretum, then turning on to Maryland Avenue. No time to appreciate the Supreme Court Building's majesty, the Capitol too would have to wait.

Men were running down the steps, but by the time frenzied orders were given to fire the whole unlikely cavalcade was stampeding down Constitution Avenue. Ignore Taft standing with his back to a lifetime's achievement, a hundred foot high belfry—on past First Street, Louisiana Avenue...

Third Street.

'News is coming in that Halliday has broken through the city's outer perimeter. Halliday is in Washington! Stay tuned.'

Fourth Street. That's the National Gallery of Art, folks, made in good old Tennessee marble. Goes all the way to Seventh.

'Washington Fire Department reports twenty-eight fires burning in all parts of the capital.'

We have the Federal Trade Commission on your right, folks. It's extremely triangular as you see, cost three million dollars to construct which I make a million bucks a side.

'Heavy fighting is reported from the Bladensburg area. Mayor Carroll has ordered all citizens remain at home. On no account go into the streets.'

Between Seventh and Ninth is the National Archives Building. Everything of importance you can get on paper is in there, folks. The Declaration of Independence, the Constitution and the Bill of Rights, to name a few, all of which can automatically be removed to safety at the touch of a button. That's scientific know-how for you.

The convoy took its first sustained fire from this spot. Fire was returned. Two paratroopers died and seventeen received wounds.

'News coming in from our field reporters suggest Halliday is closer than was first thought. Firing has been reported from the Capitol vicinity but we have no confirmation of this.

'Riot police are receiving NG support between H and Fourteenth. We have a special announcement: do not show yourselves at lighted windows. Please keep away from your windows. Stay tuned for further developments.'

You're looking at the Department of Justice on Ninth and Tenth Streets, yes indeed it covers the whole block clear to Pennsylvania Avenue. If you have time, folks, go take a look. If you have a legal problem you might just run into the Attorney General of the United States himself and if he can't fix it no-one can. Home of the FBI too and they'll be glad to show you around. They'll even teach you how to catch a spy in ten easy lectures. If you like good shooting they'll show you how in their very own basement range. Demonstrations every thirty minutes. Take the kids: they'll love it.

FBI agents protecting their HQ took a beating as did a unit of NGs on public building guard duty. Reported casualties, thirty-seven dead and wounded.

Halliday's convoy, delivering simultaneous fire from forty port-holes on each side, flattened everything that got in the way.

Let's not bother about the next building, folks. That's the Internal Revenue Service and believe me it covers thirty acres. We'll be glad to drop anyone with a tax problem.

'Mr President—we have word they're into Constitution Avenue.'

'Well?'

'Their objective can only be the White House!'

'We're surrounded by some of the finest troops in the world or are you prepared to tell me otherwise, Fouchay?'

'My job is to protect you, sir. If you remain by that window there is nothing I can do about stray bullets.'

Foxwell paled, and the strain of those long hours showed in the badly bruised look about the eyes. The gleam of discontent seldom absent from the eyes of a man who has achieved what he most wants; but there was something deeper, more danger-ous, about that gleam no man would dare to question, which not even Foxwell could consciously admit to.

Nor did he move away from the window.

'Law and order, Fouchay. Remember my words. Some day people are going to have to learn a bitter truth. They cannot have freedom *and* law and order. If they place their destiny in our hands *we* must have the freedom, they must have the law and order. This is happening because they insisted on taking all.

'If I could, Fouchay, I would throttle Halliday with one hand, crumple our Constitution with the other and ram it down his throat.

'*That damned Constitution was the death warrant of law and order.*'

And Fouchay was not a man who shocked easily.

'What d'you think you're doing?'

'We found this man looting an electrical store, sir.'

'OK so what are you doing?'

'Turning him over to the cops, sir.'

'What for!'

'To—to be charged, sir.'

'You stupid bastard, you think this is '68? Shoot him!'

'Shoot ... ? I can't do that——'

'Oh for Chrissake, give me your gun. Step back, private.'

The Marine captain took the M16 and cut down the negro still clutching the nice bright shiny toaster; then he threw the gun hard at his inferior.

'Next time I give an order, grab it!'

'Fierce fighting has broken out on K Street and in the bus terminal area. Rioting and looting are spreading in most coloured districts. White House sources confirm all looters will be shot on sight. The situation on Constitution Avenue stays confused. Unconfirmed reports give two hundred of Halliday's desperadoes killed in a shoot-out close to Maryland Avenue.

'Stay tuned for further news.'

'I'll sure be glad to get outta this container. Too bad the major didn't think to instal air-conditioning,' Fletcher shouted to former private Hands who was busy loading for him.

'You're travellin' ain't you? Seein' the world—what more d'you want?' He handed up another full M16 choking over the words. The atmosphere was pretty acrid at that.

'I want some fresh air that's what I want. Hey Golden! you know Washington, where the hell are we?'

'We're right there, baby. Just passed the US Constitution. We made it, soul cousin!'

The men who weren't manning the gun ports began checking their gear.

'What happened?' a coloured reporter was squeezing hysteria out of a twelve-year-old on H Street; between sobs the boy tried desperately to get the words right.

'We—had a fire—in the 'partment block—wasn't nothin' t'do with the trouble. Jus' a fire—we done called the Fire Department—an' no-one heeded—it got worse—and Mom she said— she said ain't nothin' else but we gotta quit—so we all quit.'

'How many?'

'I dunno—there's all around a coupla dozen families, kids and so—we jus' ran out—and these soldiers—they started shootin' and—and ...'

The reporter looked at the blazing tenement building casting its torch-light glare over a dark heap of dead and dying. Something detached itself, a woman, humped up, throwing a snail's shadow, trying to crawl out of death's range. A trail of bodies, men, women and children, led up and down H Street.

A few soldiers, gay fellows sporting yellow neckerchiefs, stood around; some were studying their handiwork, others were reloading, nice and casual.

He pressed the boy painfully hard to his side. 'Come on, kid, I'll take you someplace safe.'

'We have the following from Mayor Carroll and Police Chief Calhoun. There is no cause for alarm. Operation "Cabin Guard" is proceeding smoothly. Specific military units have been assigned to all police precincts and are now in position. General Kruppstadt has completed a survey of sensitive areas and is now believed delivering a situational report to the President.'

'I congratulate you, General. With twenty-five thousand troops at your disposal you failed to hold the enemy. He is now three blocks from the White House. You'll hear more of this later.'

Those of you lovers of postage stamps—which means philatelists —will be interested in the buildings coming up on both sides of the avenue.

On your left is the Old Post Office Building and I think you'll agree it looks like it. Across the way is the PO Department Building as of now, and, no exaggeration, it's the biggest in the world. You can mail your postcards to the folks back home right there and buy all the stamps you want. No, lady, they don't print stamps, that's another place I'll tell you about later . . .

'They're getting smarter,' Halliday observed.

Facing them across Twelfth Street, four ton trucks double-parked.

He radioed the convoy. 'Halliday: engines running, first fifty out. Kill that barricade. The rest give rapid covering fire.'

That way the assault party could operate knowing their flanks and rear were secure. They had another advantage: all street and flood-lighting had been switched off with bullets. Near darkness suits this kind of action.

Trabs appeared with a grenade launcher.

'You're gonna need this, Major.'

'Don't bother, you're a sitting target with that damned thing,' and he was away with a haversack full of grenades.

Almost before the fifty had deployed there came a series of explosions and the MG fire stopped as suddenly as it had begun.

Halliday fought like a man who assumes the charmed life as a birthright . . .

Heavy firing came from the convoy's rear. It was only to be expected. Troops were pouring down Constitution Avenue planning to box them in. The first trucks went out of control as the rear M6os poured out a devastating fire. A bearded private spat into the roadway.

'Bunchin' up like that. Why will they do it?' He slipped to one side making way for the CS detail. They fired CS into the confusion and pressure on the rear dropped to a faltering zero.

Up front the fifty were facing marines who didn't panic so easily. But even they didn't look for the ferocity with which Halliday's men fought. They did what they could, held on to the last moment, but one man, as a survivor testified later, was like the scourge of God. 'It had to be Halliday,' he said. 'With thirty-three per cent casualties we had to retreat, men were falling everywhere, and we didn't seem to be touching them.'

Ferocity.

And an enemy using every trick in the book, every inch of cover, every vantage point, every bullet. Halliday hadn't spent those months in the Cambodian jungle doing nothing. Five hundred men hadn't taken target practice every day to win fairground prizes.

By the time that fight at the barricade was over the marines were running down Twelfth Street just to live. They left over a hundred dead and wounded. Halliday's casualty was Perkins, hit in the arm.

By a stray bullet, Perkins said.

It took two minutes to clear a gap through the trucks, in which time more men were poured in from other sections, crossing Madison, Washington, Adams and Jefferson Drives, that is, across the comparatively open and tree-filled Mall. What might have developed into a dangerous flanking move against Halliday's attenuated line of march lost momentum in face of an unlikely ally.

Cars, parked along Sixth, Seventh, Ninth and Fourteenth Streets, slowed the motorized columns to a point where the occupants just had to get out and walk. As container trucks were halted with their gun ports covering these thoroughfares the defenders still had the advantage.

An armoured emplacement sited at any main intersection becomes a formidable all-round proposition as any college commander majoring in low profile operations would know.

Not that they stayed long enough to welcome the newcomers.

The trouble was, as one outraged colonel confided to the Congressional Committee, the bastards never stayed still long enough to make a fight of it.

Snap! Colonel, didn't we hear you say that in a Saigon mess-room a couple of years back?

I'm sorry about the hold-up, folks. City Tours Inc., can show you everything in Washington including our traffic problems. I guess we just have to live with it ... well we're moving off again and only five minutes behind schedule. Like I told you, there's nothing mind-bending between Twelfth and Fourteenth Streets but if your interests run that way don't forget what I told you about one of the finest aquariums in the country, right there in the Commerce Department Building yonder.

Which brings us, Ladies and Gentlemen, with a fine flourish of ruffles and tuckets, to Fifteenth Street and the President of the United States' very own backyard ...

They encountered no more barriers. That was unbelievable. For a moment Halliday suspected a trap; but the steel caterpillar raced through nothing worse than ragged small arms fire. For obvious reasons they drove with heads right down—blind driving is one of those little items a good soldier should know about.

Halliday talked to the convoy as he drove. 'We're almost there, keep bunched up, don't separate. Crash through behind me number one—when I call "accelerate" put your foot right down. If I stick, push me!'

'Your local station reporting. We have news of a tremendous battle raging in Constitution Avenue. Army sources admit Halliday is gotten through to the Twelfth Street barrier but is being held. All available troops are being rushed to this position and it looks as though Halliday's luck has run out at last.

'The whole world waits breathlessly as the regular units of the US army and Marine Corps shoot it out with renegade Halliday and his adventurers.

'And we—we have a sensational development in a day of unimaginable happenings, and remember, it all began less than twenty-four hours back. Informed Government sources are quoted as saying there is actual doubt about the identity of John Halliday. Army records appear to show Major Halliday died in a Cambodian ambush three months ago. The big question follows—*who* is leading these Americans? Is he himself an American?

'Time is out of joint for mere speculation. Right now we are receiving news of total disintegration of law and order in certain districts—there is serious rioting on Sixteenth and Euclid Streets. Across the Anacostia River police and NG units are battling with rioters in Nichols Road. Trouble is reported in Arlington and Fairfax but we have no details as of now.

'Stores are burning on Minnesota Avenue. These and other blazes rage unchecked. Fire departments in Maryland and Virginia have urgent requests to send all tenders they can spare. Hospitals are appealing for transport to help ferry the wounded to hospitals. The city's twelve ambulances are not sufficient to cope with this scale of casualties.

'Washington DC the city of light. But at 2.30 in the morning, that light is no more than a gleam in the eye of the dark forces of devastation.

'This is—America—today. Stay tuned.'

The White House complex had been completely sealed off. Impossible to get in or out of what had degenerated into an armed camp.

Hardly anyone remained in the Executive Office Building. As though some mystique attached to the person of the President, those who had not fled at the first signs of danger congregated in the White House itself.

The establishment is never less than swollen. The house servants, the First Lady's staff, telephonists, secret service agents, aides and various officials, butlers, ushers, messengers, all these and more—take just such a motley crew, frightened, confused, bewildered, gather it under one roof and stir vigorously over heated imaginations.

Muntsch was there, Fouchay and Helderman, the Defence Secretary and the Attorney General. The President's Appointments Secretary was also present, but it was not a time for making appointments.

257

Caressinger remained, virtually alone, in the Executive Office Building.

Muntsch plucked the decision out of the chaos around him. Someone had to go in there and tell Foxwell.

The President sat at his desk, making notes on the yellow jotting-pad. Muntsch wondered why the room appeared so much larger, decided its occupant had become that much smaller.

'I didn't request your presence, Muntsch.'

'For your own sake, Mr President. They're almost here. You've got two minutes to take the helicopter, and they'll be a dangerous two minutes.'

'I stay. Why do you suppose I insisted we have crack units of the Marine Corps out there! Men who fought—honourably! —in Vietnam?'

'A lot of the men Halliday fought and beat came out of Vietnam, Mr President.'

'Don't be too sure about that. I tell you these men will enjoy eating him. Now get those people out there to make less noise. This is not a refugee camp. Find Meyerbeer and tell him report to me at once.'

Muntsch closed the door like a man taking intellectual exercise.

'Well?' Helderman, smoking furiously, torn between suspicion of any man closeted with power, however briefly, and anxiety about his place in the survival stakes; for that was how it began to look.

'Well?' he repeated.

'It's true what they say,' Muntsch explained to no-one in particular, 'he wanted this place so much he'd die damned sooner than leave it.' As he hurried off to find Meyerbeer the first shots from the grounds were breaking the first windows in the White House.

The truck accelerated fast and crashed through to the Ellipse, a flattened circle of green park space divided from the rear gardens of the presidential mansion by E Street. And it was in the manner of his coming to rest at the very centre of America that Halliday showed his genius.

Followed by the garbage truck and the twelve containerized

258

lorries with the second garbage truck in rear, Halliday drove tight between trees on to the path girdling the Ellipse and circled round, closely followed by the convoy, till he was nose to tail with the city truck, so creating an almost impenetrable cordon.

No stopping to admire their geometrical progression, they were out and under the trucks, pouring fire as from the spokes of a Martian wheel into the surrounding trees. Small detachments of three or four men then advanced from twelve o'clock to twelve o'clock of a perimeter on the offensive, not deigning to wait for opposition still recovering from the audacity of Halliday's manoeuvre, but going out to search for trouble.

One man in three tossed grenade after grenade into the semi-darkness, his companions providing covering fire with two M16s apiece, a technical feat of arms they'd perfected in the jungle.

The ferocity of this attack knocked the opposition off balance and effectively reversed its purpose. Captain of Marines Cramer would admit later that, classically, a unit forming a defensive position one minute is not expected to go on the offensive the next. Logistically there should not be time enough.

Regular army-style thinking. Halliday, explaining his plan to the men on the *Carolina*, had put it another way. 'Confuse their thinking in every way and on every possible occasion.'

The clock-faced attack expanded the perimeter. As the fifteen survivors withdrew they were immediately replaced by a team of twelve 'suicide' volunteers. Each of those men humped two four-gallon drums of gasoline. Behind them, and running in parallel, twelve covers fired continuous bursts to keep unfriendly heads down.

Dodging in and out of the trees the volunteers ran, letting the gasoline spill from large holes punched in the base of the drums. Right round the Ellipse and across E street, but not closing the circle; they left a twenty yard gap opening right on to the White House.

Racowiczs, one of the volunteers, made sure the rest were clear of the area and, as a fresh wave of marines began to close in, he tossed a grenade into the pool of liquid.

Instant Valhalla, proclaiming twilight for someone. The

sudden efflorescing of that broken ring of fire would scorch the memories of those who witnessed it.

To any who lived and died only by what they could see, 20th-century materialists or whatever, that fire reanimated seeds of superstition lain dormant for so many generations. Men who had never seen the Harz mountains, the forests of Transylvania or the mysterious hills of Ireland, remembered with a flicker of atavistic hindsight that the world had not always been shaped like an ice-box, an automobile or a cathode ray tube; had been like this, a phenomenon invoking wonderment, awe—fear . . .

Forty marines died in the inferno; those who could, fled. Their comrades, crowded in Fifteenth, C and D streets, stood paralysed by the spectacle, never dreaming that Halliday and a hundred men were already on the move as Racowiczs threw his bombshell.

Association of ideas. 'That guy has to be the devil himself,' one marine officer exclaimed.

'Maybe we should offer him twice what he's getting,' a sergeant suggested.

As if Halliday had finished with them.

From the container truck roofs men with grenade launchers fired CS gas over the flames into the already shaken concentrations of marines badly lacking room to manoeuvre.

As Halliday's task force broke into the grounds proper small detachments began dropping off to set up MG posts, others hurled gas grenades to take pressure off the flanks. The main body fought like men possessed with the last coherent force covering the White House: a company of marines and Fouchay's men. Three hundred in all.

'I never saw anything like it,' Marine Lieutenant James Cobb, one of thirty-seven survivors, would testify many months later. 'We shot them, and no matter how damned near dead they were, they just kept coming. I mean, in regular warfare you just fall down and wait for a medic. It was like they wanted to get killed or nothing.'

Senator Winfield treated Mrs Bird gently.

'As chief housekeeper you were in a position to know roughly where people were in the White House on that fateful morning?'

'Not everybody.' Her homespun countenance looked badly lined from the worry of it all. She surveyed the Senate Chamber with the troubled air of a woman itching to get her hands on a duster.

'No, not everybody, there were so many people around, all over the place.'

'Of course. I'll try to be more specific. Do you recollect seeing the President and the First Lady at the end?'

'Oh yes. Mrs Foxwell had asked if I'd be kind enough to fix her a cup of coffee. I did that and took it to her myself.'

'Where was she?'

'In the Yellow Oval Room.'

'That would be on the second floor?'

'Yes, that's right.'

'She was alone?'

'Oh yes.'

'No member of her staff present at all?'

'Oh no. Her press secretary was standing in the hall, the one leading from the east wing, and I think her social secretary was present, oh and Mrs Hampshire, the lady who dealt with Mrs Foxwell's correspondence. That's all I remember though I have an idea the chief butler might have been present. It's hard to remember with all the confusion around.'

'What were they doing, just waiting?'

'No, watching television.'

'And Mrs Foxwell? You took her coffee—can you describe how you found her?'

'She was just sat in her favourite chair, reading a book. I gave her the cup of coffee, she smiled and laid down her book to take it.'

'Did she say anything?'

'No—except to thank me, of course.'

'But at this time, the Ellipse was in flames, there was the noise of heavy firing, of grenades, of shouting, a full scale attack, visible and audible. Do you mean she made no comment whatsoever on what was happening?'

'None.'

Winfield was impressed, and half inclined to disbelieve. It simply wasn't dramatic enough for his purposes. There had to be a fine ringing phrase somewhere—'one short step backward for Mankind'—that kind of thing. But the First Lady's total silence in those circumstances offended his sense of occasion.

'Can you recall the title of the book she was reading?'

'Oh yes, it was called *One Morning in the War.*'

Winfield sensed he'd committed a rare blunder. It hardly ruffled the surface dignity of the proceedings, but a lot of people were going to wonder about that book. Why the hell couldn't she have been reading the Bible or even *War and Peace*?

'And the President?'

'I only recall seeing the Vice-President outside the President's office. He was shouting a lot——'

'At anyone in particular?'

'At Mr Meyerbeer who was just going into the office.'

'Well?'

'The situation is critical, Mr President. They—they've occupied the Ellipse and fired it.'

'I can see that for myself. It isn't what I asked for.'

Meyerbeer, trembling, tried hard to match the presidential calm or his deathly inflexibility, which was which, and only trembled more violently.

'Word has gone out to the media. "Strong suspicion in official circles Halliday an impostor." General Booth will take care of the army records. That's all we can do at this moment.'

The President smiled, corpse-like, watching his last ace fly off into the whirl of time.

'Fine. It'll be enough. Every myth is forged under crisis—and grows all the stronger. We now have ours and, whatever happens, Halliday can only fail. I shall go to the Lincoln Study.'

Meyerbeer, only half comprehending the President's half shared thoughts, nodded. 'Very well, Mr President.'

As they left the room, Meyerbeer shouldering a clearway through the crowd, the first bullets shattered the french window...

* * *

The men of the Executive Protection Service fought for every tree, shrub and rose-bush. More even than the marines they were conditioned to die. Apocryphal maybe, but the story is strong how Crowley had given a new intake of recruits a helicopter tour of the city, out over the Cherry Trees around the Tidal Basin. Crowley turned to a veteran agent. 'Jump!' he ordered, and the veteran hurled himself out of the open doorway. Crowley turned to the group of astonished rookies.

'And that's what you do for the President, every waking moment of your lives. If you're doubtful you'd best turn in your gun and ID badge right now.'

When men don't fear dying to that extent there's nothing wrong with their aim.

Halliday lost forty-nine of his storming party in that final rush, some of them surely died twice over; but the executive agents only knew about dying once and they simply ceased to exist.

He called up another hundred to hold the flanks as the last agents fell in the rose garden and even under the arcade.

The battle for the White House was over.

It was three o'clock on the morning of 29 March.

'Pete Kelly taking the desk, your local radio station. 3.00 am Washington time.

'I've just returned from a tour of an embattled city that so lately lamented the fate of New York.

'Police Chief Calhoun states Halliday has one hundred thousand coloureds on his side and that looks like making the big difference. All over the city groups of these rioters are looting and burning and often hampering the work of the defence forces. In places they appear to go unchecked. Elsewhere, groups of negroes still lie where they were cut down by Cabin Guard operators. There's a grim efficiency about these men's methods. Police trucks and army jeeps scream through smoky city streets to wherever there's trouble, a kind of human fire-fighting group pouring bullets into burning passions and smouldering injustices, real or imagined, igniting at the drop of a pin.

'The city boundaries are sealed off. In spite of repeated appeals by civic and military chiefs hundreds of vehicles filled with scared families, white mostly, attempt to head for safety; these too are badly impeding military operations.

'Washington is a city of fear and I've witnessed how deep it goes. At Roosevelt Bridge I watched men claiming to be Vietnam veterans trying to break through the army barricades. From where I stood they looked very like the bearded weirdies you can see on any road out of town.

'Most of them were clubbed down on the far side of the bridge, but one broke away and began running zig-zag towards the city side—he had only one arm so he may very well have been a veteran. At any rate I heard him shout "Long live Halliday" before a National Guardsman almost at my side cut him down with a burst of automatic. He got to his knees and shouted something like "My country ... your country" before a single shot put him down for good.

'Some late news: Lerner's on Fourteenth Street is burning fiercely. Most Safeways in the riot areas are taking their usual beating and we hear of trouble spreading as far as K Street. The Statler Hilton and the Watergate have been fired. Connecticut Avenue, New York and Massachusetts Avenue are being cordoned off.

'Walter Reed Hospital is accepting casualties. The hospital, you'll recall, isn't too far from Battleground National Cemetery, diminutive reminder of the Civil War and a Union attack on Washington which almost paid off—but that was then.

'Latest information gives two thousand students from Howard surging down Georgia Avenue. Paratroop units are shaping to hold them up at Columbia Road. On top of official warnings my advice to the would-be junketeers is "trust to your transistors and go back". The mood this side the barricades is ugly and no chance of it looking beautiful for a long time to come.

'And—and we have just got word—we have—Halliday has taken the White House! Halliday is in the White House ...'

'OK, Benner, round up everyone, have them concentrated in the East Room. Maxwell, tie up the telephone system, send word to everyone. Gelby, MGs on the North Portico and a dozen

264

men covering north facing windows. Soup, your party up on
the roof right away. Able, take your detail through EOB and
bring in anybody you find. Trabs.'

'Right here, Major.'

'You stick with me.'

Halliday watched carefully as each man was rounded up. A
mere handful of GIs combed through one hundred and fifty
rooms so quickly and smoothly there were those who wondered
exactly how it was done. Well, one of the negro corporals had
once worked in the pantry so Halliday didn't need a crystal
ball for that one.

A motley crew indeed: the butler and a couple of housemen
came first, some FBI men, a nervous little man who might
have been the curator, Foxwell's doctor—passing the bearded,
bloodstained cluster of soldiers with grim dignity—third class
aides, messengers, the Press Secretary, the chief housekeeper,
Foxwell's valet, Muntsch...

Halliday stepped in his path. 'Where's Foxwell?'

Muntsch looked him up and down then spat full in his face.
The major wiped his face and started to smile.

'Kennedy wasn't so lucky.' Whatever that meant it did something to Muntsch.

'I know about you, Muntsch.'

And there was somewhat about Halliday's words that took
the starch out of Muntsch's arrogance.

'Take him away.'

More of the administrative and household staff filed past—
and Crowley...

'Where's Foxwell?'

'Find out, punk!'

'I know about you too. The man who makes Murder Inc.
look like a charity ball.'

The Defence Secretary was stiff-lipped. They'd found him
in the telephonists' powder-room. Defending democracy is
one thing, but this was something else.

'He blew his guts,' Gribble complained disgustedly.

'Did he now. I guess that wouldn't have happened if you'd
gaily waved off a few MIRVs, would it, Mr Secretary? I mean
contemplating other people's destruction doesn't move any-

body's bowels does it? Take him away before I'm sick on this fine carpet.'

'OK John, don't bother—I've got him.' Racowiczs on a roving commission, had run Foxwell to earth in the Lincoln Study. 'His wife's up here too.'

Halliday tarried long enough to give Benner guidance on the sorting process before hurrying away. The housekeeper regretted a backward glance, shook her head at sight of all those heavy boots covered in filth and—and blood—great oafs, banging into irreplaceable things...

They were bringing in a lot of stuff that had risen to the top: Meyerbeer, General Kruppstadt, Deputy Attorney General Cooper; Helderman rolled through to the East Room without a trace of concern.

Halliday, followed by Trabs and Racowiczs, strode like a man unwilling to fail his appointment with Destiny, knew exactly where to go, no hesitation, along the hall to the Lincoln Study, neighbouring that great statesman's bedroom.

The door was open.

Foxwell sat at the desk facing them. In the fireplace a small log-fire was burning, the windows were heavily curtained—a small world with a necromantic touch. There was stereo equipment, dozens of tapes, books everywhere and a man in the middle of all this sophisticated paraphernalia, seated at a desk large enough to dwarf a personality it was meant to fit.

No camera, no TV equipment to catch the historic moment when rogue and renegade met, face to face.

For all their calm, Trabs and Racowiczs had to sideglance long enough to see how Halliday was savouring this supreme moment of venture. Realized they should have known him better. Halliday had never yet taken an objective emotionally.

'You're under arrest, Foxwell.'

Foxwell's was a killer's stare; he transferred it to Halliday's companions.

'As President of the United States of America, I give my solemn word, you will go free if you turn this man over to justice.'

He wasted time searching for a trace of expression in their regard.

266

'Do any of you really think you can get away with this?'

'Every word you utter comes out of old Hollywood scripts—the rejects.'

Foxwell stood suddenly: 'You do not speak to the President of——'

'You are no longer the President. I'm not even sure you ever were. Maybe you're the President who never was. Any man who could lie, cheat, cover up, dissemble, plot, go along with any dirty deal that meant a second chance, pack a Supreme Court to get his kind of verdict, the way you did, has to be an illusion.

'Any country that could want you for President is beyond saving, Foxwell. We had another purpose, and it touches the whole of mankind. What you committed in order to become President, what you did so as to continue as President is not too important. What you're prepared to do to remain President is a small matter of looking through your armament programme; what you have in mind suggests a bigger war than the one you lost—not just to prove the size of man you think you are——'

'You're raving, Halliday.'

'I can't stop the process, but I can slow it down long enough to let the world say its prayers.

'Trabs, get him out of this room and down with the goats.'

'And what about me?'

They turned at the sound of a woman's voice, low and icy calm.

'You'll be free to leave with the others, Mrs Foxwell.'

'The sheep—and am I to be allowed to say "goodbye" to my husband?'

Even Halliday stared at the implication, that she knew exactly what was to happen.

'You have two minutes.' He stepped aside to let her pass, left them together, and partly closed the door.

'Cool,' said Racowiczs admiringly.

'Indifferent,' Halliday corrected.

History is still trying to make up its mind.

By the time they returned to the East Room Benner had

gathered up the remnant staff and a few persons of note, among them several top aides, a vociferous Vice-President and Caressinger.

Very little was said; a few women sobbed, but in general there existed an odd kind of interest in what was happening, in the men around them who had made nightmares come true.

Many of those present are now frantically writing their memoirs; whole books devoted to their miserable lives, scraped off the East Room floor to make a fondant 'I was there' a guaranteed entry to the book clubs.

The base on the Ellipse radioed they were coming under heavier fire. Halliday chose to send an emissary, and his choice represented a shrewd blow to the vitals of military morale. He sent Kruppstadt who'd helped make a mess of the defence for which he would be required to answer at a later date.

'Kruppstadt, I radioed your people to cease fire. They don't seem willing. You will go out there and tell them to hold off. We have Foxwell and a lot of VIPs. Make sure they're left in no doubt what happens if they continue the attack. Take a flag, go by way of the south portico, and go alone.'

Kruppstadt knew humiliation when he saw it. 'Can't you send somebody else?'

'That's a general talking. Listen, Kruppstadt, my RTO keeps me well-informed. Men under your command are gunning down negroes all over Washington and comparing numbers. That's your responsibility and I could shoot you for it, but this way proves there are worse things than dying. Now get out there and do your own dirty work.'

Kruppstadt, broken, like many others, on the wheel of circumstances during the Senate Investigation, would intone to the tune of a Nuremberg psalm: I had no choice.

As he left, Sweetman and Lucas were taking off in the presidential helicopter with four specialists and a maximum cargo of explosives and napalm.

In two minutes they were hovering above the Department of Justice. As they came in to land a detachment of marines began to wonder what it was about. They died without knowing. Almost before the chopper touched down Lucas and the EOD squad unloaded plastics and napalm, tossed the whole lot down a lift shaft from the top floor and while the rest scrambled out through the fire exit one man stayed long enough to drop a grenade on the concoction then he too ran like hell just making it to the roof-top as a pillar of fire leaped up the shaft; began to spread with a fearsome roar before they were two feet off the ground.

People say that much FBI documentation was reduced to ashes in the holocaust; but people, be they senators or petty crooks, should not rely on what other people say. Much of the confidential material is stored at the bottom of a far more secluded garden.

The small group found its death warrant signed and ready for delivery at the Capitol. Sweetman made a poor landing, smashing one of the skids. None of the others seemed too worried.

'This is it, fellers.' Sweetman sounded a little dejected. Hosea Smith chuckled and patted his shoulder.

'Don't you pay no mind, soul brother, we all dead sometime; what's wrong with now? Come on, let's go.'

Because they didn't shirk him Death let them right through the outside guards, across the great rotunda, through the old Senate Chamber and into the north corridor connecting with the Senate wing.

A few of the High Hundred still sat, not in session exactly, but anxious to figure in someone's book as men gravely debating the Nation's Agony when everyone else had gone home to Prudence. In fact, they were some of the most dedicated filibusterers in Congress and for proof they will keep themselves out of hell on Judgment Day, believe it.

Only Lucas and the coloured man remained now and even Hosea was bleeding from a stomach wound. They turned at the entrance to the Senate Chamber, tossed a grenade at the gathering clans then dashed in with guns blazing, collided with a hail of bullets from the gallery above. Three of the senators died at the hands of their protectors, one was badly wounded.

It was the kind of thing that used to happen in Vietnam.

*   *   *

'You people will leave the House immediately. There is nothing to fear. Simply walk out and make your way to the cordon.'

'Why are you doing this dreadful thing? What kind of a man are you?' The outburst came from the former President's head usher, Poulton, who had gooseflesh courage enough to speak out where Foxwell's henchmen preferred to keep their valour under wraps.

Halliday looked at the questioner, looked at them all; saw them for the first time as people, yet unlike him and his bloodied victors as Earthmen might be to Martians. 'Maybe,' he thought, 'maybe I do have Martian blood.' But last of all he looked at the question.

What kind of man? Not the recognizable kind, God forbid. He was sick and tired of people, those little humanoids proudly calling themselves Americans, Russians, British, Vietnamese ... A slight question of fear. The more you kiss the flag the greater the fear, of yourself and others. The kiss leading to a love match between you and the you called American, Russian, British, German, French—one bangs the big drum and deafen-dominates the other, and Foxwell International feeds your fear by feeding your pride. 'I'm an American' the other man says 'I'm a Russian. Boo! So there.' Someone's got to give. 'No you don't have to give, you've got me, Foxwell, you've got me, the Praesidium, you've got me, Chairman Mao, you've got all the top crap from Thieu down. We'll put you out front. We'll build bigger missile-systems, better submarines, distil more subtle nerve-gases—obscenities!'

And you swallow it, you *little* people from one end of the world to the other, fall on your knees in awe of a three thousand million dollar defence project or a couple of obsolete jet fighters bought cheap—and never count the cost.

Something like that flashed through Halliday's mind. Something had taken him beyond time for he seemed palpably to return to that crowded room.

'We have different conceptions of what is "dreadful". To betray nature's laws—what would that mean to you in your inch thick armour-plated sophistication?

'Looking at you, flunkeys serving their masters at cosy little dinner-parties, ladies making sweet little appointments for the First Lady—then remembering the blood and agony of Vietnam I feel sick to my soul for the future of humanity.

'Now get out—please go.'

Three hundred loyal members of the household shuffled off, and the manner of their going would not be faithfully recorded in those memoirs to come. The rôle of a whipped cur is beyond most people's self-conceit. Only the First Lady, leading the line of outcasts, paused to face Halliday. She regarded him for a long time with a touch of expression no physiognomist could have put a name to, then without a word she went her way.

Halliday had time to count the cost. Of his five hundred and thirty-seven men he had less than two hundred effectives alive. It tallied with his earlier calculations.

'Sweetman should have been back by now.'

'That's what I figured. Four trucks should be enough to get us through,' Racowiczs said.

'Let's not forget the garbage truck,' Roberts reminded him.

'We ought to be moving soon, Major.' Trabs was keeping close watch on the top men being shepherded into the great hall.

'I suppose so.'

Halliday felt very tired, very suddenly. Curiously it had to do with the way she'd looked at him. And with something else: the magnitude of what had still to be done, the effort of will, close to superhuman, needed to get through the last phase. But, they couldn't sit there forever.

Racowiczs was watching Halliday closely. 'In some ways the next phase is easiest,' he suggested.

Halliday grinned at that. 'If only because it's the last. Come on, let's put your theory to the test. See the men have five minutes to relax and then we go.'

Roberts reported he had the frequency and the major sent his message.

'Halliday: do you have that?'

'Receiving you,' a curt clipped voice.

'Listen carefully and have the following circulated. I hold Foxwell, Papadopoulos, Caressinger and seventeen officials of government—confirm.'

'Roger.'

'We leave the White House five minutes from now. Any attempt to interfere and they're dead. Confirm.'

'We have it.'

'They will be conveyed to our objective in four containerized trucks. I repeat, any attempt against us will be an attempt against them. The responsibility for the safety of Foxwell and his campaign managers is therefore yours. Confirm.'

'Roger.'

And the two children, so tangible and so intangibly a part of what it was all about. For the first time that day Halliday could give them some attention. Well, they'd lived through it, were safe and sleepy and still in Marshall and Extra's care. The air was fresh in their quarters and, until the convoy had bumped onto the Ellipse, they'd slept like innocence itself.

'How are they, Marsh?'

'Fine, Major, just fine.'

'Scared by the action?'

'Naw! What have they seen they didn't see in Vietnam?'

'I sure hate sittin' on the side-lines, Major,' Extra called as Halliday turned away.

He smiled. 'You and Marsh have the biggest part in the whole operation, Extra.'

Marshall watched him go. 'You could follow that guy all the way to hell,' with a slow wondering shake of the head.

'Where d'you think we came from, rat-brain? Now you two snuggle down and get some more sleep, ain't dawn yet by a long way. Hey Marsh, they just drank a quart of milk between 'em, how about that?'

REQUIEM

THE LAST PHASE. In Benner's words: 'There'll be nothing to it—in a way.'

The men were tired, many were wounded. The surviving medvacs did what they could in the time they had. The badly wounded, those who hadn't quite fought to the death, were shot. That was agreed procedure. No-one had any illusions about the ugliness of captivity in the special circumstances.

But Halliday was there, seemingly everywhere; not sparing himself by word or deed to prove that the incredible venture, still not a day old, was still worthwhile. Like a rare isotope he radiated an intense, almost unearthly energy against which prevails no immunity.

Charged with a new lease of life they prepared to go over the last ditch, to make the impossible dream an imperishable reality.

They got the Vice-President, Caressinger and the rest to the container vehicles; none was put with the children. Halliday, Trabs and Roberts would lead the brief convoy in the garbage truck loaded with two tons of explosives.

Ready to go and only one last detail needing attention.

Fifty gallons of petrol were splashed through the White House. A match at the front door was all it needed. Halliday saw to that.

He walked to the Ellipse without a backward glance at the flames. No-one dared fire a shot at so perfect a target, for the watchers among the smouldering trees on either side of his progress could see the man ahead of Halliday, hands raised high above him.

It was Foxwell.

The opposition stayed its hand for the first fifteen miles. They had no trouble leaving Washington; reached the Washington Memorial Parkway and then switched to Interstate 495.

Things were different at the intersection with Dulles International Access Road, the route giving a clear twelve mile run to the airport.

Firing began when they were less than two hundred yards from a makeshift barricade. Halliday took a shot in the arm and Trabs had to grab the wheel to keep them steady, but they lost speed at the worst possible moment.

Ed Roberts didn't stop to think twice. 'Keep her going, Trabs. Put your foot down.'

He was out of the cab before they could stop him. The others, flashing past, saw him firing at the MG post, saw him throwing grenades, saw him trying to draw all the fire he could —saw him succeeding.

They'd picked up speed again knowing they could do nothing for him. The convoy smashed its way through while Roberts stood his ground shooting blind until a bullet knocked the M16 clean out of his hands and they were on him before the tail of the last truck was out of sight.

'I hope he died,' Trabs made a prayer of the words.

Halliday said nothing, closed his eyes, willing it to happen.

'We can stop and patch that arm.'

Halliday tried a smile. 'You must be joking.'

'Yeah, come to think of it, I must be.'

They got to the airport at around five.

The size and a curious kind of eloquence of Dulles Airport beats most jet harbours. You could live on its ten thousand acres a lifetime and want for nothing, plus ear-plugs and brain surgery.

Just now it was quiet. All aircraft were grounded, nothing coming in or going out unless one allows for Gore Spiller's executive jet which had special clearance of course and had landed not five minutes before Halliday's arrival.

Gore the 'Pauncho' Spiller badly needed strapping into his parts these days. It's hard to be a middle-aged hero, slugging

274

it out in the steamy jungles of Hollywood's vinyl Vietnam when your stomach's looking the Vietcong in the eye before the rest of you shows up.

The things I do for my country. The literally present thought of Spiller believe it. At which juncture he was lolling in the lounge of his very own airyplane given him by his very own fan club, Honorary President Foxwell, for his services to America...

And very elegant too. The whole thing fitted out like a dude ranch with moose horns over the cocktail bar, swinging doors to the bedroom, saddle seats, not to mention Winchesters and Derringers on the wall with which our hero had won the West on Lot Seven.

There he was then, in his buckskin suit and ten and three quarters gallon stetson, high boots and, it has to be said, a pair of pearl-handled Colts slung from his Capitol Beltway.

Yessir, he was every inch a God-knows-what. Most of him was pure celluloid, and it's difficult to put a label on a reel of that stuff. The rest of him was mean. Ponder those slitted eyes that had looked on so many victims, inhuman as the slits in an armoured reconnaissance car.

Picturesquely then he awaited the travelling terminal service that would carry him straight to the airport buildings. His servant, weirdly garbed in some kind of Davy Crockett suit, was serving him an iced lager when the colonel entered.

'Mr Spiller, Colonel Ruggles at your service. I'm sorry to intrude but I have orders to bring you under guard back to the main terminal.'

Gore looked worried. 'Something wrong, Colonel?' he drawled, arousing in the colonel the uncanny sensation of watching a drive-in movie.

'Well that depends, sir. We have information Halliday is on his way here.'

'Is he now?' Gore rubbed his chin reflectively, maybe wondering if the Sioux could be trusted when he was so durned busy with the Cheyenne.

'Gonna call him out, Colonel?'

'That ain't—that is—it isn't possible, Mr Spiller. He's holding the President and most of his staff hostage as I understand it.'

'Is he now.' Gore made an effort and managed to push himself off the red plush sofa in one. 'Well I just reckon we'll have to see about that. I just reckon that.'

'If you'd care to come with me now, sir.'

'Oh I'm not going anywhere. I'm gonna see this Mr Halliday and I'm tellin' him he'd better turn in the President and everyone else or he'll have to deal with me.'

He reinforced the impression by producing one of those beautiful Colts, looking it over as if to assure himself it was all there.

'I can't let you do that, sir.' Ruggles had no doubts on the subject.

Gore narrowed his gaze like he did against his burning Western sun-lamp. 'Well now, Colonel, reckon I'm just an ornery crittur with a job to do like the next man and I have personal authority from our President's own mouth to come on over and do what I can. Now why else do you suppose I'd high-tail it all this way?'

The colonel glanced at the FAB official waiting in the doorway. The official shrugged.

'It's a question of the President's safety, Mr Spiller.'

'Well now I mind that particular, Colonel. And I'm obliged to you for recollecting it, but I'd be failing my duty to a friend and to my country if I didn't do what little all I could.'

'That's commendable, Mr Spiller. If that's your feeling I'll leave you to it. He's out there now if you care to go over.'

'You're coming, Colonel?'

'Oh no, that's more than I dare do. If Halliday saw a posse of —I mean—if I take you over myself we couldn't answer for the consequences.'

The six-gun drooped a little. 'You mean I don't get an escort?'

'Absolutely not. I'm afraid in a delicate situation like this it could be—in fact I'd strongly advise you to leave your—your side-arms back here.'

'Well now, I was hoping I might get a little moral support,' and to say truth, Gore began to look as if he could use it. What in tarnation had he gotten himself into that he could reasonably getten himself out of?

No question with Luke, his Japanese servant watching, not to mention that damned Yankee colonel and the evil-looking hombre from the FAB standing right behind him. There could be no backing out of this reel.

'Very well, Colonel. I'll be right out.' Brave words if his drawl hadn't slowed to a crawl.

Moments later he stepped out of his ol' X Bar One jet and began walking the half-mile across runway two to where Halliday and his men were supposed to be. In fact they'd stopped at the airport entrance while Trabs relayed a message through the guards.

'Tell them have two good pilots, a navigator and flight engineer ready at the terminal.'

No choice.

The four men were already waiting as they arrived.

All this under the eyes of soldiers, police and airport officials acutely conscious of what they were able to do—which was precisely nothing.

'Which two planes are fuelled and ready for take-off?' Halliday demanded.

He had to wait for an answer; the aircrew couldn't take eyes off someone who'd blown the Statue of Liberty one day and hi-jacked a president the next.

'Well?'

'Er—there's a Braniff 707 over there and a BOAC 727 lined up for London.'

'They'll do, hop on.'

The one who'd spoken shrugged and hopped on. He'd been hi-jacked twice already, what was one more or less? His companions did likewise, hung on to the garbage truck where they could and the odd, historical, little convoy roared off in quick order.

Gore Spiller, still teetering along the tarmac, watched the procession cut across his path at an angle. Breathless already from that four-forty yard walk—he was used to moseying around on a horse or a timber framed Cadillac—he swore the Durango Kid's oath and set painfully off in the new direction.

A camera team on the terminal building roof began recording the scene with a telephoto lens at about this point. The reel is to be shown twice daily in the Hall of Infamy.

'Jesus! Am I seeing things?' one cameraman took his eye

from the viewing lens and gazed vaguely about him as though waking from a difficult dream. 'There's a cowboy on the runway.'

'Naturally,' his assistant was laconic about the obvious. 'I told you when we got the call, Gore Spiller just blew in.'

His number one took another look. 'What's he doing here anyway?'

'Well since he's the fastest draw bar Danny the Drop I figure the army's been savin' him for Custer's last stand.'

But, like the airport staff and the stranded passengers crowding every permitted vantage point, their profoundest attention was concentrated on the receding convoy.

The first pale streaks of dawn were already out on reconnaissance as the trucks came to a halt between the jetliners.

One of the pilots, still recovering from that dash, gasped out an urgent question to the bearded man beside him. 'I don't understand, why only one navigator and flight engineer for two planes?'

'One of us isn't going far. Can you get one of those things off the ground without help?'

'Well, yes but——'

'That's good enough. OK you take the 707, your friend in the other.'

He was losing a lot of blood, had only a hazy view of things, yet somehow the mind still functioned. Only now there were interpolated images that came and went unbidden and always a lonely figure somewhere on a long, long beach.

Twenty-five men formed a chain, began passing the explosives from truck to plane, up the motorized stairway and into the rear baggage compartment.

Two tons of it.

Meantime the hostages were brought out and put into the 707. The camera caught Foxwell for ten seconds, his features visibly white and drawn even in that difficult light.

'That's him—hold it! keep it tight, left a little—up! he's climbing the stairway, don't lose his face, he's turning, looking back—beautiful! we got it!'

The remainder filed on and took their seats, bunching up as

close as possible, as though sensing but not believing this was to be their last ride.

Halliday, Racowiczs and Trabs left them under guard and went to meet Marshall and Extra who were carrying the children to the 727. The boy, so small for his age, seemed to be all made of eyes: such a big plane, Marsh—sure that's a *máy bay* 727, just for us. The girl, still crumpled in sleep, her head bobbing gently on Extra's shoulder.

Halliday bent over and kissed her hair, very softly: '*Chào cô* little one,' turned to the boy, 'I wish you a good future. Explain it to him sometime, Marsh.'

'I'll do that.'

'Sure you don't want me along with you, Major?' Extra looked anxious, even maternal. At any other time Halliday would have smiled at the puckered up little face.

'See the children to safety, that'll be our satisfaction, Extra.'

Extra nodded miserably at Halliday's blood-soaked sleeve. Marsh nodded once and both men turned and boarded the plane.

The three men stood by as the rest, torn, filthy and all but dropping with tiredness and reaction, filed slowly up the stairway.

No smiles, no handshakes. They had won no victories, suffered no defeats—only, mission accomplished by men too exhausted to feel.

Halliday saw every last one aboard, turned and almost stumbled across to the other jet while Racowiczs and Trabs went ahead to relieve the guards. Just as Gore Spiller came floundering along to plant himself squarely before him.

'Hold it, Halliday!'

The major paused, studied the odd-looking cowpauncher as though trying to remember something.

'You may have heard of me, Halliday. Gore Spiller. Name mean anything to you?'

It's all there, on film. The light was improving rapidly but gave nothing like the high noon wattage the scene deserved. Two shadowy figures can be seen confronting each other in the best tradition of the worst Westerns.

'Gore Spiller. Why yes, pardner, now I call to mind—heard

279

tell you're the meanest Republican this side of Little Big Rock.'

'Well now, I don't aim to swap words with your kind, Halliday. I'll just thank you to hand over the President and company nice and peaceable...'

'Hey Major, you having trouble?' Racowiczs called from the top of the ramp. Halliday, watching Spiller closely, heard but made no reply.

Suddenly he crouched and, left handed, drew his .45. Spiller crouched too, drew his Colt—and dropped it. The major smiled down on the gun, laughed, walked towards Spiller, bent to pick up the thing and handed it back with his bloodied right hand.

'That's the trouble with America, Spiller. People like you. Too many bad actors chasing too few good rôles.'

He brushed past Hollywood's greatest patriot and climbed aboard the plane.

'We continue with news and comment: official observers agree everything points to a planned operation worked out to the last detail. It becomes clearer with each hour there is nothing haphazard about Halliday's programme of destruction. Pentagon officials confirm rumours that AN Other must be responsible but no-one seems able satisfactorily to account for the complicity of so many others.

'At this hour Washington has the appearance of a bombed-out city. The Federal capital has been declared a disaster area. The declaration is long overdue.

'Fire Department officials state there is no possible chance of saving the White House.

'We have news that Halliday and the remnants of his force together with the President and high Government officials are taking off from Dulles Airport in Boeing jets, speculation about their destination swings between Cuba and Red China. Stay tuned for further details. Meantime I have the following emergency calls...'

The 727 cleared the runway and headed north. First cautious assumptions that it had to be on course for Canada proved correct.

It landed at Montreal Airport.

No-one knows precisely what happened during the final minutes and seconds of the 707. Only the pilot survived to give a partial account of events after take-off.

'Captain Silcock, the Emergency Committee appreciates you're still close enough to events to be a little shaky in your recollection, particularly in view of the injuries you sustained, but it's essential, you understand, we provide a rough sequence of what happened for the full Senate Committee to work on.'

The pilot looked what he was, a two week convalescent recovering from extensive injuries and multiple memories. He remained seated of course.

'Yes, I understand.'

'What happened from the moment you boarded the plane?'

'I was told to go forward to the flight-deck and run through the routine checking procedure.'

'Were any of Halliday's men aboard at that time?'

'Yes, I had to pass a man Halliday referred to as "Trabs" to reach the deck.'

An usher passed a photograph from the chairman to the witness.

'Is that the man?'

'I'd say it was, but he had a beard and he looked a little older.'

'What was he doing?'

'He had his back to the door leading to the flight deck. Held a gun, a rifle, I'm not sure about these things——'

'You've not had experience with——?'

'Revolvers, automatics, not the long stuff. Whatever it was he had it pointed at the group in the cabin.'

'Did you have time to recognize anyone in that group as you passed through?'

'Yes, several of the faces were familiar—the President of course, the Vice-President, Dr Caressinger and so on.'

'Was anything said by any of the victims before you reached the flight deck?'

'No, nothing.'

'Could you deduce anything from their demeanour?'

281

'They didn't seem too worried by their situation, I mean nobody looked apprehensive; I'm sure I noticed Doctor Caressinger smiling.'

'Smiling! Did that surprise you?'

'Not really. I wasn't too worried myself, at that point.'

'Why not?'

'I figured Halliday had made his first big mistake.'

'In what way?'

'Well, if this was to be a routine hi-jack with the President of the United States as one of the hostages, I didn't know of a country anywhere in the world that could afford to play Halliday's game for him. I guess that must have been in their minds too.'

'Did you have no idea what was being loaded into the plane?'

'None whatsoever; the whole business of loading occurred while I was up front.'

'I see. So you checked your instrumentation. What happened then?'

'Halliday came on to the flight deck.'

'At which point the 707 was preparing for take-off?'

'That's right.'

'Go on, Captain.'

'Halliday asked if I had radio contact with the control tower. I told him I had. Another man with him asked "Shall I monitor?" Halliday simply nodded and this guy took a head-set.'

'You're talking of the third man now?'

'Yes.'

Again there was formal evidence taken of identity and it followed that the saturnine features in the picture belonged to former Lieutenant Racowiczs. 'Except he had a long, droopy moustache.'

'Did any or all of those three men show signs of exaggerated emotions, impatience, hysteria?'

'I never saw men looking calmer. They were simply going through the motions.'

'Is that your experience of hi-jackers?'

'Definitely not. The two I had to deal with were unstable from head to foot.'

282

'Did you make any comment at this time?'

'No. Our experience in this type of situation shows it's better to say nothing. A word out of place can trigger off unwelcome responses; however calm they might seem I couldn't take chances.'

'I understand. So Halliday was first to speak.'

'Yes, he apologized for giving me so much work to do.'

'Apologized?'

'That's right. Normally my co-pilot would check out fuel, hydraulic systems and the rest. We got routine clearance and three minutes later we were airborne.'

'Heading north?'

'Yes, I thought we were meant to follow the other plane. Then he asked me—he asked me...'

'Take your time, Captain.'

'Captain, what speed is minimal with retraction of front wing flaps to give instant stalling?'

'Even then I wasn't worried. I just thought he must be.'

'But you told him.'

'I saw no reason not to.'

'Did he persist on this?'

'Yes, he asked me to show him the retraction lever and the speed indicator.'

'You did so?'

'Yes, I imagined he was simply showing an interest in the control system.'

'And of course, if you shut down the engines at the same moment that would have the aircraft dropping like a brick——'

'You might have forward thrust for about fifty yards but——'

The pilot broke off as some dim presentiment began to tell what this extraordinary man might have in mind.

'Which of these things cuts power to the engines, Captain?'

'Why?'

'I'm interested.'

'And you told him, Captain?'

283

'I still couldn't see reason not to!' An anguished cry, one of the few to bring tears to the eyes of watching millions.

'We understand, Captain.'

'So I can fly this plane, simply by holding on to this control and if I move it forward it takes me down?'

The pilot nodded.

'All I wanted to know, so keep her at minimum speed, take a turn to bring you in on a line running straight through the centre of Rock Creek Park.'

'Shouldn't we try a dummy-run—just in case?' Racowiczs asked.

'Do we need it?' Halliday asked the pilot.

'I don't think so.'

'OK. Let me know when we're running in.'

He left his seat and went aft. Trabs took his place at the pilot's side.

Feigned indifference, malevolent curiosity, that much their expressions told him as he faced them.

'We don't have much time,' he began.

'Too damned right you don't!' Papadopoulos screamed at him. 'When this is over I'm gonna take you apart with my two bare hands!'

Halliday ignored the man from ITT.

'And there isn't much more to say,' he continued. 'Let's forget you're the men who sold and soiled America, let's concentrate on the economics.

'A billion dollars for one new aircraft carrier. Nine million dollars to fight poverty. And that you were ready to cut to nothing.

'Women searching through garbage bins to help feed their children, but you have to have your new toys for Xmas.

'The death of the OEO, the war on poverty, benefits for veterans cut, medicare funds slashed, pollution control budget cut. Everything that could make this country clean, decent, above all, humane—cut.

'How could anybody be taken in? One only has to look at you and your bunch of cut-throats, to know you're not only capable of what the Democrats suspect, but a few people are dead who can testify on the Last Day how you got as far as you did. They know, and you know, Watergate was only the last chapter. Don't bother to say your prayers, no-one's interested.'

'I'm going to enjoy finding out what's back of your mind, Halliday,' Fouchay promised.

That seemed to amuse the major.

Trabs appeared in the doorway. 'We're on course, Major.'

'You'd better work fast, Fouchay. We're almost over the Pentagon.'

For the first time Caressinger spoke. 'What exactly does that mean?'

Halliday smiled. 'We're taking you home, Doctor. Special Delivery.'

Trabs would stay with them. Halliday regretted that. The two men held each other's gaze for the lesser part of an instant. It was enough to say everything. Then he climbed back to the flight deck.

'Three minutes from Rock Creek Park,' Racowiczs crisply.

'Right, get him out and into the parachute.'

Halliday took over the controls, rehearsed rapidly what had to be done. In the distance he could see the green of the Park, the Potomac beyond, silver in the light of a cloudless dawn, to his left the fiery city of Washington under a pall of smoke drifting sadly to the north-west.

Somehow Racowiczs got the bemused pilot hitched into his parachute.

They were cruising at around two hundred-fifty knots at three thousand feet and closing rapidly.

'Quickly!' Halliday shouted, not impatience but pain coloured the command blood red.

Racowiczs hustled the pilot out and along the aisle, got the emergency rear door open. Silcock, seeing the ground far below, rushing past at speed with nothing separating him from it but air, was instantly sick.

'Jump!' Racowiczs screamed. 'Go-go-go!'

The first green of the park appeared but still the terrified man clung to the door-frame; suddenly Racowiczs smashed at his knuckles with a revolver and, reactively letting go, he was pushed into space...

Half conscious, he was still floating down through the last hundred feet when it happened ...

Don't imagine Halliday had beautiful thoughts or beguiled the seconds by tuning in to the false voice of Destiny as he fought ordinary weakness to keep that plane headed for its target. He brought it down in a shallow dive from three to one thousand feet—eight hundred—at which point the park slid out of sight and there was only the river, the Lincoln Memorial and Arlington Bridge angling away to his right.

So many ways of loving one's country—six hundred—only one way to care about the world, his last conscious thought tied up with a sea-shore image as he flipped the retraction lever, cut the engines and pushed desperately on the control as it looked as though he might overshoot.

But the drop was a piece of perfection.

And the combination of loaded fuel tanks and two tons of explosives was irresistible.

As for the Pentagon, official statistics give one half of its three and a half million square feet of office space and nine of its seventeen miles of corridors as totally destroyed with graduated damage to the rest of Man's finest Death-house.

The saga begins and ends here. And if ever evil lived after a man it outlives Halliday. No fine phrases will ring through the universe in praise of his purpose or to laud the exploits of the fiendish Five Hundred. No—not in our time.

But the world is a strange ball of matter. What it shakes its head at today it may well nod to in some wiser, happier region of time to come.

'OK Ed, now let's go through it again. You hopped out of the truck and began running towards the barrier because you'd had enough—you'd had enough—you'd had enough—you'd had enough ...'